THE MOON IN OUR HANDS

ALSO BY THOMAS DYJA

Play for a Kingdom
Meet John Trow

THE MOON
IN OUR
HANDS

Thomas Dyja

CARROLL & GRAF PUBLISHERS
NEW YORK

THE MOON IN OUR HANDS

Carroll & Graf Publishers
An Imprint of Avalon Publishing Group Inc.
245 West 17th Street
New York, NY 10011

AVALON
publishing group incorporated

First Carroll & Graf edition 2005
Copyright © 2005 Kelmscott Ink, Inc.

Library of Congress Cataloging-in-Publication Data is available.

ISBN: 0-7867-1505-7

Interior design by Susan Canavan
Distributed by Publishers Group West

To my mother and father,
who showed me that
the world was made of colors

Author's Note

The Moon in Our Hands is a novel, based on events in the life of Walter White (1893–1955), who, by his own tally, between 1918 and the early 1940s investigated forty-one lynchings and eight race riots for the NAACP, using tactics similar to those that follow. Although these extraordinary journeys produced detailed reports vital to the antilynching movement, White left only brief accounts of the journeys themselves, and *The Moon in Our Hands* is an attempt to imagine one of them—his first, made at a time when two hundred African Americans were being lynched every year. As much as I like to hope that the Walter White fashioned in these pages approximates the real man, his words and thoughts are built only out of what I have read and heard and hypothesized. They are all ultimately my creations, as are the town of Sibley Springs and its inhabitants. The dedication and courage, though, surely belong to the real Walter White.

"Nobody is anything all the time."

Maya Angelou

PROLOGUE

Afterward, a man in faded overalls looked up and saw the first stars of the night flicker over the town, over the Cumberlands to the east. "Good time for doing this," he said.

The man next to him kicked aside some loops of chain, still too hot to touch. Dented felt hat well down over his ears, he lifted up his head a bit and sniffed; in the silence the February air had settled now like a snow, captured the sour smell and held it close to the ground. He nodded. "Kill a hog 'neath the dark of the moon, lard's richer." The charred mass beside them wheezed. "Greasy bastard." They shared a weak laugh and both kicked at the chain now, hoping to cool it by rolling it out of the circle of burnt ash and onto the cold grass. "This yourn?"

The first man shrugged, hands deep into his overall pockets. "I don't know." He looked it over for a few seconds in the moonless dusk, toed it like a dead snake. "You got use for it?"

"Well, yeah. Probably so," said the man in the hat. He pushed up his brim and tried to think of one. "Didn't grunt him. I'll give 'em that. Didn't make a sound at the end."

Together they stared a bit longer until the man in the overalls went in search of a different souvenir for his wife. Most of the crowd had wandered back down the hill to hop the last train, but dozens remained, the residue of a mob milling about the pyre where they could smile freely at what they'd just seen, or done. So remarkable, so entertaining had it all been, that they hated to see it end, and though maybe a few hesitated to bring this kind of fire into their own homes, most spat

XI

wisely and reassured themselves out of any doubts as they sifted through the ash for keepsakes.

Three men, less excited than the rest, shuffled together toward the vague black shape at the center of it all and stopped. A man in the long coat and tie of a country professional shook his head while one of them poked at the thing with a long stick, forcing out another wheeze.

"When you think they all leaving?" he asked no one in particular, poking again.

Someone close by called, "Who wants some of the shirt?"

The empty-handed, still pecking through the grass, trotted over to examine a yard or so of green homespun in the hands of a bearded man wearing a tailless raccoon hat. Swept up by sudden generous instincts, he tore long shreds of fabric and thrust them into outstretched hands. A shriveled woman in a shapeless, man's jacket took hers and tied it through a button-hole. Charmed by her ingenuity, the crowd recognized a fashion when it saw one, and the bearded man instantly regretted his Christian impulse. To make up for his original lack of commercial sense, each new scrap would cost a dollar. The crowd would have none of it, though, and a shoving match ensued.

Ignoring the row, the three men watched instead as an arm, cooked through, dropped off, and thumped into the grass. "Oh hell," one of them said. The cupped palm and five large-knuckled fingers, still distinguish-able as what they'd once been, rose through the blades of dead grass, though one could just as easily have seen a dark, tropical flower lying there, or some scaly, malformed tuber upturned a season ago and rejected. Decades of tool mishaps and heavy lifting had left countless scars and nicks in the surface and had so calloused the palms that any memories of tenderness from that hand seemed impossible. It appeared to beckon to them, to ask that they visit the place where boiling flesh had burst apart skin, to notice the ring that identified this limb as once belonging to a human. A man they knew. Had once known.

The men stared at the arm and did not move. Whatever lesson it hoped to impart could not be heard for the wind in the trees and the echoes of the shouting, could not be seen for the darkness sliding over them all in the absence of a moon. Unheeded, the hand did not fight when the man with the stick finally squatted down and harvested a finger with the same twist of the wrist he used when snapping melons off the vine. Another joined, grimaced a little at the crackling sound he made but smiled once he had his souvenir. Offering a white handkerchief for wrapping, the professional man said, "Someone oughta tell the family. Maybe Ludey."

Those who'd missed out on the shirt suddenly noticed the action near the corpse. As they came closer, the last of the three, a man who'd remained silent, gone without a memento, noticed something shining in the dirt. A closer squint revealed it to be a gold ring crowned with a big blue stone. He bent to put his hand over it, pushed the grass around with his right for show. "Thought I saw something," he mumbled. Curving his fingers around the discovery, he slipped it into his pocket.

Now fully satisfied, the three stepped aside so others could snap off the remaining fingers, shove freely as the competition for lesser pieces began. Halfway down the hill, one of the men said, "They don't need telling. They know."

By ten, the clearing was empty. Stars filled the sky and a very primitive quiet swept the lost hills and fields of Sibley Springs.

Part One

—

ONE

There were no stars in New York. Only on the ceiling of Grand Central Terminal, where it was perpetually a moonless night in winter. Frozen forever in solstice position, electric Betelgeuese and Aldebaran twinkled amid painted constellations such as Orion, Pegasus, and the Crab, tried with thousands of other stars scattered across a blue-green sky to fool travelers into believing they were walking the shores of Lake Como at dusk.

Swinging around a corner, swerving past a fruit peddler and a family of newly arrived Russian immigrants sampling oranges, stopping only long enough to pick up late editions of the *Sun* and the *Evening Post,* a dapper young man in a sleek brown coat and matching fedora strode through the crowds of Grand Central Terminal. The stiff gait of his short legs, the purposeful swing of his case, betrayed someone who hadn't yet caught the rhythm of mass movement, a newcomer trying to look as purposeful as he assumed every New Yorker around him to be. Finding seams with a quarterback's sense, he arrived at Track 23 well in time for *The Birmingham Special's* eight o'clock departure.

It was colder here, open to the elements at the end of the tunnel, so he flipped up the collar of his coat, tucked his papers under his arm, and let the smoke and steam swallow him as he made his way down the platform, through the couples kissing goodbye, around the porters sweeping past with carts of baggage. Springing up onto the steps of a car, he tossed his paper on a seat near the door and flipped his suitcase onto the rack. More careful with his coat, he slipped out of the sleeves, folded it, and placed it on top of the case.

With a deep breath of the welcome heat, he sat down and snapped open a newspaper. The other passengers filed in as the young man, blue-eyed and blond, fine hair parted on the left and slicked across a high forehead, read news of the Bolshevik capture of Kiev. Average height and trim statured, completely unremarkable, he called attention to himself with frequent movements—constant adjustments to his tie, twitches of his moustache, toe tapping—that together with his sharp features created a foxlike quality, an air of cunning. The lifted chin, the straight back, the polite nod he gave anyone that met his eye all but shouted for his fellow travelers to recognize the brilliance of his future, to envy him whatever adventure he was setting off on. And yet anyone who noticed him noticed as well the way his searching eyes made his obvious hope appear to be just as much a fear.

At exactly eight P.M., the train lurched out of the station.

New York to Philadelphia passed quickly; he read his two newspapers as the train rocked along, the half-empty coach, the heat, the heavy wraps soothing some travelers into an early slumber long before the porters had prepared the berths. Once through Philly the numbing effect of travel set in on him too and leaning his head against the window, the lights of Maryland flashing by, he tried to sleep, but the engine's lulling motion failed him. He tore an article out of the *Post* and folded it into his pocket. He lit on passing details—the silhouette of a late-dining family thrown against their kitchen shade, the puddle of light in front of a Packard as it struggled to keep pace with the train—but his own reflection blocked his gaze so he turned to the passengers. Up a few rows a red-faced toddler squirmed in its mother's arms and loudly agitated for the removal of her sweater while the father, escape in his eyes, asked a porter for directions to a scotch. Financial types in their chalk-stripe suits passed a flask and discussed the turmoil in the British War Office while a middle-aged Negro in a tight, vested suit of gray worsted, bowler over his eyes, feigned sleep. At the far end, a couple not much older than the young man held hands and bobbed with the rails. The gentleman was only just noticeably Negro, light-skinned with worried eyes and straightened hair; his companion, unmistakably black, chewed at the corners of her lips. Both wore high-collared, faintly ministerial clothing more than a few years out of date. A second, older woman faced them; his mother, clearly. Her black hair was streaked with white and wrapped around the back of her head. She had steeled herself against the train's motion and the well-dressed, if not affluent, white couples around them, dealing hands of gin and reading *Cosmopolitan*. With a sigh of impatience, the young blond man stood, stretched, and opened his suitcase.

Sifting through a short stack of three laundered shirts, a pair of pants, two decks of playing cards—one marked and one straight—socks, undergarments, many small boxes of Cracker Jack, and various toiletries, as well as three mechanical pencils, a package of Choco-Lax, some toothbrush and toothpaste sets, and a large red box of Mr. Chee's Genuine Oriental Fortune Cookies, he at last unearthed a copy of *The Life of Ben Harrison* by General Lew Wallace, which he leafed through as he stood.

A sudden sway of the train pushed someone into his back. It was the conductor, edging past. Nearly spherical in a deep blue, double-breasted jacket, he assumed a military air and bellowed, "Waaaaashington, D.C. Next stop—Waaaashington, D.C."

The border.

In the capital of the United States another nation called The South began, and now three hundred years of its white voodoo fluttered curtains on the back porch of every passenger's mind, the scent of loamy Delta mud and sweet, spicy flowers softened resolve and stiffened manners. Imagined sounds, a lonely fiddle, the occasional whip crack, roused the train's respectable couples, made them stroke their sensible clothes. In these parts, thoughts rarely spoken of up North were proclaimed from pulpits, and so now they murmured to each other and nodded as they stole glances at the Negroes in the car, heretofore tolerated, if most pointedly ignored. A woman in a boa giggled.

Book in hand, the young man closed his suitcase and turned toward the club car, but the conductor didn't budge. Instead, cheeks swollen around the slits of his eyes and mouth like rising dough, he stood his ground in the middle of the aisle for a long, suspicious moment. Just as the traveler opened his mouth to request passage, the conductor stepped left, allowed him just enough space to press along the seats on the right, and avoid rubbing against him as he passed.

Two cars up, at the bar, he placed his book on the velvet banquette running the side of the car, rolled a thin cigarette, and greeted the bartender, a very black man in a very white jacket who took his order for a scotch and soda, then poured it with a generous hand. The young man closed his eyes.

Back home, he thought. Back home after only two weeks, and he had to admit he was happy about it, even under these circumstances. Though Maryland outside was still chilly, he felt Southern warmth in his bones again after New York's sloppy snow, the suffocating steam heat pissing out of its radiators. Somewhere in the train a harmonica drawled, touched at times with the trills and twists that signified complicated lives amid the cotton. Every mile they traveled, he sensed the train losing its Northern sense of purpose, old ways and temperate air gaining control. The South was his, too.

Something bumped his foot. He lifted it so an empty soda bottle could roll by over the gum wads, candy wrappers, and silver foil balls littering the floor; five or ten years ago, it would have been peach pits and sandwich crusts. Sneering at the manufactured Yankee trash, he stubbed out his cigarette only a few puffs through and reflected with pride that consuming had yet to consume the South the way it had New York. In his two weeks there, it appeared to him that the work of most New Yorkers involved convincing other people to buy things so that they could buy the things that *they'd* been convinced they needed.

He closed his eyes again, but his moustache started to twitch at a sudden musty, tangy smell, like cheap hair tonic slopped on dirty clothes, and when he opened his eyes he saw the source, a tall, once-handsome man, looming over him. Though the strong and regular features could have belonged to a top salesman or lodge president, the red, spongiform nose said no on behalf of its owner, announced that drink had poisoned this body, made such sturdy brands of success a lost dream. The blotchy pinks and creams of his cheeks, the broken blood vessels lacing them, leapt out next to his blue tweed suit, and the young man started back a few inches, surprised, and repulsed as the other leaned forward, the mum in his lapel drooping dangerously near. "Yeah, you like that music, don't ya," asked the man in confidential tones, looking around to see if anyone was listening. "I do too. I wouldn't admit this to anyone I'd ever see again, but I got quite the taste for that race music." He peeked around again, thrust out a hand for shaking. "Clover. Edward Clover."

"Walter White."

"Good to meet you, White." The hand hung in space as Walter noted the red patches of eczema, the bitten nails, the hairy knuckles. He gave it a quick squeeze. "Oh sure . . ." Clover then wrapped the scaly hand around his tumbler the way he'd once surely dreamt of wrapping it around the lodge gavel and lapped at his drink. ". . . Sometimes I go down to the Seventh Ward—I'm from Philly, see? Hit Lombard Street and just listen to whatever they're fixin' up."

Does he buy himself a little colored girl while he's down there, too, wondered Walter. What exactly would they do without us? He jogged his right knee up and down.

"So how do you pay the bills, White?"

The conductor leaned in through the door. "Ten minutes to Union Station. Waaaaashington, D.C. Ten minutes."

Lingering again in the middle of the aisle, the conductor stuck his thumbs into the small pockets of his vest and squinted hard into the rows before him. As *The Birmingham Special* slowed to enter Union Station, white passengers changed seats so they'd be ringside for the show.

"Insurance," said Walter, which was passingly true. During college, he'd walked all the one-outhouse towns that ringed Atlanta selling policies for Standard Insurance. It was his days wandering those peaceful little deathtraps that had given him the idea for this mission, an eager new-man-on-the job kind of idea that was feeling impetuous now, to say the least.

"Really, Mr. Roosevelt! Insurance! Me too!" Clover poked the shoulder of a fellow member of the brotherhood of underwriters. "Which outfit?"

Walter froze at Clover's touch, at being caught out only a few hours into the journey. He couldn't say Standard. Every insurance man knew Standard was an all-Negro concern. Still standing in the aisle, the conductor's eyes flicked with nervous energy, letting everyone know how little control he'd have over himself if necessity arose. Fear always made Walter think faster. "Intercontinental Mutual," he said. Clover wrinkled his nose and looked for the name up in his bushy eyebrows. "Yes sir. Intercontinental Mutual. New outfit." Before the salesman could ask any questions, Walter pulled his shoulder away from Clover's finger and drowned him in words. "You know," he said, "I can't think of a more important profession for a young man such as myself to be a part of ..." He was speechifying now. "You teach frugality, thrift, long-term thinking. Provide for widows and orphans."

And, he couldn't help thinking, you make a good living. Walter leaned over and sharpened the crease of his pants. His greatest regret about this new job was the pitiful salary, the simple fact that there wouldn't be another suit like this one for a long time.

Clover smirked. "Well, *you're* full a spit." He scratched at the back of his left hand with great avidity, switched to the right; off the scent, it seemed, for now.

Uncomfortably far down on Walter's list of regrets was leaving Cornelia, and he was feeling uncomfortably not guilty about this. He twitched at the memory of his fiancée lowering her eyes, turning away as if slapped when he'd broken the news of the move. She'd been a better sport when he'd told her his parents couldn't afford law school or that the army had thrown him out of officer's training for being a possibly seditious mulatto. Foolish him, he'd expected her to be proud of this new job. Not having to speak with her on a daily basis had at first brought on a kind of disorienting euphoria that turned to guilt when he realized just how soon he'd become accustomed to not thinking about her. And then day after day passed without a letter. When it finally came, it was a numbing chronicle of her weekly routine, from breakfast at Papa's table to something one of her little "brownies" did in class—she called them that, "brownies," and he'd never truly admitted until this moment just how much he hated it—all the way to dinner with whatever well-off family was scheduled for that night; four pages sparsely dotted with expressions of affection so restrained as to resemble admiration or appreciation more than what they in their less buckled moments of the past four years had called love.

"Washington, D.C.!" said the conductor over the rushing steam of the train stopping.

Before leaving home today, he'd made a point to not check the mailbox, though he had dropped her photograph into his pocket, an act that right now felt more like superstition than devotion. He resisted a pale need to be reminded of her eyes, once smoky but now, to him, asleep.

"Waaaaaashington, D.C.. Make your changes!"

Make your changes. By law, Walter should have popped up and fulfilled his Negro duty, and indeed he felt the reflex to follow orders, but tonight he had to watch. He sipped his scotch and winced, fumbled the rolling of another cigarette while the conductor rounded up black passengers, stirred them out of their seats with a rough shake when entering the South hadn't been enough to wake them. From car to car he herded black men and women, families with puzzled children wondering why they had to move, through the club car and into the next, so that the new white passengers could take the seats God had always meant for them to have. How nice and warm the benches were after three hours of colored use!

Walter forced himself to stay engaged with Clover. "I'm sorry you don't agree with me, mister. It's a true calling." Leaning back, he took a drag on his cigarette, focused the superiority of his youth on the sorry man before him.

Overseeing the process from their seats, white folks nursed their drinks, their strongest protest a studied oblivion. Walter's face flushed as the contents of his car passed by. The light-skinned minister and his wife exchanged thin smiles, doing their best to appear as if they just hadn't been comfortable where they'd been sitting, as the older woman marched behind with her head high. She stared at Walter, who found something compelling to investigate on the tabletop until they passed.

Clover slouched over his drink. "A calling, huh? Well, maybe you're right." The salesman let his hands rest. "You know, Mr. Barrymore, I'll be damned if you don't remind me of myself not a few years ago."

Oh really, thought Walter? Picking a cuticle, he noticed from the corner of his eye how the man and wife gripped each other's hands.

Then the vested fellow in the bowler shuffled by as if sleepwalking, eyes all but closed despite the prods of the conductor.

"You know I'm pretty sure I've heard of, what was it? Inner-conti . . . ?"

"Intercontinental."

Jowls trembling, the conductor waved a fat finger. "You know this train will not move until *all* Nigras are in the *Nigra* car."

And yet for some reason this clear statement seemed to provoke the opposite reaction and the man only became more sluggish.

"Oh sure. That's right. Innercontinental. New firm, right?"

"Yes, sir."

"Are you deaf?" asked the conductor. "Are you a *moe*-ron?" White folks in their chairs clucked and shook their heads; the additional delay this Negro was causing proved it well enough—These niggers just didn't understand how the world worked. People would miss meetings, mail would be late, hundreds—no, thousands—of good white men and women inconvenienced because of this nigger's ignorant sloth.

"So where ya headin," asked Clover, the edges of his words softened by whisky.

"Franklin County, Tennessee." Walter watched the man's protest play out, entirely misunderstood by the all-knowing white folks. "Down by the Alabama line."

"Oh hell, I been down there. Heard they ha' some 'citemin'."

Walter's heart leapt at this sweet bit of luck! "I'll be damned!" Old salesmen had always told him that the good information comes when the other man starts to slur. Walter gave his companion an encouraging smile.

At the end of the club car, a petite woman sitting near the door that opened onto the Negroes began urgently calling for the conductor in a voice as shrill as cold gin. Attractive only because she was a sure thing, she blew boa feathers away from her mouth as she

11

waited, tapped a mule-wearing toe and pointed with distaste at something in the other coach the way she would point towards something her poodle had left at a curb. It was the minister.

"Yup. Porter up in D.C. tole me 'bout it. Runs on the N.C. & St. L. line through Sibley Springs. They gave Sibley Springs to some new fella; he got the 'Lower Middle Tennessee Terror-tory.' Thass what they call it now—your terror-tory. I got the Upper Deep South, which is your Alabama and Mississippi and Georgia, but not Atlanta." Clover scowled. "No, not Atlanta." After a beat, he looked at Walter. "Does any of this make sense to you any-more?" Clover began drifting away again. "Does *anything* make sense to you anymore?" The salesman rubbed an index finger down the velvet curtain.

The conductor glowered at the minister while the white woman waved about the tip of her boa, thrilled to be in the spot-light. "You know what he's after," Walter heard her say. "It's immoral, white mens trawlin' nigger girls."

She moved her hips back and forth slightly, in a rhythm with her words. New York was full of women, and Walter had spent two weeks watching them pass as if he were in a cage, close enough to see them and smell them, but untouchable, every one. And every morning, every pair of eyes he met on the subway, made him feel a little bit more the fool.

"So what happened in Sibley Springs?" snapped Walter. "Some excitement, you said."

Clover mumbled, "Yeah, well, they lynched some colored."

The older Negro woman put a protective arm across the accused. "He's my son!"

The "colored's" name was Cleon Quine. Walter drummed his fingers on the table, distracted himself from the scene in the other car by thinking about what was known. Aged fifty-one, a farmer, Quine had been strung up after a disagreement with three youths on the streets of Sibley Springs, Tennessee. Tortured first, then castrated, he'd finally been burned alive by the good people of the town. Other than those few, rude facts, Sibley Springs had kept its secrets, hidden the guilty behind its skirts. The article he'd torn out of the *Evening Post* had no new information, just the Association's statement.

"Didn't buy much from me, I'll tell ya that." Clover snorted. "They got those sulfur springs. Place smells like shit. Say, you haven't *touched* your drink."

Bring back the story. A couple of hours out, and he was already doing just that. That was the job Mr. Johnson had charged him with after he'd sprung the idea on them all. Mr. Johnson and Miss Ovington had stood there in the office on Fifth Avenue with their heads together, clucking, *Will he be safe?* and *Does he know what to do?* like an old married couple while John Shillady, the supposed head of the Association, wrung his hands in the corner. Issuing statements made him comfortable; this kind of thing did not. Of all the people he knew, Mr. James Weldon Johnson was the most elegant, a brilliant diplomat and composer—he would never let himself think poorly of him—but Miss Ovington, as good a person as she was, struck Walter so far as a glorified schoolteacher. He'd finally broken into their huddle, pointed at the clock and said, "I'll miss the train!" And now, a few hours later, after a speedy cab ride up to Harlem, a ham sandwich and an ill-considered packing job, here he sat. Two weeks had also made it clear to him that the NAACP needed more action and fewer theories. *Bring back all the information you can,* Mr. Johnson had told him. *We'll get it to the governor, and Dr. Du Bois will run your account in* The Crisis. *The truth will indeed save us, Walter. You will be my Corona.* He had thirty dollars and 28 cents—enough for eight days in Sibley Springs plus train fare home.

The woman's voice cut through both cars. "Your son like *hell!*"

Walter's neck prickled. He saw himself pouncing on the conductor, barking at the woman to sit back down and leave the church mice alone as he fended off the attacks of drunken white men. Mr. Johnson's mellow voice pressed down on him: *You'll be tempted Walter, but you are not justice. You work FOR justice. Your job is to prove a great crime.*

Do what you're told, thought Walter, edging closer to the window. *For once.* But if he'd kept his mouth shut at meetings, stopped trying to be in charge of everything whether or not he'd had any clue as to how, would he have become secretary of the Atlanta branch? Would Mr. Johnson have recruited him? Walter bit his lip. No matter what Mr. Johnson thought up in New York, Walter was absolutely certain that what this conductor most needed right now was a whip snap all over his damp, white ass.

"Say, she's got it goin'!" Clover turned his head. "Cozyin' up to the dusky maidens, huh?" Said with a touch of romance. He leaned forward again, thrust his nose, bright pink and porous, even closer to Walter. "Can't say that I blame him, but they're a little wild for me, Mr. Edison." Clover winked.

Walter stubbed out his cigarette. "You go on. Man like you?"

"Oh, I been tempted, believe you me." Clover's eyes fogged as he summoned some of the dark ankles he'd catalogued during his years on the road. He'd surely bed his share of widows, typists, and diner waitresses who'd let him do what he wanted as long as he rubbed their feet. As if it were the starting link in a chain of evidence, Walter called up his first attempt to cajole a kiss out of Cornelia; he could not help the minister. That was not his fight. It was on a moonlit night, magnolias perfuming the campus. They'd escaped from their dorms to nestle under a tree near Stone Hall and discussed, much to his extreme displeasure, Anthony Trollope. For three hours, she'd offered her practiced opinion of *Phineas Finn* until he'd finally grasped her hand out of desperation to have at least *touched* her. Oh yes, Mr. Clover, he thought, grinding his teeth even now at the memory, *quite* wild. Even at the best of times, after stolen kisses were allowed, she dampened every affection with a roll of her eyes or an exasperated sigh, the price, he'd once figured, for all the admiring smiles and invitations owed the campus beauty. Four years later, she was still beautiful, but Walter was in charge of nothing. They discussed their future together—always in terms of when he was successful, eventually—but he could no longer smile away the sense that she wanted more; a more secure future, more talk of a dizzy, blind love for her that he'd never felt. Chronic disappointment had set in, he knew it; the cheery expectation of marriage rubbed down into resignation. The night before he'd left Atlanta, he'd sat with her for a hour and seen nothing but memories, lost all words other than the protests necessary for a lukewarm kiss. As he remembered the scene, her thick hair, the long, fawn-colored arms, all he felt was annoyed.

"Yes, he *is* my *son*," said the older woman. Walter stole a look at the minister hunching under the protection of the two women. "He is a Negro." Her public announcement that he belonged to the lowest possible class of humanity dashed any pretense that some higher things mattered to white America. *All they care about is skin,* thought Walter. The wife's head sagged.

In the doorway, the accuser smirked, still unsatisfied. Clover, returned from his miscegenary dreams, offered Walter tobacco. Niggerhead Brand.

Maybe it was the scotch. Maybe it was Cornelia, or just life in America. Whatever it was, the magic word made him so dizzy and furious that he thrust off the layer of everyday acceptance the way a snake sheds its skin, left himself vulnerable to the shock of Negro existence. Stupid, bitter questions formed in Walter's mind. *Is this* all *that white people can do?* he wondered. *Can they talk about* anything *else? Do they have* any *idea how slovenly they are? How they* smell? This Clover with his sharp stink of boarding house cabbage and fear . . . Walter's heart threatened to burst. "Immoral," she'd said. Immoral for

15

a man to be with his wife and mother. How *twisted* were the minds of white people. His mother always said it, and she was right—that extra $\frac{1}{32}$ of Negro blood in the White family made them more than just Negroes; it made them *better.*

Loudly enough for both cars to hear, the minister said, "This is where I *belong,*" the word *belong* hanging in the air with a pungency Walter assumed only the other blacks heard. The conductor and the woman in the boa snorted.

The world should not be like this, thought Walter, twenty-four years old, still convinced that the word "should" carried power. He noticed the light from a sconce falling on his book like a heavenly shaft and remembered that he was royal. Sort of. Family lore held that his great-grandmother had been President Harrison's slave and mistress—a misalliance, legendary or not, that allowed Walter to imagine himself Harrison's descendant, and when he wandered even further up the Harrison line, his blood went beyond the White House, over the ocean and back to the English kings. And there was Cornelia, tolerating his failure, acting as if this was a job somewhere below wearing the collar; an indulged kind of profession *other* men did. Drifting down upon him now, that mantle of royalty comforted him with the feeling he was the only man here who truly owned wisdom and justice, reassured him of his rightful and impossible place in the world. He hated moments like these, but what he couldn't admit ever to anyone else was how much he loved them, how they fed his righteous passion.

He jerked up, his voice slipping high and out of control, "You son of a . . ."

Clover pulled at the hem of his jacket. "Hold on there, Sergeant York! Slow down! Let the conductor do his job. Have another drinkee."

No one moved in either car. The bartender, the conductor, the minister and his family; every passenger stared at Walter, and as the silence eagerly built he wondered what exactly his plan was, given he hadn't actually laid hands on someone since he was eight. A few hard tackles on the football field didn't count.

"Take a breath," whispered Clover, with a glance around the car. "Take a breath, General Pershing. You want some air?"

What exactly are you trying to do? Walter asked himself.

His moustache twitched to his pounding heart, and still he did not speak. His fellow passengers seemed to nod encouragement, just assumed that he was cursing the minister. A sidelong glare from the bartender confirmed Walter's fear that he'd been misunderstood. Before he said anything to correct the mistake, to reveal his true intentions, he realized that he'd come a breath away from revealing himself. Dr. Du Bois's words buzzed in his mind: *Blackness is being someone who must ride Jim Crow in Georgia.* Yet here he was, Walter White, $\frac{5}{32}$ Negro, riding unquestioned with the white men and the white women, a required act under the circumstances for which he currently felt an enveloping shame. Walter groped for the banquette and slid down. "I think a drink, maybe, yes," he said to Clover, even though he hadn't finished his first.

Disappointed murmurs collected in the corners of the car, men and women sipped at their drinks, stealing long and shameless looks at Walter. The conductor shrugged. "Ma'am, he's a Negro. Said it himself. Why would he lie about *that?*" Case closed, he plowed back up the aisle toward the engine, slowing briefly for a fresh look at Walter as he passed. *The Birmingham Special* let out a whistle and aimed at Tennessee.

The minutes rolled on. Another glass of liquor appeared, though he'd already decided not to drink it, afraid of what it might make him do next. He calmed himself with thoughts of home, his sisters.

Clover ran a thumb and forefinger over the frayed edges of his cuffs. "Yeah. Well . . ." Fully drunk at last, he peered over the edge he'd been building up the strength to confront. "I don't care if she leaves. She can stay at her mother's, if that's what she wants. I don't miss her."

Walter heard Clover speak but not his words, considered rolling another cigarette. How long, he wondered, before he'd be there? When he'd read the first story in the paper next to Mr. Johnson he'd felt a need to *see* the place, but in a way beyond witnessing. He'd done enough witnessing. Something had to be *done.*

His fingers touched Cornelia's photograph in his pocket; his stomach ached as he pictured her pursed lips, her tolerance. He may not have been rich or famous, but Walter knew he deserved more than tolerance. All his dissatisfaction stewed, and just as the train crossed a thin trestle bridge in the Shenandoahs, the mixture hit critical temperature, hardened of a sudden into a sour mass of truth. He'd known it for at least a year. When he closed his eyes, he couldn't escape the fact making itself all too clear to him now; he read the block letters behind his lids—*I don't love her.* And, he was sure, if Cornelia was honest, she'd admit the same.

As if breaking the surface after a long dive, Walter let out a rush of air and took another equally deep.

"Good riddance," said Clover, as if reading Walter's mind. The salesman let his head droop. "That's what I say. Good riddance!"

"Hear, hear!" said Walter, clinking his glass to Clover's, brothers after all. Good riddance, indeed. It was settled: he was definitely not marrying Cornelia Devers. Not only was he not ever marrying Cornelia Devers, but likely he would never see her again! The thought awakened his masculine sense of the world's constant amorous possibilities. He was free.

Clover shrugged, eyelids wavering at the weight of three drinks. "Can't figure it. Nope. Can't."

His head suddenly clear, Walter shifted around in his suit, eager to move on in a hundred different ways now. He thought about the insanity of what he'd just done by speaking out in the car. He'd nearly destroyed the entire plan before it had started, even as Mr. Johnson's words had played in his mind. *You will be there to prove a crime,* he'd said. *You do not need to prove yourself.* What if the conductor had taken one more good look and decided that his nose was a little broad, detected a suspicious thickness to his lips? The fact that he'd nearly been caught tamped him down a bit. *If they find you out, my boy, they'll kill you three times,* Mr. Johnson had said. *Once for being black, once for being white, and once for being both.*

Mr. Johnson had looked terribly grave then as he spoke, but all Walter could see then was what he saw now: the flashbulbs popping in his head, the reporters—"Mr. White, what sort of people did you encounter?" He was a bachelor again, free to accomplish the sort of large and dangerous achievement that men on the way to the altar must swear off. *Did you know that you'd be risking death for justice, Mr. White?* A parade through the streets of Harlem for busting this story wide open. Walking into Brentano's with the great James Weldon Johnson at his side and seeing a stack of his *own* autobiography . . .

The harmonica snaked around the train again, and Walter allowed himself one more sip—Clover had bought him bourbon, not scotch. He guessed that Old Ed Clover would probably jump off the train if he had any idea his drinking buddy was a Neee-gro.

Clover slurred, "That's a good idea. Relax a bit. You know what they call that? They call it 'the blues.' "

A sudden bilious wave in his stomach made Walter sit up. He couldn't even enjoy the simple pleasure of closing his eyes and listening to a harmonica without a white man explaining it to him. Usually the layer between himself and the world, the white world, grew back, stretched a little wider like a new skin, but tonight he still felt raw. The blood in his temples ached. When exactly could a black man relax? Who had Quine's body? Had he been buried right? Had there been enough left to bury?

Clover snored gently. The conductor stopped in front of them, stared at Walter, whose heart began beating quite rapidly. *You can never relax,* he told himself. *Never.* "May I help you?"

"Time you and your friend got some sleep."

"I don't really know him . . ."

"Where you headed?"

"Chattanooga. Then on to Sibley Springs."

The conductor didn't move. "You from there?"

"No sir. I'm a salesman. That's my new territory." He pulled out his tobacco bag. Another cigarette would calm him down, that and the shelter of knowing that a white man never risked affronting another white man by accusing him of being black. "One more of these and I'm turning in."

Very slowly, the conductor nodded and waddled on.

The only time Walter's father had ever whipped him was for smoking, back when he was fifteen. He knew people who'd been expelled from college for the vice of tobacco. Walter lit his final one of the night, took a deep, calming pull, and let the smoke dribble out of his nose. He was a man now, a young unmarried man with all too many sorts of hunger, already different from the man who'd boarded at Grand Central Terminal. A fattening moon cast enough light on the passing countryside for Walter to pick out details beyond his white face in the window: a slanting shack in a field, telephone poles, tall trees with low, thick limbs. He leaned back into his seat and focused on his reflection. He was also a black man, and a black man could never relax. Not until he was dead.

Two

He did not see Clover at five A.M. when he got off the train at Chattanooga. Keeping to himself the rest of the trip, Walter made the complicated connections that took him through the unexplored coves of the Cumberlands and down into Alabama's bleak fields, and then back northward on a N.C. & St. L. liner destined for Nashville. Once more he had to climb the Cumberlands, this time from the other side, riding through Sherwood, Anderson, and Monteagle—mountain hamlets.

Outside his window, shreds of midday clouds sank down from the white sky to meet fog rising up from hollows. Rainwater glazed the rocks and boulders, creating new streams among the stands of leafless trees that Walter's eyes jounced over. This was the long, last stretch of winter in southern Tennessee, the painful weeks of damp Lent, as men wondered whether the promises of Christ and the groundhog would indeed come true.

Here in these drizzly hollows, his evening ideal of a warmer, more elemental South seemed overstated; primeval came closer to the truth, a raw sort of life cooking away under the mud and dead leaves. Until the last two weeks, he'd spent his entire life around Atlanta. He'd never seen *this* South yawning before him, and now, as it happened to every black man who strayed from the guided paths, travel had turned him into an explorer in his own nation. Walter tried to enjoy the idea, fancying himself for a few miles a black Stanley weaving through the unspeakable perils of the White Continent.

More locals piled on at Cowan station, each new face taking note that he was not known. Suddenly very alone, Walter shivered with the fact that his familiarity with the dialect and resemblance to the natives would not guarantee his safety. He folded his arms, then remembered that he'd been without a wash for more than a day now, a repellent thought to him. The roll and cup of coffee at the Huntsville switch were a long time ago, and his stomach now growled for lunch. During the night, as he'd rustled in the sheets of his berth, the unpleasant image of Edward Clover had appeared. He'd decided then that insurance was not the right game to play in Sibley Springs. Instead, he'd be Walter White of the Exelento Medicine Company, producer of fine hair straightening products for men and women of all races. Some bawdy punchlines of a drummer's sort came to mind, and he blushed a very nonsalesman red.

Down from the Cumberlands, the train entered the Plateau. Trees gave way to thousands of acres of broken stalks and barren expanses, gray and shiny with muck. Bleak smears of brown and gray and wind-blown tan, the identical field repeated over and over, desolate huts made of tired wood. Sooner than he expected, the call came for Sibley Springs.

Walter stared out the window at small, chilly homes adrift on winter fields, an advertisement for Black Draught painted on a barn, a misery unrelieved and damp. Three days ago, Sibley Springs hadn't existed in the mind of a single person outside of Middle Tennessee, and from the look of the shacks they were passing now, Walter bitterly concluded that it probably hadn't represented much to those living here either. Already Mr. Johnson talked about "preventing another Sibley Springs" as if this whole town, its existence in general, had been proven a regrettable and deadly mistake. For Walter's part, he'd employed one especially squalid Georgia burg he'd once visited to represent Sibley Springs in his mind; in the end weren't they all the same? The general store guarded by drunken farmers and loafing dogs, the monument to the Confederate dead.

That the lynchers could very well live in those dingy homes he was passing, could be sitting there right now eating eggs, fully dawned on Walter, and in the course of three miles of railroad track, Sibley Springs was transformed from two simple words in his mind into an actual place. The risks of the mission gnawed at the edges of his nerves, fingers, and toes. Suddenly it wasn't surprising to Walter that such a thing had happened *here*. Happened right outside this train. The same kind of thing that would happen to any Negro who got caught pretending he was white.

Just after it entered a thatch of forest and quickly came out again, the train crossed a black iron trestle bridge over a small, slow river, then stopped with a great release of steam.

Sibley Springs.

Walter did not move. Still tapping his toes, now fingering the brim of his fedora, he sat in his seat waiting for the curtain to part, for the kicker to put up the ball. *Concentrate*, he told himself. Before games, he'd tell the team, *Breathe deep and concentrate*. He could hear the crowd. The teams lined up. Cheers boiling over. *Nothing else exists*. He flexed his biceps, tested his calves. *Forget everything that's not on this field. Look for the seams*. Cheers turning to a roar. He rotated his neck. *Exploit their weaknesses*. Walter stood up, grabbed his hat and bag. *Outsmart, but don't be afraid to outmuscle. You're on the Exelento team now.*

He grabbed a handle along the door frame of the coach and swung himself around the corner and onto the last step, the train chuffing. Through the doors of the station, dozens of people were suddenly rushing toward him with the same sound the crowds used to make before the game. They came forward, all facing the train, looking for someone, examining the disembarking passengers with the hungry, unconscious smiles of a meeting transforming itself into a mob.

It was obvious to Walter what had happened. The conductor of *The Birmingham Special* had known all along and sent word down the line. Stuck to the bottom step, he reminded himself that he'd survived a mob once before. The old torches flared to life in the dark place where he'd locked the memories, and he made himself remember that he was no longer a boy, that there were no torches. On the other hand, Mr. Johnson would never have told him to simply walk into an ambush.

The whistle blew. This was not a long stop.

Why was he doing this? He had to get back on the train!

Thousands of men had been lynched in America, and Walter suddenly wondered why he had to be one of them. No one had asked him to do this. He didn't sign on to the NAACP to die. He would tell Mr. Johnson the locals wouldn't talk. Hole up in Chattanooga for a few days. He had to think of his mother.

The whistle blew again. He reached behind for the arch of the train door with a hand and a foot.

It was the right thing to do. He could still get out of this place alive.

The train inched forward and he felt his parade in Harlem slipping away, imagined Alexander in his armor—at twenty-four he had conquered the world. And here he was, afraid to step off a train. How would he ever look Mr. Johnson in the eye, or his father?

He released his grip on the moving train, stumbling once and for all onto the platform. Righting himself, Walter stood tall to face his executioners. Nearly all women, they wore thin, drab coats over ankle-length dresses of dark cotton or wool. They waved no weapons. In fact, they didn't even appear particularly angry and once they had a good look at him, their heads craned away as one, a flock of dun field birds searching for something new to run from or eat. To his immense relief and profound embarrassment, Walter realized he was not who or what they wanted. As the train ground forward, a heavy bag hit the platform and with a unanimous cluck of satisfaction, the women shuffled toward it, boys and girls continuing to chatter and flirt on the fringes as word spread into the depot that the mail had arrived. Walter scolded himself, wondered if anyone had noticed him quaver.

Out came the stationmaster, white-haired with muttonchop whiskers along both jaws, the rooster of the yard high-stepping around the hen house. Waving his arms, he shouted gruff warnings to the women to stop ripping at the mailbag. Walter grabbed his sleeve and the NAACP spy became an Exelento salesman, pouring forth words. "I believe you're the man I need to see!" The stationmaster, well into his eighties, lowered his head so he could peer over his rimless glasses at the man accosting him. The medal on his jacket looked suspiciously Confederate in origin. "I'm guessing you're the stationmaster, right?"

"Yes, sir, and I'm a goddamned busy one right now so what do you *need?*"

Walter stuck out a hand. "I'm White. Walter White. With the Exelento Medicine Company. This is my new territory, and I'm waiting for my samples to arrive so I can get a move on here and start selling. Has a case arrived for me? My name's White? Walter White? Ring a bell . . . ?" The stationmaster cast a glance toward the women, all clamoring for news from their soldier boys, then back at Walter with annoyance. "I didn't catch your name . . . ?"

"Drake," he said. "If you have to know. Now I asked *you,* what do . . ."

"A pleasure, Mr. Drake. I'm Walter White."

"Yes. I *know.*" Plumes of impatient breath steamed down from Drake's nostrils.

"I'm only saying that to remind you. Should we check for it?"

"No. Whatever it is, it ain't here," said Drake, deliberately, pecking his head a little forward at each word. "You drummers think the whole world . . ."

"It hasn't come in yet then," Walter said. "Because it is coming here. It was supposed to be here already. Listen, . . ." He tugged at Drake's sleeve one more time as the stationmaster tried to slip away. "Here's what I'll do. What times are the trains?"

"Eight A.M., two P.M. just gone, and the six o'clock." Drake pulled back his arm. "Come back when . . ."

"Six P.M. All right then, I'll come back and check if it's arrived on the later train. A salesman's nothing without his samples, you know. Much obliged."

Whether he was waving him away or acknowledging his thanks, Walter could not tell as Drake marched over to the mailbag and began pulling it and the crowd of women behind him. He let the parade of mail and females pass, leaned against a wall, and caught his breath for a moment before he entered the station. The sample case was the best excuse he could think of for staying around this hell hole for a few days.

The women thronged around Drake. All around were the signs of a great move, consisting largely, it appeared, of medical apparatus. Huge wicker chairs with high, rounded backs perfect for the aged or tubercular had been piled up to the ceiling along one wall, while in a corner, four stiff wheelchairs circled a stack of wooden boxes all stencilled with the odd legend "SIB. SP. SPA." Walter picked up the last copy of the *Nashville Banner* from a little boy in tattered overalls, hugging his knees as he manned a low crate beside a hospital gurney topped with yet more boxes. Head lolling to one side, eyes uncomfortably far apart on his jaundiced face, the boy glanced up when Walter put down a nickel for the two-cent paper. The boy continued gazing up and scratching at one of his outsized ears with languid strokes as Walter waited for his three cents. At last, the boy's jaw slipped open into a gape, drool creeping over the edge of his lip. Walter gulped and tapped the crate with a finger. "Keep the change." Then he stepped out of the station for his first look at the real Sibley Springs.

Despite the numerous steeples puncturing the sky, it was possible that the Lord had already damned this town to Hell, stripped this corner of the planet down to dreary browns and grays and shades of dirty white. Walter could detect very few signs of life, only the plumes of chimney smoke curling up from every home and building, strings connecting the town to the clouds above. A thick bank of trees lined the river to his left and continued following the water's curve in the distance, broken only by an opening for some structure or bridge at about ten o'clock. Otherwise, the land sat naked and newborn, embarrassed by its lack of covering. Everything that may once have grown here looked to have been chopped down and planed to build the wooden buildings scattered about, yet unlike a plowed field where flatness is the point, this town felt like a newly shaven face, puckered and uncomfortable with exposure. Accustomed to Atlanta and New York, Walter White looked for the places to hide in, the corners where you could get yourself lost, but Sibley Springs had none. Some low hills rose to the right. An arrow-shaped sign also stencilled SIB. SP. SPA pointed in the direction of a pair of wagon ruts that disappeared into another bit of forest. A couple of blocks straight ahead on a pocked road stood a patch of two-story buildings, a few made of brick, which added up to downtown Sibley Springs. Except for a smattering of people huddled under a porch in front of one of the buildings and a single wagon next to it, no one walked the streets, no cars or horses disturbed the gray sheen on the road or the silence. Pale, enervating light filtered through pasty clouds, and a faint disagreeable odor floated in the humid air—brimstone. Quite possibly, God had nothing to do with this place.

"You like it?"

An old black woman spoke this from under a bright red wrap. Her skin was a polished, reddish brown, and she sat in a large oaken chair, beside a table covered with a collection of what he took to be small white stones, though the sign at her feet—"PEARLS FOR SALE *by A. L. Timmons*"—explained otherwise. She gestured with her head toward the other side of the station, where mean little shacks huddled together alongside another rutted path, their frames exposed in places. "Back there's where the niggers live." A white person would have taken this as a point of information, but what she was saying was that she'd spent years looking at those better homes across the tracks and had found no reason why she shouldn't have had the chance to live in one of them. Only one squat bungalow, painted dark green, its horizontal boards all securely fastened, gave any appearance of warmth and solidity.

"Whatcha have there, Auntie?" He cringed as he spoke, disgusted that he had to speak this way to his own people.

"They pearls." Miss Timmons tapped the board. "You see the sign?"

Walter White, Exelento salesman, would have to humor her. He bent over the table, pretended to take in this treasure of glowing pearls—all shapes, sizes, and colors, from the blue that edged summer clouds to the pink of sunset to weak lemonade. Some were snowy white, others cast dove gray or silver; teardrops and oblongs, strange shapes and perfect spheres, even squares, from the size of a young sweet pea to some grape-sized curiosities. Walter peeked up ahead at the building with people in front of it and figured it for the general store. During his insurance days he'd always made the general store the first stop; storekeepers knew everyone in town and everything about them—how much money they had, what they bought, and why.

"Very nice. Where'd you get them?" With its subtle accusation, Walter judged it a properly suspicious remark for a white man to make in this situation.

Miss Timmons worked her lips a little, disappointed with his lack of consumer interest. "Pearlymussels," she said, and lifted an arm toward the river. "In the Elk. You got yourself a sweetheart? These go-o-o-od for that." The woman leaned forward and began to work the pearls with long, root-like fingers, picking them up, examining them, straightening them.

With a slight pang, Walter answered to himself. Feigning interest in the pearls, he picked up a few as he reviewed the next steps in the plan. Plain folks are suspicious folks. He'd ask no questions, take a room, wait for his samples for as long as it took for the town to tell him its secrets—Shillady had given him twenty-five dollars of the thirty he had, enough for a week. Then he'd get the hell out. If they wanted to tell him everything today, he'd be on the six o'clock train.

"What you doing here?" Miss Timmons asked.

He itched to see the place right away: the burnt pole, the tree, whatever form the cross had taken that day. Like a tourist hunting for an out-of-the way chapel or hard-to-find statue, Walter craned his head over the woman's shoulder as if it might be just *there,* over on the next block, hidden somewhere in plain sight. "I'm a salesman, Auntie. Exelento Hair Straightener."

She snorted, waved an angry hand at him. "Get out a here with that. Black man's hair *supposed* to be kinky."

Walter smiled and touched his own hair, light and wavy when not greased down. In college, they'd called him "Fuzzy." He sniffed at the sulfurous aroma, a rotten egg tang that could not be ignored, as if the whole town had just spoiled. "What is that?"

She giggled in a high and girlish way, surprising from a woman so old. "That smell? That's the springs." She pointed in the direction of the SIB. SP. SPA arrow. "They shuttin' 'em down for good this week. Nobody comin' anymore."

Walter noticed the pair of beaded moccasins on her feet. "I like those." Miss Timmons was old enough to have been a slave. Which meant that she most likely had been.

"Cherokee. One quarter of me is Cherokee Indian."

"Anywhere a man can get something to eat?"

Without hesitation, Miss Timmons said, "No," then giggled again.

Walter blinked, nervously twitched his moustache at her brutal simplicity. Tipping his fedora, he stepped into the crossroads and opened the paper. Bolsheviks striking in Germany, civil war in Finland. What else was new, he thought?

Germans launch aerial attack against eastern shores of England.

Slowing down, he realized the Boche had tried the same thing three weeks ago, before he'd moved to New York.

Italian troops break through at Asiago.

Walter stopped and checked the date of the paper—January 30, 1918. The boy had sold him a paper three weeks old. Feeling his connection to civilization growing thinner, Walter stuck the paper under his arm and forged ahead with a swagger he considered befitting a cocky salesman but which really wasn't all that different from his own. He dodged puddles for a block until he saw three teenaged boys leaning against a shed. An alarm went off in his head. He lengthened his strides and made a great show of ignoring their presence as he watched them from the corner of his eye. They muttered among themselves as a woman, statuesque with a massive bosom and airs to match, crossed in front of him. Though her weight would cut a few years off her life expectancy she still had a nice spring in her step, and the quality of her clothes indicated access to adequate doctoring if so needed. Figuring her for somewhere between the ages of forty-five and fifty, Walter decided that he'd have approved her application for a policy.

Coming to the paved stretch of the business center, Walter noticed he shuffling gait of the middle-aged man digging a post hole in front of the Baptist church; a barber's pallor as he stared out of his window toward the empty field across the street; gaunt women, scabs on their arms and legs, skin cast the same gray as plaster, standing before the empty stores; all utterly uninsurable. The woman, obviously a "leading citizen" of the town, stood out as a healthy exception. Young men his age were conspicuously rare.

Also absent were any Negroes whatsoever, save for Miss Timmons. All the way from the station not a single tanned face, a single olive face, let alone a black one, and as he arrived at the main intersection, the feeling washed over him of bobbing alone on a great white sea, that lonely moment he sometimes had in New York when he realized he was the only Negro in a subway car or in a restaurant, not that anyone ever knew. He wondered if every black person had already moved up to Cleveland and Chicago. Sometimes that happened; an entire black population or close enough to it would just pick up and leave after a lynching like Quine's. If not, they were probably in hiding.

Someone had splashed the words CLOSED FOREVER in red paint across the boarded windows of a butcher store, an unusual act of honesty amid all the other vacant stores and splintering signs, the evidence of widespread bankruptcy and failure. Although the view from the station could be read as a town yet in its pioneer infancy, these signs of past life proved that in fact Sibley Springs was stillborn, a dead, or at least dying, place past all hopes it may once have had for a future. The white clouds pressing down, the way the cold made him pull in his arms and stomach all compressed Walter into his own thoughts, and that was not a place he chose to go unless forced. He focused on a tall, emaciated man outside the Sibley Springs Farmers Bank wracked by a coughing fit, his clothes flapping like flags in a storm. *You're just passing through,* he told himself, trying to shoo the fear. He didn't have to live here. He'd get the story and get out.

Standing across the street from Vine's General Store, Walter took a good look before making his first contact with the natives. Once blue, its façade had largely peeled down to the raw wood, and a painted list—ladies' notions, nails, seeds, hardware, and the like—faded away on both sides of the thick, oaken doors. The two figures he'd seen in the distance, farmers keeping dry under the porch as they sat on bales of hay and barrels, both stared at him through bleary eyes. The guards of the sanctuary, thought Walter; the liquored-up dirt farmers. Assumptions confirmed, he shook his head back and forth an inch in rueful satisfaction. A fat man, with the sly and greedy eyes of a pig huddled close to his nose, tossed a rock up and down in a way that Walter couldn't decide was menacing or simply diversion.

Three large dogs braced together with a heavy chain raised their heads and growled at his approach. The second farmer, a leathery fellow in a brown homespun suit, barely held on to them as they stood up. Walter would have to get past them to enter the gates.

Somewhere along this street, Cleon Quine had been beaten and hauled off to be burned—that fact felt very real now to Walter, and he imagined himself in the dead man's skin, walking down the street, consumed with whether the grocer would extend him a further scrap of credit so he could give his babies milk when the local thugs accuse him of something. Without warning, they attack him. He doesn't run, though. God bless him, he pulls out a gun and sends two of them to Hell. The rocks, the rough boards of what sidewalk there was, the dogs arching toward him all explained much, and it struck him now as a wonder that Quine was the only Negro they'd slaughtered here recently. Walter tried to feel the fear Quine felt, fear compressing into resignation and then the diamond clarity of death's acceptance. As the dog handler smiled a toothless smile at Walter's reluctance, something much more profound than hunger ground at his stomach; the fear of a soldier, the constant awareness of death's proximity. The fear of a black man in the South. He gave the knot of his tie an adjustment. He'd make them pay.

A buckboard wagon sat hitched to a team of two mules. Three generations of women in coats all cut from the same bolt of cloth, as gray and plain as the mud, silently waited in the drizzle for someone inside to finish shopping. In the eighties at one end down to the thirties at the other, all three were much too thin, remarkable for the similarity of their frowns and furrows, prime examples, thought Walter, of that legendary Southern womanhood, which had to be defended no matter the cost to human life or justice. Hard living had left them sinew, dried of anything soft. The middle woman, probably in her sixties, sat erect and impatient, observing him with an eye at once wary but also entertained by something new to look at. She brought something up in her throat and spat it out violently between the haunches of one of the mules.

Under the woman's eye, Walter tipped his hat and swaggered toward the store with a confident smile.

The dog man leaned forward, and the other man pushed back against his barrel, a pair of brand-new, unmuddied brogans propped on a bale. Walter went straight up to him and pointed at his shoes. "Hell, friend . . . ," he shouted above the dogs. "That's a bee-yoo-tiful pair a shoes you got on." His voice sounded overdone to his ears. "Regular Sunday shoes, those are."

The man looked over his belly to see what had happened to his feet, then grunted once he got the idea. "Shet them dogs up!" The leathery man gave the chain a rattle, and the dogs stopped. The pig-eyed farmer waved his trotters around a couple times, clearly pleased with his footwear, then motioned back with his head at Vine's. "Just got 'em today."

The cue. Walter gingerly stepped past the assembly, tapped the man's shoes as he went. "Well, let me take a look-see at whatever else friend Vine's put up here." Walter tipped his cap, "Good day gentlemen," turned back—"And the same to you, ladies"—then pushed open the door.

After a few seconds, his eyes adjusted, and Walter could see long, full rows of shelves and counters stretching down both sides of the store, shovels and brooms, pots and pans hanging down from beams. Bolts of fabric and a glass cabinet made of dozens of drawers, each packed with buttons, thread, and other notions, dominated a far corner while shoeboxes, stacked ceiling high, formed the back wall. Above them a coat, some pairs of overalls, and a dress floated in spectral fashion. Tools of every sort—garden, field, woodshop, metal—gleamed from cases and swung from nails, while the right side of the store held the comestible and medicinal. A larder of glass jars, crockery pots, barrels of wheat and rice, packaged goods in boxes and tin cans belied the overwhelming sense of want just outside the doors. Colors began to pull out of the dim light: the fiery orange of a Wheatena box, hot-red shovel handles, bolts of indigo and violet sateen, as if all the bright shades of life had been stolen or maybe just pawned to three men in the center of all this, sitting before a black stove that crackled as smoke seeped through its seams. A copper pot caught all the light from one of the kerosene lamps and glowed like a gong in this treasure room, almost Oriental in its fullness.

The store's smell was even more exotic. Though sweetened by spices and fresh paint, a miasma of unwashed bodies, passed wind, and rotting produce hung almost visible in the still air. The foulness would not have surprised Walter if he'd encountered it in a Shanghai opium den or a Calcutta slum, and he forced down a gag, fought the desire to wipe away at his coat, which he decided would never lose this stink.

Walter leaned against one side of the doorframe, crossed one leg in front of the other in a casual way, and held the door open behind in case a quick exit became necessary. "So fellas," he said, low and monotone so they couldn't catch the small tremor in his voice, "Whaddya do for fun around here?"

The sudden daylight had made the men by the stove recoil, and they squinted at him, shading their eyes with the cards dealt them as they tried to identify the stranger. A fourth man, meat-featured and obviously the proprietor in his striped shirt and white apron, rubbed his nose on his cuff as he ambled toward him. In his forties, running to a kind of middle-aged, middle-class softness common in the North, Mr. Vine, as Walter assumed this man was, presented a more anomalous type here, a man who did not work with his hands. And yet Walter knew that with the bludgeoning force of commerce behind him, Storekeeper Vine didn't need strong hands or bullets to bring a man to his knees; all he had to do was cut off his credit.

Halfway down, a shocked look came over Vine's face. He stopped. The grocer's eyes widened, then squeezed shut, and after a large intake of breath, he sneezed hard and freely at Walter, who imagined a wave of infectious particles raining over him. One of the men said, "God bless you," but Vine ignored the politesse, and he cleared his sinuses with a loud, inward snort. "What can I do ya, mister?" He jiggled a finger in his ear to stop the itching inside his head, then tucked his hands under his apron atop his belly. A long piece of slick black hair, usually combed over the bald spot but flung forward by the violent sneeze, had jumped the part and now hung down to his neck. Sucking his teeth in a lazy, threatening manner, he regarded this unfamiliar customer.

You are so alone here, thought Walter, who nearly had to stifle a laugh at the absurdity of all this. On the shelves of Vine's General Store, so many other black faces widening their banjo eyes at his presence there, offering their comfort. Just to Walter's right, the Aunt Jemima, Mammy of Us All, leered down at him from the shelf right next to Rastus, both insanely eager to lend their support with a nice, hot breakfast and an eternity of docile service. And look there, to the left! It was the crafty Gold Dust Twins, waving as they scampered about, trying to keep clear of the alligator eating the little pickanniny girl on the competitor's box of soap. Lonely indeed . . .

The trick's gonna be on them, he told himself. He was calling the plays now. With a loud thump, he dropped his suitcase and grinned a Buy Me smile wide enough to embarrass every goddamn Cream of Wheat–offering Rastus on the shelf. "No, my friends," said Walter, his voice suddenly hale and resolute. "I'd rather ask what can I do for *you*."

THREE

Taking their seats, the four men displayed all the energy of turtles sunning on a log, but the violence crackling in the store's swampy air came from no simple box variety. These were snappers. Walter held his ground. Eyes slowly measured him, judged whether he could be eaten or not, if there was any need for them to shove off their stools and splash away to escape.

"I'm Walter Francis White. I represent the Exelento Medicine Company and its line of hair straightening products."

A few feet away, a match flared, revealing a pink, pointy nose and two feral eyes staring at the flame. The man wore a wrinkled white shirt, bow tie, and blue police-style jacket. Small irregular shadows marked his cheeks and brow. Lean as a strip of smoked meat, he seemed to have collapsed into himself, free arm wrapped around his chest, legs crossed high at the thighs, torso bent, either holding his parts together or containing violent emotions. The leather strap of a Sam Browne holster cut across his chest under his arms. He regarded the fire with a lover's interest, wondering, it seemed, while the flame worked down toward his thumb and finger, whether to consume the object of his affection or to let it consume him. Again, Walter couldn't tell whether this was a warning or merely primitive entertainment.

Vine stomped over and blew out the match. "Goddamn ya, Nip!" The feather of smoke tickled the grocer's nose into another great sneeze.

"Jus' playin'," said Nip in a spiked accent, all briars and biting vermin. When he opened his mouth for a soundless, mean-hearted laugh, he showed tiny teeth and resembled less a turtle than a possum caught in lantern light. The patch on his shoulder read *Bank Security*. Walter couldn't imagine trusting him with a nickel.

"You gonna set this place on fire!" Vine said.

A thin grease monkey in a tan jumper smirked. Hands black and grimy, he set down his cards to squeeze an old baseball with his right hand. He tested different grips, holding the ball with an athlete's natural command, snapping his wrist when something felt right. Shallow wrinkles at the corners of his eyes and nose put him on the other side of thirty, somewhere past the age Walter could ever imagine being. Lost in his own haze, the man rhythmically worked his undershot jaw back and forth, watery eyes focused on the baseball as if faced with one of life's great mysteries. At the moment when Walter figured him the village idiot, the man turned a look on him so cold and dead-eyed that if Walter had been standing in the batter's box, he'd be getting ready to duck the next pitch.

Walter addressed him, hoping for some purchase with a fellow athlete. "Call me Walter."

"All right, Waaaaaalter," his name stretched out with a testing mockery. But it wasn't the pitcher speaking. All attention slid to the last man in the room, pushing his chair back onto its two hind legs in a most satisfied way, his fingers laced and resting atop the large spare tire inflating the midsection of his checked flannel shirt. Much of his reddish-blond hair had thinned to show scalp, the darker marks of middle age overshadowed the freckles on his fleshy cheeks, and yet his impish grin, the disarming twinkle in the eye signaled that he was about to be a naughty boy. Probing his tongue around his teeth, he leaned over and spat something brown into the open maw of the stove. "Probbim is, we don't have too many kinky-haired types around here right about now."

The speaker rocked back and forth a few times, begging for a challenge. Without question, this was the Big Man of Sibley Springs. Walter wished the chair would give way and send this razorback squealing onto the floor. How many of these had he seen during his days selling in the field, bullies growing tall and thick in Southern towns like a nuisance plant allowed to run wild out of an affectionate sympathy for a native species. A dog, white with black and tan spots, not all that different from the ones bawling outside, shifted on the ground next to him, lifted its head in wary curiosity and got something out of the Big Man's pocket popped into his mouth for his trouble. The Big Man grinned even wider now, checking both sides to make sure everyone else was grinning too.

Walter felt the ground beneath him give way. Torn between spoiling for a fight and tiptoeing quietly back out the door, he pushed forward, stared them down, even as he tried to case the room for exits. "Well, I must point out that a goodly portion of our users are in no way members of Ham's dusky tribe. They are proud white men and certainly a goodly portion of their spouses who desire the elegance and sophistication of straight hair."

The pitcher released a loud burst of flatulence that passed without remarks of either disgust or admiration. All four, plus the hound, glowered at the newcomer, who felt his skin blush. Nip shifted in his seat, allowing his revolver to slip into plain view. Walter considered the fact that this whole escapade could be over in second, over with him dead. Affecting the chummy tone of a salesman trying to worm his way into a sucker's confidence, a tone that for all the talk around the office of uplifting the people, he'd used more than once during his days at Standard, Walter clapped his hands and said, "Gentleman, I am tired and I'm going to spare you a pitch none of us is interested in hearing right now."

The muscles of one side of Nip's face pressed together into an ugly squint. His hands twitched and touched and fussed until he struck another match, apparently the only way to quiet them. No life insurance policy for old Nip, thought Walter; somebody'd strangle him if he didn't blow himself up first, some Fourth of July. "Well," said Nip, "that's the smartest thing I heard you say."

"Second smartest." Walter held up a finger. "Here's the smartest—Where's a man get a drink around here?"

The four looked at each other, and then fell into cheap, knee-slapping laughter. Nip cawed, "That's more like it!" while the dog laid its head back down on the floor with a jangle of its chain.

Walter exhaled. Though he'd been a pretty good quarterback at AU, able to read a defense and juke his way to where he needed to go, it'd been a few years since a first down had sent the invigorating rush of progress through his bones. His fingers wiggled and his toes tapped as if he were driving the varsity forward, inside the twenty now and knocking on the door. Time for the next play.

"Looks like you're having yourselves a card game." He stepped into the circle, put a foot up on a chair next to the half barrel they were playing on so he could survey the high stakes—a pile of matches. Momentum was everything in football; time to punch the ball into the end zone. "I got me a brand-new deck and a pocket full of cash. How 'bout some poker, fellas?" Walter pinched up some of the matches, burnt and otherwise, between his thumb and forefinger, then let them sprinkle back down to the table. "And maybe this time," he said, rolling his eyes because Walter White, sassy Caucasian salesman extraordinaire, did not suffer fools, ". . . maybe this time, with *real* money . . ."

The four scratched their necks and examined the floor until

the pitcher sent his stiff little moustache horizontal with a small and genuine smile, as if he'd been unexpectedly amused. Patting the table in front of Walter, he introduced himself in a probationary way as Hillman Chew, then returned with a blank stare to his baseball, still smiling at Walter's spunk. Vine set down a glass full of clear liquid that Walter could smell from the table.

Touchdown! He was a lion tamer! He was Daniel in the lion's den! The fantasy of addressing a roomful of crackers in such an insulting tone had come true and now, having done it, Walter could say he knew the sensation of flying. "It's a pleasure, Hillman." Walter beamed with a smile as genuine as Hillman's. "Mr. Vine, how's about a round for the house?"

The men grumbled thanks while Walter laid his coat on a reasonably clean stretch of the counter. Settling into his chair, he wondered what Miss Ovington would say when she saw his expense report. "So where's the best place to stay?"

No one answered, and Walter decided to ignore the question too, reaching into his suitcase for his tobacco bag and the comfort of a cigarette. As he unzipped it, though, he realized that Nip's jaw had dropped and Hillman squinted at him with the most extreme emotion he'd shown so far, a kind of fearful amazement. "What's the news, fellas?"

Hillman pointed. "What the hell is *that*?"

Now Walter pointed in a dumb show. The tobacco? No. The bag? No. The fastener? They all nodded. A quick review of their clothing revealed that every closure was a button or a tie. Apparently the new wartime technology hadn't reached Sibley Springs. "It's called a separable fastener. Everybody's using them now." Walter handed the bag over to Hillman, who received it as if it were a thing of great power. Holding it with his fingertips, he brought the fastener close to his ear to better appreciate the sound of its teeth meshing and unmeshing.

Nip snarled. "Well now, you had enough turns. Hand the damn

thing over." Walter gently removed the bag from Hillman and gave it to Nip, who sniffed at it with his possum's nose. The sense that he was on the football field playing a game evaporated from Walter as he watched them work the fastener. Deep in another country, he'd discovered a lost tribe in the heart of America. Its chief, the Big Man, tugged the bag away from Nip. One run up and down the teeth was enough for him to rule it a worthless invention.

"Gonna replace buttons," said Walter, reclaiming his tobacco.

Hillman put a hand to his chest, affronted. "Hell, I *lahke* my buttons."

Nip's face twisted as if he had caught the suspicious tang of Yankees and Washington Dee Cee on the metal fastener. "Ain't nobody tellin' me how I'm gonna close my pants. No goddamn way."

"Well, nobody's passing a law . . ."

"Damn right nobody's passing a law 'bout no *sep-ar-able fasteners.*" The others nodded. Vine's eye, though, had a craven spark —he'd already calculated the appeal of people replacing all their clothing.

The room returned to an uncomfortable silence. The Big Man, more swollen than strong, clenched and unclenched his fists in an ominous manner while Nip rubbed his scarred hands as if they were sore. The revolver on his hip shined a cool, oily black.

Somewhere back in the store, a clock that had surely been ticking the whole time began to toll the seconds in Walter's mind. After rolling his cigarette, he cracked open the trick deck, confident no one here would catch on, then spread the cards across the makeshift table, glad to have something for his jittery fingers to do. "Alrighty. Time for poker, my boys." His boys. The sort of men he and his friends dreamt of destroying, the sort who chased them in their nightmares. Walter contemplated breaking the ice with some raunchy tales, but experience had taught him that if you waited out white folks long enough, they'd tell you just about anything you could ever want to know about them, and then some things you didn't. Even so, the silence gathering over them, thick as cigar smoke, made him anxious. Hillman fussed with the baseball, and the Big Man squirmed in some kind of posterior discomfort. Nip continued to burn matches. Maybe they were saying nothing because that they had nothing to say, because their minds were empty save for only the most base and immediate topics required for their survival.

"Five-card draw," he declared. "Nickel to play; dime to open." Or else, thought Walter, each man was deciding whether to string him up, light him on fire, or drag him behind a truck. The clock ticked louder in Walter's ear; no, it was his heartbeat. He piled up words to hide behind—"You know, that's the only game I ever seen 'em play in Nawlins. Five-card draw. Atlanta, Memphis: you see a lot of stud. Seven card you go to D.C. . . ."—flipping out cards until Hillman abruptly scraped his chair forward across the planks and folded his arms with great ceremony.

"I got a question for you, Mister."

Walter braced himself. "Alrighty. Shoot."

The pitcher looked from man to man, nodding his head as if he'd finally worked up the gumption to ask the question they were all thinking. "Who you say is the best pitcher in the 'Merican League?"

"Oh, I thought you had a *real* stumper there, Hillman. That's easy. Walter Johnson. Hell, best in *both* leagues." Both *white* leagues, that was. Anybody who'd ever seen Joe Williams knew he was the best in the world, and Walter had seen him.

Hillman's hard look crumbled. He slapped the table, pointed at Nip. "Ha! I told you!" then pointed at Walter, "You is *right,* son!" Then, regaining his balance, he hooded his eyes suspiciously and tossed out his follow up. "You ever been to a ball game?"

"Senators, once. Johnson against Eddie Cicotte."

"I'll be damned," whispered Hillman. Walter may as well have been the Big Train himself from the way Hillman stared at him,

43

awe-struck by the fortune that had not only brought to his side a man who shared his opinion on Johnson, but a human being who'd actually breathed in his general proximity. The seals, Hillman's at least, had been broken. "I *will* be damned."

"Sure. Had a big meeting in D.C.. Had the day free so I went over to Griffith Stadium, bought my ducat. Walked right in." It was as amazing to him at the time as it was now to Hillman.

"Yeah," said the Big Man. "*Ah* been to Nawlins." He let the fact set out there for a spell so everyone could understand that the cosmopolite in their midst didn't have one on *him*. Stomach spreading his suspenders, he leaned his chair back again and stroked the dog's head. "Went there once, me an' Billy Stoker. Didn't think much of it," he said, relieving the others of ever having to think about New Orleans themselves.

Hillman seemed to not have heard a word he said. "You get to go on the field?"

"Naw. But I'll tell ya, you could just about put this entire town inside that stadium. You know, that Johnson's a big ole boy."

The Big Man snorted, but Hillman's eyes glazed in wonder as he tried to imagine such a thing. "Shee-yit. You *seen* him. Jes' shee-*yit*."

"Yes sir, I have. Mr. Vine, you wanna open?" The storekeeper shook his head. He still hadn't flipped his lock back into place, and as disgusting as it would be to touch, the disorder of it hanging there so disturbed Walter that he finally had to look away.

"Hillman? Nip?" Both passed, but the Big Man lifted the corners of his cards with the bulbous tips of his fingers and studied the garbage Walter had dealt him. He'd need a bone soon, or else he'd turn nasty. "Are you the mayor?" Walter asked. "Somethin' tells me you the mayor a this town."

The other four barked quick laughs, which started the dog barking too. Rocking forward, the Big Man accepted the mistake as his due. "Naw. I got me a piece of propitty off to the west I farm with my Dora. I let her take care a mama. No, Ludey Fentress ain't no mayor." Ludey chuckled, waved a finger to shush his dog Poke, then tossed a dime onto the five nickels. Flattery was clearly his weakness.

Walter took a broad, anxious wipe across his forehead. "Oh man, somebody holdin' somethin'." He slung a dime into the pot. "I'm in. Boys?"

Vine and Hillman both looked queasy at the prospect of losing ten cents, but in the end they tossed in too. When not looking at his cards, Hillman stared at Walter, who returned some nods of the head and winks until it felt odd to do so. A few more seconds passed as Nip mulled the value of staying in. "Christ, you is *slow*. You understand what he's askin' you to do?" asked Ludey with a grin. He snuck a look at Walter to see if his high roller act was making an impression on the fancy out-of-towner. "Huh? He askin' you to *bet*."

Nip's face twisted in its slow tic, as if he was riding out a burst of pain. At last he flung a dime into the pot with a pair of untrimmed fingernails grown well past the pads, then deflected Ludey's sourness by turning it on his neighbor. "You goin' to the big leagues now, Hillman?" He laughed wickedly. "Just don't tell 'em 'bout Cowan, OK? You tell 'em Cowan got lucky." He folded his arms and winked at Ludey. "Why you throw that curve to Clancy I will never know, but that's done and done. Everybody sayin' Birdie Frennet orter be startin' this year 'stead a you, but I tells 'em, 'No suh! Ol' Hillman still got a little somethin' in that arm.' "

Hillman ignored the bait, like any athlete being goaded by a fan, though the way he now rotated his right shoulder told Walter that he'd had some problems last season. Shamed in front of his new friend, he kept his eyes on his hand, asked for three new cards to go with the pair of fours Walter saw he had. If Ludey was a wild boar and Nip a possum, the pitcher had a cat's grace, sat with his back straight. It was more than his interest in Walter that made him seem the least of evils in this room; he'd actually smiled about something that did not involve injuring or insulting someone else.

45

Hillman shook his head again, said to no one in particular, "I gotta tell mah boys. They gotta meet a man who shook hands with Walter Johnson."

"Now I didn't say . . ."

Paying no heed the interruption, Hillman suggested he stay at a place called Mitchell's. "It's back up by the station? Or else . . ." He mulled something, then thought better of whatever it was. "Well, naw, I think Mitchell's best." He stated the larger portion of his thoughts in question form. "I seen drummers staying there. He probably the cleanest?" The words PULLET'S GARAGE were sewn over his breast pocket.

Walter filled in the blanks on his own—Hillman had dreamed of the big leagues, but no one had discovered him down here in the sticks and now his arm was going and all that was left was the girl who'd started to sour on him about four days after the wedding, her and the pig and the ten kids all rolling around together in a shack. The insurance man in Walter smelled the reek of stomach problems out of Hillman's mouth, unfiltered by the shaggy moustache; took note of the greasy skin, the stubble, the hair, cut wildly uneven and uncombed—all proof he was losing interest in appearances. Dead by fifty, decided Walter. Maybe forty-five if he started up with Vine's moonshine; Walter still hadn't worked up the courage to attack his own glass.

Nip held up two fingers, praying for Clubs. Though Walter had sat through enough sermons to know that outward beauty did not indicate a beautiful soul, in this case he felt confident that Satan had crawled out of Nip's dark heart and pulled his fingers through the man's skin, twisted it into gorges and ravines to prove demonic ownership. He did wear a wedding band, though, leading Walter to consider what the wife looked like to settle for such deformity. From the look of Nip's crumpled clothes, she wasn't one for housekeeping, and Nip didn't seem to care. Walter assigned him a slovenly, bitter woman that he slapped around when the spirit moved. He pictured Nip flipping the fatal match, Quine's black toes tightening up as the flames tried to grab hold. Walter tossed him Diamonds.

Ludey tapped the table twice. "Mitchell one of our resident holy men. Eeeee-vangelical, is what he is." Then he raised his glass accusingly at the storekeeper. "Bax, ain't you got any of that Jack Daniel's? This is misrable stuff."

Vine shrugged. "Boys can't get so much sugar." He pointed up to the heavens, or the top of the mountains. "The war."

"When I was a boy five year old, me an' Billy Stoker had ourselves a still out in the woods," said Ludey. "We'd use the old peelin's from my mama's potatoes to make me some *po*-tent shine." He laughed as if he owned all the truth in the room, knew all there was worth knowing. As Ludey told it, the sheriff allegedly caught them and told Pappy, who'd tanned his ass until dear Mama had threatened the Sheriff with a sword given to her by General Nathan Bedford Forrest himself. Ludey Fentress's unwavering fascination with his own bloated self, his mounds of what was obviously bullshit, would in Walter's professional policy-writing opinion add twenty years to his life. And though he'd suffer through every day of them with gout and swollen bowels and every other ailment a fat, selfish man is prey to, such revenge was not enough today with bits of Cleon Quine still floating in the winds of Sibley Springs.

"Say, where can I buy a newspaper?"

Poke whined, a piercing sound that went straight to Walter's spine, and Ludey tried to settle the dog. "What you gonna do with a *nyooo*spaper?"

Nip said, "I think Timmons used to take the Nashville paper."

"Not anymore."

"No. No, he don't." Nip looked wronged, and he flinched when Walter finally lit his cigarette.

"What happened to him?" asked Walter. "Mr. Vine, how many?" Vine waved three fingers.

"Died in a fire," said Nip, grimacing, rubbing his shoulder. "American man don't need no books anyways."

Hillman licked his moustache. "I think Clem at the depot got one?"

"Yeah, I bought it."

Hillman squinted at Walter like a pitcher confused by his catcher's signs. "So there you go. You got a newspaper."

Now it was Walter's jaw that dropped, appalled by such aggressive stupidity. "I guess I do."

Ludey regarded his cards with distaste. Walter had made sure to give him nothing. "We ain't seen many you drummers lately. That fella in Memphis opened up that, whatchu call it . . . ?"

"Piggly Wiggly," said Vine.

"Yeah, Piggly Wiggly. That just about gonna put everybody out of business," said Ludey with an old pol's pompous certainty. "You too. You know I been there. Manager gave me a tour. Gonna fatten up them fat cats," he continued, sounding as if he were accusing Walter of playing some key role in the great Piggly Wiggly conspiracy.

Reading the marked cards, Walter knew that Vine had a pair of jacks, but the dealer held queens and Vine had stomach enough for only one round of betting. Ludey called. An elderly woman walked in just as Walter showed his cards and pulled in the $1.15 pot. Vine got up, made his sale and returned with the unfortunate news that he'd just sold his last bottle of Black Draught.

The reaction would have been calmer if he'd told them he was a Bolshevik. While the North ran on coal, the South ran on Black Draught, the single most potent laxative then created by Man and a necessary aid for avoiding autointoxication, that dreaded bodywide spread of poisons caused by accumulated waste matter. Everyone wanted to avoid autointoxication, but Southerners led the way, and Ludey, whose clubbed fingers indicated an unhealthy reliance on laxatives, appeared to be on the movement's vanguard.

"God damn it, Vine!" he snarled. "Why the hell didn't you hold it back? You know I need it!"

Vine discovered the hair dangling off his head and shoved it back up with an insulted huff. "Well, if you're not, Ludey, you kin pay up and do your business somewheres else." The threat silenced Fentress.

Shuffling with slow hands, Walter congratulated himself for counting on the white people to not stop themselves, to never consider their words or who heard them. It was time to float something about Cleon Quine . . .

But just then a child's scream pierced the room. Poke growled as a young black boy, dark, maybe seven at the oldest, in overalls faded nearly to white, tumbled in through a back door. Right behind, a white boy about the same age waving an open catalogue of some sort yelled at him to stop. Walter held his breath at the sight of another Negro. The white boy wore knickers, a clean blue shirt and a necklace strung with small human teeth.

Vine leapt out of his seat, his voice gone deep and parental. "What the hell's going on, Edgar? Why's Booney screaming? Booney, what happened?"

The black boy hid behind Vine's legs and pointed at Edgar, who couldn't keep from grinning despite the absence of all four front teeth, clearly the ones he now sported around his neck. "Edgar showed me the book and I asked him to stop but he just keep on showing me the book."

Vine yanked the catalogue away from Edgar. After a heavy sigh, the grocer whacked Edgar on the side of the head. "I told you not to show the coffin book to niggers." He was trying to be reasonable with the boy. "They don't like it, son. They spook." Hillman shook his head in disapproval, and Nip clucked too. "Go on home, Edgar."

Edgar stalked off to perpetrate more acts of petty violence, while Booney, his side taken, stood a few feet away from Vine and stared at the men, especially Walter, whose mouth had gone dry. Could he tell? A white person had never found him out, but black folks always had an easier time and a little boy wouldn't be afraid to speak the truth. He remained outside the circle, one notch down from Poke, waiting for a way to please. If Booney was lucky, he wouldn't understand yet why it was a deadly insult to identify a man as being like him, why he shouldn't just open his mouth and ask why a Negro man was playing cards with them. But that kind of luck would cost Walter his life.

Wrinkling his nose into a sneer, he summoned all the power and insolence and lack of concern he'd seen as a child on the faces of white men and stared down the boy. "Ah, Dr. Livingstone, I presume." The men laughed because it was mean, not because they understood the reference, and Vine told Booney to get on home, but the boy stayed put, continued to stare at Walter. "Come on boys, let's play some cards." He turned around to deal a fresh hand, but he still felt Booney's eyes burning into his back. Walter's toes tapped. "So here's a little joke I heard on the train coming down here. It's a bit raw for a minor, though." He gestured toward Booney in hopes they'd run him out.

Instead, the others stared at Walter, waiting for him to begin. He threw a thumb in Booney's direction. Vine finally caught on. "Edgar's gone. It's all right."

"What about *him*?"

The men laughed, and Nip especially leered at the boy. "Oh hell, Booney prolly already gettin' it wet more'n you."

Booney had a blank expression. He had no idea what they were talking about.

Stomach souring, Walter began telling the joke, an ugly thing he'd heard once in the locker room. "Well, there's this farmer girl, see . . ." His eyes danced over the shelves and labels as he wished the little boy away. *Aunt Jemima and Uncle Rastus, pray for us. Most Holy Gold Dust Twins, commit us to thy divine mercy.*

Something caught Walter's eye next to Vine's register, something long and thick floating in a Mason jar full of a light, yellow liquid. He couldn't tell whether it was a root of some kind or a sausage, maybe a type of rural barroom treat. They were waiting for the rest of the story. "And she's home all alone while her parents are . . ."

The white hot blast of what it was stopped him. He breathed hard, swallowed back the vomit. As the black finger floated in the formaldehyde and Walter's head buzzed, muffled all sounds, he asked himself, asked the empty heavens, whether they'd cut this finger off while he was still alive.

"While her parents are where?" asked Nip.

Walter fanned himself with the cards to hide his shaking hands. These were the men who killed Cleon Quine. "While her parents are in town bringing in the crop. And the only person who stays behind is the uh. The uh . . ." He lost the thread as the finger floated before him, on display like the last pickle in the jar. Was it for sale, he wondered? Was he really sitting among humans? "The butcher."

"What's the butcher there for?"

"He was looking at the hogs."

"All right."

"So the butcher's there and the girl says . . ." He'd expected to find the devil, but not behind the first door he pushed open. Was he behind *every* door in Sibley Springs?

The fact that he should have stayed on the train slapped him. He noticed that the door wasn't locked. He could still jump up, get the hell out of this store and this town and sell insurance to nice middle-class black folks for the rest of his life like any sane man would do. Cornelia was a beautiful woman.

"Dammit, White. For a normal-sized fella you sure act like one a them little jumpy guys." said Ludey. "You got reason to be nervous?" Poke sniffed Walter's leg.

The air hung still in the room. Walter didn't know whether to laugh or cry. Sawdust under Booney's shuffling feet made the only sound.

"I said, you got reason to be nervous?"

Walter caught the suspicion forming on Ludey's voice like a rime of ice. "Fellas, I'm jes' afraid I'm gonna become as bad a poker player as y'all."

Much laughter, a round of bets, drinks all around on Walter White.

"Sorry boys, but listen, I straight out forget the punchline on that joke." The pain in his gut throbbed, but a quick glance at Booney suddenly sent him lurching away from doubt, toward anger, which would be much more dangerous. He remembered the poor minister on the train, the mob marching toward the house, convinced himself he could take on this whole room. What good sense he still had told him that he had to get the information now, before he totally lost control, before he tried something stupid like he did on the train and got *himself* lynched. He was close enough already. "I been meaning to ask you, Vine. What the hell is that in the jar?"

Nip perked up; he'd been disappointed that the dirty joke had petered out. "Oh, that's just a little souvenir from our lynchin' party." The others exchanged looks, not certain whether it was wise or not to offer that. "A little warning to the niggers that they better keep in line and that this here's a civilized white man's town." He crossed his legs in his prim way and folded himself forward, rocking again.

Hillman said without affect, "It's a finger."

Walter realized he was looking at Booney straight on now, that they were looking at each other, and all Walter wanted to do was grab the little boy and sweep him out of his miserable future here. Little black boys have so few days in the Garden, years when they can believe that all God's children are the same in His eyes, years before someone explains with a rock or a stick that in fact little black boys and their mommies and daddies are all garbage on this earth. *When did you find out, Booney? When did they teach you?* wondered Walter. Was it last week, the fire off in the distance that your mama wouldn't let you go see? Would it be enough to accomplish here, if he ran out and saved this one small, sweet life? For a time, his nose had become acclimated to the store's foul stench, but now it rose into his eyes, down into his lungs, and he gagged again. He couldn't nod at him, or smile. No, instead he had to say, "What the hell you looking at, boy? You never seen men playing poker before?"

Booney didn't move. Worse yet, he didn't flinch, showed no sign of pain, any indication that this was an unusual or unacceptable manner of being spoken to, that the conversation was a catalogue of horrors.

Nip lit another match, unable to hold himself back any longer. "Yeah, we had some trouble last week." Walter tingled with disgust, still surprised that he was staring at the very men who'd killed Cleon Quine. Of course, it wasn't a very big town; the odds had been on his side. The good news was that if they copped to everything he could get out of this pit on the evening train and not have to close his eyes once in Sibley Springs. "Last week, right about this time."

Ludey launched a hock of spit into the fire and said with the defiantly bland tone of a cop on the stand, "There was what you call an incident, and we got involved."

Nip struck another, and the images of torches coming down Houston Street, flames circling his house, finally overran Walter. It was hard to see fire as an objective force once men have threatened you with it and after that night when he was twelve, fire had become a personal matter for him. He'd learned from it, let his anger smolder all the time, and once in a while, as if a hot wind was passing over, it would burst into flame. Right now he couldn't see a single reason why these men should exist on the same planet as him. He tapped his chin as if coaxing something out of his memory, then said absently, "Oh, you know I think I read something about it. Some folks here said it was a shame. Is that the kind of nigger-lovin' town this is?" Walter leaned over and blew out the match.

Nip slammed his scarred hands down on the table and shot up off his stool, knocking the butt of his revolver hard into the board. "Hell no! That's the kind of shit them Northern papers write. He killed Trick and J. C., dammit! Shot Dickie Stiles just next to the heart!"

Walter looked at his cards, but no one cared that much about playing now. Even if Ludey and Hillman let Nip walk point on this, the fact that they weren't stopping him meant they'd been waiting to tell *someone* about the lynching, and they were watching him for his reaction as much as he was watching them. Walter whistled a few lines of "Hail, Hail, the Gang's All Here." Down the counter some ways, Vine sneezed. He'd jumped off the log as soon as the topic of Cleon Quine came up and now attended to messy showcases and empty drawers.

Walter didn't want the anger to pass. He pictured his hands around Nip's neck, a bullet entering Ludey's head. "Well, that's a damn shame. Makes me goddamn angry to hear." He certainly wasn't lying to them. Walter White won football games and debates. He knew he should've been president of the United States some day, but that could never happen. Sitting on the edge of his seat, Walter knew more than ever in his life that it would *never* happen. *Details,* Mr. Johnson's voice reminded him. *You need details.* Though Walter knew sugar was called for, the words came out bitter. "But shit, there's lynchings all over and they're all the same from what I can tell. What was so special about *yours*?"

"What makes you such a goddamned pro-fessor 'bout lynchin's? And here you are lookin' at the boys what did it!"

Hillman grabbed up the baseball again, his delivery slow and unemotional as he gazed at something far away over all their shoulders. "Easy, boys. My friend Walter here don't mean no harm now." Walter couldn't tell if Hillman was just playing diplomat or whether there was enough in what he'd just said to hide behind, whether this lyncher would protect him from the others if it ever came to that.

His bow tie out of whack, brow twisted, temper bloomed on Nip's tortured skin in half a dozen shades of red and pink. He had bigger things than Walter's attitude on his mind, but his lips opened and closed like a bass trying to make sense of the bait, seemingly unable to explain to his companions what exactly those things were. "Just, well . . . Just Quine's boy, that Fortune, he deserve some watching. That's all. They're having a funeral tonight, I heard." Ludey nodded. "That right, Booney?"

They all turned but now that they needed him, the little boy had run off. Walter needed to find out where and when the funeral was. Hillman had cooled him down enough to see that despite his own warning to himself, he'd done it again, he'd pushed Nip too hard, raised hackles higher than he should have and shut him down when he could have had the whole story right now if only he'd sat back and listened. *You are NOT justice*, he heard Mr. Johnson say. *You work FOR justice!* Hillman had saved him already, without even knowing it.

Ludey weighed in with another wad into the flames. "I don't like the idea of all them niggers in one place."

"You gotta let 'em bury their dead, Ludey," said Vine.

"Hell, Bax, you just wanted to sell 'em a coffin." Ludey tendered Walter a very pointed look. "I wouldn't try to sell that straightener to the niggers here. I'da keep outa that part a town, if'n I was you. This town has a long history of hospitality, with the spa and all, so we's always *pleased* to see visitors, but . . ." He darkened. ". . . they's parts of town you just don't want to go."

"Well, you boys have certainly made this traveler welcome, and I appre . . ."

Hillman crinkled an eye. "You like hunting?"

"Well, I haven't in a while, but . . ."

"'Cause we got some nice hunting and fishing around here? You might want to stop by the spa, too. 'Fore it closes down?"

Booney came running in through the front door, splashing light again. "Mistuh Ludey. You mama tells me to tells you they not waiting for you no longer and if'n you wants a ride home you better git along wit them."

Ludey swiveled around. "Oh, for chrissakes." He coughed and cursed the nerve of his womenfolk as he gathered up his loose change and whatever matches Nip hadn't burned.

The party was breaking up. They knew more than they'd told, and Walter had thrown away a precious chance to get them to confess to everything. He'd have to stay over for the funeral anyway, so he'd swallow his disgust and discouragement, scout around town, and be back tomorrow. Before it was all over, though, Walter decided to give the natives one more show. He opened up his suitcase, unwrapped his package of Choco-Lax, and handed three disks of it to Ludey. "Listen, my friend. I just happen to have some samples of a very special preparation created in Vienna and captured from the Kaiser that the American government will allow in the future to be sold here in the States. You cannot currently buy this product in stores or through the Postal System. It is . . . *not* . . . *available.*" Ludey looked at his laxative and the others stared with such envy and longing that Walter found himself doling out the rest of the package. "My friends, I can tell you from personal experience that this is the stuff of miracles. It has the sweet, smooth taste of chocolate, but it will prevent autointoxication as well as any glassful of Black Draught. Take three of these medicated discs and I dare you to come back here tomorrow and tell me you are not fully and completely purged." He estimated that a triple dose would leave them with a memorable evening. Walter turned to Vine, whose face had puckered. "It's not available on these shores yet, Mr. Vine. I'm not stealing business from you, I assure you. I just want to make my friends happy and healthy."

With thanks, Ludey heaved himself up. His left leg remained straight, unbent at the knee. Noticing Walter's stare, he slapped his thigh. "Don't got a kneecap. Some drunk Indian kicked it apart for me." Saying his farewells, he shoved the door open and limped out.

When the coast was clear, Nip shook his head and muttered, "Drunk Indian . . ."

Back in his own haze, Hillman squeezed the baseball, ran a finger over the red stitching. Nip asked Vine for some aspirin powder. On the counter, the finger pointed downward in its jar. Walter had to get out of this room now. Out before he fainted or reached for a shovel. He broke in between the grocer and Nip. "Mr. Vine, how much I owe you for the refreshment?"

Vine fixed Walter in his sights. "Fi' dollars."

"You gotta be . . ." He'd figured he was into Vine for two bucks at the most, but as Walter's color rose at the robbery he noticed that Vine didn't blink; things in Sibley Springs cost what Vine said they cost. "Alrighty then. Five dollars. Here you go." He counted out the bills.

Hillman now stood between him and the door. "I was thinking," said the pitcher, tilting his head in a sheepish way. "We don't got a fancy house like them Mitchells, but Janie keep it clean, and I'd be honored . . ."

Hands up to stop this plan before it went any further, Walter protested. "You don't want a drummer round your house, Hillman. Anyhow, I got sample cases coming and if they show up, I'm on my way at six."

The pitcher looked a little crestfallen at the prospect. "Well, I sure hope you can stay awhile. Good huntin' 'round here."

"I can't tell you how much I appreciate your hospitality. The Mitchells? They set up for my sort. I doubt Janie'd be too happy if you showed up with me, anyhoo. Listen, if my cases didn't arrive, I'll see you tomorrow and give you a chance to win back your money. Now which way is it to the Mitchells?" Shoulder to shoulder, a disappointed Hillman guided Walter to the door.

FOUR

Standing on the porch, Walter breathed deeply of Sibley Springs' sulfurous air and thanked God that he'd brought gifts for the headhunters. The sunlight and the white clouds and the inexplicable logic of America—that the guardians of civilization were those who strung up humans, made trophies of their fingers—had him dizzy again, and he leaned against one of the posts. His own smell rose up to his nose. Though he'd steamed dry around the stove, Walter prayed for the chalky skies to open and wash away the filth. He prayed for them to cleanse him of that clammy, primal urge to violence. He prayed for courage.

The dog handler had fallen asleep, as had the hounds. The other man whittled with no apparent plan at a small piece of wood. Walter had a few more hours of light before dusk, so he planned a long walk to get the lay of the land and hopefully find the site. Then, following Hillman's advice, he'd get a room at the Mitchell House and finally eat something. After dinner, he'd work up some excuse to run out so he could find Quine's funeral and either present himself to the black folks, if the time was right, or sneak around and learn what he could.

Buttoning his coat, Walter took a right out the door and headed toward the river. Hillman had pointed out Mitchell's in the distance, a large two-story home down the block from the depot. Setting his course as a loop around the river side of the town, maybe a look at the gap in the trees to the south, and then back up around to the boarding house, Walter stepped off the porch and made his way toward the trees. On the corner, he passed the unguarded Farmers Bank, two stories of yellow brick apparently closed for the day. A few doors down, Pullet's Garage and Livery looked closed too, or at least asleep; bricks kept the wide doors blocked open and a large black Studebaker that seated at least five took up most of the space inside. Nothing moved among the leather harnesses, the bridles, and the car parts that were day by day turning them into curios.

He needed only a minute to clear downtown Sibley Springs and pass a group of four homes along two sides of the dirt road that a tilted sign identified as Main Street. Much more substantial than the shacks he'd passed earlier in the train, these had porches wrapped around them perfect for games of checkers and lemonade on summer afternoons. They didn't compare in Walter's mind to his parents' immaculate gingerbread on Houston Street, the finest for many blocks in Atlanta, often mistaken for a white man's home by embarrassed salesmen. He pictured his mother tugging weeds from amid the flowerbeds; his father, thin and tanned dark from working his postal route—an upper-middle-class profession for a Negro—as he polished the carriage out front. Walter slumped his shoulders, pretended that his father had just put his arm around him.

By now cold nibbled his toes and he stopped to wipe off his shoes; the puddles and muck and wet gravel were destroying a perfectly new pair of oxfords. As he wiped, he wondered if the Association would reimburse for the damage. In front of the Sibley Springs mansions, painted rocks outlined paths and driveways, edged patches of what might be flowers in a few months' time. He guessed at what his mother and father were doing at that moment. Poor people when compared with so many whites, his parents had made a castle of sorts out of that house on Houston Street, made it the family keep, a wiry postman and his stout hard-working teacher wife fighting endlessly against the darkness around them like ancient royalty. Their vision of themselves, Walter knew, was less romantic. They made a great point of wanting nothing more than what was Right. Upright Congregationalists, the Harvard Library on their shelves, they walked firmly through the house like New England abolitionists plucked out of time; prim, conservative, strict of hand, though generous of heart with him and his brothers and sisters. He pictured his father, the most Northern of them all, emotions always in check, and flushed at the thought that he would never have come so close to erupting the way Walter had. So far this trip, the further South he went, the less control he seemed to have over his own lesser emotions. Walter blamed the town; Sibley Springs would suck hope for humanity's triumph out of anyone who passed through, black or white.

To his right, the trees opened, as he'd seen from the station. He'd been hoping for a park or maybe a band shell in the clearing, but instead, two city blocks of blackened wood and steel, the charred ruins of a sizable building, lay in a heap like some dragon felled from the sky. A disastrous fire or explosion had taken place here years ago. Grass and weeds grew over twisted girders and bare threads of vine had lashed themselves to the lower beams, everything of value long stripped from the building's bones. On the ground, a scree of glass shards and broken brick lay scattered amid puddles of long standing water.

This had to be where Quine was lynched. Walter's heart raced until he remembered that one of the few facts they knew was that it had been done outside of town. Of course, the swells wouldn't have wanted it done under their noses—the oily stink of burning human flesh would have put them off their cured ham and gravy. With some disappointment, he kicked at the rubble, flipping over a board that turned out to be a large sign. Singed along the bottom, but still legible, it read "Timmons Flour Mill," with a painted hand pointing right above the word "Entrance." Obviously, Timmons the news-paper reader had owned all of this, not Miss Timmons the pearl lady; Walter wondered if Nip's pyromania had destroyed it. A wide and once well-traveled road led away along the river on the other side.

It all struck Walter as a testament to the colossal sloth of Sibley Springs. Having picked the bones of the wreckage clean, the town was now content to let the elements take the rest away. A squirrel hopped from the top of one fallen post to another. It stared for a few moments as Walter made welcoming sounds with his lips; then it dashed away.

He walked on, past the ruins of the mill to where the road nar-rowed down to a path. A smaller structure waited for him at its end. As he could start to hear the river, Walter made out a curved wooden platform maybe thirty feet long, elevated, with a colonnade on each side bridged to its partner by a wooden beam on top. Though poorly cared for, the arcade was intact. A white sign the size of a window pane announced in black gothic lettering *The Vale of the Confederate Dead.*

If the town had no statue of Stonewall Jackson in the square, at least there was this oddity. Walter climbed up three steps onto the wooden boards. Rain and cold snaps and hot summer sun had boiled off whitewash, and left the wood gray and exposed, the remaining flecks of paint caught in the swirls of grain. Where plaster had stood for stone, it crumbled to the touch. From this platform, many a Rebel veteran had delivered grandiloquent speeches extolling the virtuous life Robert E. Lee, the unblemished soul of Jefferson Davis, the bravery of the Boys in Gray, while pinched women nibbled tea sandwiches out of hampers and the children waved small Confed-erate flags. Walter raised up something from his throat and spat on the spot where he stood.

They certainly hadn't burned Cleon Quine here. This was holy ground. He continued down the platform, examining the columns. Dried vines waiting for the rejuvenation of spring clung eye-level on each and crawled through the rafters overhead. In the warmer months, foliage swallowed this structure. Here in bleak winter, though, gray faded letters uncovered by leaves listed all the men of the area who had served in the War. Manster Frolly. Giles Porter. Alfred Fox.

He stopped reading and hopped down. Speaking their names, even thinking them, brought them back to life; Walter preferred his Confederate Dead in Hell.

The path now led directly to the river's edge. Here at Sibley Springs the banks of the Elk River, for most of its way a sluggish brown run, tightened and the river moved quickly, swirling into white around some large rocks, but slowed short of ever frothing into rapids. Pines lining both banks provided minimal cover; that job was for the profusion of bare branches and bushes waiting for spring. In the center of the river, just south, a thin island had built up around an outcropping of large boulders. The trees and branches were thicker there; no one ever crossed the Elk to visit them. The landscape was done in a melancholy palette: the mash of black and brown leaves iced with a coating of mist, the dense patches of dried tan reeds.

Spent by the last hour, only the beginning of the mission, Walter scouted for a thick stand of thorny bushes where he could hide for a quiet minute along the banks of the river and get his heart right. He hadn't slept well in his tiny berth, wrapped for eighteen hours within the unreal time of the traveler. He'd decided to part ways with his sweetheart of four years and then found himself face to face with the murderers he'd been trying to investigate. So much had happened so fast—he'd discovered most of what he needed to know in the first hours here—that he felt like he'd already been in Sibley Springs for a full day, and there was more tonight with the funeral. He hoped he'd get what he needed there.

As he edged down the steep path toward the water, Walter saw a person sitting on the bank maybe ten yards away. Black, seventeen or eighteen, just about a man but still immature in some of his movements, he swung his knees back and forth as he lifted each mussel out of the bucket next to him, opened it with his stout knife, and then prodded around the insides.

If the boy had been white, Walter would have crept back up the bank, but instead he stepped closer, noticed the pair of black, store-bought slacks protected from the mud with a burlap bag tucked beneath the rump. The white shirt, ironed into crisp lines, identified him to Walter as a servant. The boy was weeping, the tears rolling down his cheeks with the same slow progress of the raindrops on the tree trunks and leaves.

His instinct was to wonder what made the boy cry, but as Walter stood up and saw the Negro shacks in the distance, through the empty bushes, he asked himself what reason the boy had to do anything but cry. The leafless trees, the murky sky left Walter exposed, unable to escape his own thoughts. Up North, everyone was too busy to think, but not down here. For at least a day after the riot, he'd wanted to do nothing but cry; it had taken a while for the anger to grow back where there'd once been happiness and understanding, and then anger seemed to be the only emotion worth having. He would sit for long stretches and remember what the gun had felt like in his hand, the power it had given him after such a searing betrayal. He couldn't look at a white person after that, after that finger was pointed toward their house, and every time he passed a mirror, he would stop and stare, twitch his nose, mug with his lips, unconvinced that his white skin was truly connected to him. His parents finally steered him to considering the fluke of their white faces as if it were an unfortunate health condition not to be remarked upon, and over time they guided him to a better place of the heart. They taught him that there was good and bad in every person of every race. He grew up rejecting violence by rejecting it violently, with passionate words and constant action meant to hide the hatred that stiffened his bones. You turned anger into conviction, he reminded himself. Walter White will keep moving up. Empty mussel shells clattered ahead. With his upper arm, the boy wiped at his brow, but not his tears. Here at the side of the river, that finger floating in his mind, Nip's cackle in his ears, Walter delivered his daily speech to himself: *You are moving up and taking your people with you. Success will be your revenge. The freedom of your people will be your revenge.*

He debated talking to the boy, fighting with the spoken word against this gloomy tide of introspection, but it was too late, and the waters too high. There were worse things than anger, thought Walter. There were days when the whole joke seemed to be on you, days when the scales dropped from your eyes so you could see just how unfair the setup was, and a sadness gripped you that made it hard to breathe, made living the rest of your life seem impossible. Anger changed nothing, so bitterness took over. He'd get sour then, and a bristling sort of edginess tempted him to snap his fingers under every white nose not in the name of justice, but out of pure spite, out of a taste for those just deserts they kept promising. *Those* are the blues, Mr. Clover. Walter pulled the brim of his hat down over his eyes. What was he going to do against that, a voice asked him. What did he really think he could do against the white man?

His hands clutched Nip's throat again, a feeling far better than accepting death, better than the chains wrapped around him, better than allowing the flames to rise. The death of a warrior was not a suicide.

So quick to kill, the voice said. *Fool*, you *are the white man*. That was the proof. That was the monster in him—his whiteness.

Maybe he wasn't the right man for this job. Walter picked up his suitcase and headed for Mitchell's boarding house, while the young man cried alone.

FIVE

A low, wire fence of the sort used to pen chickens bounded the Mitchell House, a wide, two-story building, as far as Walter could tell, free of any peeling paint, broken windows, unattached gutters or rot. No dogs or pigs rutted about the lawns. That this home was not down by the river, not among the more generous estates of Main Street but a property among the rest of Sibley Springs' dilapidation, made its maintenance stand out as a sign of possible enlightenment within, and the fence, worthless for actual defense, appeared then more as a wall, the gate a crossing over into a slightly better land.

A sprightly tuba oompah, accompaniment to a polka, greeted Walter as he swung open the gate. Just inside stood a white post with a sign—*The Office of Dr. Darius Moody*—and past it, straight down to about five feet before the house, ran a broad concrete path between the two halves of the lawn. Walter imagined boys playing on them, lobbing a football, laying out bases when not practicing the tuba. Directly in front of the house, the walk split to allow a young tree some chance of growing into a tall and moody willow. The paths then led to separate flights of steps up to one porch that stretched across the building's front. A large turretted room anchored one corner. Brittle, empty bushes and patches of dirt wreathed the house with a promise of gardens.

As Walter paused at the willow and wondered which path to take, the music stopped. He went up the porch, out of the damp, and was about to enter the foyer when a girl, chubby and squinting, six or seven years old, blocked his entrance. She wore a baglike dress made of faded red gingham and was much too small to be the one handling the now-silent tuba. With a mound of tummy pushed forward defensively like a palace guard, she asked, "Who *are* you?" She was a mouth breather, her expression not cross so much as puzzled, as if she'd been promised that the party would have a pony and the pony wasn't there.

"Walter White," he said, extending a hand. "A pleasure to meet you." The girl allowed hers to be shaken then let it fall back to her side.

"I've met Jesus Christ."

"Lucky you. Whereabouts?"

"My sister Gladys met him too."

"How very good for Gladys." He considered patting the girl's head, but the long, stringy brown hair, free of ribbons, shone with a particularly oily sheen, and he could not bring himself to touch it.

"The preacher is coming Sunday from Winchester. Whar you from? He's stayin' here for the night."

Hop had warned him that the Mitchells were "Eeeeevangelicals," and while the hypocrisy of Christians beseeching God as they tortured Negroes had stopped galling him the way it had in college, still it made him grit his teeth. So obvious was the sacrilege that he now simply regarded most white Christians as pagans, no better than Druids or Hindus worshipping stone idols and cows, and any goodness derived from their devotions to their Great White God as purely accidental. Nothing on earth is as poorly served as the Lord's name, and there were times when Walter looked forward to Judgment Day; the surprised expressions of millions of white faces would light up the heavens.

"Move aside, Goose. Let him through." A lanky man in black pants and a red musician's jacket with the word "Timmons" embroidered in gold across the chest grabbed one of Goose's shoulders and swung her to the side like another gate, allowing Walter's entrance into a foyer. "Go tend the hens." She scrambled away as Mr. Mitchell, revealed now as the tuba player in the family, gave Walter a slow head-to-toe looking over. "You wanna be staying here?" Mitchell had a long, sallow face, unruly blonde eyebrows, and a sizable Roman nose similar to Hillman's. Like everyone else in Sibley Springs, he had fetid breath, and, also like everyone else, Walter could not tell if his doleful countenance expressed annoyance at being disturbed or a more chronic state of melancholy.

"I do, yes."

Mitchell did not move. After the encouraging appearance of the building's exterior, Walter found this a sorry welcome, and a peek into the sitting room dashed any hopes he had for a comfortable resting place. Many, many years ago some family had made of this building a fine, warm hearth, but it wasn't clear whether the Mitchells had been that family. The house exuded a loose sense of ownership; either the current tenants lived atop the past or the Mitchells had undergone some trauma that had forced them to reduce their circumstances by a devastating degree. Five pieces of furniture sat well away from the walls—two chairs, a settee, and two end tables, all in heavy oak stained a dark brown, the seats upholstered in a red stripe once respectable before the years of tears and stains. The tables, the mantels, the floor, all sat bare. Up along the top of the walls, the rose paper had begun to peel away and its floral pattern now brought to mind not so much live flowers as dried bouquets from long-ago parties. Brown coronas of dirt circled the ghosts of oval frames; a formidable range of head grease smudged the paper where a larger sofa most certainly had gone flush to the wall. Carved lintels and intricate moldings tried to keep up appearances, but their handiwork felt strained and obvious amid so much evidence of loss, and it was not clear whether this was through financial poverty or just a poverty of soul, the effect of some Puritan cleansing. Whatever strength Mitchell had, he apparently applied it to the exterior; Walter wondered if he was a widower.

"You here for the spa?"

"No."

"It's closing." His eyes flicked away from Walter to a battered tuba in a crate. The rest of him tottered like a man old before his time. It didn't matter that no one in this town had bought insurance from Clover; none of them would have passed the physical.

"Yes, I know." Perturbed that Mitchell had not offered to take his bag, or even welcomed him inside, it then dawned on Walter that Mitchell wanted some sense of his identity. He remembered that he wasn't himself, couldn't be himself. As tired as he was, up since four-thirty that morning, this would not be a place where he could truly rest. "My name is Walter White. I represent the Exelento Medicine Company. I'm waiting for some samples to arrive and I may be here for a few days."

Mitchell nodded for a bit. "Two dollars a night. For another fifty cents, we'll feed you. We keep chickens, so they's eggs."

Walter's stomach rumbled at the thought of food. Though the poker game had boosted his holdings $1.15, Vine's gouging on the bar tab had left him with only $26.93. On the other hand, he already knew who killed Quine. A visit to the funeral tonight, another few hands of poker at Vine's tomorrow, and he'd have what he came for. One night would probably do it, had better do it. "Alright, then."

Without another word, Mitchell turned and started up a flight of stairs in the foyer with the plod common to domesticated animals or prisoners serving long sentences, pausing at each step before he hauled up the other leg. Above, in a room on the second floor, a woman's voice whispered urgently, feet shuffling as she spoke. At the top of the stairs Mitchell held out an arm through an open door, the first sign of hospitality he'd ventured, to display Goose busily shoving a thin pillow into a case while a woman, clearly her mother, made the bed. Smoothing over a trio of cigarette burns in the sheet with her cracked, red hands, she gave Mitchell a deadly look for walking in on the scene. "This my wife, Pettey." Walter couldn't help grimacing at the prospect of slipping his body between such gray, possibly unwashed, linen.

Pettey nodded toward her guest because she had to. "Hi do," she said, turning immediately back to the sheets. Chopped straight across the brow in child's bangs, her lifeless brown hair hung down to her shoulders on the sides and back, swaying like a wet dishrag on the line as she moved. Her skin was the same pasty gray as the sheets. A strong candidate for Wine of Cardui, the cracker woman's absinthe, sister product of Black Draught, Pettey sighed and grimaced in ways that she surely thought were invisible to the outside world, but which indicated a female disquiet fermenting into gothic proportions. "I'm afixin' cold plate tonight."

Unable to consider eating this woman's food, especially served cold, Walter kissed off his fifty cents and put his hopes on something edible, and free, at the funeral. "Thank you, ma'am, but if it's all the same, my stomach's still riled from the traveling."

She slapped a pillow hard a few times to produce the desired fluffiness. Goose and Mitchell both flinched; Walter saw them meet eyes. "I'll set a place anyways." Evidently one did not say no to Pettey Mitchell, so Walter thanked her. "You share a bathroom with the other folks on this floor. Shy, did you show him?" The question prodded the leaning Shy, not one to waste energy, off the door frame. Then, as if no one else were in the room, she said, "Why didn't he show the man that, that's what I'd like to know? I tell him every time."

Guided by Shy, Walter visited the small, barely passable lavatory, then took possession of his quarters, tested the bed, pushed aside the thin muslin curtains to see the train depot down the road. A brassy bellow from downstairs signaled the resumption of tuba practice. Two small photographs of slumbering babies hung near the door, the only decoration in the room. Goose, who hadn't left yet, caught Walter staring. "That's Mama's brother and sister."

"How nice." He looked a little closer. Each child rested in a small bank of flowers.

"They dead."

"I'm sorry."

"In the picture. They dead in the picture. They was twins." Walter reared back as he suddenly noticed the edges of the coffins, their tiny fingers forced around crosses. Goose squinted up with him; she needed glasses badly. "April and May. My Granny made Mama name me June, but I called myself Goose when I was a baby so evibody call me that. They call me Goose."

Walter nodded. He imagined her round stomach, which resembled the breast of a fat goose, had helped the name stick. She toyed with the handles of his bag, which he grabbed away from her, albeit with a smile, leaving her sitting on the side of his bed, shoulders in a hunch until a fresh, seemingly impish, thought came to her. Leaning over, Goose whispered to him like a conspirator, "I kin get ya an extry towel." She stopped for a breath. "I know Daddy bought some new ones down by Vine's last week . . ."

Given the thinness of this place, the people, the sheets, the clothes, he guessed the towels would be no better. The only sign of life was Shy's tuba, running up and down the scales. Even the poorest black home had a richer spirit. "Well, yes, that would be nice. But only if it doesn't get you in trouble."

Goose shrugged her shoulders as if trouble didn't really matter to her. "Where's the farthest you ever been?"

Saying New York City was grounds for lynching in most places; Berlin was a safer answer. "Oh, I guess the furthest was Washington, D.C."

"Yeah? One man last week said he been in Washington District of Columbia. That's the true name, of course," she added, tossing a sophisticated look his way. "He drew me a likeness of the president's house. I still have it." She nodded as if he'd shown some disbelief. "I do. In my pocket." The pictures he would take down before he went to sleep, but how, he wondered, would he get rid of Goose? "Oh lordy, there was *people* here last week. A lady stayed in this here room. She from Winchester. She was sooooo pretty." Goose brightened at the memory, touched the side of her chin with the tips of two fingers as if posing for a magazine drawing. "She let me use her brush and mirror, and they was both real silver." She shook her head. "Lots a people had pretty things. Daddy say he gonna give me something pretty someday."

Walter pretended she wasn't there.

"Do you like it here?" Goose waited a moment out of politeness, then continued. "Can I see a picture of your family?"

He imagined what would happen if he pulled out Cornelia's photo from his pocket. "Sorry, Miss. I didn't bring one." As hungry as this little girl was for any sign of life from the world outside, Walter absolved himself of having to care. She had the entire power of the South behind her precious womanhood. Goose Mitchell would not ever have to worry about being raped by a carload of drunken farmers or watching her husband or father or brother strung up like a winter hog for not stepping into the gutter in time for a white woman to walk by.

"What's your favorite song?"

The answer popped out of his mouth before he had a chance to think: "You'll Never Know the Good Fellow I Am Till I've Gone Away." He'd sung it to Cornelia the night before he left for New York, the sentiment surely true. Would she cry when he told her? Probably not. Even so, the best tack was a letter. He thought of the minister and his wife on the train, casually holding hands. As much as he envied them, he couldn't imagine trusting someone so deeply who didn't know firsthand the uniqueness of the Whites' lives. Certainly not Cornelia, whom after four years he—and here he tested out the past tense—had never trusted as much as any of his sisters. The weight lifted off his shoulders, set him bouncing on his toes even more than normal.

Goose wrinkled her nose. "How's it go?"

Sotto voce, he started, "Oh, you'll never know, you'll never know, just what a good fellow I am . . ." Walter had completed two verses of the little nothing when he looked down and saw Goose smiling as if she'd caught him out at something. He stopped and straightened his tie in an attempt to regain some dignity.

"Why'd ya stop?"

"I think you get the idea."

The tuba went silent. Pettey called up from downstairs, "Goose! Scipio come by to see you. And Booney!"

As Goose hopped off the bed, Walter could hear the deep baritone and slow drawl of a Negro out of the rows, slavish tones that made Walter's neck stiffen. He edged toward the door to try to get a look. Friendships between little white girls and black men weren't that unusual in The South, but the mention of Booney made Walter doubt that coincidence had brought by this Scipio. Craning his head around the frame, peering down the stairs, he saw a large man, bald, thick-chested, in overalls and three jackets of different colors and sizes layered on top of each other for warmth. A big dark field hand, he clutched his hat to his chest as he paid tribute to these lifeless white people; Walter noticed him sneak a glance up the stairs. The return of a hammer was an excuse—Scipio was looking for him.

Shy, his tuba wrapped around his gut like a yawning brass serpent, delivered a flaccid reprimand for the tool's late return. After scraping apologies to Shy, Scipio turned and addressed Walter directly. "Oh my, Missus Pettey, I didn't know ya had a new guest!

I'se so sorry fo' bargin' in on you! You just visitin' our town, Mistuh . . . ?"

Goose jumped around Scipio, saying his name over and over. "Scipio! Scipio! Scipio! Scipio! Scip . . ."

"Now Miss Goose, you gotta let the man talk. Mistuh . . . ?"

"White. Walter White. Yes. I represent the Exelento Medicine Company."

Scipio's face broke into the wide smile of a cakewalk dancer, his teeth huge and white, his tongue pink. Walter couldn't separate the disgust he held for the man from the pity. "You make that hair straightener! Oh, the culud folks be mighty grateful to you fo' that preparation. And that pomade? Yes, sir! Fahn!"

"Thank you," said Walter. He couldn't tell yet if Scipio knew. "I'll be sure to pass on the compliments at the Home Office."

Though she had stopped repeating his name, Goose continued to tug down with a regular beat on Scipio's outermost jacket. It annoyed Walter to even watch, but with a hand as vast as his patience with this girl, Scipio gently pulled her fingers away. "If it wasn't Febrary, I'd asay you got a hopper in your pants, Miss Goose. How's about I tell you one of the old stories? Maybe that'll sitcha down. Mistuh Shy, you mind?"

Shy nodded that it was fine, the bell of the tuba moving slightly up and down with his head. "A short one."

"Dass all right? Good. Goose, Booney . . ." The little boy had not taken his eyes off Walter since he'd come creeping in behind Scipio. "You chirrun sit here on the step. Mistuh White, how you feel 'bout stories?"

Walter gripped the banister, but didn't say a word.

"Well, you might want give a listen. Tell your granchirrun you heard a nigger man once tell you the finest story you ever heard."

Scipio grinned. Walter's heart pounded as Shy and Pettey left the foyer.

"Alrighty. Now Goose, I don't think I ever tole you this one." He rubbed his hands together and leaned in close to the children. "You see, Brer Rabbit and Brer Fox and Brer Bear all be different coluhs. Brer Bear, he be dark as the bottom of a grave at the midnight hour. He do all his best work when de moon up and everybody else is sleeping." Goose giggled as Scipio gave up the job of narrator for a moment so he could lumber about the foyer on his tip toes, arms outstretched like a bear, hands hanging down, sniffing at the walls. "He slip aroun' and do what he got to do when the sun don't shine and he do fine. Yas, he do mo' than fine, and don't you think Brer Rabbit didn't see'd dat cause he did."

Goose mugged a bear's face too, though Scipio had already slipped out of Brer Bear's skin and had started to slink his head ominously from one shoulder to the other. "Now dere's Brer Fox. He don't make Brer Rabbit any happier. Brer Fox be a most comely shade of white, jes' like he be lightly toasted, jes' tetched by the sun. When the sun up, he skippin' around, not afraid a nothin'. Takin' what's his, you know what I mean?"

"I never heard this one before," said Booney, who'd wrinkled up his nose.

"You think you heard all the stories?" Scipio slapped his own knee and laughed. "You jes' a boy!" Booney sank away, stung.

"What about Brer Rabbit?" asked Goose.

"Well, now you done named the probbim, Miss Goose. Brer Rabbit ain't got no real coluh."

As soon as he said that, Scipio stared directly at Walter for a few very long seconds and Walter understood immediately that he knew. He knew if not who Walter was exactly, then he knew *what* he was.

Turning back to the children, Scipio continued. "He jes' somewheres in between, which is pretty much nowheres, if'n you ast me. He don't belong to no one, no wheres, no hows." Scipio was not changing into any character for Brer Rabbit; that role was already taken by someone else in the house. "He cain't hide out at night cause the moon cotch his light fur and showed him out. In the daytime he too dark. Ain't gonna get anythin' past Brer Fox in the daytime, and he jes' stand out like a black cloud on a sunny day.

"So Brer Rabbit decide he need a new coluh." Everyone watched Scipio, who now avoided Walter's eyes. "He slip into Brer Bear's tree one day while the other one asleepin' and steal his fur. Well that Brer Rabbit, he *loves* Brer Bear's fur! He be sneakin around at night, takin' what Brer Bear's and livin' high."

Scipio pulled a mournful face. "But that wasn't enough for Brer Rabbit. Too much ain't never enough for him. So the next night he go out and while Brer Fox be sleepin he steal out *his* fur too! And now here's where this is one strange story 'cause it gots three endings and each one a them is true and we gotta decide which one is *most* true. All right? You wit' me?"

The children screamed out, "Yes!"

Scipio held up one huge finger. "The fust is that Brer Fox goes out a day and finds Brer Rabbit aprancin' aroun in his skin and eats him up for it!"

Goose and Booney both made scared faces.

"The second is that that poor little thief Brer Rabbit puts on Brer Fox's skin and cain't get it off, and when Brer Bear comes by he eats him oncet and for all.

"An' three is sort a like two, 'cept he cain't get outa Brer Bear's fur, and it's Brer Fox that eats him up jes' for being a big ole brown bear."

Scipio dropped his Uncle Remus voice, let the smile melt away, and once again looked straight up at Walter. "So, Mistuh White. Which one *you* think is the ending?"

Walter worked his lips and tongue to get some moisture back into his mouth. "I think you underestimate ole Brer Rabbit."

Scipio howled another one of his darky laughs. "Oh, das a good one Mistuh White! Das a good one! Unda-estamate Brer Rabbit!" Then he got serious very quickly. "But the probbim, Mistuh White, is that Brer Rabbit is always *over*estamatin' his own self."

Before the dialogue went any further, a door across the hall cracked open, and a white girl about Walter's age with blonde hair in long, gentle waves, one of them dropping over a green eye, stuck out her head. "Could y'all keep it down jes' a little? Mah Auntie Dorcas is trying to have her rest . . ." After looking down toward the foyer, she looked across toward Walter and made a small smile with a crinkled nose to show that she wasn't all that angry about the disruption.

Shy came back into the foyer. Bending at the waist, he brushed Scipio and Booney toward the door with the bell of the tuba. "You best be gone."

"Yassuh. You right. We funeralizin' him tonight at his home." Scipio looked up to Walter to make sure he'd heard. "'Bout seven-thirty."

The news hung for a silent moment, time enough for Shy to become cranky. "All right. Git now. You too, Booney. Git home to your mama." But Scipio had delivered his message. He nodded to Walter gravely as he left, assumed a watermelon-eatin' smile for Pettey and Shy as he walked out.

Though he hadn't felt her there, Walter found Goose at his side, bearing an extra towel. "Her name's Louisa. She's here with her brother Tate and her auntie for the spa." He ushered his companion out of the room.

Six

Walter latched the door behind Goose, removed his coat and jacket and shoes and sank into the mattress with a painful creak of the springs. Before Scipio's visit he'd been ready for a good nap, but someone knowing he wasn't who he said he was had jolted him awake, and the question of what would happen to Brer Rabbit filled up the room. Though he didn't know yet what exactly this Scipio had in mind, according to him, it wasn't a matter of whether Walter would be eaten here; it was just a matter of who'd do the eating. On the other hand, brashness overtaking fear, he decided that he'd just beaten the crackers at Vine's and he'd do it again tomorrow. Walter folded his arms and stared ahead at the blank wall, reassured himself that the game had only started. No matter whether Scipio had delivered a warning or issued a threat, and even if he'd pushed it too far with Nip, still no one had a clue who he really was or what he was up to. Brer Rabbit was definitely winning.

He reached over into the suitcase for his notebook, small and easy to stash in case of trouble, and scribbled down the names of the guilty and what he knew of the story to this point. His stomach cramping, Walter remembered the Cracker Jack and tore open a box to snack on as he wrote. At first the sugary popcorn felt so light that he gobbled it by the handful and contemplated another box before deciding to bring the rest to the service for the children.

Munching a peanut with greater restraint, he looked at what he'd written down—a short list of names, a fleshed-out description of the scene the office already had. No airtight confessions, just Nip saying that they did it. Even though he was sure those men had lynched Cleon Quine, on paper what he'd learned so far represented just a few lines of black ink on a whole sea of white, no proof enough to bring anyone in for questioning let alone convict them. He really wasn't anywhere as close as he had felt in Vine's store. Annoyed with the quantity of effort success in life required, all the obstacles to proving one's worth, Walter tossed the empty candy box aside and began pacing.

After four steps, he hit a wall and turned his thoughts to Scipio. A regular mule-whippin', cotton-pickin' sharecropper most likely, Scipio sucked up to the Mitchells, and so, Walter assumed, he probably crawled around on his belly when it came to any other whites, too. Every black man had to crawl once in a while, but Walter spied a glee in Scipio's case that repelled him, an ease with the social yoke, an acceptance of the torn jacket and disintegrating shoes. Walter looked down at his own shoes, their beautiful oxblood leather, imagined with pleasure the books already stacking up in his new room in Harlem. While some who assumed membership in Dr. Du Bois's Talented Tenth thought mostly of the compliment it conferred—and Walter could call to mind a few familiar faces—seeing Scipio and Booney had reminded him of the responsibilities of good fortune and realized aspirations. Well, mostly realized. No, he wasn't a lawyer, that hadn't been possible, but his job, quite literally now, was to help poor, downtrodden Negroes such as Scipio, worrying his hat to shreds in front of soulless Charlie. His shoes, those fine new books, were part of his armor for the fight. From now on, his future would not be based on the fears and desires of his woman. She would have to fit into *his* life. Walter reflected that maybe Dr. Du Bois had gotten it slightly wrong: there weren't more than a tenth of the white people in America as talented, positive, creative, and strong as him and Mr. Johnson. Maybe there was only a talented tenth of the human race that made everything possible for the other 90 percent. On the other hand, he thought, that Scipio accused him of overestimating himself. Was he just a messenger boy, delivering news of the funeral? He wondered what reason Scipio could have to dislike him—after all, wasn't he here to help? Maybe it was simply the fact that he was mixed race. Many God-fearing Negroes assumed that made one a bastard.

Stowing the notebook, Walter was suddenly taken with a chill. The sun could no longer pretend it held the skies; uncertain dusk had claimed the stage. Time for changing into something else, but was it both day and night, or neither? Was being in-between a void, or was it something tangible, with a fluid identity of its own? He shook his head clean of the collegiate questions, stirred up some guilty working man's impatience, and thinking of his desk back in New York piled with press releases and letters to donors, he became suddenly desperate for a telephone. A line to the outside world would let him get some work done, and the question of whether Brer Rabbit really belonged to no one, no wheres, no hows would take care of itself. He considered writing the very difficult letter that had to be written to Cornelia, but decided he would need more strength for that, as well as access to liquor.

Pettey had changed her mind about the cold plate; the smell of greens on the boil slithered under the door. Walter put his coat over his shoulders for warmth and paced more. Such a chilly home, he thought. No one had ever papered this room, so the white walls emphasized the cold of winter and coal rationing; numbed the mind and heart to the tiny coffins on the wall, to the plates clattering downstairs as the sun weakened outside, to the low, artless sound of the tuba that Walter was very quickly coming to detest. He slid a finger over the greasy top of the night table. The stories brought out of the finest white homes by the folks who worked them, the unflushed toilets, the filthy clothes strewn about the floors, the food left out to rot, were legend in Atlanta. Walter figured the same held everywhere—the great white mansions were spotless only because of the black people who cleaned them. Miss Timmons probably would have shined this place dull if she'd spent her life in it. Cautiously, as if reaching into a rat hole, he slid his hand under the blanket to test the sheets and found them rough, but not foul.

With no intention of cleaning up the Mitchells' dirt, Walter decided to take care of his own needs. Down to his undershirt, he grabbed his kit and his extra towel, peeked around to see if anyone was coming, then scooted over to the open door of the bathroom. At the very moment he passed the girl's door, it swung open and her smiling face, a wide and very full set of lips painted dusky rose, confronted him. Her skin was smooth and creamy pink, lightly downed on the cheeks, her hair as blonde as his. She most certainly did not hail from around here. Walter took in the trim satin shoes. Her dress, a simple blue frock of royal blue embroidered down the front with white *fleur de lis,* was much too fine for the Mitchell House, but he guessed it was as casual as her evening wear ran. For a Southern belle, her mammy had taught her well—once again he saw her smile with restraint and possibly even sincerity, neither beset by vapors nor beaming that intimidating and ultimately insufferable grin of Southern indomitability.

"Hello," she said. Her eyes became smaller, slanted in an Oriental fashion, when she smiled. "I'm Louisa Warren. This is my brother Tate."

Beside her, a boy around eleven in blue knickers and a matching jacket buttoned with brass glanced up at him only long enough to decide that Walter did not merit his attentions. A remarkable attitude, thought Walter, for an absurd little boy wearing a red tam o'shanter. His shoes were freshly shined, and his dainty hands, all soft and clean, showed no sign that he'd been the one to shine them. Through clenched teeth, he sniffed and whined something about being hungry, and Walter desperately wanted to knock the wee tam off his head.

Louisa must have seen the look in his eyes. She shrugged her shoulders. "He's on a Scott binge. We're currently living through *Quentin Durwood*. The little prince will only answer to the name Captain Clutterbuck." Tate kicked at her shin, but she ignored him. "Will you be at dinner?"

Walter's carnal tastes had never included white women, and for this he was regularly grateful because dating across The Line meant immediate social death, those bony rear ends more a source of trouble than excitement. One had to be doubly careful, consider not just what you said and how you said it, but where your eyes fell. If nothing else, he thought, Cornelia had been supremely safe and had satisfied, if only aesthetically, his demand for a little flesh on the bones. She also came from a good family, which had its significant privileges, especially for a young man rising. Most of all, he liked a sense that a girl could have fun and still know her place, that she liked the chase and knew when to get caught. Aside from being highly white, this Louisa had a freshness that defied his categories, a modern sort of independence Walter hadn't come across yet.

"Parlez-vous français?"

Walter realized that he hadn't said a word. "Oh, I'm sorry. No. I don't think so. I've been traveling." He felt the chill on his arms; he was standing in his undershirt, all his toiletries bunched up in front of his chest. If he was ever exposed in Sibley Springs, this encounter would be tantamount to rape. Flustered, he pointed with a free finger toward the bathroom. "If I may . . ."

Pushing Tate toward the stairs, Louisa shrugged again. That he wouldn't be attending dinner made no difference to her. "Alright, then. Come along, Captain." Walter found himself a little peeved by this; even if one doesn't care about whom he rejects, vanity still demands some disappointment from the rejected party. Swirling around the bolster, she said, "Good night, Mr. White."

Walter offered a "good night" in return, then took his time in the bathroom, lingered at the mirror as he enjoyed a hot shave and a good scrubbing. He had no plans to go down while the Warrens were still eating, so he went back to his room and removed his pants so as not to crease them. Downstairs, Pettey instructed Shy to pack up the tuba; Goose rambled on about Lula Dean's undeserved gift of a pencil in school today and how much she didn't feel like feeding the chickens tonight because one pecked at her yesterday. It all sounded so normal to Walter, so human, but he reminded himself that it was not. It was *white*.

Parting the bedroom curtains, Walter saw the moon hardening over the town in a deep blue sky. The lights in the homes, the smoke from chimneys gave the appearance of warm rest, and yet somewhere out there a man had been tortured and burned, and Walter felt driven to find that place somewhere on this featureless land. Sitting in limbo wearing only his undershorts, Walter trimmed his nails as he waited for the full night. Only then, he thought, could he become his true self with his people. You will hide in the darkness with them, and then you will bring them light. The whistle of the six o'clock train made him start. Somehow he'd have to stop at the station on the way to the funeral.

Walter's stomach growled. The Cracker Jack was not enough. He'd have to eat some of Pettey's greens or faint before he got out the door. Without buffing his nails—he'd sit down for a proper man-icure when he got back to New York—he dressed, tied his tie, and went down to the dining room, another severe chamber, this one adorned with a photo of a girl and a larger-than-life portrait of Jesus

Christ that stared at the diners from behind Pettey's shoulder. Though he told himself he was glad to see that Louisa and her brother had left already, he asked after them, a question which made Goose smile broadly as she slurped some milk.

"She could be your Lou."

Walking into the kitchen to fetch Walter's plate, Pettey pointed at her lips and remonstrated with a single, dangerous, "Goose . . ." Her breath was no sweeter than Shy's. As she went into the kitchen, the woman's thoughts slipped out again: "That girl had better learn to . . ." The rest was muffled by the swinging door. She seemed to have no filter between her mind and her mouth.

"What's a 'Lou'?"

Goose licked milk off her upper lip. "A sweetheart."

"I don't think so," said Walter.

"Was the sun still up when you combed your hair," she asked without breaking stride.

"I believe so," he said. "Why do you ask?" He thanked Pettey for the tepid greens and the cold chicken leg.

"Because it's bad luck to comb your hair after dark."

The only other guest was not really a guest but the resident doctor, Darius Moody, an elderly man with swaying ear lobes and a waxy complexion that seemed to be melting away from his skull. Walter wrote him down as benign enough, smiling indulgently and gripping the lapels of his frock coat like Daniel Webster as Goose sang in a nasal voice, "Had a little sweetheart just so high, Tra la la sic a li de o. I loved him better than chicken pie, Tra la la sic a li de o. Gladys taught me that."

"She with your mama?" asked Walter.

The noise in the kitchen stopped. "No. She's over there." Goose pointed to the girl on the wall, tall, thin-legged and grim, wearing the same dress Goose had on right now. Tight-lipped, with hard, elusive eyes, Gladys showed signs of a coming beauty. "She's dead too. That's her room you're sleeping in."

Before Walter could think much about that, Dr. Moody asked in a deep, burled voice, "Anyone told you about the. nigger they lynched?"

His professional mien left Walter sniffing at the crossroads, unsure which track he should follow. Was he being ironic, one of the town's few "intellectuals" passing sour judgment? His soft tie did lend him the sense of an old aesthete. Or had he been a part of it too? He'd be a good witness in court. "Bits and pieces. No one's told me the whole story."

The doctor jumped at the opportunity. "Well, when I first saw him, they had him in chains, you know. Pulled him off the train and dragged . . ."

Elbows on the table, Goose set her chin into her hands, eager to hear all the details, when Shy did something that shocked Walter: He covered Goose's ears and over her voluble protests sent her out of the room. The doctor seemed surprised and looked at Shy for a few seconds.

Shaking his head, Shy held up his hands. "All respect, Doctor, I'd ruther not talk about that jes' now."

Here in the land where children were often forced to attend lynchings for their character-building qualities, Walter debated whether he could even make quick, commending eye contact with Shy, whether that was too risky. Would Walter White, Exelento salesman, do such a thing? Hardly. Word would get out that he was a nigger-lover. That would shut him down, if not get him killed. Maybe being an evangelical was better than nothing down here. At least, reflected Walter, Shy and Pettey had actually allowed Scipio inside their home, a statement in these days after a lynching. Even if the black guest was a shufflin' coon, grateful that they didn't beat him, they did regard him as a human; a lesser sort, but a human all the same. Walter looked up at Jesus' head looming over Pettey's seat. How grateful we are, he thought, for such sorry crumbs.

Of course he still needed to hear the story, and Moody would know where the lynching happened, so he found himself in the unfortunate position of trying to convince the doctor to overlook Shy's wise house rules. "Well, Doctor, I would be interested in hearing about all that. Like I said, I've heard bits and pieces, but I'd love to get the whole story from someone distinguished such as yourself. Someone who'd give an objective view of it."

Mitchell shot him an angry look, and Walter mulled whether the hotel owner actually deserved his sympathies. Simso Clark, the grocer's pug-nosed boy, had been his best friend when he was thirteen. He'd taught Walter all his card tricks, always played on the same team, and Walter had seen what happened to him when the whole world was put on his shoulders the way white folks do to their sons.

To hell with you, thought Walter. And fuck Simso Clark. Over and over he'd been taught the lesson that good white people existed, that men were all the same under the skin, and yet so far in this life it seemed to him that those who considered themselves white did good only to be congratulated, or to not look bad. Where were the ones who did good in silence? Walter chewed his cheek as Shy quarreled with Goose about taking ginseng smoke after dinner. Pettey discussed with someone Walter soon realized was herself what to serve the preacher on Sunday. Even the best, like Miss Ovington up at the national office, were kind in a way that polished the porcelain of their white skin, proved their superiority by their kindness and largesse. They'd be your friends right up until it cost them.

Mitchell pointed a finger at him. "Say. You in the market for some land? I got a little piece I'm awillin' to let go, and in fact I know of a big parcel off on the pike west a town."

Live here? Walter couldn't help but to give this a laugh. "Well now, I've just arrived in Sibley Springs. Seems like a lovely town but I'm not quite ready to settle down." He lifted his fork and waved it. "I'm a traveler, see? Could be a nice town to end up in, though." Walter thought he saw envy amid Mitchell's generally peevish expression. "Let me look around and get back to you. Would that be all right?" Traveling with a guide could make things easier. "Maybe you can show me around?"

"Makes sense." Mitchell shrugged.

Finished with his dinner, Dr. Moody softly belched and then gestured to Walter with a wink that he'd fill him in later.

SEVEN

Four boxes of Cracker Jack in his pocket, Walter interrupted Shy Mitchell's final practice of the night to tell him that he needed to stop by the depot to check on his samples. Then he'd probably stretch his legs with a long walk and a few cigarettes. Shy nodded once, then laid a gloomy cheek on the tuba—toward the end of dinner Pettey had reminded him that the man from Sewanee would be picking it up first thing in the morning and he was to give her the five dollars immediately upon receipt. And no, he did not want the uniform. Also, the Warren children's aunt, the as-yet unseen Miss Dorcas, had complained earlier in the day of Shy's excessive practicing, so he would have to apologize to her. Walter imagined Miss Dorcas as one of the heavyweight battleships of the Southern navy. Louisa Warren's future.

Close to seven, a light still burned in the depot, but when Walter reached it, he found the station doors locked. Through the window, Clem's crate, lonely and tragic as Tiny Tim's crutch at the cold Cratchit hearth, struck just one of many unsettling notes among the abandoned wheelchairs and long shadows. Farther back, to the left, in the ticket office facing the platform, Drake performed some clerical task with great concentration. Walter walked around the station to the ticket window where he waited for Drake to stop counting.

The stationmaster moved his lips as he counted, a whispering sound that reminded Walter of the old women praying in the pews of the First Congregational Church. Just as Walter was about to open his mouth, Drake, without looking up, said, ". . . 10, 11, 12. Didn't come. 13, 14. Try tomorrow. 15, 16, 17 . . ."

Walter pulled an expression of distress and muttered a minor curse.

". . . 19, 20, 21, You got a place to stay? 22, 23 . . ."

"Yes, thank you. I'm at the Mitchell House."

Question answered, Drake no longer acknowledged his presence, which was fine by Walter. All that mattered was keeping the story afloat.

Now he had to get to the Quines'. With Drake still in the station, Walter saw no option other than sneaking over to the river and making his way along the bank, under the bridge, until he was well into the Negro part of town where he could safely come out of the woods. Leaving the station behind, Walter strolled downtown, past the Mitchells', but then at the next street, he bore left. While he could well imagine Booney's happy face as the boy held a box of Cracker Jack, the popcorn and peanuts shifting with each step warned of his approach as if he were a rattlesnake.

By the end of dusk, the clouds had broken, torn apart the way one pulls apart cotton, and now as night established itself smaller bolls drifted past the growing moon, gray at the center, then lighter and finally rimmed in silver. The moon, soon full, cast diamonds across the wet leaves and stones. Yet as welcome as it was after such an oppressive day, Walter could not consider it a friend in the cleared fields where he walked between the last shaky homes east of Mitchell's and the woods along the river. Nor could his white skin. If caught, his pallor lit by the moon, he'd have to talk fast to explain why he was there, no matter if the Mitchells and the boys at the General Store could vouch for him. As he hurried toward the relative safety of the river bank, he remembered something he'd once heard in an old African story—white men

90

were white and larval because they'd been created at night, but black men had been created in the full light of the sun.

He entered the woods close to where the servant boy had been shucking mussels that afternoon, picked his steps with care on the narrow trail slick with mud. He was a football field away from the bridge when he heard the first dog baying out.

Walter could not move his legs. Many times he'd imagined what dogs on the hunt sounded like, but life in Sweet Auburn had never featured posses, and no matter that he'd told himself they'd be here, included them in all his dire scenarios, the wailing of these hounds tore at him, clawed at his confidence, cut into his bones. The bawls of each dog rose up into the wind, swirled around with the others and made a constant wave of cruel desire so pitiful that if one didn't know that they were trailing human quarry, he'd be forced to pity them. He squeezed his eyes shut, tried to bear the sound and find enough calm in himself to move forward. Everywhere else, God's creatures were supposed to be the black man's allies against the white world, but here in the South the dogs sent a different message: They were happy to cling to the white man's company, eager to hunt innocents in return for scraps. The shadows of branches seemed to beg to hold the lynch rope, and suddenly Walter had the horrible sense that all of nature would whore itself to the white man if given the chance.

Finally able to push himself on, Walter tiptoed to the thickest tree he could find and leaned sideways against it, wondered who they were after now. This was why Shy wanted Scipio to get home before dark—the white men of this town had a reign of terror going, certainly a curfew. Had there been more lynchings that no one had heard about? His mind unfolded the prospect of saving hundreds of lives here, liberating an entire county with what he was doing. There would be speaking engagements! With eyes and ears open, Walter chronicled all he could of this terrorized town, turned its horrors into gory details sure to elicit gasps from eager audiences. As the dogs approached, Walter picked out at least three from their different pitches, and then heard human voices behind them.

The first was Nip's. "Where'd he go?"

Followed by Ludey, breathing heavily as he tried to keep hold of Poke. "Maybe it wasn't him."

"Drake said he didn't get on the six o'clock."

Suddenly Walter could not breathe.

"Yeah. An' Poke got a good whiff a him at the store."

Many things are possible in this life. We may be mowed down by a runaway truck, fall out a window, be struck by lightning during a sudden, unexpected squall and as much as we admit that such things can take place, that they surely happen to other people, the possibility that we should fall victim to any of them almost always comes as a shock.

And so with Walter, when he realized that *he* was the one being hunted. That his sudden paralysis was the product of a very real threat, not a silly panic like at the depot this afternoon.

Only yards away now from the dogs, Walter sipped at the cold air, the dogs tearing apart the night and his smug assumptions that membership in the Talented Tenth conferred value in a small Southern town, that subtle gradations of class and skin color meant something.

It was over for him here. Walter had to get out of Sibley Springs immediately. And yet he couldn't move. He'd been hunted once before. He'd pretended for years to forget all but the fact of it, but now the same terror and shame at being terrified returned. He was swallowed by the world. Once before he'd been told that he was nothing but a nigger like every other nigger in the U.S.A., and he'd come to believe that he'd learned his lessons from the experience, that he'd let the hatred and the anger propel him forward into this life of dignified ambition. But among these trees, a man on borrowed time, the simple pain of it returned and he didn't care about his oxblood leather shoes or the stack of books in his room. He was just a nigger again. Just a pair of furtive eyes that took everything in this magnificent world that pissed him off only because he wanted so much more of it and collapsed it into two simple piles: Things that would help him survive and things that would kill him.

Their barking at a regular pace, maybe twenty yards from the crest leading down to the bank and closing, the dogs finally forced Walter into doing something. Abandoning his reluctance to muddy his coat, he curled up into a ball underneath the winter bones of a large oak where he tried to remember if he'd left anything with a scent at the store. He certainly had back at the Mitchell House. Had Shy or Dr. Moody turned him in? Just minutes ago, they'd given no clue they were onto him. He slowly pulled his hands up to his mouth to hide his breath steaming in the moonlight. Damp seeped through his coat, and the corner of a Cracker Jack box jutted painfully into his ribs, and still he held his place, moving nothing, trying to disappear.

The dogs were very close now. Walter heard their paws scratch at the mulch of leaves, the panicked breathing against their tight collars, their slobbering jowls.

And then Nip again. "He ain't gonna be out now. He be out later."

The dogs hadn't stopped barking, yet neither had they picked up their pace. Ludey said, "Too smart to be down there."

How flattering, thought Walter, but not true. Nothing he'd learned at AU had prepared him for crawling along a riverbank, dodging lynchers. Only that night when he and his entire family had been cornered, preparing themselves to be burned alive, had he felt so betrayed. Every moment since, he'd loudly trumpeted the White family's creed that their black blood in fact exalted them, but he did not feel exalted right now: He felt ashamed, reduced by both his whiteness and his blackness. He was completely alone.

"It's only seven. We got time. Sumbitch can't git away with Poke on im."

The dogs sniffed along the crest for another endless minute and then turned away back toward town. Walter let his muscles release, sank further into the mud for a few seconds as he calculated his next moves. He hadn't heard Hillman's voice, a fact he held to with both hands. Should he go back to the Mitchells' right now? Get his bag and try to hide until he could hop the morning train? Running off blindly into the night was suicide. He had something for Mr. Johnson, but not enough. Not really. Still, survival was the ultimate goal here, to live to fight again, and that was currently in question. Running away from Sibley Springs, although it meant failure, was the only reasonable course of action. No one had asked him to die. He had to run somewhere and do it now. A stiff breeze shook the tops of the bare trees, rattled them together so loudly that Walter looked up through the broken clouds and branches to see the stars, to see the North Star brightly anchoring the drinking gourd that thousands of his people had followed to freedom.

The branches shook again, thin fingers pointing to make sure he'd seen the message in the sky.

Isn't this why you came, he taunted himself. *To see it again? To feel it again. To see if you're strong enough to fight back this time.*

He looked up river, past the bridge.

To prove you belong somewhere.

He was only a hundred yards from the safety of the Negro part of town.

To prove you are black.

He pinched his arm. Fourth and goal; leave the philosophy to Dr. Du Bois. Walter reassembled the broken pieces of the plan. He'd get to the funeral, hide there, and gather what information he could. At least he'd come back to New York with more, and he'd be safe for the night. Probably.

Even in the dark, Walter could see the dirt on his coat, the leaves sticking to him as if he'd been tarred and feathered. Wasting no more time, he stepped quickly along the bank and quietly over the rocks under the bridge until he was fifty yards along, parallel to the Negro part of town. Where he belonged.

Coming up on the low ridge, he peeked over. Darker here, the small shacks and windowless homes, boards pulling away from their frames, all shuddered in the cold. Higher now, the moon left a sheen on puddles and roofs, created shadows. Aside from the dogs still barking on the other side of the tracks, the town was quiet. Walter dodged along the road, shadow to shadow, in search of the Quine house.

At the end of the main strip, one road back from the railroad tracks, a well-lit house suddenly pushed back against the night, the voices of many people emerging from the silence. Walter stepped up his pace.

EIGHT

Stowing himself behind a dense thicket of sumac nearby, Walter watched figures file into the house he'd seen from the station. Nothing but a simple, porched bungalow with a scrim of decorative trim along the eaves, it wouldn't turn a head in Atlanta, but as large as any five of the shacks surrounding it combined, the Quine home was a mansion here in the Negro section of Sibley Springs. Bare shrubs grew along the front. A woman announced that the service was about to start. Cigarettes flew over the porch railing into the bushes. The final stragglers wandered in, and the door closed.

After a brief silence, a man's voice rolled into an old, slow song.

"Oh, don't you want to go to the gospel feast?"

If you didn't, you'd better have had a good reason, because this man wasn't singing for pennies or critics. His rough, powerful voice rubbed hard like burlap against weak human flesh.

"The promised land where all is peace."

He sang alone, carving each line of the song out of some moment in his life. Walter tried to guess how long it would be before Ludey returned with the dogs. Already a fidgety man, kneeling behind the bush, Walter now felt the questions multiplying and swamping him: Where could he hide? He told himself that the folks here would hide him, but would he make it until the morning train? And what if they *wouldn't* hide him? What then? What if they didn't want to risk their lives? Asking himself the same questions over and over and listening to the same frightening answers, he finally admitted that the man huddled under this sumac knew nothing, really. Asking the same questions black men and women stealing away to freedom had asked for centuries, Walter no longer felt modern or talented or unique. His knees ached. An unpleasant cool sweat pooled at his temples, even in the night chill. He could die tonight. It was not some close call with friends in a part of town they should have known better than to go to, a hypothetical situation discussed morbidly over drinks—no, he was being hunted for a second time.

"My home is over Jordan," declared the singer.

At the moment when Walter thought he'd have to burst screaming out of the bushes, the sadness of the spiritual settled onto his shoulders, whispered into his ear. *Someone has been here before, it said. We have been in the valley you're walking through. We paved its road. And you'll continue walking too, but as long as this song calls into the night you can loosen your grip on your pain. You are part of something greater than your troubles.*

With the slow rhythm of a mother rocking her child, the song closed Walter's eyes and settled his heart. His body set root. He was tired, up since four-thirty. His head felt vague and packed with cotton. He'd barely slept on the train . . .

The song was "Deep River." He'd heard it once at a poorly-attended concert during his sophmore year. For as long as he could remember, Walter's church had sung out of hymnals, sooner willing to eat dirt than be caught moanin' in the moonlight like this man, no matter if white folks in Paris and New York were paying money to listen to such things. For all their beauty, the spirituals sounded to him too precious for the modern world, offered as proof of Negro artistic potential rather than Negro achievement. He could never listen to one without imagining first-nighters in Boston and London whispering, "And now if he could only be trained to perform real music," as they reached for their top hats.

His eyes opened. Walter pinched himself hard again and stood up, resisting sleep. On light steps he approached the house, crept up to the porch where a window had been cracked open to let some air into the living room, overheated by all the mourners. Walter squatted just under the sill so he could peek in.

Seen through a pane of fogged glass, around an edge of curtain, the assembly was a welcome drink of water. A roomful of Negro faces in all the colors he identified as his own—edible shades of chocolate, coffee, and overbaked bread; earth tones from sand and fawn to deep cherrywood—and yet none his exactly, or even all that close; he was lighter by far than anyone in the house. The variety of tones welcomed him, put him at ease in a way his mind could accept. *How brilliant the Negro mind,* thought Walter, *how rich the vocabulary needed to describe a society of colors.* In this room, beauty wore a thousand shades other than peaches and cream, let its hair grow wide, tall, braided, straightened or curled; each surpassing the wavy allure of blonde tresses. Even for such a somber event, women put color to their faces, combined indigos and reds with mahogany and copper, while the white of the men's cuffs set off their hands, framed them for a viewer able to understand this multiple knowledge of beauty.

He'd expected them all to have their eyes closed as they swayed with the song, but instead the mourners sat as still as any Sunday morning gathering at the First Congregational Church. Some younger mothers tried to distract infants swaddled in thin blankets, and two or three bored children already bounced in their seats. Walter suddenly felt better about bringing the Cracker Jack. When the singer, who he saw now was the preacher as well, finished a verse, only a few elderly men and women stepped forward with *"I'll walk into heaven and take my seat . . ."* and these voices soon dwindled away into an uncomfortable silence. A very round woman in a purple shawl finally informed the minister, whom she addressed as Reverend Keyes, that Reverend Lewis had never been much for singing and others confirmed this. For all their variety, most of those gathered were comfortably in the middle of the palette, their hair natural and neat, and those on the other edges in either direction still stood out here, even among their own. The bad news—and it was quite bad—was that Walter couldn't hide here; in fact, this room would provide the opposite of cover. If he *really* wanted to hide, he had to sneak back to some white place, take his chances with the Mitchells.

Thanking her for the observation, Reverend Keyes considered the music finished and collected himself for a moment before his eulogy. Compact, with only enough neck to sustain a white collar cutting into his jaw where his long sideburns ended, he glowered at the congregation from behind small, oval glasses clinging to the tip of his broad nose. If some preachers thought a man to Heaven and others lured them with honey, Reverend Keyes, with the biceps of a man who regularly wrestled with more than just angels, appeared able and willing to fling his brothers to salvation.

Unlike every other funeral Walter had ever been to, no one wept or moaned. Instead, a sense of required attendance held the mourners down quiet in the seats, a reserve unusual even in his own straitlaced church back in Atlanta. There was no coffin; apparently there hadn't been enough left to put away.

"We need to talk tonight about a rich man," Keyes began, clutching a Bible to his chest, his deep voice raggedy with emotion, trilling like a banner torn by the wind. He opened his arms as if gathering everyone close.

A rich man you all know.
A rich man you all recognize.
A man who worked hard.

Loooooved the Lord's creation.
*Loved the **things** of this world.*

A man with gray streaks in his tall and frizzed hair finally rewarded the preacher with, "Oh yes he did," in a tone that made Walter wonder whether the statement had been meant as a compliment. A chill rippled though him. He suspected that crouching on the porch in a wet coat was exactly what the germs he'd encountered the last day and a half had been waiting for.

The gentle conversation from the pulpit ended and now, line by line, each sentence of Reverend Keyes became more of a definite statement, each timed with a short breath, a tap of his foot, a nod of his head that together beat his rhythm as a few more solitary words returned to him from around the room.

Worked the fields, made the earth fruitful.
Um hm.
***Glorified** it.*
Yes.
***Multiplied** it.*
Yes!
When he wasn't in the fields, he was in his home
*Counting the **fruits** of his labor.*

Mourners nodded, heads swiveled around as if noticing their surroundings for the first time, a home groaning under the weight of middle-class life, the heavy furniture, the shelves of bric-a-brac, an upright piano against the far wall, the border of an oriental rug. Despite Walter's imaginings, Cleon Quine had not been some poor, country boy. He wouldn't have had to beg credit for milk. His mourners, on the other hand, Walter figured to be largely poor sharecroppers, maybe some servants like the boy he'd seen before.

As long as the spa was open, these were the lifters and the carriers, the cleaners and the polishers, those who built and those who knocked down. Well aware of the gap, the assembled, for all their colors and dignity, had dressed for this night with more energy than affluence, and they sat like poor cousins amid the evidence of Cleon's comfortable life, resentment singeing their response.

They liked where Keyes was going. Twos and threes now buoyed him up as he hit his beats harder.

> *He was a riiiiich man.*
> Yes, he was.
> *Owned hundreds of acres.*
> He did.
> *This man had a goood wife,*
> Come on, Preacher!
> *Two children,*
> Two of them.
> *Son **and** a daughter.*
> Yes, Lord.
> *He had a fiiiine house.*

On top of the piano sat a brass clock stopped forever at 4:38, its works revealed under a glass bell, the same kind, Walter recalled, as the one in which his mother always kept an arrangement of silk flowers. He scribbled down the time of Quine's death in his notebook as the preacher stormed Heaven. Beside the piano stood a waist-high case containing mostly books of identical binding—some series probably bought on subscription. A sudden chill set Walter's teeth chattering. The room reminded him of the stuffy parlor of his childhood, where he longed to be right now, safe and surrounded by his family. With no corpse present, no spirit to be hijacked, the Quines had apparently loosened the proscription on mirrors and photographs; as well as a large mirror on one of the walls and numerous framed images on tabletops, a portrait of Booker T. Washington hung over the bookcase. Walter couldn't help but shake his head a little, mournfully, at Quine's poor choice of hero. And there, next to the preacher, enshrined on a chair in front of the congregation, a tinted photograph of the man he took to be Cleon Quine stared out at a three-quarter angle, looking past them leftward, toward Walter.

Quine looked to be in his forties at the time of the photograph, with short hair giving way at the temples to rows of furrows across his brow, dark and seeded with concern like a plowed spring field. Captured in his Sunday best, he wore a black suit and a tie in a wide, loose knot. He did not have the faraway look common in photographs, the emotionless gaze of someone waiting for the experience to end. Instead, Cleon Quine seemed to glare at the photographer, suspicious not of the strange hoodoo of the camera but of how much the whole thing would cost him. His features were broad and rounded and, if the tinter was to be believed, colored a deep brown cut with a minimum of white blood. Walter judged him to be handsome, in *that* way, and even from the other side of a window inferred from Quine's hostile gaze that he'd been a hard case; just looking at his photograph made Walter embarrassed to be crouching under his window sill, hiding from white men's dogs instead of wrestling them.

Up to this point, Reverend Keyes hadn't strayed from his spot, only moved to keep his rhythm, sometimes leaned his head back for a breath, but now he took a large step forward. His voice louder, its harsh edges dug deeper to turn the soil, ready the field.

> *Now one day the devil meet the Lord,*
> Come on, Preacher!
> *And that serpent says the only reason that rich man love the Lord*
> *Is because he's so blessed,*

He is.
*Because the Lord has **rewarded** him.*
Tell it!
*Well, **No** sir!*

Fans danced in the assembly, bright colors fluttering like butterfly wings as the more generously proportioned sisters and mothers started to feel the heat.

*The Lord **knew** that man,*
He did.
***Trusted** that man,*
Trusted him!
***Belieeeeved** in that man.*
Believed!
Church, you all know that the Lord giveth.
He does.
And the Lord taketh away.

"Oh yes we do," said one of the few young men in the room, brushed by the Spirit even though he lurked motionless against the back wall.

Left him with nothing,
Nothing.
Shivering in the field without a coin.
Shivering.
And the Devil laugh and say,
*Loooooook at him **now**.*
Look at him!
*Loooooook at that sinner agettin' ready to **sin,***
*But the Lord said, **Wait!***

Keyes held up a hand as if stopping traffic and the whole room held its breath. His words were gentle now, almost a whisper.

Wait for my child to speak.

Walter realized that until now, he'd never even wondered what Cleon Quine had looked like. He'd been a symbol, just like this town, like the men in Vine's who'd probably killed him. The pain had been spread across black America. They'd all taken their share of Cleon, used him to sing about their own troubles, but no one had really thought about *him*. In the front sat a woman in a long black dress layered with rows of black lace. A black satin belt with a buckle also wrapped in black satin cut across her middle. A veil hid her face. Supported by a young woman in her early twenties on one side and a boy with straightened hair, around seventeen, on the other, she had to be the widow.

> *Back down on earth that man was confuuuused.*
> Confused.
> *He **prayed***
> Prayed.
> *And he **wept***
> Oh yeah.
> *And he **groaned.***

"Groaned," said a woman, eyes pressed closed, sitting directly behind the widow. Walter had never seen a woman as thin, with the individual fibers of her muscles visible in her jaw, the eyes deeply set in her skull. Dressed in clean if simple clothes, she appeared to be in fine health. She held a long hand out to her side and grasped important words as they came, held them tight, then let them go.

105

But his misery was unrelieeeeved and
*He was **angry**.*
Yes sir!
He was angry because alllllllll he'd ever done was right.
That's right.
*Did I say he was a **good** man?*

"Yes you did!" A pigtailed toddler in a neat blue dress lifted up a corner of an antimacassar until her older sister slapped her hand.

He was a good man and he was confused like we're alllll confused,
Yes!
*Wondering what **we** done wrong,*
Tell it!
*Wondering why **we** the oooones to suffer.*

The preacher's face contorted with the pain of the question. Walter had never seen such a display of emotion in his house, and particularly of a religious sort. His parents simply would not have it. Sundays, when they weren't all across the street in church, they were kneeling in the parlor and silently praying like Puritans. As he'd grown older, he'd indulged their austere devotions but he'd never experienced the alternative, and he'd never ventured this far outside the walls of propriety his parents had built around themselves, around their youngest son. Unprotected from the wild dangers of rural white America, Walter also stood exposed to certain unknown comforts. He touched the window and let the flame of the Spirit catch a little on his dried-up Congregationalist soul, moving his head with the reverend. As much as a part of him wanted to be back home, he was twenty-four; he needed to be away from there, he knew that. Away from Cornelia. In fact, where he most longed to be was in *there,* in the Quines' parlor. Among his people.

*And he finally **threw** up his hands because he couldn't answer
that question.*
Not with his mind,
No sir.
Not with his heart.

Leaning in toward the window, flipping his own hand back and forth
like one of the fans, Walter realized that the boy he'd seen sitting
beside the widow was the boy down by the river shucking mussels.
He hadn't been watching some servant; he'd intruded on the private
mourning of a son. The assumption he'd made curdled in him.
Although dark like his father, the son inherited what Walter had to
assume were his mother's finer features. He was not crying now. Not
touching her, arms folded, staring at the ceiling, now the floor, young
Quine seemed alone in this room.

So he called out to the Heavens
"How shall man be just with God?"

Walter wondered if he had looked like that after the riot. The torrent
rushed on—

I can-not contend with the Lord's mountains.
Uh uh.
*I can-not **move** the sun and stars.*
You can't.
*I can-not spread the **sea** upon the earth.*
No way.
***Do You knooooow Lord, what it's like to be a good man and
suffer?***

Walter remembered his work, pushed back against the words. He wasn't here to lose himself. The AU, FCC, NAACP man paddled hard against the tide by taking in detail, as much as he could, no matter how irrelevant it seemed here in the shadow of his imminent death. The daughter appeared to Walter a few inches taller than him, an observation he made with some vain chagrin. One arm twined with her mother's, she continued to incline toward her. She favored Cleon in the fullness of her features. His usual taste was for sharper, mixed features, yet the curves of this woman's nose and lips gave a sense of plenty. Impassive and elegant, her expression remained bounded by wistful sadness on one end and a resolve to show no emotion on the other. Walter credited Cleon's discipline: with a face like his, a house like this, there had to have been strict rules and they had produced an almost regal young woman. She clutched an unusual green handkerchief, a homespun rag or towel of some sort, in her masculine right hand.

The man sitting next to her was huge, his blue suit nowhere as fine as any the Quines wore. The swatch of homespun slipped out of the daughter's hand and when the man bent over to pick it up off the floor, he revealed his bald head to be Scipio's.

> *Right here the Devil rubbed his hands together,*
> *Ready to win a soul,*

Reverend Keyes measured out an extra beat here; the ground had been plowed. It was time for the planting. He started the next sentence low, rising in volume with each word.

> *But the man shook his head and said,*
> *No matter what,*
> No matter!
> *I shall dieth,*
> You will!
> *And I shall wasteth away.*

108

"Oh yes!" shouted Miss Timmons, the pearl lady, who hit the floor with her cane.

Scipio had told Walter where and when the funeral was going to be, so he wasn't surprised to see him, but in his suit he appeared dignified, nothing like the man who'd staggered through the Mitchells' foyer in imitation of Brer Bear.

The preacher let the words rain, let the Spirit drench the room with glory.

> *I shall give up the ghost.*
> Give it up!
> *Yet even in my grave*
> Um hm.
> *I shall belong to the Lord*
> Amen!
> *Until I live again!*

Hands shot up and the shouts of Amen nearly swallowed the preacher's words. Only Scipio was not waving. Instead, his hand crept over to the daughter's and rested atop it. Walter squinted through the collective heat of all the mourners, further fogging the edges of the window to see that she did not respond. Scipio checked her face with a quick, nervous glance. Though she didn't shrug off his comfort or brush it away, she made no sign of returning his affections.

> *Well, the Lord heard his servant Job.*
> That's right.
> *Heard his faith.*
> Um hm.
> *And rewarded him a hundredfold.*
> Praise Him!

But He also heard him ask the question,
Heard him.
Heard him ask if He knew what it was to be a natural born man.

Though his mind felt clear, the cold had not left Walter and a sneeze built in his nose. He lost the preacher's train as he bit his lip, stopping himself from what would be a sure giveaway. Scipio lifted his head and cased the room. Walter tasted blood on his tongue as the preacher recounted Christ's birth and how the straw became as down, and the animals became a choir until he said,

*With His blood He wrote a **new** promise!*
A new one!
*A promise that we **will** be born again!*

And at the words "born again," the room burst open again into full shout, allowing Walter to sneeze into his sleeve. The people now rocked in time to the preacher, the fans rose into the skies as if a breeze had scattered the butterflies. He tried to get a glimpse of the widow, but he couldn't see through her veil, just the hands in her laps as she turned the wedding ring on her left hand with the fingers of the right. The preacher's voice raced along, barely leaving spaces for the congregation to speak their souls, and Walter closed his eyes, swept up.

He was crucified,
Yes!
Hung upon that rude, wooden cross,
That cross!
Lynched as true as any man ever was,
Yes!
But he came ALIVE again!

The room roared approval, all standing, waving arms as they shouted the triumph, while outside, Walter's arms pushed up too, giving glory against his stolid upbringing, his new and fashionable life in Harlem, his worldly ambitions, his better judgment. His mother would cluck if she saw him slumming this way.

The Romans could kill his body, but they could not kill HIM!

Hallelujahs showered on them all. Feet stomped. Walter did not forget that a brace of hounds was out searching for him, that he could be minutes away from being lynched, that he needed to hide. But these men and women closed his eyes and rocked him between the knowledge and the hope that he was indeed part of something beautiful and more powerful than evil, that he belonged to the side of goodness in a way beyond simply knowing what goodness was. When he opened his eyes, Scipio was staring at him from his seat. He was smiling.

He rolllllled back the rock!
Yeah!
He waaaaalked the streets of Galilee!
Walked them!
He was born into the spirit,
Yes Lord!
Born by his death!
Born again!
*You see, no **tree** can kill us!*
No, man!
*No **fire** can kill us!*

All the forces had been brought to bear for this moment by Reverend Keyes. He'd assembled hearts and faith and biblical words to meet with the brutal reality of their lives, made Christ one with them and exalted them all, put them into Heaven together to praise and triumph—as Walter crouched under the sill and decided what to do.

Though they gamble for our garments and spit upon our faces, we shall live!
Yes!
Despite the rope!
Yes!
Despite the nails!
Yes!
Despite the flames!
Yes!
If we are born again, our chains shall be the wings that lift us up to Heaven!

The preacher swung his arms and stamped as he yelled out,

We SHALL be born again!
We SHALL be born again!

The crowd shouted "Jesus," screamed "Amen" and "Yes Lord" in the knowledge that they *would* be born again, that they *would* be rewarded for their suffering, for being right.

Walter ventured a look over the windowsill, saw Scipio still staring in his direction and went down as if he'd heard gunfire.

We are here because of another man the Lord blessed with riches.
Um hm.
Blessed with a loving wife named Dulcet.
That's right.

Like Job, he was blessed with two children,
Blessed.
Ellanice and Fortune.

Subdued hums and yesses calmed the room

But Thou hast shewed thy people hard things, Lord.
Hard.
Thou hast made us to drink the wiiiine of astonishment.
Say it.
Cleon Quine did not get his three score and ten years.
Uh uh.

This was a trap of some sort, Walter was sure of it now. He started to strip off his shining, righteous robe as if he'd been caught out.

I have been told he only got 51 years before his days were con-sumed like smoke, his bones burned as a hearth.
Yes.

But where else could he go?

Two regular trains,
two special trains.
25 minutes of fire returned him to dust,
Uh huh.
floated him across the 2137 acres he'd once owned
and boasted of.
Ummmm.

What would he have accomplished if he couldn't even enter a room of black folks?

And yet.

And yet we read, "But though I give my body to be burned, and have not charity, it profiteth me nothing."

His own people. Keyes took a final breath, shaking his head in sad regret for all that had transpired, for the sins of all involved, including Cleon's. Sweat rolled down into his eyes.

Oh, the legions of the Devil are infinite.
They are.
Many say that they wore white faces that day,
They did.
But the Lord's ways are not our ways,
No sir.

And the robe did not come off so easily.

Beareth all things!
Believeth all things!
Hopeth all things!
Endureth all things!
I am not so much a race man as I am a grace man!
That's right.

Walter rose up again, his face framed in the pane of glass. He had a right to claim this world, even if he claimed Dvořák and Voltaire, too. Scipio continued to smile ominously, but Walter resisted the urge to drop back down out of sight. Instead, he locked eyes with the other man and the two glared as Reverend Keyes wound to his grand finish.

The only color I care about is the snowy white of that robe Jesus holds for me in Heaven, because uplifting a man to a bigger house on a bigger hill is NOT our business.

It's not.

Uplifting a man so his pockets bulge and his heart shrinks is NOT our business.

No sir!

Uplifting a man so that he's so high he can't see the shoulders of the brothers and sisters he's standing on is NOT our business.

Amen!

No! Call me when you're lifting men up to Heaven!

Call me!

Call me when you're raising all who believe to the House of the Lord!

Call me!

Then I'll bear all my load and more.

Bear it!

I will carry my burden and more until He leads us all to the verdant fields beside that quiet river of peace!

And at this, Walter let out a generous sneeze that banged his head against the sill and brought all the rest of the eyes in the room to the window.

NINE

Walter turned the knob. He belonged here. No matter what Scipio had in mind, Walter had a right to be with the people for whom he was risking his life. His father said there were as many ways to be black as there were shades of skin. The bristling crowd opened up a circle as he entered, gave wide berth to this white man spying on Cleon's memorial. Scipio obviously hadn't mentioned that he was coming. In the parlor light, Walter saw that leaves and branches still stuck to his coat and the sopping cuffs of his trousers tolled heavily against his ankles. He removed his hat.

"Good evening," he said.

As much as Walter desperately wanted someone to rush forward and call him brother, no one moved or spoke. He should have just hidden in the hills. Some weary mothers and middle-aged men offered the darting, guilty eyes they reserved for the presence of white people. A few young men who'd decided to take their chances here rather than in the battlefields of Europe stood near the door, thought they saw a white man having a laugh. So did the old women squeezed into coal, and they clicked their tongues.

"Reverend, my apologies for this most unseemly interruption."

Pulled up short before his finale, Reverend Keyes hadn't budged since Walter's head struck the window. He did not look happy; his

117

expression in a barroom or alley would have sent most men the other way. Across the room, Scipio smiled at Walter with the indulgent smile of Brer Bear, feeling a little sorry for Brer Rabbit before he gobbles him up. Before Walter could even think about convincing these people to help the cause and the NAACP, he'd need them to keep his secret. He'd need them to protect *him*. Had Brer Bear underestimated him, he wondered? Or had he overestimated himself?

"Mrs. Quine, may I enter?"

His smart suit and tailored coat, hardly standard garb for Night Riders in Tennessee, home state of the Ku Klux Klan, begin to raise the question in the faces of the mourners as to why a white man would come bearing any kindness. A few squinted at Walter, wondering if his skin somehow lied.

He decided not to lead with news that Nip and Ludey were out searching for him. "My name is Walter White. I apologize for my dress, but I had to come along the river to get here."

Dulcet Quine lifted the veil. Grief sat poorly on her, had taken the deep, motherly lines of constant smiling and a life of enforced generosity, a life spent taking care of everyone from her husband down to the babies of rich white folk, and turned them into a brittle wince. "Did my Cleon know you?"

"No, ma'am. I did not have the pleasure of knowing your husband." Walter stopped and coughed. On the train down, he'd imagined this next moment as something great. Damp and threatened as he was, he still pictured the crowd rushing him with a cheer of gratitude and relief. They'd pull off his coat, set him down at the head of the table with a plate of fried chicken and grits. Mustering all the drama he could, Walter faced the roomful of country folks and remembered his royal English blood as he declaimed, "I . . . am the field secretary of the NAACP, the National Association for the Advancement of Colored People. I've come to investigate this crime."

Walter waited for the rush. Scipio folded his arms and snorted derisively while everyone else remained in the exact position they'd been in prior to his announcement.

He didn't have time to feel embarrassed or defensive. You came here to save these people, he thought. They *should* help you—Walter White, descendant of a president, star salesman, champion debater who should be arguing before the Supreme Court. Who should be on the Supreme Court. A decorative plate painted with the Statue of Liberty hung on a wall by the piano. Freedom is the best product in the world to sell. Start fighting for your life. Start selling. "Are all of you familiar with the NAACP?

Heads nodded here and there, and Walter pointed to them. "Good. For those who do not know, the NAACP stands for the National Association for the Advancement of Colored People. It is a national organization committed to securing the rights and advancing the interests of the Negro in America."

People exchanged glances, still too curious about him to pay too much attention to what he was saying. Mrs. Quine had not taken her eyes off Walter, but her son Fortune probed his tongue around his mouth, ran a finger between his collar and his neck, and otherwise expressed boredom. Ellanice stood close to her suitor, the only sign so far that she felt anything for him.

Walter pulled out the boxes of Cracker Jack and held them out. "Here. These are for the children. Is Booney here?"

The extremely thin woman called out, "He's my boy. He's home asleep." She narrowed her eyes. "Why *you* want to know?"

"Because I'd like to be sure he gets some."

The woman chewed that over. "So why you givin' out candy now?" she asked. "Booney told me you was playin' cards with those segurs at Vine's."

The two girls Walter had noticed during the sermon came forward, the older hauling her toddler sister under the arms like a calf or a sack of rice, as she checked her mother for reassurance. A more daring boy dashed up and snatched a box before Walter changed his mind.

With one left, Walter walked up to the thin woman, her arms drawn up to her chest in defense, and he pressed the Cracker Jack into her hands. "Would you be so kind as to tell me your name?"

She resisted the temptation to sneak a look at the box and instead lifted her chin. "Mrs. Tansy Portis."

He needed to score some points before Miss Tansy came up with anything else or Scipio got into it. "Well, Mrs. Portis, I work in the New York office of the NAACP," said Walter. He tucked his hands on his hips, threw his voice forward to the back of the room and speechified over her head, reeling out the sentences before anyone could counter. "I grew up in Sweet Auburn, in Atlanta, where my mother and father still live. Married now more than 30 years. I'm a graduate of Atlanta University and until recently was employed by the Standard Insurance Company. I'd venture that more than a few of you have policies with that concern." Some hands went up and the tension eased at Walter's résumé, one that could only belong to a black man. His claim of legitimate birth here among these churchgoing people also scored points—bastardy was not becoming a good Christian. Scipio scowled on, but for the first time, Ellanice broke her mask, batted her long eyelashes in puzzlement and leaned her head in to hear. "Now my colleagues, *Dr. William Burghardt Du Bois and Mr. James Weldon Johnson . . .*"—All right, "colleagues" *was* an overstatement, but sometimes the facts had to be stretched to serve the truth. Walter's passionate delivery of these names—important to those familiar with them and impressive-sounding to those who were not—rattled the glass in Dr. Washington's frame, and he felt justified as the Quine house became more animated, and he edged a bit closer to action. If he said enough fast enough and enough of it was right . . . ". . . They believe it is crucial that the true story of what happened here in Sibley Springs be exposed. That those who lynched Cleon Quine be brought to *justice.*"

Unconvinced, Scipio folded his arms. His massive chest made it appear that he held them out genie-style. "So then why you stayin' at Mitchell House? Hmmm? No black man stays at Mitchell House. What you playin', White?"

Though Brer Bear could probably eat this rabbit whenever he had a mind to, Walter took comfort in the fact that he'd have to have a mind first, and Scipio hadn't proved that. Nor had anyone tried to stop him. Walter pulled off his coat and hung it on a rack before he was soaked to the skin. He wondered if he could ask for some tea before he ended up with pneumonia. "Brother," he said as if summoning up patience for someone thick in the head. "I've got a job here. I have been sent here *specifically* to get those boys at Vine's and every other white man or woman who had a hand in this lynching to confess the whole story. I know the men responsible. They're already talking to me. As soon as I have all the information, I'll take it back to New York!" The silence created by Scipio's fear let Walter's voice ring off the walls. Men and women nodded, embers of the preacher's sermon still smoldering in them. Planting his feet, Walter gripped his lapels—he had the floor now. The room was his to be had. "We will take it to the governor of Tennessee and get each and every one of Cleon Quine's murders prosecuted!"

Someone shouted out, "That's right!"

"We will publish the report in *The Crisis*! We'll make this a *national* issue!"

"You tell them!"

He shook his fist. "We will tell the president he must condemn it!"

"Tell *all* of 'em!"

"What happened here in Sibley Springs must be *punished*! Instead of *representing* tragedy, with your help we can make Cleon's death shed light on the path to freedom! *You* can help us end lynching for good!"

Much of the congregation applauded. Heads nodded with the

possibility of something other than acquiescence and servility. Walter held back a greedy smile. Letting off all that steam, going from being hunted outsider to at last taking up all the space that he'd always imagined would be his made him a little drunk. A man with a checked vest and white whiskers dusting his jaw stood out into the aisle between the seats. "So what we supposed to do?"

"First, any of you who saw what happened, please tell me the details." Walter stepped further into the room, down the aisle, stopping to shake hands with his questioner, and then down to the front where the preacher stood, aghast at the treacherous turn the proceedings had taken.

"Second, you must . . ." He looked at Scipio. ". . . You must keep my secret until I leave. You can all have a good laugh after I'm gone, but you must not let on that I've been here or who I am or why I'm here. I've told the white folks that I'm here selling hair straightener." This idea—pulling a roscoe on the entire white population of Sibley Springs—was very well received, and the children had reached the prizes in the Cracker Jack, adding to the high spirits.

"I'm sorry that I have to do this now, . . ." he gestured to the photograph of Cleon. ". . . but we don't have much time. I think the men at Vine's may already be onto me; I had to dodge their dogs on the way here."

The room suddenly went dead silent, and Scipio, a good six inches taller than Walter, stepped away from Ellanice so he could loom over him. "You mean to tell me you *already* got 'em riled? And you gonna tell me you did it for us?" Walter swallowed hard as Scipio circled him. "Well, thanks so much, *Brother* White! I mean, if'n you walk out a this town alive, then you gonna run some story in your paper and get a trial and I'm tellin' you that's only gonna kill more of us. They gonna take it out of us for helpin' you. You gonna leave us all with less than *nothin*." Scipio palmed the jewels of frightened sweat on his bald head. "Cleon's gone and now you done rattled up all them white folks even more. You see, . . ." He tried to hide his panic, slowed down and took on a more reasonable tone. ". . . we had this all worked out."

Scipio seemed not to notice that Fortune and Ellanice exchanged glances at his last line—the first thing anyone had said that grabbed Fortune's attention. Dulcet creased her brow and others rubbed their jaws at Scipio's arguable version of Sibley Springs' Negro history, doubters such as Mrs. Portis, whose pained expression seemed to remember things that Scipio hadn't taken into account. Still, the silence spoke. Everyone had a story, and Scipio made a point—they *were* the living, the survivors. It would be good to keep it that way.

"If'n we lay low a few days, let me get word out to the good white folks aroun' that we don't want to see any more probbims for anybody and it'll all blow over."

Brought to the top of a mountain, the Negroes of Sibley Springs saw two cities before them. Without a doubt, living another day, living until you were called by God, not sent up by the Devil, had its attractions. But if it meant a diet of nothing but fear and corn flour, a man had to think hard. Blown by winds from both sides, the mourners and family remained, the way most people stay all their lives, frozen between two reasonable positions.

Walter sensed everything slipping away, saw himself running from the dogs, all alone once again. "So that's it?" He had nothing but words to fight with. He wouldn't beg, but he could bluff. Walking back down the aisle with slow, deliberate steps, Walter picked up his coat. "Scipio speaks for all of you? Well, whether you believe it or not, you're free to stay slaves if that's what you want. Me? I'd rather go outside and face those dogs awaitin' on me." He took his time putting on his coat, fussed with the brim of his hat and prayed someone would speak. The room remained quiet. When he finally reached the door, he turned. "This is a different world, my friends. When our boys get back from Europe, they'll expect us to have done something better. They'll expect us to have put up a fight as good as the one they're giving."

Nothing. Trembling some at the prospect of returning to New York on the run with only what he had, he reached for the door-knob. Plotting his escape felt like more than he could handle right now, but what choice did he have? Should he splash back along the riverbank, he wondered, or had Drake finally left? He was going to die tonight. His mother hadn't wanted him to leave Atlanta in the first place; his father and Mr. Johnson had had to convince her.

Dulcet spoke. "He was going to the bank."

TEN

Walter sagged inside his coat and turned around.

Ellanice nearly screamed, her royal face collapsing in anger, "Mama, don't speak to him!"

"Oh, Neecie." Dulcet had sat down, exhausted with the memory and her daughter's pride. "He was going to the bank to buy a piece of property. Neecie was with him." Everyone looked to Ellanice, but she didn't speak, the scene suddenly fresh to her again. She held the rag to her cheek, trying to rebuild her shattered calm. Scipio reached out and put a hand on her shoulder, but she shrugged it away, and he stepped back as if slapped. Dulcet went on. "Neecie said three boys standing in front of Vine's started up with them, began insulting her. Cleon was not . . ." She began to cry. ". . . he was not a man who allowed words to pass. The boys threw stones at them. Then he pulled out a rifle. Shot two of the boys dead. Hurt the other one bad. Cleon and Neecie come racing back in the wagon. Lord, he kissed us all, then took off to Reverend Lewis's house. That's the last time I saw him alive."

Hands in his pockets as if passing time in pleasant conversation, Fortune stared at the ceiling as he took over for his mother, oddly disconnected with the pain of this scene. His voice was lower than Walter expected. "Papa and Reverend Lewis went off toward

McMinnville. Two days later, they's dragging Papa through the streets in chains. Ellanice saw that. Yes you did, Neecie. No black folks saw what happened up on the hill, though." He tapped his toes, scratched at his cheek. Some of the fire in Cleon's photograph had taken the place of the afternoon's riverside tears, but Fortune's vacant expression lacked the resolve of his father's; Cleon had never had a suit as nice as that boy's when he was seventeen. Nor had Walter, and they were probably both the better for it, probably better for not being so pretty. If the father had seemed to believe not so deep down that if he stared at something long enough it would do what he wanted it to do, the son's eyes burned only to provide cover for emotions he didn't understand. "I want to kill them," he said with no particular emphasis, no passion. Nip and Ludey were right to be afraid of him. Anger and panic had touched a boy with no sense yet of who he was, an incendiary combination. "I want to find Reverend Lewis . . ." Fortune glared at the preacher. ". . . We'll put together an army. I want to kill them."

Scipio bulled back into the family knot. "You see! You and this boy gonna get us all killed!"

Dulcet held up her left hand. "Somebody stole all that money out of his pockets. Tore the wedding ring off his finger." The jar leapt into Walter's mind. "Eighteen carat with a blue stone. That's all I want now." She held her son's hands. "No more dead men. I just want my Cleon's ring. Want our money and our justice. Neecie, trust him. Why would they be after him if he wasn't for us?"

Her emotion carried the day. Brer Rabbit had won, at least for now. Even with the dogs out there, Walter had to visit the site. "I want to see where it happened." He looked at Ellanice, quite striking in her sorrow. "Could you take me there?"

She turned from him to her mother. "There's dogs, Mama."

"Take him, Neecie," said Dulcet. "Take him there.

• • •

Ellanice pulled a woolen shawl off a hat rack, then held the front door open for Walter. After pausing to pick up a sturdy branch for use as a walking stick, she led him around the house and onto a path that took them away from the town, into the fields that began just outside the black settlement. They didn't speak. Ellanice strode as far as her skirt allowed her and Walter soon found himself in the unpleasant position of trying to keep up with a woman. Her hair hung behind her, long and straight and thick, in a single wide plait held by a gold pin, and she had rediscovered her placid expression, a beautifully polished surface that Walter had begun to view as a challenge on more than one level. Securing the shawl with her left hand, Ellanice planted the stick and pushed forward into the wind with the other, her chin high, eyes looking ahead in private thought as if Walter were simply a hound accompanying Artemis on a tramp through her fields.

"How far do you think it is?" he called ahead. Walter needed to get back to Mitchell's. He also needed to catch his breath.

Still crunching through the corn stubble, she pointed up to a low rise. "Just past that hill. Top of the one after." Walter judged it to be a ten-minute hike. He took a deep breath, then upped his pace. The moon was high now, spreading a fragile light on the land. Without turning, Ellanice said, "What makes you so sure they're after *you*?" She hid the softness in her husky voice beneath a withering tone. Under other circumstances, it might have been a perfect voice for secrets and consolation, although sweet nothings were hard to imagine coming from her. She was not a woman who giggled.

"I was walking along the river when I heard the dogs and two men I met at Vine's talking about somebody hiding in the woods and coming out for him later. You know someone else they could be looking for?"

127

Ellanice shrugged. "Maybe they're talking about Reverend Lewis."

She offered nothing more. Walter would have to chase her with words. "Who was Reverend Lewis?"

"Our preacher."

"Then who's Reverend Keyes?"

"The Methodist."

"He gave a good sermon."

She stopped and faced him. "You think?" Her voice was sharp now. "I especially liked when he mentioned how many acres we owned." Ellanice never seemed to blink unless she chose to. Slashing at some ankle-high stalks with her staff, she continued on ahead. "How you can give yourself to burn and still have no charity. Papa was surely no church man, but he and the Reverend saw it all the same way. They were Tuskegee men."

"Your father went to Tuskegee?"

She snorted. "Papa didn't learn to *read* until he was twenty-two. No. Fortune and I come up, all he talked about was Mr. Booker T. Washington and how great Mr. Washington was and how we should all listen to Mr. Washington." Her voice went deeper. "If a colored man works for himself, makes money, the white man will *respect* him." Ellanice glared at Walter as if he had come up with the idea. "He believed that," she said with wonder. "Worked and saved and bought, and all that did was make *everybody* hate him."

She turned and began walking again. Mounting the hill now, Walter felt weak from his worsening cold and from tussling with this woman. As the lights of the town emerged below them at the top of the first rise, he sneezed. The night was getting on. He had to pull some details out of her and hide himself as soon as he could. There was no time to step lightly. "What did he think of Scipio?"

"You should *live* to be as good a man as Scipio." She sounded defensive, and not at all winded by the climb. "That man cares about folks living and dying, not fool theories you toss around up North. National Association of White Folks Lovin' Niggers. Men like Scipio pay for that kind of crap with their blood. My father did."

"Like freedom? You think that's a fool theory? That's what your father died for. He died for us."

"Don't you do that!" She turned and waved the idea off with a pointed finger, then aimed it at his eyes. "Don't you turn him into no Jesus Christ because Papa wasn't no Jesus Christ, I'll tell you that! He didn't die for *you*."

"He was a soldier in a new . . ."

Ellanice laughed at him in a scornful way that made him feel younger than her by many hard years. "Let me stop you, college boy. Maybe you didn't learn this at 'Lanta University, but fact is, *nothing's* gonna change. *Naw*-thin. White Man always gonna have us. You can love him, you can hate him, you can pretend he ain't there, but he always gonna be there so you better just *deal*."

"With respect, Miss Quine, I don't see *you* wet nursing in the Big House. I mean, the world changed enough for you to wear that satin blouse and that gold pin in your hair." Her nostrils flared. "Something *must* be working somewhere. At least for *you*." The wind bit a little more; an excuse for Ellanice to wrap the shawl around her head as she walked away. "Let me ask you one thing. What would your father have wanted?" She took longer strides, lifting up her hem, but Walter kept close after her. "Would he have wanted justice, or would he want you apologizing to the good white folks?"

Beneath her shawl, Ellanice went ahead in silence toward the top of the next hill. This was not going well. Walter sighed and trudged after her, looking mostly at the mud and the corn stalks below his feet until he saw her shoes next to his. She'd been waiting.

"When we were young, he took us on a trip to New York City," she said in a calmer tone. As much as she obviously thought on these things, Ellanice did not often have the chance to speak

129

them. "That's where he bought Mama and him those rings. You'd think folks here'd be proud of a black man reaching up and seeing the world. No." She shook her head. "No. Just talk about how he selled out. White folks? Well, he was just a nigger to them like every *other* nigger in Sibley Springs. 'Cept, of course, he had money and that made them hate him even more 'cause they're all lazy-ass segurs living on bad land they don't know enough to not bother farming. He kept Washington up on the wall so he could curse at it. Reverend Lewis was his only friend around here. Daddy tried to build us a bigger house up around the top of the hill, but funny thing is, kept on getting burnt down. Don't you think that's funny? Could've been anybody in town set it." She looked at him firmly, to make sure he understood her point. "Anybody."

"So where do you think Reverend Lewis is?"

"Ran off with Daddy, but he didn't get caught." Speaking of Reverend Lewis, Ellanice had the look on her face that Scipio dreamt of seeing some day. She met the eyes of someone much taller than she was, someone she felt safe with. Someone not there. "Folks think he still living out in the woods, puttin' together some kind of fight back, and that's just about the last bit of hope most black folks here got."

"I hate to ask you this, but . . ."

"You want me to tell you what happened." She curled her lip in disgust, as if he were some cub reporter dogging a byline. "We told you too much already." Now only a stand of low pines stood between them and the summit. "Just past that shed of trees," she said from under her shawl.

Through the branches Walter could see the moon fully revealed, the gray shadows of craters; tides were pulled, crops planted, months counted by the regularity of its mysteries. More stars had thickened the sky since he'd seen the drinking gourd. In all his time in New

York, he hadn't noticed the moon, couldn't see the stars if he wanted to. In fact, he hadn't really noticed it much back in Atlanta, either, but one couldn't hide from it here.

As soon as she realized what he was staring at, Ellanice turned away. "It's bad luck to look at the moon through branches. And don't count the stars." Walter kept staring though, an unwitting show of courage in the face of folk wisdom that seemed to embarrass her once she noticed her companion's indifference. "That's the saying, you know. Besides, . . ." She lifted her nose, proud once more of the depths of her oppression as she started toward the summit, ". . . you don't look like you ever have much bad luck."

Too insulted to speak, Walter had only begun to assemble a response when they reached a charred blot of land, a black square in the field the size of one of the small Negro homes down the hill. Ellanice pointed. "Here."

They had arrived at Golgotha. No skulls littered the spot, no rocks or buzzards or signs that the Devil had reserved this place for his work, just a patch of blackened grass and a low mound of dirt that Walter, unwilling to step inside now paced around instead. The earth seemed unfazed; discolored maybe, but not overly disturbed. It had merely made another everyday accommodation to the needs of Evil. In the summer, low stalks of corn would push through this soil and by August, no one would know where it had happened. Quine's murder would be folded back into the regular process of things, confirming his daughter's belief that nothing would ever change.

Walter ventured a few steps toward the center, where the small pile of ashy dirt marked the site of Quine's last breath. He had seen the finger, Quine's photograph, met the men who'd done it, but until now he'd kept the gruesome detail caged separately. For everyone in the NAACP office, this whole lynching had been largely a matter of representation, one horror made to stand for all the horrors of Negro life, yet never really touching what Quine the man had experienced.

Walter closed his eyes, opened the cages and allowed everything he'd learned here to pounce together and recreate Quine's Passion. Slavering, grinning white faces, savages dancing around a fire. The final, imprisoning clank of the chains. Flames crackling. Fathers holding their young sons up to see the man writhe. The fire embraces the feet, then the legs, leaps higher, licks at his balls, the hair crinkling off, please God, dead or insane by then, burning from this high spot as a beacon for merciless Sibley Springs.

The words formed in Walter's mind. He saw the images, felt disgust, but the more he squeezed his eyes shut and tried to restage this lynching, the real desolation of this other man floated further out of reach. His own past intruded.

So here you are, came the thought. Here you are. *Go ahead and chain yourself up.*

For eleven years he'd buried the memories but now they pushed Quine aside. A house on a nice street in Atlanta came into focus, windows open to whatever breeze passed by during that September heat wave. A young man, thirteen years old, itching under the tension of the last few weeks, opens the door, looks at the thermometer and then checks the front page of the paper for the temperature of the town: false accounts of Negro men assaulting white women. Tussles on the streetcars, a sense of boiling disorder, a disquiet that makes him move and tap and twitch. His best friend, a rough-edged white boy name Simso Clark, is nowhere to be found. That evening, the young man goes out with his father in their wagon and suddenly a flood of people courses down the street throwing stones, mobbing every black face in their path. He feels his father go rigid with fear. They see a lame man stoned to death. They pull an old woman into the wagon just seconds before the mob catches her. The boy calls out for Simso, but he's gone, disappeared, and the boy is worried that something has happened to him, that Simso has been caught in the terror. As if he'd dreamt it all, the next day passes without incident, but he is lost in a fog. There is nothing real anymore, no reason to keep doing other than to do. The family performs the motions of life while dreading the sunset, knowing that when the moon comes, when the stars twinkle their messages from the angels, the white mobs will move on them. All is silent until midnight. A roar begins a few blocks away. It charges down Houston Street. Something like lightning hits the house. Mother and his five sisters run upstairs. Father pulls down shades, stacks chairs and tables against the windows. Walter wonders which way to go. He is thirteen. He doesn't want to leave his mother, shouldn't have to hold a gun, but Father yanks him by the collar and hands him a gun. The sudden weight almost pulls Walter to the ground. He kneels at a window next to Father. Rocks shatter the street lamp on the corner and now only the approaching torches light the street. Faces come closer. White faces . . .

"We rode into town on the wagon for the meeting with Palgrave."

Ellanice had let the shawl fall to her shoulders, and the wind tried to lift her plait of hair, tugged at her cowl. Walter realized that his eyes were closed. He opened them, tried to place this woman staring at him. He felt the strain of panic in his eyes, tasted the tears that had rolled over his lips. He shook his head clear. "I seem to be catching a cold. Who's Palgrave?"

"The lawyer working the deal. Papa hitched up the mules in front of Vine's, and there were those three boys." Her expression recoiled from the memory. "They started in, jawin' at Papa and me." She stepped inside the great stain of fire and blood. "They said some things about me. Papa got out of the wagon. I told him not to!" Ellanice shook her fingers like the branches on the trees, shaking in the wind; long, expressive, elegant fingers that bowed back in protest. "I don't care what no man say about me! But Papa give it back, you know? Then the boys start heaving rocks at us. He pulled me down into the wagon. Then he grabbed his rifle—Papa was the only black man in the county crazy enough to carry a gun. Three shots. Then ladies screaming, and those boys crying like babies. Papa jumped back into the wagon and we raced on back home. He got some clothes and ammunition and then he ran to the Reverend's."

Walter expected her to collapse in tears, the same kind of tears he had just shed, but Ellanice was made of stronger stuff, and the bland smile of Louisa Warren came to mind. How foolish she seemed compared with this woman, one whose confidence did not come from her ability to send Vandy frat men swooning. Cornelia only aspired to such reserve. Ellanice wore the solemnity Walter saw on the faces of all great black women, a knowledge that suffering creates this world, that suffering is this world, and, like the mountains and the trees, wherever they are, the works of Man will be built on them and of them. He wanted to sink into her, but he was ashamed of needing her strength. He had come to comfort *her,* save *her,* but her sadness only made Walter want her to comfort *him.*

"We heard bits of news the next two days. A posse went out from the town and most everybody in the county went alookin' for them. Black folks kept off the streets. Finally we heard Papa been caught up near McMinnville and they were bringing him back on the train. Momma told me to stay home, but I ran out, and I met it, watched them pull him down the steps of the car. He wasn't walking. I don't know if they'd broken his legs or if he just wouldn't walk." That thought made her smile a little. "Just a rag around his modesty and his green jacket." She held up the piece of green homespun she had pulled out of her pocket. "I wiped his face of the blood with some of it."

Walter wiped his brow, damp despite the cold.

"Only the white folks know what happened next. Papa *hated* white people." She gazed hard at his pale face, illuminated by the moon.

He said nothing, just looked up and she looked up with him, watched the clouds trying to sneak under the moon's eye. It cast colors where there should have been none: the blue of the night sky, misty grays and whites from cloud and fog. Silver rims on blades of grass; the dead black place where it had been burned away. Too cold for birds or frogs or crickets, only the scratching sound of windblown chaff, the swirl of quick air flapping their coats and shawls, disturbed their thoughts. The clouds, bunched together as they edged past, reminded Walter of passengers on the Underground Railroad, immigrants stealing out of the land they loved to find what they loved even more. It was hard not to see the dead in the shadows, and with Ellanice, whether she liked him or not, Walter was allowed his sorrow, allowed to have pain and not told to buck up, get over it and put up a stiff upper lip because she understood that he bucked up, got over, and stiffened his lip every day of his life. He had a sudden, sad urge to kiss her, an urge with only an incidental connection to romance, but there was too much of Ellanice, and Cornelia still lingered, the flaws being searched for and catalogued, the memories crumbling but not yet gone.

"You know, this is black man's time," she said. "Back in the day this was about the only time he had to rest—the dead of night. The only show he ever got to enjoy with his hands free."

Walter hid his hands. To him, white still lived best in these larval hours of weak moonlight; the white of hoods and of pale, protected skin. He craved a cigarette.

"Papa used to always tell me and Fortune about this magic land up in the mountains. He called it Diddy Wah Diddy." She smiled. "Swore it really existed. Really. Somewhere in the Cumberlands. He didn't mean Sewanee where all the rich white folks are. He said it was up in the coves. A long time ago some people had just all started to live together and marry up and now they hid out there. Up in Diddy Wah Diddy, there's just two kinds of people—men and women. No one cares what color you are." She pulled the shawl up around her shoulders. "I don't know if that sounds good or not."

The faint sound of dogs bawling drifted up to the hill, shocked them out of their thoughts.

"I'm sorry for saying you've never had any bad luck," said Ellanice, already starting to trot back down the hill.

"Well, it's *all* about luck, isn't it?"

ELEVEN

Any more delay would kill him. The two loped down the hill, stopping briefly as Ellanice twisted two green sprigs off a tree. Damp wind cut into their faces, and Walter nearly stumbled more than once. At the bottom, slightly out of breath, Ellanice asked him if he wanted to hide in their home until morning.

"No. I think everyone will be safer if I get back to Mitchell's." The depot had gone black; at least he wouldn't have to bushwhack along the riverbank again. "And you may be right. They may be looking for your Reverend Lewis." Walter didn't mention that they were keeping an eye on Fortune, too. "What about Scipio?"

"What about him?"

"He's not happy about my being here."

Ellanice pulled the shawl back over her head. "Scipio does a little bit of everything and it all adds up to something important for most folks here. He'd like to be the big man in town. Seein' as Mama's for you . . ." A pause. ". . . An' me, he'll leave you be for now. Finding her ring would give her some peace. Here." She handed one of the branches to Walter. "Put this under your pillow. It'll take off the bad luck from looking through the trees."

"Thank you," he said, though he doubted that he'd be sleeping on a pillow tonight.

Ellanice hesitated, looked at the ground, then said, quickly, "Thank *you*." She left before he could say anything more.

It was getting on to ten. Back in New York, he'd be finishing a chapter, stubbing out the final cigarette of the day. Here in Negro Sibley Springs, the shacks were battened down for sleep or hiding, tucked in for the night save for the Quine house and the one lamp burning in its living room. The distractions of Ellanice and the cause were gone, and he was thrown back onto his own survival. They'd accepted him for now, but they couldn't hide him, so where exactly *would* he sleep? Or would he be on the run all night? With the Mitchell House only two blocks away and the depot closed, he had a good shot at getting back to his room undetected. Once there, he could hopefully hide until the morning train. Of course, if Shy Mitchell had turned him in, he'd simply be walking into his own grave. Walter twisted the branch in his fingers. Shy had appeared sincerely repulsed by Dr. Moody, done what any sane man would have done and led Goose out of the room. As queasy as it made him to think, Walter had no one else to trust.

Shrugging into the upturned collar of his coat, eyes under the brim of his hat, he crossed the tracks, then crept along the wall of the building where the platform ended, staying in the shadows as he slid around the corner.

As he passed the west wall of the station, just about to take off for the Mitchells', Walter noticed two dots of light coming up the spa road and getting larger, dancing along like will o' the wisps.

Headlamps.

The faint puttering of a truck reached him from the lights. He didn't have long to decide. Sibley Spring had no street lamps, and the headlamps' beams hadn't yet touched him yet—he was still in the dark. Scuttling to the front of the building and around the corner, he pressed himself face first against the wall so the entire depot stood between him and the truck. As long as they kept their eyes on the road, they'd drive right past him.

No barking dogs. Just the moist sound of tires slopping over the road's thin coating of mud. Walter stared at the bricks in front of his face, frantically hoping that the truck belonged to some farmer heading home. The engine's putter became more muscular as it approached, became closer to the pant of something large being held back, like the panting dogs.

He closed his eyes, pressed his cheek against the brick.

The sound of the engine built. Walter closed his eyes. It was almost at the station. The puttering, the pant, rattled in his head, no longer anything natural, soon so loud that he couldn't imagine it getting any louder and then it crested. He held his breath, waited for it to pass by, waited for it to get softer and softer as it faded away behind him.

But the engine remained where it was.

Walter held the same breath. The light of the car wasn't shining on him; he could tell that. But there was still the moon.

The sound didn't move. He'd have to breathe. His heartbeat thudded in his head.

The gears shifted into park.

Then Nip's voice. "White?"

Could he possibly pretend he wasn't here? Were they wondering if it was him, or whether there was anyone here at all?

"Why-yet." Nip spoke with a playtime tone, a teasing, hide and seek sarcasm that made Walter shiver. "Is that you, White? You takin' a piss over there?" With his head turned away from the truck, he stared off beyond the tracks toward the Negro homes. The laughter of a truckful of men forced the air to trickle out of his nose. A final scream of self-preservation told him he could still run, that he could make the Quines' or hide up in the hills.

Then a gun cocked, a double-barrel shotgun.

Pulling away from the wall, he turned to face a pickup truck splattered with mud up to its windows, vibrating with the engine's labors. The headlamps shone forward, but the moon made a mass of human shapes armed with rifles just visible in the bed. Heavy chains rattled with the whimpering of dogs.

"Well, come on over here, you sumbitch."

It was pointless to resist now, and the faint hope that cooperation might even buy him a few minutes to find an escape convinced him to take a few slow steps forward. Ellanice's branch fell out of his hand.

"Get in the truck," hollered Hillman. Wearing a baseball cap, he sat in the bed as Nip tended to at least five dogs next to a father and son. The boy, thirteen or so, swam under what had been his father's wool-lined cap, bouncing his bottom on his gloveless hands as Pa checked the chambers of his shotgun.

Apparently they didn't want to kill him right there.

The driver, Ludey Fentress, leaned out the window. "Hell, we been out looking for you half the night. Et some dinner, come back out." He shrugged, as if he were awful sorry that it had to happen this way, but his hands were tied. "Nip and Hillman here *insisted* on it."

With his possum nose pink from the cold and especially sharp, Nip pulled back his lips as he spoke, showing his little teeth. "We gonna on a little *cooooon* hunt, Mr. White. Thought you'd like to attend."

Nodding hard in agreement, Hillman said, "I didn't bag nowheres near my limit this year." The men sniggered.

They were a cool bunch. Stupid as mules inside Vine's, but out here, with guns in their hands, they were playing with *him* now.

Pulling him up into the truck, Hillman made space between himself and the boy, who tilted back an empty bottle for its dregs of Chero-Cola. He licked at the opening, sticking his tongue in the tiny hole for every possible drop, making the small, unconscious grunting noises of a feeding animal. The father pulled the bottle out of his hand and flipped it over the side.

"Boys, this is Mr. Walter White," said Hillman with a shocking joy. Before the father-and-son executioners could introduce themselves, Ludey shifted gears with a jolt that threw them all onto each other.

The truck rumbled out of town and northward, along a road to the west of the hill where Quine had been burned. Though the moon had crested and begun to slide away, it still had enough strength to show Walter the young trees, the faint rows where corn and melons would grow in a few months' time. But he'd never seen them. He wouldn't see spring or the Fourth of July or his mother's birthday. He had tickets to see Barrymore next week at the Shubert, but his seat would be empty. All his worst fears of the last few hours were coming true. The spiritual yearned sadly in his head, and he held himself as tightly as he could, wondering how painful it would be, whether he would be tortured first or if they'd just shoot him and leave him for the pigs.

Fool, said that voice, *you didn't have to do this. You asked for it.*

He pictured his mother weeping, his sisters collapsing when they heard the news. His father and brother huddled in the corner, their shoulders shaking. Black crepe on the door of the house. When all that became too much to bear, he rolled through the Lord's Prayer over and over again. A death that accomplishes nothing is just a death. He wouldn't even be a martyr for the cause. Cornelia would go into mourning for a man who no longer loved her.

What the hell had made him think this would all work?

Revealed now as the most cunning of them all, Hillman pinched the elbow of Walter's coat. "That's a mighty fancy outfit you got on. Hope it don't get all tored up." The two other men and the boy laughed, the dogs howled in sympathy. One of them—Walter thought it was Poke but he had no ability to tell the hounds apart—sniffed at his leg, wagged his tail a bit as if expecting a treat. Instead, Walter sneezed, let the song carry him along, and he even swayed a little.

Hillman pointed at the dog nosing at Walter. "Makin' friends with Poke, are ya? Lookee, Nip. Poke lahkes him."

Like Walter, the boy had the sniffles and wiped his nose on the sleeve of his plaid jacket. He had two big gapped front teeth and freckles, a fresh-faced young American about to learn his civic duty. He eagerly shared some inside dirt. "Ludey say his 'ficial name is Nathan Bedford Forrest. Right, Paw?"

Paw had dead eyes and did not share in the festive mood of the others. He just nodded yes; killing niggers was serious business for him. Both father and son wore new boots. Walter marveled at the foolish things he was noticing: people's shoes, their teeth, the bizarre quality of his own lynching. Was it really happening to him? He'd studied ancient Greek and organic chemistry, had descended from kings. Or was this a long, awful dream he would wake from, soaked in sweat, perfectly safe. Unable to remember what came after *That promised land where all is peace,* he returned to the Lord's Prayer. Despite the rope, despite the flames.

Hillman bent over, then slowly straightened up, examining a pin between his thumb and forefinger. "How'd *you* git here?" He extended his arm so his prisoner could see it. "Find a pin, find a friend. That's what they say."

Brown teeth gleamed through Hillman's moustache as he made a gift of the pin to Walter. "Here," he said, and laughed. Walter did not thank him, as his bowels edged close to failure. Traveling at this speed, the truck's open bed became even colder. As they entered a stretch of anonymous forest, banks of scraggly trees on both sides, Poke again snuffled his nose under Walter's hand. Nip gave his own dog a few hollow thumps on the ribs. "I 'spect you gonna git mighty acquainted with all these fellers by the end of the night."

The men laughed once again laughed, and Walter suddenly felt disgusted not with them but with himself. *So what are you gonna do about this, Mr. NAACP? Where's that white man anger you're so scared of?*

They could kill him, but he was the only one who could make himself die less than a man. At least Quine had taken a couple down.

Walter resolved not to die quietly. Staring into the dark of the passing night, he scouted for vulnerabilities. Nip could be tipped over and out of the truck. The boy had a loose grip on his rifle. There was no way to know whether it was loaded, but if worse came to worst, Walter could swing it like a club. And he had the pin in his hand . . .

The other voice now spoke. *You're a gambling man—what are the odds that you kill seven men with a straight pin and then drive this Ford truck north? And then what?* Though the words could have been Scipio's, the voice was his own, and he asked himself whether it really mattered how you died?

Walter hummed the spiritual, squeezed the pin so it pierced his palm.

Hillman cocked his head, trying to place the melody. "What's that song?"

Ludey took a right off the road onto a gravel path. In a small clearing within the forest, he switched off the truck.

TWELVE

The engine whirred down to silence. Ludey growled at them to get out.

The father and son in the back flipped over the side, while Nip helped hand the dogs down to Hillman. Walter cased the forest. Fifty yards away, beyond the first rows of trees, everything sank into black. If he could get into the woods, he'd have a chance. Fifty yards. Half a football field. He kept his movements to a minimum, squeezed the pin harder to keep alert. Ludey stayed in the cab as the other men readied the dogs for whatever was about to be done to him.

Fifty yards. The field at AU didn't have this kind of high, whipping grass, but Walter figured he could make it in eight seconds. Fifty yards and he'd be free. He wound himself into a coil. Sorry to disappoint, thought Walter.

Now!

He sprung over the side and put his face straight into the double barrel of a shotgun held by Hillman.

"Here," said Hillman.

Walter didn't move. The pitcher squinted down toward him, poked the rifle at him again. "Here. Take it."

"Jesus Christ, Hillman! You like to kill that man?" The father

145

sounded frustrated. "I'm atryin' to teach my son 'bout huntin' and you 'bout to blow a man's head off in front of him!"

Hillman ducked his head under the bill of his baseball cap. Two "S"s twined on the front. "Sorry, White." Then he called over to the father—"Sorry, Toomer! Don't ever do that, Curtis! Mind yore daddy!" Hillman put the rifle in Walter's hands and whispered, "Just take it. Damn Toomer shoulda been schoolteacher instead of a carpenter."

Walter took the gun and let the pin fall to the ground, though the new weight in his arms made even less sense to him.

Hillman rearranged his cap. "Whatchu you looking at me *that* way fer? You said you wanted to do some hunting, right? Well, season's almost over and I only got me but 22 coons this year and a dozen possums. Nip took but nine."

Walter grabbed at the side of the truck.

They were taking him hunting.

All at once he was hungry, thirsty, in need of a bathroom and the possessor of a growing erection. Reeling from all that life reentering his body, he hooted up to the stars as the other men had just minutes before.

Ludey slammed the truck door. "What's so goddamn funny? Hillman had me and Nip out looking for you since after supper." He came closer, said hopefully, "Hey, you drunk?"

And! And he had a gun! Hillman pressed some shot into his pockets. "I said it before, I sure hope that nice suit a yourn don't get all tored up in the woods."

Righteous evil presented all its possibilities to Walter, and he considered each in its turn, so many and so wonderful, with less a heavy sense of responsibility than sheer glee. He stuck his cartridges in, snapped the gun shut, all the while telling himself that it was for protection, that he had to do it or they'd start asking questions, but the images skipped about his mind so pleasantly—Ludey on his knees in front of him, begging for his life; Nip crawling on his belly. At Hillman, though, Walter's vengeful fantasy sputtered. Humanity occasionally flickered in Hillman's eyes, expressed a tentative knowledge that the satisfaction of his needs may not have been the sole purpose of the universe.

Nip had traded his uniform for a pair of faded overalls and a red plaid jacket missing three buttons. A torn breast pocket flapped as he moved. It was at least two sizes too small. Walter wondered how Mrs. Nip could let him out of the house like that. "You look pretty excited to get out there."

The resurrected Walter White, Cumberland's representative of the Exelento Medicine Corporation, beamed. "I been looking forward to this for a loooong time."

"I bet you have."

"Nip, my friend, you have no idea."

By now, the dogs were whining and squirming about, knotting themselves up in their chains, so Nip and Hillman set them loose as Ludey did the honors himself with Poke, né Nathan Bedford Forrest. Under the cloud of their cold and eager breathing, they took off in a pack toward the forest wall, Poke in the lead and then two similar white, black and tans, and two gray and black coonhounds behind him, all barking a rather perfunctory bark every few seconds, a warning to any raccoons or possums that the game was on. As they neared the trees, they broke off. Poke dashed straight ahead into the darkness on his own, the black and tans went left and the grays to the right, their barks increasingly muted by the dense bush.

Barking coonhounds sound a lot less terrifying to a man with a gun in his hands. Assuming the game was to rush into the woods, firing at anything that moved or breathed, Walter began to trot after them, glad for a reason to burn off some of the joy that had replaced his recent bowel-loosening fear. He was not just alive, but safe among Quine's murderers, a sick irony that mixed some guilt into Walter's relief.

"Lookee, Curtis! See 'em, boy?" cackled Nip. "He runnin' out there like a-one of the dogs! Ain' that funny?"

Hillman cackled, "Where you goin', White?" with a finger in his mouth as he shoved a fresh plug of tobacco up under the lip. "Ain't you ever been coon hunting before?" He wore the same coveralls and pea coat he'd had on at the store.

Walter stopped. His hunting experience consisted of chucking rocks at sparrows when he was a boy. "No, I haven't. Mostly birds."

"Well, this part's sorter like fishin'," Hillman explained, forgiving Walter's ignorance. "We send them dogs out and when we's ahear 'em barkin' faster and then go into bawlin', then you know you got somethin' on the line, see? Then we go in there with some lamps and find what they's atreed."

Nip took a seat on the running board of the truck and pulled a brown jug out from behind the seat. Hillman, Walter, and the boy Curtis passed. None of them was wearing Dulcet's ring. Not Nip. Not Ludey. It could have already been sold. When, he wondered, would the shooting start? Suddenly Ludey dashed off toward the dogs.

Walter resisted the temptation to put him in his sights. "Well, so where's he going?" he asked Hillman.

The pitcher shot out a tester wad of spit. "Well, you oughta know. *You* gave him that chocolate. He ate it right up. We been stopping the truck all night. I'm surprised we made it here all the way from the station." Though Walter expected the whole group to burst out laughing, they nodded in sympathy. The ebb and flow of a man's intestines were no laughing matter here. "Does its job. You were right about that. Savin' mine till Tuesday."

"Glad to help," said Walter, with a wink. Then he realized that Ludey had just run full out into the woods when this afternoon he supposedly had a fused knee. "What happened to his leg? I thought . . . ?"

The other men ignored the question; Walter could come to his own conclusion—none of them was about to call Ludey Fentress a liar.

Hefting the gun, Walter remembered a rifle being so much heavier. Back then, in his knickers, he hadn't believed that a couple bullets would do anything to stop the crowd from burning down their home, but the truth was that someone shooting from another house had scared the mob away. The gun deserved respect; it *had* done its job. Those raccoons scrambling up tree trunks out there in the forest knew life was not a gentle process. Man was a violent animal, but protecting oneself was not violence. Strictly speaking. Once this little hunting party started up, he could even up the score. An eye for an eye, the Bible said, though he couldn't remember his father ever reading that passage on a Sunday afternoon in the parlor. He was itching to get started on something, anything. "So how long we wait?"

Hillman let a few seconds pass. "Don't know."

Nip patted the empty space on the running board. "Come on up ahere, Curtis. Sit on next to Uncle Nip."

Before the boy could move, Toomer said, "You ain't his uncle." Toomer stared into the trees with an intensity unmatched by any of the other hunters. Even though he was out here in the wild with his gun, his boy and a jug of moonshine, a situation that Walter imagined to be White Man's Paradise, Toomer silently ground at his jaw, tension in his thin lips, tight grip on his gun.

"Don't mean he cain't sit next to me." Nip smiled his feral way. "Come on, boy. I ain't gonna bite cha." Curtis didn't know whether to lift a foot or not. "I like boys." Nip had his shoulders up to his ears, twisting his body, tapping his knees together as he winged. "Pleeeease. Just for a minute."

So that was Nip's deal. Walter had to walk away. He'd once spent three months as a bellhop at the Piedmont Hotel, and more than once he'd escorted slathering white "uncles" with their puzzled "nieces" to their rooms. He'd get a big tip pressed into his palm and take an order for two root beer floats to be sent up in an hour or so. Sometimes they'd have "nephews." That was white Christian morality: murderers and perverts. Walter squeezed at the trigger just a little, just to know what it would feel like.

"Come on now, Roy," said Nip. "Daddy's cold."

Before Curtis could move either way, Ludey returned, hitching up his pants. At the sight of him, Nip sat up straight and glared into the night, as if he'd never said a word to Curtis. "So Toomer . . . ," said Ludey in a mischievous tone. "Why'd you wait so long to get Curtis out here ahuntin'?" He'd weep when he saw the gun in his face, thought Walter. Probably piss himself.

Toomer's jacket had worn through at his hip, at other places a loose meeting of thread held the denim together. It draped off him as if it couldn't support its own weight any longer; Toomer had probably carried a few pounds more when it was new. Shifting on his feet, he just barely unclenched his jaw. "Some boys just don't take to guns, that's all."

Nip nodded. "Nothin' like takin' a boy out inta the woods the first time."

Toomer showed no sign of hearing Nip. "We's arunnin' low. Coon or two would stretch us a week. Curtis gotta learn."

Curtis finally moved, but to his father's side, not Nip's. Toomer put a hand on the boy's shoulder as Walter's father always did to him and the two suddenly looked desperate, not blood-thirsty. Walter's mood lost some of its bouyancy. The others took steps away from Toomer and Curtis, acted as though they were straining to hear the dogs, but their quick and complete isolation of the father and son made poverty seem like a highly infectious disease.

"Gotta take care of yourn. Gotta *deserve* a son," said Nip.

Ludey brightened as if a squirrel had hopped into one of his traps. "Well, that's some kinda thing for you to say."

Hillman stepped in front of Nip, protecting him. "Aw hell, Lude, you don't gotta bring that . . ."

Folding his arm over his chest in a manner that Walter found girlish, Nip ignored the wince Ludey's comment caused and took his pain out instead on Toomer. "So if you so poor, why'd you buy the fancy shoes?"

Toomer hissed, "'Cause we didn't *have* none. Everybody bought the rest!"

Nip grunted, then leaned on the wheel guard, his vision wandering far from all of this as he rested his chin on his arms.

Hillman steered Walter away from town business. "So, you get a chance to see the spa today?"

"No, I didn't. I'm meaning to tomorrow."

"Yeah, you should. See that Vale of Confederate Dead, too. That's a moving sight."

"Oh yeah?" Walter sneezed.

"Bless you. 'Course, my granddaddy was in Turney's First Tennessee?"

"You don't say."

Ludey swigged Nip's shine, wiped his lip. "Oh hell, *everybody's* granddaddy was in Turney's First Tennessee. Don't pay him no mind, White. Company C. Mountain Boys." Other people's stories didn't interest him, but as he replaced the stopper in the jug, he let an earnestness enter his voice that made him sound almost like a normal adult, unconcerned for once that every word he spoke somehow asserted his primacy. "See, that colonnade there got the names of all the fallen from Sibley Springs 'scribed on it. Did you know Franklin County left the Union before the whole rest of the state?"

"I did not, but it sure makes sense now that I've seen the place."

"Oh sure." Ludey affected a smug, teacherly posture, hands in pockets, rocking on his heels. "General Forrest operated in these parts."

"Curtis mentioned about Poke."

"Me and Billy Stoker used to steal nails and wood when they was building the Vale. Shit, they didn't know *what* they was doing. We built another one, a good one, in the woods, and we'd drink our shine out there, you know? Got tore down by some mountain boys 'cause they caught us with some a their girls." He shifted gears at the flare from one of Nip's matches. "My mama once watered Forrest's horse. That's a true story. Gave her his sword." Hillman bit a fingernail, steeled himself for what appeared to be a familiar tale to the Ludey Fentress Gang. As Ludey spun his mother's chance encounter with the rebel guerrilla into the fulcrum of the War, the men, slightly forlorn, grinned and nodded for the thousandth time at this tale of dubious truth and meager interest. Where was the violent bacchanal Walter expected, the visit to the belly of the beast? Ludey blabbed on, invited him to see the Fentress Excalibur hanging over his fireplace.

Warming himself with the image of Fentress gripping prison bars, Walter politely declined, but he remained curious. "Billy Stoker still live around here?"

Ludey dragged a toe around in the mud. "Naw, he joined the navy when he turn eighteen. Never heard from him then. Probably got hisself shot."

He went silent at that; sad, despite the drop of venom he put in the saying, and everyone else stayed that way too, mourning the fact that Ludey's pleasant memories were a good twenty years old, and he was lucky to have those. A night breeze shook the empty treetops. Walter yawned. Apparently there wouldn't be any scheming and plotting tonight, either; no review of the grand plan that kept Sibley Springs under their thumbs.

The Big Man took a swig off the jug. "Say," he leered over at Walter, suddenly cheerful again. "You have a look at that Louisa Warren over at Mitchell's?" His thick tongue popped out of his mouth like an eel from it cave, slobbered around his lips as Ludey's eyes rolled in feigned ecstasy above. "I'd lahke to have me a piece a that . . ."

Such a vast, white mountain of demands, thought Walter. Surely the constant threat that he would attack made Ludey the Big Man, but he figured the ability to feel nothing, no pain, no sympathy or empathy or respect, helped Ludey, too. He imagined Ludey Fentress backing that girl into a corner, his fat lips going slack as he leaned into her face. "Aw, leave off her," he warned, a gentlemanly sentiment no self-respecting salesman would utter. Walter immediately asked himself where exactly that had come from.

Back from his daydreams, Nip snickered. "Look like Froggy here already been acourtin'."

Ludey didn't take kindly to opposition; he squinted at Walter as if he were trying to see more there.

"He's right, Lude," said Hillman. "She not that kind a girl. Them Warrens is properlike."

Thank God for Hillman, thought Walter. Whatever misplaced sense of gallantry had made him defend her, Walter dismissed Miss Warren with a wave of his hand. "She's a snack for you. You growing corn this spring, or cotton?"

Luckily Ludey cared more about his back pocket than the front of his pants. Without another word about Miss Warren he launched into a short discourse on the sorry economics of cotton growing and how a man could go bust before he even knew that somebody had left the gate open. Walter understood only enough to nod empathetically. Hillman claimed his Uncle Dick had invited him to move to Gassaway where they just had a fine year of corn, and Nip spoke up for the value of Duroc hogs.

The group sank back into silence, another enervating stretch that lasted even longer than the ones at Vine's. They'd lost any suspicions about him, were maybe even bored with him already, and Walter had to remind himself that these men had indeed killed Cleon Quine.

The sheer dullness of this outing had Walter thinking about bed again, and he was suddenly loath to puncture the relative calm of this gathering with more questions. It had been a long day, but it would end with him in charge of the situation, white and black. Now he needed sleep to think straight. He'd gotten a reprieve.

Toomer whispered to Curtis, "Well, go on and ask him."

Ducking his head back and forth, the boy never actually looked at Walter as he addressed him. "Hillman says you're some kinda important businessman and you's Walter Johnson's best friend an' you got a separable fastener an' all . . ."

"Well, I don't know about . . ."

"You ever been to a *moving* picture?" Curtis had a hopeful look, and the other men watched over the boy's shoulder.

"Sure. All the time."

Curtis lit up, melting Walter just a bit. "All the time? Really?" He checked back with Toomer, who had the distant, satisfied expression of a father experiencing a pleasure through his son. "What's it like?"

When did you last eat? thought Walter. It dawned on him that he'd personally never missed a meal in his life, had never gone hungry longer than it took to stroll into the kitchen. For a strangely guilty moment Walter wished that he hadn't given away all the Cracker Jack.

"OK. Well, . . ." Each man inched up closer with a subtle shift of position or an inexplicable need to look inside the cab window until they had arrayed themselves in a semicircle around Walter, his back to the truck. "First, you sit in a nice soft chair in this big room, with a whole crowd of other people."

Nip looked suspicious. "Any niggers?"

"No niggers," Walter reassured him, amazed by such relentless bile, by the smeared and shattered lens through which Nip saw the world. "Maybe some upstairs, way up where they can barely see a thing and there's just benches or crates to sit on, but, no sir. No niggers downstairs."

Satisfied, Nip stuffed his matchbox into a pocket and nodded for him to continue. "Little Roy'd love this."

"I bet he would. You can buy some kind of candy to eat if you want, too, then the lights go real low and the whole room is dark and someone starts playing the organ." Curtis knit his brow. "It's like a piano. Kind of. Anyway, everybody's facing what they call a screen." He turned now toward the truck, as if they were all staring at a huge, two-story movie screen. "It's a big white wall, least two stories, about the size of . . ." Walter tried to think of a comparison they could understand. ". . . About the size of Mitchell's."

Ludey spat. He wasn't buying, but this was so out of his ken that he couldn't conjure up a lie to top it. "Like Hell."

"Would I lie to you boys?" Reluctantly, he looked away from the screen. "Hillman, would I lie?"

"I don't think he would, Ludey. He *been* to places."

"So up on this screen all of a sudden there comes on these pictures. They're black and white." He squinted as he thought about this, trying to be more precise, explaining flowers to a blind child. "I mean there's no color. Does that make sense? There's all kinds of gray and white and black, but no red or blue, so if like if there was a movie of Sibley Springs . . ." It's all black and white already, he thought. ". . . Or, say, the forest in the summertime . . ."

Nip broke in. "We seen foe-toe-graphs before, Walter. We ain't *stupid.*"

"All right, so you get the idea. Except they're moving. The actors and actresses wear costumes and do the parts, and you sit and watch. Like a play."

This comparison brought blank stares, and it dawned on Walter that none of these men had ever seen a play, had probably never read a book; in fact, earlier in the day Nip had all but boasted of it. Ludey plucked a piece of tobacco off his tongue. "So you just sit the whole time?"

"Well yeah, everything's going on up on the screen."

"I don't like that. I like to do something when I spectate." The others shrugged, more amenable to the concept.

Curtis scratched at a sizable patch of discolored skin on his cheek. Even if that roundworm ever cleared up, no one would ever insure the Toomers. "What's the best movie you ever seen, Mr. White?"

"I like Chaplin and Barrymore." No smiles or nods— the names meant nothing to them. "I guess I'd say *Narrow Trail* starring William S. Hart."

The audience stared at him, at the imaginary screen behind him, then back to Walter. None of them had the courage to ask until Curtis scratched some more at his cheek and said, "So what *happens?*"

Where the hell did those dogs go, wondered Walter, increasingly uncomfortable. If these ignoble savages couldn't form the thought that they were barely humans or admit it to themselves, they could sense it, sense that they were only a notch above scavengers, at best scratching a living off the surface of the earth, their brains as fallow as their farms. Without coloreds to sit on, this lot would be racing to stay ahead of the chimpanzees. Veering closer to pity than he felt comfortable with, Walter stepped back into the center of the group. "All right, well there's this cowboy named Ice Harding. He's a real outlaw type . . ."

And so the curtains parted and the movie began. Rapt, the five stood and spat and watched Walter act out the story of the doleful William S. Hart's failed attempt to straighten his evil ways with the love of a good woman. At first Nip appeared confused, squinting at Walter and then back at the others as if he trying to see what they were seeing until he finally settled on hovering close to Curtis, once even dreamily leaning in toward the boy's dirty hair. Just as Ice Harding was riding Fritz the Horse across a ravine on a fallen tree a hundred feet long, the distant barking of actual, live dogs shattered the drama.

Hillman gave Nip a sour look. "Damn it! This is the best part!"

"Ain't *my* fault, Hillman. You the one wanted to go huntin' with White."

The pitcher gave him a wink and a spit, said, "Well, yeah." Walter took his shotgun, looked back over the truck at the hill in the distance, not towering over the clearing but gently pushing over the crest of the trees around them. He couldn't look Hillman in the eye, didn't know how to handle the kind intentions of a killer.

Hillman lit a kerosene lamp. "That's where they lynched Cleon." An odd word stuck out there. "Oh really?" *They?*

Nip lit a lamp on the other side, waited for the match to burn out on the pads of his fingers. "Yeah, that's where *we* done it." He gave Hillman a reproachful look, snuffed the thought Walter had started to have, an oddly hopeful one that he couldn't bring himself to put into words. "Had to be done, see?" Crouching with the lamp held out forward, the small man looked like Jocko the lawn jockey poking at Hillman with his free hand. "Man got out of his wagon, started saying things at Trick and J. C. no nigger ever said to a white man and then he shoots 'em in cold blood. What the hell else you gonna do?"

Ludey already way up ahead, Hillman, Walter, and Nip started walking quickly toward the trees. The light of the lamp created shadows in the wrinkles of Hillman's face. He looked old now. "Well, Nip, they threw the rocks at him. Called his daughter some pretty foul things."

The other men had waited for them at the edge of the forest. Nip showed his best possum face, straightened up as best he could through a wince that manifested a profound wave of pain. "Nigger don't speak to a white man that way in Sibley Springs." Then the edge dropped off his voice like icicles falling during a thaw. "They was *always* doing that. Everybody knowed that. Cleon shoulda kept his head. Them boys was dirt. Little Roy kept 'way from 'em. Me an'

Cloda never had to say a word. Little Roy always a good boy . . ." Shaking his head, Nip spat hard and stomped off, mumbling curses to the trees.

Toomer nodded. "They was bad fish." He wagged a finger at Curtis. "You ever act up like those boys, I'll whip your ass but good. Hear?"

"Fact is," said Hillman, "everybody hated all *three* of them dead men." Ludey had stopped at the treeline, already sweating from the trot after the dogs. "Ain't that right, Ludey? Everybody was glad to be shed of Trick and J. C. as much as Quine. You hear all that singin' an' shoutin' from the funeral?"

The pace of the dogs picked up, each barked sharply twice a second or so.

Walter gripped the stock of the gun, put his finger in the trigger. Tired or not, there'd never be a better time. "So what the hell exactly happened there?"

Hillman looked at Ludey. "He was on his way to Palgrave's, wasn't he? Buyin' some more land."

Ludey glared as he walked past. "I'm gonna get me a *cooooon.*" Then, his injury regained, he limped off behind the light of his oil lamp.

THIRTEEN

Hillman shook his head as he walked. "Nip ain't the same since the fire at Timmons. Bank job his first reg'lar since."

"Where's Little Roy?"

"He dead." Hillman waved his lamp in front of his face. "Cloda, that was his wife, and Little Roy his son and Nip, they all was working at Timmons and them two died? He got burned up pretty bad, too. Doc Moody say he'll be in pain rest a his natural life. That's true." He shrugged his shoulders, scowled at either fate or this new, damaged Nip, Walter couldn't tell which. "That's his jacket Nip wearin'. Fact is, he don't say much that's good anymore. Half crazy from missin' em, I think. Only people he half nice to is boys."

Hillman may well have said that Nip was a woman, so hard was it for Walter to move the little rat of a man in his mind from killer to victim of any sort. He tried to imagine the newly wed Nip skipping through the pansies with his wife, working a sugar tit into a baby's mouth, and while the pictures were all imaginary, Walter knew they were more real now than any vengeful fantasies he'd had of killing the lonely, rumpled, hateful Nip, desperate for a boy to pretend he was his son.

"Where your people from?" asked Hillman.

Walter stayed close. He hadn't taken a lamp and so was bound to

159

the three who had, nor was he about to leave Hillman's side until he had the whole story of Cleon's death and a confession. Getting on the morning train was still the goal. "Atlanta," he said. "Going back, my grandmother lived on the Harrison territory back up in Indiana, but mostly Georgia."

"I'll be damned. Indiana, huh?" Hillman turned to him as they parted around a tree. "Bread and butter," he said out loud. "My uncle Dick says Gassaway's a damn sight better than Sibley Springs. You ever been there?"

"Nope."

"Got a baseball team, too. You ever play any baseball?"

"Centerfield in college. Football's more my game, though. Quarterback."

Hillman frowned and nodded. "Yeah? Well, we's more for baseball 'round here. Some folks follow that Sewanee team, but not so much down the mountain." He sniffed at the air, searching for a whiff of spring, a taste of leather and dirt. "Good nines in Cowan. Monteagle. Soon's all this mud dries up, we start throwin'. Dick say they need a new pitcher up in Gassaway. Say, you married?"

"Naw. Too much traveling. Hard to stay tied down."

Hillman spat off to the left. "Well, don't you go hurryin'. Yeah, and don't have no kids while yore at it. I got me four, and hell if I know what to do with 'em." After a few more steps he said, "Shee-yit," shaking his head. "Naw, they's good kids. Harry and Peter went damn crazy when they heard about you and the Big Train. Johnnie didn't say nuthin. He's none too smart." Hillman sniffed, then said, "But you gotta love whatever God gives you, right?" He was sorry he'd gone there. "So what's Johnson's motion like? I seen a picture oncet, but . . ."

Walter cut him off and wrenched the topic back to the reason he was there. "Tell me about the lynching."

Hillman's face fell. He'd heard what Walter asked, but he ignored it. Instead, rotating his arms for a few seconds as if loosening it up, he finally said, "Hey, you heard of this colored pitcher Joe Williams?"

We define ourselves by our affections, twine our favorite books or foods or people into our identities so much so that when someone else shows an interest in that topic the wall is breached, a link created that exists despite every other difference. A shared passion is the simplest way into another person's heart, no matter how dark that other heart may be, and now, hearing Williams's name, Walter's eyes opened wide and he forgot everything but the smooth wind up and snap release of his favorite Negro League pitcher. "Hell yes! In Birmingham! You can talk about Johnson all you want, but Williams? That man can *throw*! I saw him once against . . ."

"You seen him?"

Hillman seemed more confused than suspicious as to why Walter would attend a Negro League game, and Walter quickly regrouped. "Well, he was coming through town and I'd heard about him."

The other man shrugged; he just wanted to know more about Joe Williams. "What kind a motion he got?"

"Sidearm, mostly. And he has a killer drop ball. You gotta understand—he's big. Six five or so."

Hillman whistled. "Damn!"

For a couple minutes, they shot the breeze like two men in the stands of Griffith Stadium eating peanuts on a sunny afternoon, finding general agreement on the merits of Tris Speaker and Heinie Groh, grinning at their mutual distaste for the duplicitous Hal Chase; Walter was even able to wheedle out of Hillman the fact that he despised Ty Cobb and his snarling, spikes-up style of play, a small, but telling detail in Walter's book.

"I'd love to see a big league game," said Hillman in the wistful way one might say they wanted to fly to the moon.

"You know, Walter Johnson really isn't my friend."

The pitcher shrugged into a shoulder like a boy caught out. "Close enough fer me."

Walter looked at Hillman, whose eyes searched ahead as they had before in the store. As remarkable as it was, he had ideas and tastes in common with this man, and after this first uncomplicated, unfraught conversation in Sibley Springs, he had the urge to talk more, to test the ice with more opinions, describe things he had a feeling Hillman would appreciate, like John Henry Lloyd's reflexes at short, the way Bruce Petway threw runners out without even getting up from his crouch, though that would take them over more than one border, into places Walter couldn't go. He knew he couldn't do it, but still, he sensed some kind of value in this Hillman. How, Walter wondered, could he have lynched Cleon Quine? Hillman may have been simply staring into the trees for a raccoon, but what Walter saw now was the man next to him trying to find a way out of Sibley Springs. "Anything's possible, Hillman. You think you gonna move up with your uncle?"

"I don't know." The pitcher sniffed. "Town ain't like when I came up. And that Birdie Frennet's 'bout seventeen years old. Got a helluva a fastball, but see, his motion's too wide." Hillman stopped to imitate Frennet's enormous leg kick. "See? He does that? Takes away from his . . ."

Walter broke in. "Yeah, that'll throw you off." He sensed something out in the dark behind Hillman, and there was Simso Clark, cracking a peanut and smiling an innocent smile. Don't be a sucker, said Simso. "Listen, tell me about this lynching now."

Again ignoring his companion, Hillman held up his hand for Walter to stop. He pointed up. "Look at that moon! God*damn*! I used to come out here by myself? Maybe bring Harry, but then Ludey got the truck . . ."

"Hillman."

Sincerely puzzled, Hillman asked, "You *really* want to hear about it?"

Walter felt pained to press, but yet he had to, wanted to. "Well, hell, sure I do. That's big news, that is. Drummer like me likes to get the story."

"All right." Hillman spat and started to walk again. "Well, you heard about the boys throwing rocks at Cleon and Neecie? Some folks was saying that Cleon liked to throw the bones himself and them boys and him had some business to settle and that's what it was all about, but I don't believe 'em. Cleon done worked too much to ever gamble, if'n you ask me." Ahead of them, three lamps bobbed and swayed, sometimes racing ahead and then coming closer as they walked. Two would cross, as if trading paths, or meet up for a few seconds, and Walter could hear Toomer having a quick chat with Ludey, or Nip and Ludey grunt at each other. Past ten feet, the lamplight watered into gray and there were so many trees that the walk was a constant maze. The two picked their ways through, sometimes together, other times separating around tree trunks, an event Hillman tried to avoid at all costs.

"Me and Ludey and Nip was in Vine's when we heard the shots? We pulled Trick onto the porch. He died right there. Then we got Dickie. Quine just run off in the wagon then, and everybody was ascreaming bloody murder. Bread and butter. County sheriff up in McMinnville? He wouldn't send nobody down."

To this point, Hillman had sounded like his usual slightly slow and querulous self, but looking at Walter, who was offering his full attentions—the full attentions of a man who'd been to a moving picture, a man who'd seen the Big Train pitch—he swelled up his voice as if he were puffing out his chest and his tone hardened. "Like Ludey told you, we got involved. Oh yeah, we got involved. Word got out 'round these parts, see? Ole Lude got up a posse and we all went off ahuntin' Quine. Finally holed him up in a barn outside McMinnville. Had a gunfight? Shot him in the leg. Yup, Nip done that. Nip a great shot. Bread and butter. County sheriff don't wanna do a thing, so's me and Ludey and Nip put him on a train back here? Bread and butter. Town was full already when we got there. We pull Quine off the train, and we was figurrin' to do the job in front of Vine's. Ludey got the chain in his hand an' all but there's some people, like the Timmons widow? She says get this show out of town."

Walter couldn't tell which lamp belonged to whom. The rhythm of the dogs picked up now, and so did the pace of Walter's heart. Trotting through the black forest, the hunt on, the lynching, his own memories; he was breathing heavily again, coughing, squeezing the shotgun, his weakening bravado wondering who he'd kill if he aimed at the lamp bobbing up ahead to the right, but who he really felt like was that boy again, thirteen years old. He wouldn't be using the gun tonight, either. "Then what?"

"Well, we said, OK, let's take him up on the hill so we made him walk it? Mostly he got dragged 'cause he wasn't walking much by then."

The dogs added a new sound to the barking, a bawling relation to the howl of a wolf that expressed great longing of a particularly vicious sort. The problem was that all the dogs were doing it, and in three different directions. Walter heard Ludey's voice claim that Poke was up ahead, but Nip's voice said no, that was Andy and Lickbone; Poke was to the right. Through the cursing, and the rising sense that all was becoming very confused, Walter prodded Hillman to continue, trying to commit to memory all that he admitted, wanting to believe the story even as he hoped it wasn't true, hoped he hadn't once again made the mistake of letting in a dirty white heart.

"Yeah, well, once we got him up the hill, some boys chained him up to a pole some folks run up and set up there." That was the mound of dirt. Hillman shook his head in wonder now, but with no joy. "I never seen so many people in one place in my whole life. I'm used to pitching games in front of a crowd, maybe couple hunnert people? But there was thousands of people going up that hill and they was crazy.

Bread and butter. Well, once he was chained up, everybody piled up wood and branches and soaked it up with kerosene and was like to do it right off, but then somebody said, and I remember his 'xact words, he said, 'Let's have some fun with the nigger.' So we started another fire next to him? Heated up some long bars of pig iron. Bread and butter. Goddamn, where is Nip? You see him?"

Walter had stopped breathing. The white faces come closer and closer until the torches shine down on them, and he recognizes one. Lower to the ground than all the rest, eyes flooded with a wild joy, his pal Simso Clark points at their house and screams, "Let's get the niggers!" Father hands him a gun and says with no fear or anger, just stating a fact, "Son, don't shoot until the first man puts his foot on the lawn and then—don't you miss!" He is thirteen years old, aiming a gun at his best friend, trying to be a man, trying not to shit his pants, sick to his stomach, too stunned at seeing his world tipped over to be angry just yet. Stunned, and not at all convinced that he'll be able to do what his father has told him to do, wishing he was upstairs with his mother and embarrassed by the fact. Only thirteen years old.

"Well, once the bars was glowing, one fella picks up a bar and makes a feint at Cleon and that sumbitch, I gotta hand it to him, he grabbed the damn thing. Burnt the palm of his hand right off. People just dived in after that. Poked him in the stomach, on the neck and the legs, just shoving these hot iron bars into him. Took about half an hour. Last one they did was this big one and some boys just rammed that right into his, well, you know, his gentiles? Cleon just kept aswearing at everybody and agroanin'. He asked to be shot, but nobody did it. Bread and butter. Finally I threw some more coal oil on him and his pants and shoes and he just went up."

The dogs were now barking three or four times a second, in three different directions. Hillman yelped, "Hot damn!" and forgetting his charge, dashed off toward the sound, leaving Walter to vomit out of sight.

Killing his family would have been a natural thing to those people, to Simso, a thing as natural as hunting coons. Niggers were prey animals. You could like a fox or raccoon, think they were a smart, handsome animal with admirable, interesting qualities. You could even have one as a pet and develop a perfectly understandable affection for it. But its real job was to be hunted. To hunt a nigger was not a betrayal, it was the natural order. Like the hours when he believed the dogs were tracking him, he'd felt most black when he was prey, most pressed into that part of himself, as if he had a separate compartment in his mind and body reserved For Colored Only. On that night, he'd been told that his luck was to be prey, and the world was vaguely sorry about that. It was nothing personal. It was just the way the world worked. Would Hillman shoot him if he found out who he really was? Of course. Probably. A bitter memory of Ellanice on the hill kept him from getting down to "Maybe not." She was right: Nothing had changed in the world since 1906.

When Walter lifted his head, he could still see the lamps ahead, though he had to move slowly around the trees that now loomed up only a few seconds before he'd walk into them. He could do it. He was a man. He was in a position to fight back now. If any of them were shot here, it would just go down as a terrible hunting accident, no need for an article in *The Crisis,* for a trial, and yet even as he had that thought he imagined telling his parents that he'd killed a man. Walter stumbled ahead, realized he had to pick a light to follow if he planned on getting out of this forest tonight. Ahead, a chaos of barking and shouting and chains rattling, even some laughter; for all he knew, this was what a lynching sounded like. The night in Atlanta had had the same kind of build.

Two lamps split left, but one went right, and Walter chose that one to follow. It was slower, and soon he could tell that it had stopped, and only one voice and one dog bawled and talked to their prey. In a few more steps, he saw Ludey preoccupied with Poke, paws on the trunk, howling up at two yellow, irridescent eyes gleaming down from above. With his clubbed fingers, he was having trouble managing the lamp and getting his fingers on the trigger. Ludey looked around for help and just as he was about to call over to Walter the yellow eyes in the tree zipped through the branches onto another tree and with a great flurry of movement, both raccoon and dog shot away again, pulling Ludey with them in chase.

Walter trotted behind and in just a second or two, Poke's bawling turned into a kind of squeal, a sound of complete, terror-stricken surprise, and then a great splash. Up ahead Ludey cried, "Oh my . . .!" which turned into a cry of shock, and Walter heard the man's large body clearly falling down some height, rolling down a hill, and the lamp went out.

Taking careful steps to avoid his own fall, Walter edged ahead through the thinning trees toward the sound of Ludey's cries, the weird, fierce shrieks of two animals tearing at each other in the water, until the trees opened up and under what light remained from the moon, he saw Ludey flailing in the water of a small but evidently very deep pond at the bottom of a steep, ten-foot slope. A couple of strokes away, the raccoon had taken the upper hand in his battle with Poke and was now on top of the dog, who was trying desperately to hold his head about the water, the blubbering yowls increasingly muffled by Ludey's own shouts.

"Help me! Jesus! Help me!"

Walter lifted his shotgun so that Ludey's head was within the cup of its sight. Kill him, he thought. The raccoon hopped off the dog's back and swam away as Ludey glubbed and splashed his way to the floating body of his dead pet.

Hidden behind the trunk of a tree, Walter saw terror in Ludey's eyes.

Save him, thought Walter.

But would Ludey become a better man if saved? Or would he

only become worse? Was Hillman lying? Instead of a fat, aging man thrashing away, Walter saw in an instant the young Ludey with the same look of terror on his face as his Daddy came closer with the whip, felt the suffocating panic of an empty future farming dead, dry land, watched Billy Stoker leave town. For the first time, Walter wondered what it was like to *be* Ludey Fentress. He wondered not so he could write an insurance policy on him or take him at poker or marvel at his godforsaken whiteness. A piercing understanding of the fear and boredom, the loneliness and the need to stand on top of something, anything, had leapt onto Walter the way the raccoon had pounced on Poke, pushed him off his own easy hatred, and now Walter was drowning too.

That could be the face of Christ.

Or it could be the face of the devil. *Does the devil ever wear the face of Christ?* screamed Walter's mind as Ludey yelped incoherently now, too frightened to cry or make a word. Does Jesus lynch? How can man be just with God? How do we *know*?

Ludey's head ducked down under the roiled water, and then popped back up, cried what sounded like, *Mama!*

What are you going to do, he asked himself? Drowning in the depths of his own heart, grabbing for purchase in the murkiest of waters, he asked himself if he was justice, or vengeance. Though I give my body to be burned, and have not charity. *What are you going to do?*

Ludey's howls weakened, his arms no longer thrashing as much as reaching up now, toward the light of the waning moon.

You will be as evil as them. Walter slowly, very slowly, opened up his coat, let it slip off his shoulders. He is drowning. You are letting him drown.

Two men crashed through the forest with their lamps from the left, and Walter shouted out, "It's Ludey! We have to save him!"

He pulled off his jacket, slid down the side of the short cliff and splashed into the water with Toomer and Hillman. The three all grabbed ahold of Ludey and tugged him to shore, Poke's body floating behind them in the wake.

Fourteen

The dog's head bounced up and down on Walter's shaking thigh as Nip floored the truck toward the Mitchell House and Dr. Moody. A few hours ago, the idea of a wet dog carcass lying on his pants leg would have sent him vomiting out the window, but right now he was as wet and cold as Poke's body, his suit saturated with pond water. Ludey lolled his head onto Walter's shoulder and it just didn't seem to matter anymore.

Nip reached across, grabbed the placket of Ludey's shirt and shook him awake. "We're gonna get you to the doctor, Ludey. You're gonna be fine."

Roused, Ludey's eyes opened wide, and he thrust his head forward, searching for something ahead in the light, something beyond the dead dog he cradled in his arms. The motion made him lose a chin. For a moment Walter saw that pitiable boy's face on him again, querulous, wondering from which direction the next dreadful event would be arriving. He smelled of shit.

"You're a damn hero. You don't find him, Ludey's as dead as Poke there. The big man can't swim a lick."

Too exhausted from dragging Ludey through the woods, shivering toward what felt like pneumonia, Walter didn't answer. He closed his eyes and half-pretended he was asleep, wondered if anyone had seen him watching Ludey drown. Had Ludey himself noticed the man standing among the trees, holding his gun, smiling a tight, satisfied smile as he thrashed for his life? The thought kept Walter from nodding off. The fatal swim had left the dog's fur smooth. Walter distracted himself by following its tides and sworls around the chops and ears, all the different colored hairs dead in unison. In the end, he'd had no difference with Poke, just a hungry old coonhound that had probably slept through the lynching of Cleon Quine. The hairs around his muzzle and eyes were graying; he'd been around a long time.

They hadn't been able to pry Poke out of Ludey's arms, a refusal that had delayed the evacuation. After spurting out some water, Ludey had come back to, but his breakdown over Poke had put him back on his knees. Only after promising that Nip would walk in front of Ludey, holding Poke's body in view of him at all times, would he allow himself to be hauled back to his feet and assisted staggering through the woods. And Ludey's continued inability to control his bowels also complicated matters. Right at the base of the dog's ear, the hair broke in four directions, like currents in the ocean or wind-blown grass.

The dog's head rose up off Walter's leg and Ludey's face came down to meet the body halfway. Hardly threatening now, the Big Man pushed into Poke's ribs. The carcass took his tears. Walter pictured Billy-less Ludey alone with his crone of a mother and crone-to-be wife, the father rocking on the porch, too old to administer the lash. Though Ludey'd had to choose between being a mule or a mule driver, there'd always been Poke, his unquestioning partner.

Walter shook some sense back into his head as the grown man wept over a dead dog. He hadn't cried this way for Quine, that much was certain. He hadn't been laid too low by *that* tragedy. Walter sternly told himself that only the true mourners deserved his sympathy. In fact, for the most part he regretted that Ludey *had* survived;

there'd been just enough of something his father would call "Christian" in his bones that had moved him at all, and was that done largely to cover up why he was standing there doing nothing? He tried to understand how he could be disappointed and relieved at the same time. Seeing the why of people didn't mean that they shouldn't be punished or held accountable or absolved. And he decided that held for Hillman, too. It was done—Hillman had given him the story, all wrapped up like he'd told it a thousand times. Walter would be on that morning train with enough information to get the investigation going, for a grand jury to subpoena: Nip August, Ludey Fentress, Hillman Chew, Baxter Vine. They'd all been there, done something, played some role.

And in the gray of pondering what exactly that something had been, Walter slipped off, woken a few minutes later by the truck coming to an abrupt stop in front of the Mitchell House. Hillman and the others piled out, speaking loudly enough that a light on the lower floor went on without Hillman ever reaching the other door on the porch to ring Dr. Moody's bell. From the truck, Walter could see the tall, slightly bent figure of Moody waving them in, a blanket wrapped like a shawl over his shoulders. After Hillman wrested away Poke's body, Walter and Nip got under Ludey's shoulders and helped him down the path and up the steps into Dr. Moody's office.

In his bathrobe, lit by the light of the oil lamp, Moody had a yellow cast, his eyes sunk deep into his skull. He pointed over Ludey's shoulder and snapped, "Get that goddamned dog out of here! And shut the door!"

A puddle formed beneath them on Dr. Moody's floor as Nip explained the circumstances of their visit, Ludey's near-drowning and Walter's discovery and rescue.

Walter wanted to say that Hillman and Toomer had jumped into the water first, that they'd swum to Ludey and pulled him in and he'd maybe floated a leg, shoved the mass in the general direction of shore

173

but even if he'd wanted to come clean, he was too tired. All he could manage was a chesty cough.

Dr. Moody gave him a cross look. "Christ almighty, you're about to catch pneumonia! Get out of those clothes!" He handed him a blanket. "You can fetch your things in the morning. Just get upstairs to bed! We'll handle Fentress." The doctor sniffed at Ludey. "Jesus, Ludey, you take more laxative? I've told you you must educate your *own* bowels!"

As Walter stripped down, Nip appeared to want to say something to him. He winced as he often did, rubbed his chest, searching for something in his brain, and in the end settling for a nod in Walter's direction. Stumbling out the door of Dr. Moody's office, naked under his blanket, Walter walked into a knot made of Hillman, the Toomers, and Shy Mitchell, wearing a set of red longjohns and unlaced boots. Without a word, Walter continued through them toward the stairs and the bed in his barren little room that seemed so wonderful right now. Hillman stopped him with a surprisingly heavy arm around his shoulder. "Glad you pulled into Sibley Springs, White. Real glad." The others all nodded their heads, welcoming him into the life of the town.

Toomer said, "That's right."

Had they all been at the lynching, too, pulling or pushing or poking with hot irons? Stacking wood. Lighting the fire. Had any of them just watched, like he just had, with their own tight, satisfied smiles, wondering whether they were murderers, too? Or whether they were just doing the bidding of divine justice?

Curtis stared at him in awe. They liked him. They thought he was a fine fellow, which made him feel guilty, sullied him, and yet at the same time their warmth made them seem if not acceptable, then at least explicable. Maybe even salvageable.

The boy asked, "If I come by tomorrow, will you finish *Narrow Trail?*" Even now, roundworm was surely eating away at his guts, thought Walter as he walked past him. Hillman, the man who claimed to have thrown the oil on the fire, a man he actually found it hard to hate, tipped his cap goodnight. Was evil curable in someone like him or always cause for execution? He reminded himself that Hillman liked the hair-straightener salesman he was playing, not him.

Shy handed him another quilt and a nightdress. "Goose was asking after you." He stayed at his side as Walter slowly took the steps. The nightdress was warm, as if Shy had just been wearing it.

All Walter could say at the door was, "Please wake me for the early train."

Inside, he lit his lamp. *You will be back in New York tomorrow,* he told himself. *You got the story.*

In spite of everything, he lay back on the pillow, the case cool to his head, and smiled. He had done it. He would get the justice he had promised he would for Cleon Quine. Walter reached over for his notebook and began jotting down facts in a dazed, imprecise hand so he'd remember what Hillman had told him. The room remained cold, but Walter began to imagine a warmer day, maybe as soon as this week, and he stopped writing. Instead, he saw himself walking into the White House for a meeting with Wilson, telling that bespectacled Southern bastard the amazing story of this night and Wilson nodding gravely, finally seeing the regrettable error of his ways. *Please forgive me,* says Wilson. *I shall make a speech of apology to the nation.* Walter's face on the cover of *The Crisis. Well, Dr. Du Bois, I believe that a man's courage must never flag in the face of adversity. It has been the hallmark of our people to stand under fire, be they the bullets of our nation's enemies, or the bullets of our fellow countrymen. President Wilson, meet Miss Ellanice Quine. Miss Quine, the President of the United States.* Little Booney well rewarded with a bowl of ice cream in the White House kitchen while Simso Clark is hauled away in prison stripes. Louisa Warren pushing Cornelia aside to stare through the window. It was all coming back to New York, and the fight would begin. If never

President White, he would be remembered for other things—proud, beautiful, righteous things. The glorious life of Walter Francis White, descendent of presidents and kings, had begun, and the world would be better for it.

He closed his eyes, but the words continued to echo in his head, and he saw Ellanice, saw Dulcet's ring. The finger floating in the jar. A roll of hard-earned money stolen out of a dead man's hand.

New thoughts circled him, weightier ones. *Why do you get to live?* a voice asked. *Why do you get have a glorious life?* Walter hadn't killed anyone, but a man had nearly died by his inaction.

But he *should* have died, thought Walter.

The voice snapped back, *Do you know for sure he should have died? Is not doing anything just another way of being violent?* He couldn't escape the questions. How do you work for justice when you don't know what justice truly is? When you've lost the ability to trust?

That boy back in Atlanta had believed up till then that race did not matter, that every heart pursued its own ways, no matter the color of the skin. But since then he'd learned to define blackness by suspicion, by losing the ability to do exactly what he was asking the world to do. He missed that hope now, missed the clean air he used to breathe before he and his parents had slammed the doors shut on so much of the world.

Like a bird straying into the room, a thought entered Walter's mind that could not be chased back out, one he'd been trying not to have—Hillman didn't do it. No matter how easy it made things, how obvious it seemed, he simply could not believe that man had lynched Cleon Quine. The evil it would take to do such a thing would show itself in every word, in every action he took. Evil men can't manage to be friendly even to their own friends, can't love their own families, not the way Hillman seemed to. *For God's sake,* thought Walter, *he liked Joe Williams!* Believing this had a bracing edge, and he could feel that invigorating challenge to the bones that comes with doing the hard thing.

A fierce chill ran from the base of his skull down to his toes and then back up, settling into a cold that set his jaw chattering. This had been the longest day of Walter's life. Digusting as it was, he picked Shy's nightshirt off the floor and slipped it over his head, the foreign smell of another man's body enveloping him, another man who happened to be white. The sharp, acrid smell he associated with white folks rose high into his nose and Walter shrank from the nightshirt even though he was in it. If we were all black, he wondered, would we all be killing each other over something else?

The extra layer began to work its effect. The chills finally ended. Pulled down by the unsolvable weight of his thoughts, Walter said good night to the dead babies and fell asleep.

Part Two

FIFTEEN

When Walter woke up the next morning, he did not immediately open his eyes. He heard voices downstairs, felt warm
and entirely uninterested in moving from beneath his blanket, with
his head still a bit woolly and in need of some steam. The view from
behind his eyelids was promising—bright, even a little rosy as the
morning sun poured into his room. On a day like this at home, he
might go for minutes. He could breathe and piss and brush his teeth
and eat some toast and listen to the birds and for those sweet
moments he would just be. And then he'd scan the headlines in the
newspaper, or look out the window and see the faces of people passing
by on the streets below, and suddenly he'd have to choose again. All
those small, shining things that for five or ten minutes seemed the
whole essence of being would suddenly recede behind the blaring
realization, memory shouting in his ear, that the choice had been
made for him. He was a specific kind of man—a *black* man. He
couldn't imagine that any white man had ever once had to consider
when he woke up that he was white.

Today Walter White became a Negro when he finally opened his
eyes and sat up in bed in the Mitchells' unfamiliar guest room.

Outside, a train chuffed into the station. Walter looked at the
watch on his wrist. It was eight A.M.

Shoving aside the blanket, he jumped out of bed and pulled Shy Mitchell's nightshirt over his head. Naked now, he looked around for his clothes, but they were nowhere to be seen, and then he remembered that everything was drying out in Dr. Moody's office. No matter how fast he sprinted down there, he'd never get dressed and packed in time to make a train that was already sitting in the station. Walter was stuck here until at least two P.M. He sneezed, sat down on the bed and told himself that it wasn't a bad thing—he could have some breakfast and some tea, sniff out whatever else he could on the lynching, as long as he was still here, and go back to New York with as damning a report as he'd ever dreamed of collecting.

But first, he'd have to put Shy's nightshirt back on. As he slipped it back over his head, Ludey's panicked face returned with it, twisted in fear as the man flailed in the water, and so too did the unsettling combination of guilt and satisfaction with which Walter had gone to bed. While his cold had so far done nothing more than stuff his nose and make him sneeze, he hadn't shaken off the confusion surrounding last night's events. He'd let a man nearly die, albeit one he hated, and taken the confession of Quine's killer—one that could very likely put a man in jail, even though Walter believed, for only the most circumstantial reasons, that he was innocent. A review of his notes did some good; written in a drunkard's scrawl, he'd managed to capture Hillman's story in full, though he'd not captured Hillman's complicated nature or that he liked Joe Williams. Nor did his notes address his sense that Hillman hadn't done it. The notes did not mention Ludey's near-death, Walter's unanswerable question as to what he should have done at the pond, or who had the Quines' money. In the light of day, his expansive sympathies of the night before seemed as much the product of sleep deprivation as any examination of human souls. The facts, he reminded himself, were all that Mr. Johnson had asked. The NAACP was not paying him to untie his own moral knots while lynchers walked free. That's what God was for. Walter relied on the sunny morning and the force of reason to burn more certainty into his mind, convince him that these were indeed the facts so he could board the two P.M.

The smell of something approximating coffee had worked its way up to the room. Walter decided to retrieve his effects from Dr. Moody. Wearing a fresh pair of socks under Shy's gamey nightshirt, he sheepishly tiptoed down the stairs, praying that Miss Warren and her loathsome charge had already eaten their coddled eggs and moved on to their next amusement. The dining room was empty, though he could hear Pettey anxiously darting about the kitchen, sharply addressing an empty room. There on the table sat his pants, neatly folded along with his undergarments, his jacket and shirt pressed and set over the backs of chairs. Before he had to engage anyone in conversation, he snatched his clothing as if he were stealing someone else's and hopped back upstairs to the bathroom where he brushed his teeth and ran a razor over his chin.

In no hurry, Walter looked closely at his face. With his thin lips and sharp nose, he resembled all the other Scottish Anglo-Saxons around here, a resemblance more than natural since that was what he mostly was. He wriggled the lobes of his ears, which jutted out at an angle that stopped just short of being noticeable, lifted and dropped his eyebrows a few times, twitched his moustache. As he turned his head to the side, testing the closeness of his shave on his jaw, an odd phenomenon occurred. Since his eyes usually latched on to darker men and women for community, often the sight of a white man confronting him in the mirror gave him a sudden shock, yet this morning the trim, white, eager face greeting him appeared to belong to someone else altogether. Walter White could not recognize himself at all in the mirror, had no clue who that was there. Had he seen that face before? Yes, he had to admit that he'd indeed run across it, run across it fairly frequently. But did he inhabit those blue eyes, had he just asked those fingers to wave? It seemed impossible.

That is what *you* look like, he said to himself. That is *you*.

For once his puzzlement had nothing to do with race. Despite its youth, that mass there in the mirror, that corporeal *thing,* already seemed to be rotting somehow, its all-too-brief existence made evident in the thinning hair above the temples. As much as he, this mind that was thinking, had considered death by fire and by lynching and by any number of other tortures, he had never considered the universal transience of humans, black and white. He had never seen the possibly chance connection between their bodies and whatever ignited the spirit of wisdom and goodness. He could not help but touch his face as these considerations fogged the bathroom, and he stared into the eyes of this other man, elated, frightened, and yet calm, held trancelike by the gaze meeting his.

Pettey called up, "Mr. White!" in a rasp she tried to file down with inflections of good manners.

With a start he turned to the door and when he looked back in the mirror he saw himself, Walter Francis White, twenty-four years old, field secretary of the NAACP, his body filled with all the memories and passions that he'd brought down here on *The Birmingham Special.*

"Mr. White!"

Walter put on his shirt and buttoned a few buttons before he opened the door. "Yes, Mrs. Mitchell! I'll be down in a moment!" He gave the mirror a final check, rubbing his chin one more time before he tied his tie, then made his way down, uncertain as to what had just happened.

Breakfast awaited in fine style, much finer than last night's collard greens had given him to expect. Two fried eggs, some grits, and a sausage; by Sibley Springs standards, and even Harlem standards, a wealth of food considering wartime shortages, rail tie-ups, and coal rationing. Pettey stood next to the table, assuming the kind of service position he'd given up on here at the Mitchell House. Unlike last night, when she'd merely dropped a plate in front of him, this morning she held her place with a genuine smile that appeared forced only because Pettey had to force every smile she made. Each tooth stood separately from its neighbor, as if the distance had been measured, and she inclined her head with curiosity as he dipped a toast point into the yolk. He hadn't noticed until now that her head craned permanently forward and the low rise of an incipient widow's hump pushed up the back collar of her cotton dress, a faded blue and yellow check as wearily cheerful as Pettey's smile.

"Hope you enjoy your breakfast."

The deference, while welcome, also unnerved Walter. He munched and grinned and nodded all at once, unsure as to why he deserved the royal treatment, Mitchell style.

"Takes a good man to do what you did last night. That's a *Christian* thing to do."

The eggs and toast congealed in his mouth. "Is that coffee," was as much as he could manage through his eggs.

Glad to have a purpose, Pettey scooted into the kitchen, to be replaced by Goose, who carried a book of unusual width and a look of disbelief.

"Did you really save Mr. Ludey's life last night?"

Walter stuffed a bite of sausage into his mouth so he could shrug noncommittally, roll his head from side to side in a wordless show of humility, lack of knowledge, or whatever else the little girl wanted to read in his face other than an out-and-out Yes. Despite her mother's admiration, Goose did not seem fully convinced that this had been a good idea. As Pettey placed a cracked enamel mug before him, steaming with some watery, brown liquid, Goose folded her arms and said crossly, "You missed Louisa."

After a sip of coffee, he said, "So?"

"She left early with Tate and her auntie for a walk."

"Well that's just fine, Goose." Her candor allowed Walter to be equally blunt. "But what do I care?"

Pettey shoved herself between the two and pointed at his plate as he stuck his fork into the final inch of sausage. "Now Goose, you leave Mr. White alone. He's feeling tired from all he done. You go practice your Sacred Harp. Preacher gonna want to hear you singin' tomorrow."

Shy walked past without a word, a slight that left Pettey with a disagreeable look and Walter with some concern for Shy, once he was out of earshot.

"He was kind to lend me his nightshirt. Please tell him I'm grateful."

Pushing back his chair, Walter peeked around the door frame. There stood Shy, his tuba in a box next to him as he stared out the window, waiting for the new owner; he didn't want to have to watch this scene play out.

"Why don't he ever listen to me?" asked Pettey. Walter thought she was talking to him and turned around, but she was facing the photo of her dead daughter, his empty plate gripped tight. A finger from her other hand followed the curve of her Gladys's chin.

Walter got up quietly from the table, trying not to disturb anyone or anything in this joyless house, and went to the hall where he announced to Shy that he had to go to the station to check for his cases and that he'd be back for lunch before the two o'clock train. Shy didn't say a word. Walter opened the door and walked into the mild air of the morning in search of brighter places.

A night without rain or snow had dried some of the puddles in the streets, and the sun's conviction grew as the minutes passed; while Hillman still could not take his mitt outside, he could be excused for rubbing a little oil on the palm and pounding a ball into the pocket a couple of times. A vast improvement over Friday's drear, the clear sky cast a more forgiving light on Sibley Springs, made plants and flowers seem possible, and since it was Saturday, a few more children were about. Walter decided to go straight to

Vine's in hopes of more details that would make sense of Hillman's story.

As in most small Southern towns, Saturday in Sibley Springs was market day. Those folks Walter passed along the two blocks to the general store appeared to have dressed with just a little more flair— many women had green ribbons of a familiar fabric tied in their hair or buttonholes, and shiny shoes were surprisingly common, reflecting an overall mood certainly lifted from yesterday's gloom. As nice as it was to see a happier town, though, Walter could not forget that the grease of Cleon's body still stained a thatch of grass on the hill behind him. Terrible violence had recently flowed through these streets, and yet men and women greeted each other with no sign that it had ever happened, no eyes averted in embarrassment or shame.

As he walked, he heard more than a few people singing lines of music in an unusual, droning manner, jouncing bars heavy on rhythm and with only the most rudimentary melody expressed as "fa," "sol," and "la." So lacking in subtlety or any kind of layers or patterns, Walter figured it could only be some sort of white, Christian music peculiar to this area. More than once, one of the singers saw him pass and, still singing, gestured with their heads to their companions that they should notice the stranger, offering Walter a kind greeting that he returned with a tip of his hat and a blush.

More so than yesterday, as if a sign of spring, Negroes also walked the streets, and to his great relief, they studiously ignored him, but to such a degree that he became concerned that their lack of interest in a stranger would be considered suspect. Near the bank, he noticed Ellanice, striking in a long, black coat, trimmed in a boa similar to the one belonging to the minister's accuser on *The Birmingham Special*. With the warmer temperature, she had left it unbuttoned to reveal a black and white spotted frock that expressed more disdain for her surroundings than a sense of mourning. Though she never caught his eye, Walter was certain that she'd seen him. He was sure that every Negro he passed, both familiar from the memorial and those he'd never seen, had their eyes on him, curious about how he was able to walk the streets today after being chased last night, watching to see if his plan was real. Both sides of Sibley Springs, he felt, now had him under their scrutiny.

The scene in front of Vine's was much the way Walter had come across it yesterday. One man held the dogs under the over-hang, the other whittled, and what he now knew to be the Fen-tress wagon, with its load of shriven womanhood, sat in the mud, yoked to a gray mule. In mid-grovel to Mother Fentress, Scipio, who'd probably been waiting for Walter all morning, stared down at something in the road as he clenched Booney firmly by the hand. Mother Fentress pointed down at the same spot and hollered at Scipio, "Tell the boy to take it! It's a penny, dammit. Ain't every little nigger got use fer a penny?"

Scipio thwacked the back of Booney's head. "G'wan boy! You heard Miz Fentress. She been so kind as to give you a coin and you be dumb as a mule, jes' astandin' there alookin' at it!"

While Scipio had not employed an especially refined accent last night at the Quine house, he'd reverted now to an antic, minstrel show dialect. Knowing Scipio's subservience was a survival show only made Walter more disgusted by it. Eating your own was a way to survive too, but that did not make it acceptable human behavior.

Accustomed to the changing winds that swept through Sibley Springs, Booney slowly bent over and picked up the coin with two fingers.

"There," said Scipio. "Ain't that nice? Now you say thank you. Miz Fentress, all the black folks know jes' how much you care 'bout us."

Before Scipio could get too far with his next expression of fealty, Mother Fentress turned away without acknowledgment to greet her son's savior.

"So you're the one."

The leathery dog handler plucked a small pipe out of his mouth and pointed the stem at Walter. "A-yup. That's him fer sure."

The pig-eyed whittler smiled from his barrel as if they were old friends, the flesh piling up on both sides of his mouth in a jolly way. "Hi do, Walter."

Squeezing the brow of her puckered face, Mother Fentress regarded Walter. "You're the one that saved my Ludey from drownden, ain'cha?"

A smug, small pursing of the lips slowly spread out into a smile across Scipio's face as he and Walter locked eyes. Christmas had come early for him.

"Glory be! I knowed you was *that* kinda man the minute I sets eye on you, Mistuh White, I truly did!" He ratcheted his voice up a notch so that every Negro in the county could hear him. "Yes sir! Mistuh White done saved the life of Ludey Fentress! Shout it from the rooftops! Lord Jesus! Mistuh White saved Mistuh Ludey Fentress from a certain *death*! Mistuh Fentress no longer be alive if not for Mistuh Waltuh White!"

Mother Fentress glared at Scipio from the buckboard. "Oh shet the hell up." She turned back to Walter. "Don't let him bother you—he's a good nigger, but even the best of 'em get on yer nerves 'ventually." In a collective warning, every white person around stared at Scipio. Telling himself that it was to keep in character, Walter stared as well, confused and queasy by the complexities of his alliances. "I just want to thank you. He sick abed right now, but doctor say he'll be fine." Mother nudged the woman on her left, a few inches taller than her and slightly less wrinkled. "Dora? Thank the man for savin' yore husband."

From her ability to stare silently into space for generous amounts of time, Dora appeared at first well beaten down, even possibly a mute, and she offered Walter only the slightest nod of appreciation.

The smirk at the corner of her mouth, though, and the slight roll of her eyes toward the train station gave a sense that she was less oppressed by the Fentresses than just sick of the dreadful family she'd been stuck with, and possibly even as annoyed as Scipio was that Walter hadn't let Ludey die. Though an apology seemed in order, he reminded himself that he really hadn't done anything to save the man, and that he himself was still trying to manage in deep water.

Walter tipped his hat to the ladies. "It was all any man would do."

"He can't farm for piss, but he's my boy, and I love him."

He turned to Vine's door. "I really have to see Mr. Vine before I go."

Despite the warning from the white folks standing around, Scipio couldn't help himself. "You leavin' Mistuh White? So soon?"

Once again Walter took advantage of the situation to give Scipio a withering glare before addressing Mother Fentress. "Unfortunately, I suspect my cases were directed to Chattanooga, so I'll be on the two o'clock train."

"Dat's a shame. One day, and you was becoming a part of the town already, Mistuh White. Meetin' so many peepers. White folks *and* black folks." Walter had to consciously keep himself from bouncing on his toes. "For sure. Whole lotta people come through jes' meddlin' when we can take care of our own. Ain't that right, Miz Fentress?"

Walter had to get away from him. "Mrs. Fentress. Ma'am," he said as he entered the dark of the store without a word to Scipio. The fat man reached over to give him a friendly tap on the arm as he passed.

The breaking weather had brought light into Vine's as well, along with more customers. Rather than a den of thieves, today the store felt like an actual place of commerce as Baxter worked the counters alongside a thin man, bald on top, with a tonsure that made him look older than his thirty or so years. As soon as he walked in, Walter noticed the exceptionally thin woman browsing the food section.

They made only the briefest eye contact as he strode to the potbellied stove and took a seat before a checkerboard. She had to be there to watch him.

Baxter also took notice of her. He walked away from the people he'd been waiting on, a shabbily dressed white woman and her little boy, to yell over to his employee, set to display his derring-do to a bucktoothed teenaged girl by mounting a ladder in pursuit of paraffin blocks. "Feldon, she can wait! Go notice Tansy!"

Every head in the store swiveled toward the black woman who continued to stand, hands in her pockets, gazing up at the same Aunt Jemimas and Rastuses that Walter had, their dark faces shining on boxes she couldn't afford to buy, boxes Vine most likely wouldn't even let her touch. As Feldon scrambled over to dissuade her from larceny or any physical contact with the inventory, Vine caught Walter's eye and winked. "It's the hero! Set a spell, Brother."

"Hey, Baxter. Hillman and Nip comin' by?"

"They workin'."

If they weren't coming by, he'd have to find some other people to verify Hillman's story. Rather than face Tansy, Walter sat so he faced Vine, whose smile disappeared as soon as he returned to his customer. It seemed that the wall of shoeboxes had gotten smaller than it had been yesterday. In a whisper, not of discretion but of weakness, the woman handed Baxter a five-dollar bill and said, "This ain't all, but it's some."

Vine plucked it away with the same two-fingered grab of distaste Booney had used when retrieving Mother Fentress's penny. "So you found some too, huh?" Waving it in the woman's face, he sneezed, then leered at her as if she'd proposed some licentious exchange. Flipping it over, Vine examined the bill's veracity, all but testing it with a bite of his incisors and fully enjoying the torture of this poor woman whose son stood motionless with the total obedience of one too hungry to make trouble. Curves of dirt crusted the edges of his mouth. His overalls lacked buttons, were merely tied together at the bib. He had no hat, no gloves, and dark, bony hands like a coal miner's or mechanic's, dark as a condition of life. Walter wondered if he'd been sifting through dirt for seeds, crawling through the mud while his mother searched for greens under the dead leaves.

The boy's eyes registered Walter, but they knew too much to be curious. Too young to know that there might be any other way of living, a boy who woke up to hunger every morning the way Walter woke to the sun. Wheeling around the stagnant air of Vine's, a hearty winter fly landed on the corner of the boy's eye and sucked the salt. The boy continued to stare, the gaze sharpening a little, priming to absorb a blow.

"Mr. Baxter, Lanny need those boots fer true."

Walter snuck a look at the boy's feet, bound in rags as if he were one of Napoleon's army, stumbling through the Russian snow.

"I was ahopin' I could sign." Stunned with the absurdity of her suggestion, the woman looked to her own shoes bursting out at the soles, and said, "But I don't 'spect that's asomethin' you could manage . . ." Her voice trailed off.

Baxter scratched at his bald spot as if she'd presented him with a difficult puzzle, and in fact she had: Should he risk a dollar fifty and let them have shoes on credit, possibly keeping this five-year-old boy from death by pleurisy, influenza, pneumonia, or one of a hundred other diseases he could get in the next few months, or keep that dollar fifty safe in the bank and let the boy absorb the risk. Walter's years at Standard Insurance turning life stories into actuarial tables, boiling down widows and decades of hard work and final moments of fear into pure numbers so Heman Perry and the board could assess risk and make sound financial decisions felt right now like nothing more than mathematics. Never had he been so proud to be field secretary of the NAACP. But the NAACP and its reports and brochures didn't seem like enough to Walter next to the sight of Curtis licking the rim of his bottle of Chero-Cola like it was holy water, the face of this boy shivering gently at the side of his mother as she begged for credit.

After some ruefully humming, Baxter said, "I'm arunnin' a business here, Say-ra, not some relief board." Walter turned away, examined the shelves, counted biscuit tins and jiggled the change in his pocket. "It ain't mine to take care a yourn. That's your business." Walter stood up and reminded himself that he was here to get the story of Cleon Quine's lynching. At two o'clock he would let Sibley Springs sink back down into Hell.

Up at the front of the store, Feldon kept Miss Portis from handling the merchandise. Before he brought any item down off the shelf, he demanded that she produce the necessary amount of money to purchase it, then he would hold it in front of her an arm's length away so she could admire it from afar and make her choice on faith.

Sauntering over to the counter, Walter positioned himself next to the jar. Miss Portis had done her best to ignore it, but once he picked it up and regarded the last piece of Quine, her attentions swayed away from the canned goods.

Were there other bits of Quine, he wondered, floating in similar jars on curio shelves and mantels around Sibley Springs? He pictured men and women in the homes picking up their own jars and looking at the underside of Quine's ear, his thumb, his big toe. Did it make them happy? Were any of them ashamed?

By now Feldon stared at him and the jar as well. This could have been you, Walter told himself. This could have been your mother's finger or your father's. If not for the other shots that night, the mob could have burned them out and torn them to pieces. He looked up at the little white boy.

To his surprise, Feldon appeared embarrassed, as if he wished Walter would just put it back down and out of sight as he waited, or at least pretended to wait, on this black woman. "Sir, that's, um . . ."

His unease, though, elevated Miss Portis to humanity and so Walter brandished it a bit as she looked from Feldon to the jar then to Walter, who now beheld the jar as if it were Yorick's skull. " 'He hath borne me on his back a thousand times,' " thought Walter.

The silence from the front had made Baxter stop his petty calculations, and now Walter placed the jar, finger swaying in the liquid like a bit of driftwood carried on the sea, a butterfly hesitantly approaching a flower, back on the counter. And as he turned, all eyes on him, he very carefully and oh-so-accidentally knocked it onto the floor.

Formaldehyde and shattered glass splattered in all directions, as if a rock had been dropped into some kind of deadly pool, while the black crescent of Cleon's finger lay in the middle, released from captivity, free at last.

Walter fell on his knees to sweep at the glass with his hands. "Oh Christ, Bax! I'm sorry!" Feldon and Vine both ran over to help, but Walter snatched the finger, held it in his palm, held Cleon Quine and let his body take as much of that as he could. It was heavy with the unmistakable mass of flesh. A vision of this finger stroking Ellanice's face, gripping a plow handle, flashed in his mind as Baxter extended his palm, a look of supreme discomfort on his face.

"Here, give me that thing. No use you getting dirty with it." Vine plucked the digit from him. Walter expected them to be angry and they were, but it was hard to tell exactly what they were angry about. "It's a foul thing," mumbled Vine in a vague enough way that Walter was unsure what the grocer considered foul, Quine's nigger finger or the fact that he'd had it in a jar on his counter. Miss Portis's mouth tilted up at the edges.

"Bax, I gotta run over to the station and check on my case. You let me know how much I owe ya, all right?"

Vine waved him off, too distracted with getting the odor of formaldehyde out of his store, and Walter was about to make his escape when an idea struck him, one that he could only whisper. He kneeled back down. "Hey Bax. How much would you take for that?"

Quine's finger stuck out of the breast pocket of Vine's apron, ebony against the white cotton. As if shocked, electrically, by Walter's inquiry, Vine pulled his head back, but did not respond. He crouched, waiting to hear more.

"It's a helluva a thing and I'd sure like to have it."

A battle of sorts, hardly moral, played out on Baxter's face, as the value of a dollar and all that it represented to a businessman like Vine lay siege to whatever worth a dead Negro's finger had for him. It was a rout. "Two dollars."

He'd have $23.43 after he paid Mitchell, and with no intention of being in Sibley Springs by 2:01 this afternoon, Walter nodded and removed the bills from his wallet. A receipt seemed out of the question, but Mr. Johnson would understand. Vine stopped sweeping for a moment to wrap the finger in some wax paper and hand it to its new owner.

At the door, Walter stopped. "I really am sorry about that, Bax."

The boy and his mother hadn't moved an inch. The green ribbon in the buttonhole of her jacket hung in a limp knot.

SIXTEEN

The Fentress wagon had moved along by the time Walter left the store, Cleon's finger close to his body in his jacket pocket. Scipio had left as well, without a doubt spreading word throughout the other side of the tracks of Ludey's fortunate rescue. As Walter walked back through town toward the depot, he felt the weight of the finger on his hip, and when he didn't think too hard about what exactly it was, he derived a comfort of sorts from it, as if he now had some greater leverage with the black men and women of this town. He considered the logistics of getting it to Dulcet Quine but had no workable plan by the time he reached the station, where large trucks piled with more wicker chairs and spa paraphernalia dwarfed Miss Timmons. She sat in the same place behind the same table, watching the activity with bemused interest, occasionally issuing directives that the draymen ignored. Walter doffed his hat and was about to walk straight into the station when the pearls caught his eye.

"You see something new today, Mr. White?" She extended her fingers over the long edge of the table and waved them over her wares. "'Cause they the same batch today I had yesterday."

And yet they looked different to Walter. Today, he noticed their luster and how they seemed to make it possible to touch the wintry sky, the low bands of soft blue and yellow and rose that hung on the horizon. These were not a jeweler's pearls, the identical white balls strung around wealthy women's necks, the tight choker Cornelia had for grand events. Each of these pearls had its own character and color, expressed one of the infinite ways of being beautiful. He could not speak at first as he lifted individual pearls off the table with care, letting his fingers roll over their silky finish. Then the surprise of things so beautiful in this grim outpost finally struck him with its full force. He imagined them resting into the clefts of Ellanice's throat, or dangling from her ears, but she probably owned a few ropes of the anonymous type. Miss Warren most certainly did, but as far as he knew, neither his mother nor his sister owned a pearl. "How much are they?"

Miss Timmons dropped her voice into a more earnest range. "I sell 'em to you fer a quarter apiece."

He stepped away. "You playing with me now. That's what you're doing. Just playing with me."

"It's a buyer's market, Mr. White. I thought you was some kind a businessman." She winked. "Hell, you get 'em for free right over there if'n you feel like sticking your hands in the cold water." Lifting a large oblong, Miss Timmons squinted at it with a professional's sceptical eye. "This all I got for a while. My pearlyman gone amissin' this mornin', didn't come by."

Walter did some rapid math—he could afford three: a blush oval about the size of a baby's fingernail for his mother and two silvery blue spheres for contingencies, amorous or otherwise. Cornelia would sniff at them. *Would have sniffed,* he reminded himself with a fresh burst of relief; the next woman would be the kind who would smile.

"I'm aguessin' he gone on a trip," said Miss Timmons as she took his coins. "Some kind of journey, and he gonna bring me back the biggest damn pearlies you ever seen!" She stamped a moccasin down for emphasis.

Walter slipped the pearls into his jacket pocket, right onto the finger of Cleon Quine, which he realized as soon as he heard them scratch across the waxy paper. His first instinct was to dig them out and switch them to the other side, but fishing around so in front of Miss Timmons did not strike Walter as appropriate. Instead, he wished her well and slid sideways into the station, past two draymen hauling a stainless steel tub through the door, the odd mixture of objects brewing in his pocket.

If possible, even more spa detritus had been heaped into the station, more boxes, lengths of copper piping, a crate of spigots. Walter couldn't guess what was left for Miss Warren and her brother to actually visit. He took note of Clem, his inventory restocked with a torn and muddied copy of the *Winchester Herald and Truth*. An old woman, her head slipping down between her shoulders, sat bundled in a wheelchair as a black woman wearing a blue wool coat and the white cap of a medical attendant took bites from a thick slice of bread. Walter found Drake pointing a young black man with a red hat toward a stack of spa boxes that would have to be on the platform for the next train. He'd been at the funeral the night before, one of the men leaning against the back wall, eyeing Walter, and he eyed him again now, glancing away from the stationmaster.

"What the hell you lookin' at, Carter?"

Walter burst in between them with a rousing tone, so Carter wouldn't be tempted to answer. "Speaking of which," exclaimed the resurrected Walter White of the Exelento Medicine Company, "is the two o'clock on time?"

Not pleased by the interruption, Drake ignored him and continued giving instructions to a distracted Carter. "Carter, what in *hell* you lookin' at?"

Walter turned to walk away, but Drake shouted orders in a voice that once rang over the fields of Chickamauga. "You don't go nowhere! I'll be done with this boy in a minute and then I can answer your question. First, I wanna know what Carter here's so much more interested in than what I got to say to him when I need a job done. Hmmm?"

Walter gave Carter a look that Drake would have assumed expressed all manner of disgust and anger with such an uppity nigro but really asked with a slight shift of the eyes if he wanted to live this way his entire life. Carter pursed his lips and shrugged. "Nuthin', suh. Time for all us here to get on with our jobs *right away.*"

One ear cocked at Carter's surprisingly industrious statement, Drake finished his explanation and dismissed the porter, who did not look back. "Now *you* want to know if the two o'clock's on time. Well, no. It's on time for six. T'ain't no two o'clock on Saturday, jes' eight and six."

Four more hours in Sibley Springs. Genuinely annoyed, Walter failed to stay in character. "Why didn't you tell me?"

"Did you ask?" Engaged by Walter's anger, the old man folded his arms and got a little closer; Drake did not avoid confrontation. "Hmmm? Did you?"

It was good, thought Walter, that one is continually reminded to respect your elders. "Mr. Drake, you are entirely correct. I did not."

That seemed to placate the stationmaster, who pulled his face away from Walter's and regarded him as he worked his lips in and out of a pucker. "Well, that's right. You did not. You just assumed."

Fifty-odd years ago, without the liver spots and the white hair, Drake had probably been sitting tall and straight and riding through these same parts alongside General Forrest, ambushing Yankees and then, once the first four years of this unending War had been lost, he'd spent happy days spent terrorizing the local darkies. Though he didn't know everyone's credit history and personal habits the way Vine did, he had to have been around since there'd been a Sibley Springs. He'd certainly been at the station when Cleon's death train pulled in. He could confirm whether Hillman, Nip, and Ludey had played Satan that day and masterminded it all.

Walter gestured to the stacks of chairs and the gurneys, the old woman in the wheelchair. "Quite a scene you got going in here. Looks like a hospital."

Drake blew a rude sound through his lips. "Had a goddamned circus here last week."

Walter tugged back to see if he really had a bite. "Whatchu talking about? That boy Quine?" That fifty-one-year-old "boy." He returned Drake's sound with an equally rude one of his own. "Hell, I aheared all about that."

"Well then, you don't need to hear about it from me."

Drake turned away, but Walter followed him. "I mean, I just heared talking. Nobody told me what happened *here.*"

Just short of the postal window, Drake stopped and faced him. "I had three specials acome in here full of every damn drunken farmer from a hundred miles away jes' awantin' to burn somethin'. *That's* what happened here." He noticed Walter's doubtful expression. "That's right. Some mean boys. I'll take my hat off to the ladies of this town. They said take that man out a here, and you kill him some-place else, because Sibley Springs will not be host to that kind of scene. We have fine people come here for the spa." Drake nodded his head sharply, as if Walter had just been told exactly which corner of Heaven he'd found himself in. "Damnedest thing was the daughter." Here the stationmaster's face changed into something younger and smoother. "Not a tear. When she tore off a piece a that nigger's jacket and awiped off his face, you couldn't hear a word. That was a damn sorry day, and I carried the Stars and Bars into battle under Albert Sidney Johnston."

"So was it Ludey and those boys? I heard Jimmy shot him in the leg and . . ."

Drake cut him short by whisking off his hat and parting his hair to reveal a nasty cut in his scalp. "See that? Happened this morning." Disgusted, Walter pulled away. "Yeah, well, go ahead and heal it."

"What?"

Drake pushed his scalp up closer to Walter's face. "G'wan, I said. Heal it." Walter gave him an offended expression, his features screwed tight. "If you cain't heal it, then you ain't Jesus Christ, and He's about the only one whose business it is who did what and who didn't. Everybody gonna take it to the Lord, and then we see who done right." Drake opened the door to the back run, but just as he was about to shut it, he poked his head through, looked at Walter for an extra moment. "Somethin' about you I don't like."

The door slammed. Walter scratched the back of his neck, the hair prickling. Down the road, the red stripe of the barber's pole caught his eye.

Walter White loved a haircut. Though he spent a goodly amount of time and money maintaining a well-groomed exterior, getting a haircut pleased him for the experience itself and not just the proof that he understood what constituted fine living. He was not alone in this innocent, calming pleasure; as he approached Sibley Springs's lone barber, many a happy hour among dozens of other men in the leather seats of Herndon's on Peachtree Street came to mind, watching the crystal in the chandeliers twinkle as the gentle tug of comb and scissors, the pressure of the manicurist buffing his fingernails, lulled him into drowsiness. Alonzo Herndon, the richest black man in Atlanta, had made his fortune that way, by allowing men to indulge themselves harmlessly amid the splendor of his barbershop.

Sundy's lacked the opulence of Herndon's, and the crowd as well. A cowbell clanged in the frame when Walter pushed open the door, and it echoed through the room. The same gaunt man he'd seen yesterday staring across the road appeared from behind a curtain, black combs sticking out of the breast pocket of his smock just as Cleon's finger had peeked out of Vine's. Walter tapped his jacket to hear the rattle of the pearls against the paper. The lame man that he and his father had seen beaten the night of the riot had been a bootblack from Herndon's shop.

The barber swiped a towel across the seat to prove his hygenic practice then gestured for Walter to sit down. "Hi do."

"I'm well," said Walter. "How you?"

Sundy shrugged as if it didn't really matter how he felt. Moving slowly in his long apron, he exuded a more medical or even funereal competence rather than anything having to do with style. Such a gloomy barber didn't inspire confidence; at least Herndon's men were uniformly energetic and friendly, willing to keep their mouths shut all the way through a haircut and a shave, if that's what you liked, or else natter on about nearly any topic you could devise. Sundy wore his hair slicked down shiny and flat, a simple cut that someone without much experience in the tonsorial arts and sciences, probably Mrs. Sundy, could maintain for him. Shallow drifts of hair had gathered under the chairs and along the baseboard of the wall of sinks and mirrors. Walter saw himself shiver with disgust in the large mirror that faced them both on the opposite wall. Avoiding any contact between his shoes and the loose hair, he hung up his coat, but kept his jacket on.

"What can I do for you?"

"Just a trim." He sat down, let Sundy wrap the towel around his neck and fasten the cloth. "Busy day for you?"

The barber took a few snips before he answered. "Not so bad. Just the boy that sweeps for me ain't come in yet." As sluggish an appearance as he offered, once Sundy had the scissors in his hands, he worked energetically, chattering the shears.

Eyes closed, Walter hmphed in sympathy. "Colored boy?"

"Yup." Sundy offered nothing more, though Walter could tell that he'd had something involving pork for breakfast. Thankfully that was the only bad smell coming off him; his clothes and smock gave off no stink and Sundy himself was odorless, details not to be taken for granted in a barbershop.

"Probably still hiding out at home. Seems like a lot of the Negroes around here still lying low."

The scissors stopped. Walter opened his eyes and saw the comb and scissors in midair as Sundy regarded the man below him in the chair. The scene bounced off the facing mirror and repeated itself infinitely before them, each twitch of Walter's hand, the slight wavering of the shears, seen a thousand times before they finally disappeared in the distance. The men silently stared at each other. Walter knew that he'd dropped something into the canyon yawning behind them and they were waiting for it to land. He leaned forward slightly in his seat, frightened for a second that falling backward into that void was really possible. Sundy blinked and began snipping again. "Yeah, well, can't say as I blame 'em. That was the point, wasn't it? To scare the hell out of 'em."

"I guess." Walter let a few second pass. "You see it?"

The scissors stopped again, but this time when he looked up, Walter saw Sundy looking past him into the mirror at himself, much the way he'd been looking out his window yesterday. "Yeah. I seen it." Then he turned his attentions back to Walter's head with more aggression, tugging a little harder as he combed it up for cutting. "The man they lynched was the father of the boy that sweeps for me." Before Walter could say anything, Sundy had a few questions of his own. "Wherebouts you from?"

"Oh, I'm a salesman. Just passing through the town. On my way this evening back to Chattanooga."

A long touring car, shiny and black, chugged by in the street. After only a day in Sibley Springs, Walter had grown accustomed to a less motorized world, so this Studebaker came as a message from civilization. He perked up to watch it pass, and though he hoped to see a well-heeled, begoggled motorist behind the wheel, instead a man in a blue pea coat and a baseball cap leaned into the windshield, gripping the wheel close to his chest as if tested by its operation.

Walter said, "I'll be damned. That's Hillman." He stopped himself from calling out to him.

Sundy didn't respond, but he stopped cutting and pointed the comb as they looked at each other in the mirror. No blue and gold ring on his finger. "You're the one that saved Fentress, ain'cha?"

"I was there."

"You fall in with those boys?" Sundy's tone was disapproving; the boys at Vine's certainly had a bad enough reputation.

"I'm not gonna be here long enough to fall in with anybody, like you said. I mean, a traveling man need to find a little fun, don't he?"

Sundy scowled. Clearly, Ludey's rescue had given Walter a position in town, but Sundy didn't seem to think much of it. "Well, some of the fun folks been havin' here I'd aruther they have somewheres else. Fortune's a good boy. Works hard."

"What the hell did they do to him, anyways? Wasn't Hillman and them the ones that done it?"

The barber turned to the wall and took a sip of something from a glass. "Lemme tell you somethin'," he said, waving the scissors at the mirror. "My grandfather was in the War. First Tennessee."

Walter leapt in. "The Mountain Boys!"

"That's right. Well, every time he come by, we'd try to get him to tell me and my brothers about the War." The scissors were now still. "Everybody else's granpappy seen the War and told them stories, and we jes' didn't see what he was holdin' back on us until he finally just set us down one night and said, 'Boys, I seen things I don't want you to even imagine so jes' stop askin' me cause I ain't atellin'.'"

Sundy considered the issue closed with that anecdote and resumed trimming the back of Walter's neck, a catlike, tickling sensation that under normal circumstances was one of his favorite moments of a haircut. Today, though, it was an annoyance. The barber pressed close along the right side, and Walter could feel his leg bang against Cleon's finger as his jacket hung over the side of the chair.

More details—gory, gruesome details—would shock the world into paying attention. Another witness to Hillman's presence would let him shrug off the burden of complexity he'd woken up with on his shoulders. In a reasonable time and a logical place, Walter could have told him the truth, explained his mission, but now he would have to stop looking in the mirror with Sundy and make him look just at himself and his town.

"I've seen men burned alive in my day," said Walter. "Keeps you awake."

"Damn right it does."

"I've seen more."

The metallic clatter of Sundy throwing the comb and scissors into the sink made Walter start, and the barber looked at him again in the mirror, a hand on each arm of the chair as he pulled his head down close to Walter's shoulder so he could hiss into his ear with a mad grin. "You want to hear 'bout how Quine's eyes melted? Is that what you want to hear? Well, they melted right out a his sockets, brother. Just melted down his cheeks." Sundy's fingers waved the drops down a thousand times; so much movement that the mirror almost twinkled with it. "And his tongue swolled up and his fingers twisted around so's you didn't know whether it was the fire dancin' in him or he was tryin' to pray. That enough for you?"

Walter's jacket pocket felt very heavy now. He nodded.

"Better be." The barber twitched around the eyes and took another sip from his glass. "Some folks here didn't like it so much, but what the hell was a man gonna do? All those people come to town."

Sundy clipped over the ears, and Walter kept silent for the eyebrows.

"Fortune a good boy. Been coming here for three years. Always on time." The barber tapped Walter's shoulder and put a mirror to the back of his head. "There. That's all you need."

Walter looked down at the floor. Sundy had on a pair of shiny black shoes. Brand-new. "Looks fine. Real good."

• • •

If Sundy had trimmed his hair the day before, Walter would have walked out of the shop with only the terrifying image of Cleon Quine's last minutes. But on this morning of lemony skies and the slightest promise of spring, he skirted puddles with Barber Sundy's hopeful repugnance for the events of the past week on his mind, how the image seemed to haunt the white man as it would now forever haunt him. Mr. Johnson dispatched you to find facts, he thought, not One Good Man. Every town had its One Good Man. Sometimes he was the town lawyer who let Cuffy read his law books late at night once he was done sweeping and cleaning and painting and shoeing the horses and repairing the roof. Or he was the kindly doctor who let Tom read his medical books late at night when Tom was finished with his eighteen hours of polishing, scrubbing, washing, taking out, taking in, putting up, holding, and fetching. The One Good Man's goodness was all too often defined not by any active virtue but by an absence of palpable evil, or an eagerness to extend a little once he'd gotten all of his, and that didn't strike Walter as quite enough for his admiration and thanks. The Catholics had built and furnished Purgatory precisely to house all those Good Men.

And yet, this encounter with another white man who appeared not entirely corrupted had disarmed Walter. It wouldn't be long before he'd pry behind the smile and the pretty words to find the man's motivations, but for a few more minutes at least, he allowed a hope to flutter in him that maybe Barber Sundy was a man of moral fiber; a limp, loosely woven fiber, but of fiber nonetheless. That possibly Shy Mitchell's choice to send his girl out of the room rather than have her listen to details of Cleon's lynching indicated a true Christian heart. That the old Rebel Drake had disapproved of the whole thing. That Hillman was innocent, that he wasn't another Simso Clark. Remembering that Shy had offered to show him around the town, Walter headed back to the Mitchell House and tried to seal his thoughts for now with the usually comforting QED that white people were at best patronizing and self-serving and incapable of approaching the essential morality of the Negro, a bitter, easy concept that today failed to settle matters for him.

SEVENTEEN

Within a block of the Mitchell House, Walter saw the Studebaker Hillman had been driving parked in front, but no
Hillman in the driver's seat. In the yard, Shy flipped shovelfuls of
what had to be heavy mud; time, Walter assumed, to plant tulip
bulbs or aerate the soil, but once inside the gate, he noticed the
wooden crate that had once held the tuba he'd sold as well as a
rising gray mound of mucky dirt at Shy's side. No bulbs. Wearing
a pair of cowboystyle dungarees and a brown corduroy jacket,
Shy dug with vigor, as if trying to inter something before it came
back to life. Walter chased away some dark thoughts, judged that
nothing human could fit in the crate, before he walked up to the
innkeeper.

"Whose car's that?"

Startled, Mitchell stood up straight, registered Walter's presence
then set back to digging. "Miz Dorcas," he said. "Hillman jes' brung
it 'round for them."

Walter smirked; that made sense. "What're you buryin'?"

"Some old things."

Not sure what to expect, Walter looked into the crate. At the
bottom lay Shy's red band jacket, tidily folded, the embroidered
"Timmons" shouting out in gold. Sleeping in this man's house for

209

one night, eating his food, had shorn Walter of his reticence. "Oh hell, Shy. That's a fine coat. What're you doing that for?"

"No need for it anymore."

"Well, maybe it'll get cold or something."

Mitchell drove the blade of the shovel deep into the dirt. "It's cold right now, and I ain't awearin' it."

"Seems a shame." The innkeeper ignored him, worked the shovel out of the ground. His ring finger boasted only a thin gold band; no blue stone. Walter rubbed his hands together briskly, trying to impart some energy to the scene. "Now listen. I just found out my train's not leaving until six tonight, so I was wondering if you might have time to show me that land you were telling me about yesterday."

A load of wet soil thumped onto the dirt pile. "Cain't now."

Shy was not to be distracted. A few more loads convinced Walter that he was not so much doing a chore as digging a grave for a loved one. Soon the hole was a good two feet deep and at least as wide, able to accept the crate at any time. Befitting the solemn occasion, Walter removed his hat. "Shame about your tuba, Shy. Seem like you really enjoyed it."

He stopped digging. Leaning his chin on the butt of his shovel, Shy warily nosed the air outside the rim of his cave, a cross look on his face at all times. "I was in a band once."

"Timmons."

Shy's eyes opened up as if he'd been sleeping all the time Walter had been in town, as if the letters were not stitched on the jacket between them. "Yup! Mill band. Sixteen pieces. Strings. Played Sundays. Bank holidays."

"Bet you were a good outfit."

"*Hell* yes," said Shy. "Look at that uniform. Timmons didn't spend a penny on something that warn't worth it." He knelt down and ran a finger on the letters. "Said he sent to Memphis for 'em."

"What kind of mill was it? I saw the wreck down the river. That's what that is, right?"

"Yeah." Shy stood up, leaned his chin back on the shovel; he seemed finished with digging. "Flour mill. Went up about three year ago. One spark and all that grain went up. Brought a firetruck down from Nashville on the train, but when they seen how far gone it was, they just took the horses off to let 'em walk around a bit. Didn't bother with the engine."

As Shy slipped into his memories, apparently forgiving the guest for his eagerness to chat with Dr. Moody last night, Walter fingered the brass buttons of the jacket. Shy was right—it was actually quite fine, well-crafted of warm wool. He thought about adding it to his morning's shopping, but with $20.43 after the haircut and a New York ticket still to buy, Walter found the limits of his sympathies. "Probably 'bout thirty people got kilt. More jes' got burnt up. That friend a yourn, Nip? He probably abeen happier if'n he'd a jes' died right there." Shy shrugged. "Anybody with any sense got out a town then."

"You in it?"

"Got out." Shy rubbed his nose with his finger, sniffed. "Old man Timmons got burnt up. Family just said to hell with the town. They all moved to Atlanta and Cincinnati, just come down for the springs, visit the widow. Course that's finished too. Everybody just saying to hell with it, now."

"Well, you were lucky to have the house, right? You and Pettey keep a nice place here."

"This where Pettey grew up. You asleepin' in the nursery. Her Paw used be at the mill too. Had a paper job. Made a nice dollar." Shy suddenly became very interested in the hole again, evening the walls with the blade so he didn't have to look at Walter. "Pettey's a good woman. But she don't always like havin' to share the home she growed up in. Know what I'm sayin'? An' Gladys an' all." Walter nodded. "You owe me two-fifty."

"Of course." Walter dug into his pocket. "Here. I'm sorry . . ."

"You don't have to give it to me now." The innkeeper turned away, as if pained by the sight of money. "I'm jes' sayin'." He thrust the blade into the dirt. Like everyone else in Sibley Springs, he hid in plain sight. "Nobody in this town got any idea of what's acomin' next. Warrens not comin' no more. That was a reg'lar piece a money."

Walter let some of the Exelento can-do spirit shine through. "Well, Shy, I see a lot of opportunity around here. This is a fine place to settle down in."

Shy gave him a man-to-man look. "Friend, in this town you either gotta pray or kill things. Sell your hair howdy-do and move along is what I'm atellin' you. Don't buy my land. You're a young man. You don't know what it's like to not have pretty things for your babies. God willing you never will." He turned away. "Satan starts you lookin' at those who can with *murderous* eyes."

Ellanice's satin blouse came to Walter's mind, Fortune's fine blue suit.

"I heard you had a full house here last week. That musta put a few dollars in the bank."

"Yeah." Walter stole a look at the Shy's feet. The fresh layer of muck on his boots had been applied atop many older layers, a detail Walter found for some reason very cheering. "There's always one last hot day before winter."

The two men stood over the hole and the box next to it.

"You sure you want to do this?"

Shy didn't shrug right away, but when he did, he did so as if he was exhausted. "Say, you think you could you run Miss Louisa and Tate and Goose up to the spa? Goose, she take the waters up there 'count a her breathin. They needs somebody to drive 'em. Pettey done afixed up box lunch . . ."

"Will we be back in time for the six o'clock?"

"Course."

The Studebaker sat in the street, like a groomed horse saddled and ready to run; polished, miraculously mud-free. Often Walter despaired that he'd ever own such a huge and beautiful thing. "It would be my pleasure, Shy."

EIGHTEEN

Miss Dorcas had a fine car—there was no disputing that. Sitting behind the wheel, Walter rolled his palm over the shiny gear knobs, tapped a few gauges with the same anticipation he'd had when his father had first brought home the family buggy and he'd climbed up to the board. No one had said a word as to why such a luxury suddenly graced the White house drive; the relief on his mother's face spoke enough for all of them. The Whites had heard their last muttered curses from white Atlantans accusing them of lovin' niggers for sitting in the back of the streetcar, the place where they in fact "belonged." And on the days when they sat with up front with the whites, bitter black people who knew them, and knew better, hissed up at them for trying to pass. The White family did a lot of walking. Rubbing the nubby leather of the seat, he thought, You *will* have a car like this. Success is very often just a measure of escape.

The car listed hard to the right. A strained alto next to him, like a man's voice squeezed up into a falsetto, said, "Ah pre-suuuume you will be escorting our pah-ty to the spa?"

Finding himself sliding down the seat toward the full bulk of Miss Dorcas, Walter grabbed the wheel and edged himself back up as the visiting royalty piled into the car. A rather morose little Goose trailed behind them wearing an old-fashioned bonnet that came out a good six inches on the sides of her face like blinders. She was forced to sweep her head back and forth in a wide arc to see where she was hauling the wicker lunch hamper. Tate made no effort to assist. All these trappings of entitlement and her place within them, like Walter's an undefined position between servant and guest, had addled the girl into a rare silence.

Walter tipped his hat to the car's owner as she settled her haunches and straightened the yards of wool surrounding them. "Yes, ma'am. It's my pleasure." She seemed familiar to him beyond just her type of petty Southern aristocrat, raised on English silver and tales of the lost plantation. The smell of lily toilet water nearly choked him. Then he realized that he'd seen her yesterday afternoon on Main Street, the big bosomed "leading citizen" to whom he'd mentally issued a policy.

"We ah most grateful to *yew.*"

Tate squirmed in the back, delivered a kick to the seat that vibrated Walter's kidneys. "Awntie, tell the man not to drahve too quickly, for I shall well and truly be sick upon him if he does so."

Louisa uttered a reproach, surprising, but also gratifying to Walter. Miss Dorcas lowered her chin an inch, sharing with her substitute driver a look of exasperation that evidenced a seed of wit beneath her many well-wrapped pounds of gracious living. After letting the boy's order hang in the brisk air, she said with only the appearance of conviction, "You heard the Captain. *Allez.*"

Walter craned his head around the back seat and tipped his hat. "Miss Warren? Are you ready?" She nodded demurely within her fur collar, a border of fox that snuggled around her ears and down to her chin in a manner that he had to admit he found quite fetching. For a white girl. He reminded himself to ask her if she'd seen any of the lynching; the Warrens had been in town when it happened and

216

having the testimony of people educated to even a passing degree would be useful. "Goose?"

Before they had each half-heartedly agreed, Miss Dorcas boomed, "All right, then. Ah am *quite* bloody cold!"

Hardly an expert driver, Walter did know his way around an automobile enough to get the Studebaker pointed down the road and moving toward the spa without serious incident. The chugging of the car under his posterior imparted a cheering sense of power, and the news that he was still alive and doing his job made him smile as he rearranged the rearview mirror in such a way that required it to include Miss Warren within its responsibilities.

Louisa shouted from the back, "You seem in a good mood today, Mr. White." Walter caught the words as they scattered in the wind; Hillman had not bothered to put up the top, folded around the rear part of the frame like the leathery wings of a flying mammal.

Walter noted the most charming opening, the opportunity it afforded him to speak pleasantly. "I have been meaning to see the spa before my departure and given the chance to accompany such a fine group of ladies . . ." Another fierce kick throbbed his kidneys. ". . . and, of course, young Tate, I found this most fortuitous." The wind rushing around the dash scattered his thin hair. "Such a handsome day must be enjoyed, don't you believe?" He imagined a white, verandah'd mansion at the end of the road, moss swaying in the long, old branches as women under parasols drank their water and chattered knowingly about—dare they admit, even a little bored with—the South of France.

"Yew ah a traveler for a cosmetics concern, ah you not?" Glittering earrings swayed on the powdered lobes of Miss Dorcas. "That is the *aperçu* of yo' business, yes?" Although the jewelry and the furs smelled of money, the scent was sharp and unmellowed, her rudimentary French strangled by the rural flavor of her accent, an affected blend of dusty summer cotton fields and winters in London.

He dodged rather than answer. "I'll be heading to the home office today on the six P.M. train. Originally, I was to work this territory, but it seems a vacancy in management has opened and . . ." The falsity of what he was saying struck him as well as the considerable risks grasping at any Negro man driving two white women and two white children under a false identity.

He finished the sentence with a shrug that Miss Dorcas took for the seemly arrogance due any young man on the rise. "*Certainement* most fortunate fo' yew." She dabbed at her brow with a handkerchief. "Ah, *oui, oui, oui,* the self-made man," she said with the curiosity of one regarding a new strain of tea rose.

Set loose from Pettey's strictures, Goose whistled in disbelief at something not immediately apparent and ventured a liberty. "Them's is most pretty earrings, Miss Dorcas! Woo-eee! Gawd, Ah'd *love* those." Miss Dorcas brushed at the plateau of her bosoms, ignoring Goose's compliment.

A rocky stretch of road set them all bouncing, and soon Tate mewled, "Awntie!" from the back. "Awntie, this man is an ut-tah barbarian!" Seen next to the young laird, Goose was rising in Walter's estimation.

Turning her head as far as she could around the collar of her coat and the girth of her neck, Miss Dorcas expressed her profound displeasure. "Yew may be president of the United States someday, Tate," she snapped. "Yew ah *that* sorter boy from *that* sorter family. Now yew behave!"

Walter bit his tongue very hard as he made a needlessly abrupt right turn at the spa entrance that sent Louisa and Goose hurtling into Tate. In a day, Walter's nose had acclimated to the noxious sulfur stink pervading the air of Sibley Springs, but now, as they neared the front entrance, the odor became almost visible, a pungent rotting that eroded one's ability to think about much else. What he drove through now were more of the shaggy pines that predominated in this belt of the South, and the building he pulled up before was no Delta mansion but a one-story log cousin to a hunting lodge tucked back into the trees behind a line of flatbed trucks. Even more of the paraphernalia he'd seen at the depot—gurneys, wicker baskets, wheelchairs, steel sinks—lay strewn about the yard that had been cut into the forest. Black men, some of whom Walter remembered from last night, stopped to watch as the Studebaker unloaded its passengers. They snuck doubtful, threatening glances as Carter had.

The entire spa stood on stilts about three feet tall, and down its short steps came a woman in a nurse's uniform and a blue wool cape whose age put her between Walter and Miss Dorcas. Her bearing and her forwardness in meeting Miss Dorcas halfway up the walk, how she grasped her hand with two of hers, marked her as a woman of importance in this place. "Welcome, Miss Dorcas! Welcome, Miss Louisa! It means so much that you would come for our last day."

The party made their way up the steps, Walter carrying the hamper for Goose, up and into the lodge, a most rustic affair. Only the cold drafts killed the ripe smell of wet wood. As busy as the spa appeared, with draymen and nurses wheeling and hauling objects about, it seemed that Miss Dorcas and Company were the only clients today. Another nurse, this one in a long gray coat, greeted them from behind an ornate mahogany desk that blocked passage to the hallway behind and all the doors to the rooms where the healing action of the sulfur waters had once, and for this last time, taken place. The more Walter looked, the more the spa showed itself to be less rustic than dilapidated, preparing for its abandonment. Long cracks webbed the plaster, and the same stains that indicated in the Mitchell House where frames had once hung edged similar bright rectangles of white amid the dingy walls. A pile of thin face towels had been thrown into one corner, torn and soiled sheets into another. Masses of cobwebs blurred the rough joints of the exposed log beams splintering overhead. What the building lacked in height, the log beams only pressing the ceiling down further, it made up for in sheer area; Walter counted eight rooms on each side before the hall ended in two arrows pointing in opposite directions toward other health-giving activities. All these things, combined with the stench of putrefaction, made the spa feel to him eminently more like a place that one sought healing *from* rather than in.

The nurse in the coat sprang up quickly. With nothing else in front of her atop the massive desk, apparently she'd been waiting just for them. "Halloo, Nurse Mansley!" said Miss Dorcas, and before the nurse could speak she held up a finger. "*Vous ne se parlent*. Not a word, Ah tell you. Not a word, or Ah shall weep." Relieved, Nurse Mansley guided her down the hall without a thought to the rest of them.

Louisa sighed, her hands still in the pockets of her black coat, as her aunt departed. The involuntary wrinkling of the girl's nose mirrored Walter's own discomfort in this dying place. "Tate, are you taking some water? Goose is."

Still in her bonnet, Goose had wandered over to the towels and sheets, and Walter hoped that she wouldn't touch any of them. "Paw say I have to," she said.

Tate, in a pair of brown knickers with his black socks up to his knees, a passably masculine outfit, lifted his chin and closed his eyes in a defiant pose.

"Oh, good Christ," said Louisa, after blowing on her hands. "*Captain,* are you taking some water? Dew pray tell me, mah laird," she asked, looking to the heavens in supplication. "I hang on thine every word."

Rather than firing back any sibling fury, the stung Tate wilted to the left like a heavy flower and said, "Ah shall inform Awnt Dorcas of your attitude befaw the help," staring at Walter as he spoke.

Louisa strode over and grabbed his sleeve. He pushed her hand off and yelled, "Ah'll take mah stand!"

She folded her arms again. "Come and have one glass with us."

"I'll not have water from the spout where that nigger Quine also drank."

"They say it makes you live forever . . ."

"I shall live forever in my poems!" He grabbed a lapel and declaimed,

> *Yeoman, rise and see*
> *The world this age has handed thee.*
> *For every passing year doth take our hearts*
> *To faster and more Northern parts.*

Walter turned to Louisa. "Did he write that?"

She shrugged. "Probably." Waving over to Goose, who had stood tummy forward and agog throughout the fraternal spat, Louisa walked past the desk and down the hall. "You stay here then, Captain, and hope nobody accidentally kills you. Come along, Goose. Mr. White?"

They made their way toward the two arrows, Louisa's rubbers squeaking on the tiles. As he passed each room, Walter peeked in and saw steel and copper tubs, sinks and spigots, some torn out and some in place, shockingly erect as they jutted out of the walls. Like the wreck of the flour mill, the spa was being stripped of everything that could have any possible value. "Miss Louisa, may I ask you something?"

Her curiosity piqued, glad to have some of her passing interest returned, she affected a thin veneer of propriety. "Why, yes, you may, Mr. White."

"Well . . ." Walter looked from floor to ceiling to wall, unable to find the proper description. "I'm wondering why exactly you come here."

"*Came* here." She smiled, though, having enjoyed the question.

"We came here four times a year, once a season, because it's what we remember. It's where the Warrens came. More folks go up into the mountains, especially around Sewanee. But this is where the Warrens go."

Assuming he'd follow, Louisa did not stop at the end of the hall but executed a crisp turn toward what the right arrow termed the "Fountain Room," weaving through workers and nurses the way he had run through broken fields in his football days. Rather than expecting others to move aside as she plowed through her course, she anticipated where others would be and made the slight adjustment that afforded them both ample room to pass. It was a small thing, but one that could not be taught. Walter had to admit that his heretofore grim view of Miss Warren was somewhat undeserved, based on little more than her white skin and blonde hair. The dire effects of crossing The Line could not reason away his curiosity, brewing now since he'd begun evicting Cornelia from his heart.

Louisa stopped at a set of swinging doors to make sure her entire party had arrived unscathed. Taking note of her thin nose, her cheeks flushed a pale rose, Walter had to rummage a bit to find the personality of Mr. Walter White, Exelento salesman, and even then he could only summon a halting, seemingly abashed version. "Have you ever played football," he asked, instantly embarrassed by the stupidity of the question and by her puzzled expression. "Because you really made your way around those people."

Her smile forgave him, as woman are always forgiving the minor stupidities of men. "I feel we must walk lightly in this life, don't you? Do a little calculus before each time we speak or act." She pushed open the door and shepherded them into a large room made to seem even larger by the enormous mirrors hanging on each wall. In the center, the focus of the entire spa, stood a tall enamel cylinder out of which protruded at least a dozen faucets dripping the famed restorative waters of Sibley Springs. The heavy mineral content had stained the once-snowy enamel beneath each faucet into a downward plume of the most pungent yellow-green. Tin cups lay scattered in no kind of order across the tiled floor, on the tables and lounge chairs surrounding the fountain, as if a roomful of patients had evacuated in a rush.

A veteran of the process, Louisa picked up a random, dusty cup with her thin fingers. Filling it from one of the taps, she handed it to Goose, who accepted with thanks and remained at Louisa's side as she took big gulps. The next was for Walter; Louisa inclined her head gently as she handed it to him. He imagined the leper who'd left it there as she shuffled off, the tubercular biddy coughing phlegm . . . Certainly, this was the font of Sibley Springs's odor, one of the many cracks in the world that opened onto Hell. Breathing through his mouth, Walter accepted with a "Dank you" and raised the cup to his lips.

Louisa giggled at his nasal accent, and the gag that came after. "It is overwhelming, isn't it? I guess I've become quite used to it bah now." She drew her own mug and sat down at a wicker chair, wincing at her own first sip. "Gad! It's awful!" They laughed. Walter sat down beside her. "I do think it is a pleasure to see oneself through the eyes of someone else. All the things one has done one's entire life suddenly seem so, Ah don't know. Optional." She held up the mug and grimaced. "Lahke drinking *this*."

"Are you a college student?"

"No," she said, smacking her lips and looking down into her water.

"I was wondering after you mentioned calculus . . ."

She pressed the tips of her fingers to her mouth and tightened the sides of her neck as if she'd been caught out at a trick. "I've been reading a book of trigonometry, that's all. I imagine college is great fun."

"All but calculus, which I found a positive trial."

Yesterday Walter had guessed her to be around his age, but the closer he looked the younger she became; nothing resembling crowsfeet at her eyes, and the commanding independence she'd thrown about before had begun to retreat under his attentions. She was probably college age right now, young enough to be Ludey's daughter.

Goose spilled a good half cup of water on herself as she watched the two young people chat. She wore the same dress of faded pink she'd had on the day before and had removed her bonnet, holding it in her free hand. "Oh, Goose." Scooting up from her seat, Louisa wiped at the girl with a towel. "You must be more careful. Won't you? Please?" Goose giggled and walked away a few steps, her head very obviously tilted in their direction so she could hear. "So you attended college?"

"I went to a school down in Georgia. You wouldn't have heard of it."

"I haven't met a salesman who could do much more than add a column or figure credit."

"I'm not really a salesman."

Had he just said that?

Intrigued, Louisa squinted. "Really?"

The lies didn't bubble out in the usual way. In fact, no words came for a moment. Walter suddenly stood up straight and saw himself in the mirror, saw that man that he'd seen early that morning in the bathroom at Mitchell's, that vehicle carting him about. As he stared at the handsome, blonde-haired, blue-eyed white couple facing him, a couple he was part of, he caught Louisa doing the same with a quick look from the corner of her eye. "I mean, I don't plan on being one all my life. I wanted to be a lawyer, but my family couldn't afford it so I went into insurance." For all the risks and reasons not to, he burst to tell her the truth, the truth in this case so much better than his lies. Walter White had, by any estimate—and no matter Cornelia's air of sufferance—a life both interesting and ambitious. He was a comer, a colleague of important people such as Mr. Johnson and Dr. Du Bois, in regular contact with wealthy white men who were familiar to the most exclusive corridors of power, men who treated him like an equal as much as they treated anyone that way, and he wanted to tell her all this not to shock her or enlighten her or sharpen her sense of justice, but in order to do what he'd wanted to do with every pretty *Negro* girl he'd ever met—to impress her. And here he was, stuck with his idiotic Exelento story. "Then I went into what I'm doing now. It seemed like an unusual opportunity."

Hiding behind his mug, the stink clearing his rhuemy head, he regretted choosing such a low-rent occupation when, wearing his whiteness, at least he could have credibly pretended to be a man of compelling interest. A sign across the room said *Gosmer Sibley Gazebo* in a gothic lettering different from the clinical type of the rest of the spa signage. It indicated a door beyond the fountain. "Miss Warren, would you like to walk? Maybe eat our lunch? I think I've had enough water, and I've been told the gazebo is quite pleasant."

"It's not much. Sort of sad, Ah actually think. People like such *sad* things." But with no further protest she put down her cup and now let him lead the way through the door and back outside. Another set of wooden steps took them to a gravel path that went into the wall of pines marching on the spa. Whatever sunlight remained on this brighter day could not fight its way through the boughs, and some alarm blared in his mind that he was about to enter the woods alone with a pretty young white woman about whom he knew nothing.

"I know yawl wanna be alone," shouted Goose from the steps, "but my paw told me not to leave your side, Miss Louisa."

Walter and Louisa looked away from each other, both embarrassed, and Louisa called back for her young charge, assured her that she was of course invited on their brief expedition back into the woods.

Now he would be entering the woods alone with *two* white females. Two members of white Southern womanhood that he realized that he would protect with great conviction from any harm. The first steps led his imagination on a perilous hike into a snake-ridden forest, but within only ten yards the trees were cleared and the gravel path took them to a gazebo in the same depressed circumstances as the Vale. Long ago the scene of summer band concerts and the late night grapplings of lovers, the octagon now served mostly as a shelter for small animals. Countless wasp nests hung up under the eaves of the roof, papery globes crafted at the expense of the gazebo that housed them.

Louisa, the back of her coat moving up and down in a way Walter found especially attractive, walked the circumference as the boards creaked. Spinning on her toes, she held her hands out, offering it all to Walter. "Well, here it is. Ah don't think Gosmer Sibley would be happy."

Walter pictured the side chops of some spectral Rebel colonel standing on end over the two people gracing his gazebo. "I think it needs a new coat of whitewash."

Louisa pointed at small holes that pocked the post closest to her. "And then there's the termites." With a hard shove, she sent a length of railing flying off into the grass. Surprised, Goose and Walter stopped what they were doing. "Ah fear things here may be well beyond repair."

"Well, it will serve our purpose, yes? Are you ready for lunch?" As he knelt to lay down the hamper, a board beneath him snapped and his foot plunged through the weak floor, scraping his leg, the sharp boards barking off the bone, and he bit his lip to prevent a florid run of poolhall cursing. Goose and Louisa hurried over to lift him up the few inches to safety. His dignity more scraped than anything else, Walter muttered, "I've come around to your way of thinking, Miss Warren. I think tearing this down would make *very* good sense."

Her generous lips pursed, Louisa dusted off the front of his coat with brisk, maternal strokes. "No one tears anything down around here, Mr. White. They let it rot." Walter's heart beat faster at her touch, heat rose on his cheeks. His moustache felt wispy and boyish, and he couldn't help twitching it. Louisa removed her hand and regarded him with amusement. "You've turned a most fetching new color, Mr. White. Very becoming." He felt the red all the way to his ears. "Have you read *Vanity Fair*? Ah think it is mah favorite book." Memories of Cornelia and that long night parsing Trollope sent a shiver up Walter's spine. Wandering off to the other side of the gazebo, Louisa laughed as if remembering a joke. "That Becky Sharp is a *pistol*." She walked idly on, minding Goose, as if this were her backyard. Considering how many years the Warren had probably been coming here, it may as well have been.

The blush in his face ebbed. "It's been a while since I read it, but I must say that I detect a bit of Miss Sharp in you."

Goose opened the latch of the hamper. "Mama gave us hard-boiled eggs and they's . . ."

"Oh, hardly. Ah think I'm more like Miss Austen's Emma."

"You're that good a person?"

"Well, they's nothing else but hard-boiled eggs," said Goose. "We got hard-boiled eggs."

"To the dismay of mah aunt Dorcas, Ah think Ah'm only just good enough."

Walter had done quite enough to warrant lynching already, so he decided to fly again. "I think it is better to be only just *bad* enough." Cornelia probably would have darted away at the first line of such banter, but Louisa smiled as if he'd only said something suitably flirtatious under the circumstances and took slow, considered steps toward him in the center. This, thought Walter, is what we imagine birds to be like, these beautiful white creatures that fly and sing. But black women must live the reality of a bird's life, scraping through the dirt for food, exhausting themselves for their short flights, everything done to survive. "I wouldn't mind taking a hand at writing a novel someday. I was a bit of a rhymester in my school days."

"Oh lookee! They's some cider. I'm agonna start eating if nobody minds," Goose answered.

"Ah would certainly read your book, Mr. White."

"Well, thank you very much." He twined a bit of vine in his fingers and wished Goose would leave them, or at least stuff herself silly with eggs. "And what does the future hold for *you,* Miss Warren?"

Faced with such a serious question, Louisa looked decidedly at sea. "I've yet to make a choice." Walter imagined her in a smock, trying her hand at sculpting or watercolors, pen to tongue as she ponders a worthy rhyme. Smart, but ultimately willing to serve by being fully in charge of her assigned realm, she would make a superb wife. For someone. Someone white.

"There's no need to rush." He wanted to have splendid parties, filled with sparkling people. She was the sort of woman who simply knew how things should be. Loving Ellanice, on the other hand, for all her depth, would be like loving all the pain of the earth. Was it possible, he wondered, to remember who you were, what had happened to you, and still have joy?

"These eggs is goo-*ood*!" Goose made a damp munching sound that spoiled the edges of Walter's mood. He imagined the eggs up in her teeth and the corners of her gums. She was absolutely getting a toothbrush when they got home. "Mama can *sho* bile an egg."

He gestured at the hamper. "Egg?"

They laughed a private laugh. Louisa took an egg and tapped the shell with a spoon.

"What's funny?" asked Goose.

"Nothing, dear," said Louisa. "These are perfectly de*lic*ious eggs."

From the line of trees, Tate's reedy voice called, "Louisa!" Walter started as if caught, tense the way he'd been last night when he'd heard the dogs. "Is that . . . man back there with you? That nigger Scipio has come alooking for him though what business a white man would have with him I do not know."

With no further announcement, Scipio barged down the path and onto the gazebo, which cracked audibly under the heavy tread of his nailed boots like hammer blows on the wood. Goose ran to him and Scipio didn't hesitate to pick her up and swing her around for a few revolutions until he finally put her down, saying, "I got to talk to Mistuh White, Miss Goose. Mistuh Drake sent me over." He switched to Walter, speaking without any of the accent he'd used in the street; this was last night's Scipio, the man he was when he was at home. "Seems like they's some news about your bags, Mistuh White. Why don't you come with me? I'll give you a lift back to the station."

So soon? Walter wondered what would she say if he told her who he was, what she would say if he said right now that he was on a secret mission. He had no interest in passing, had never thought of it seriously in the past, and remained uninterested now, so the question was whether she could see not a black man or white man, but just a man. He'd forgotten about the finger in his pocket, but once again it weighed heavily, bouncing against the pearls, and he fell back to earth. Apparently, joy and remembering were *not* possible together. Or was that, he thought, what being a Negro was all about?

No matter what, Walter had no plans to go back with Scipio, a man he did not trust or like. He'd get back to the station on his own. "Thank you for bringing the message, but I'll be accompanying Miss Warren and Miss Dorcas home." Walter turned away.

"They's trouble with yo' bag! You hear me? You gotta come double quick." Scipio grabbed his arm.

The gazebo went silent. Scipio's hand jumped off Walter's sleeve as if burned and Tate squeaked, "Now see he-ah!"

"Please forgive me Mistuh White, Miss Warren. Suh, I didn't mean . . ."

Walter tried to get a look at Louisa's expression, but Scipio blocked him.

"It's all right, Scipio . . ."

Tate stomped over, indignant, laughable with his knickered petulance, but very dangerous if he shouted any louder. "Something *must* be done about this niggah! Just because Quine had the nerve to come up he-ah and put his mouth to the faucet don't mean . . ."

Walter peered around Scipio, desperate to see Louisa's reaction to the kind of deadly idiocy a black man endured every day. She looked at Tate with distaste, but that told him nothing. Louisa couldn't be judged by her face.

Goose screamed out a defense. "You leave him alone!"

Drops of sweat appeared on Scipio's head. "Mistuh White, I would never . . ."

"No wonder nobody's coming to this place . . ."

Walter looked back toward the spa to see if anyone had noticed what was going on. Extending a calm hand, he said, "Now Tate, Goose is right. Scipio's a good boy. Wouldn't ever mean to harm a man, now would you, Scipio?"

The two men stared at each other.

"No suh. Never. I just come to help you out, Mistuh White. Bring you back to the station 'cause there's *trouble* with yo' bag." Scipio's eyes stayed locked on Walter's. The third use of the word "trouble" finally sank into Walter's head and made him think at last of his own well-being instead of Louisa's reaction to this highly unpleasant scene.

At last she stepped closer. "Of course, you meant no harm, Scipio. Tate, leave him alone." Louisa looked to Walter, who still couldn't find a purchase on her expression. "It's all right, Mr. White. Ah kin drive the car just fine; Aunt Dorcas just prefers a man driving.

We most certainly understand. I'll see Goose home safely." She smiled a most pleasant smile, perfectly appropriate under the circumstances and disappointing.

"I hope I'll see you again," said Walter, still not moving.

Scipio spoke for him. "I thinks Mistuh Drake may get him on a special coming through any minute." He looked at Walter again. "But only if we leave this second."

"Yes," she said. "That would be a great pleasure for me."

As they walked away around the building, toward a rough wagon hitched to a mule, Goose shouted out, "Goodbye, Lou!" her giggles more like the whoop of some ungainly bird of the forest floor. Walter repeated Louisa's words over and over to himself. Seeing Scipio ahead straightening up from the servile bend he affected around white folks, he realized that he hadn't asked her a thing about the lynching.

Nineteen

Walter resisted an impulse to slap Scipio on the back and share a laugh at how Rabbit and Bear had just pulled one on the white folks. Once well away from the spa, he finally folded his arms and said, "You're welcome."

Scipio cracked a leather strip off the hindquarters of the mule pulling them. "Yeah, well you pretty goddamn welcome too."

"What should I thank *you* for? I just saved your ass back there. I'm here to save *your* life."

The eyes bulged out of Scipio's sockets, and he made his lips go slack as the infuriating darkie accent returned. "Oh thankee Mistuh White! Thankee fo' savin' that son a bitch Ludey Fentress! Thankee so much fo' sippin' the waters with dat fine little white girl! It's made all the difference fo' us po' darkies!"

Blushing, moustache bobbing up and down, Walter hissed, "You bastard."

"You ain't savin' mah life, White; I'm just trying to survive *you*. Fortune got all riled up and now he's missin'. You better get your oc-to-roon self outa this town, you hear me?"

Walter sat back. "Where'd he go?"

"Well if'n we knew that, he wouldn't be missin', would he?" Rolling his eyes, Scipio cracked the lash again. "Christ, you is *stupid,* ainchu? You just walk in here an' think you gonna *fix* things for all us po' country folk."

"We want to put the people responsible in jail. We want to stop lynching and you're crushing the soul of every Negro in Sibley Springs by . . ."

"I'm takin' you to Mitchell's." The mule rolled into a trot. "You go upstairs an' get your bag and wait at the station for the six o'clock."

"Chasing me out of town, huh? Well then, what are you gonna do about finding Fortune?" Walter dug into his pocket and pulled out the crumpled roll of wax paper. "I've done more for the Quines in one morning than you've done in a week. Here." He thrust the finger at Scipio. "Give this to Ellanice. At least they'll have something to bury now."

Scipio recoiled. "Get that outa here! That ain't no Quine anymore; that's some white man's charm, is what that is. You so white you don't even know the difference."

The insult landed, but Walter didn't give him the satisfaction of knowing. "What are you gonna do about Dulcet's ring and their money?"

"Listen, you figure out yet that ole Cleon wasn't anybody's favorite nigger? He had money an' he wasn't too happy about plantin' it in another man's field, an' now Dulcie's crying about her gold ring while people on their knees pickin' seeds outa mule shit 'cause it's too dear to waste and I'm supposed to go up against the white man? You a goddamn crazy man, is what you is."

"You're in over your head, Scipio."

"No, White. You in over *yo'* haid. Fortune wants to kill hisself some white men. He wants to go chase after that Reverend Lewis who had a big enough mouth but never did anything but read his newspaper and talk."

"He's a young man trying to find his future, Scipio. You don't see that. Burghardt—you know, Dr. Du Bois—would be able to help him go to a good . . ."

"Who's all these people you always talkin' about? And why do I *care*? I knowed Fortune since he was a boy, and he always set nice an' quiet right up to when he bust out, and believe me, that boy's bustin' out right now. You clear on what that bustin' out gonna do fo' us all, White? I'm already hearin' your friends talkin' about a posse to find him. Do you understand, Mr. College Man, what gonna happen? They gonna burn us *down*. They gonna hunt us in the *bushes*. You probably don't have a lot of that in Nooo York City, do you? Mommas hidin' their babies. Families with old folks layin' in the bushes, prayin' they don't get sliced up and burned up by a pack o' white mens. I ain't riskin' every black life in this town for Fortune. No sir. Let the ones who lives here deal with it, and you go back up No'th. Get yo' shoes shined."

Walter chewed at the inside of his cheek, tapped his fingers on his seat. Scipio may have been right, but what about the Quines? If the very people he had come to defend were not defended, then he wouldn't have achieved anything here, really. As far as Scipio was concerned, Fortune was on his own. Walter was suddenly positive that he was the only man who could save the Quine family. It was too late to run now, even if his job was officially done. Shillady had given him enough money for a week—he could afford one more night to find Fortune Quine. To prove Hillman innocent of the crimes he claimed for himself.

"Scipio, you know who you're named after?" He didn't wait for an answer. "A long time ago . . ."

"Scipio done conquered Africa. Beat down the one nigger ever beat the white man. Yeah, I get it. And you be Hannibal, right? Ooooh, you so *smart,* White. Done give yo'self the best part in the show." The driver caught Walter's surprise. "Maybe we ain't all country niggers huh? You so busy in New York, doing your important things that going help every single nigger an' his mama. Well, crick crack, things ain't always been like this. Not here. Nope. Once there was a terrible storm, see? Knocked down all the trees in the forest and the houses and especially Brer Fox's house and all the houses of his family, see?"

"I don't have time for none a Shy's niggah tales right now."

Scipio ignored him. "Them moles was so happy to come out and nobody both'rin' them, see? Nobody eatin' them. Nobody stealin' away they sisters and daughters and mothers and forcin' theyselves on them. So these is good times for the moles, man. They be building houses and writing Constitutions and going to Mole School and everythings going fine, 'cept Brer Fox ain't so happy 'cause he not living in the big house anymore. Naw, he just got a cave like everybody else now, but he don't like that. So you know what kind a tricky thing he done, Brer Fox? It was so sharp, I gotta tell you. So sharp."

He used the same storyteller inflection Walter heard yesterday at the Mitchells', but the summers in the fields and the winters watching black children die, his calculated groveling, had all whetted Scipio's words to an edge.

"Well, what he done was walk into Moletown and just start eatin' up the moles. Yep. Just et 'em up. Eat the papas and the mammys and the little babies. Not all at once now, 'cause that wouldn't be sportin'. No they just eat 'em up one by one, but mostly in front of all the other moles so they get the idea. And suddenly them moles got pretty hard to find. They dug themselves new holes 'cause they ain't all got cash money to train theyselves up to Chicago or New York or Pittsburgh and some of them . . ." Scipio shook his head and smiling as if he couldn't believe it himself. "Some of them goddamn moles actually *like* it here. Can you believe that? They like it! It's their home, see? They whole lives spent here fishing in the river and working the ground, and they want to keep on livin' here without becoming no meal."

The smoke of Sibley Springs could be seen now, but not the town. "No real wisdom in that story, is there, Scipio? Mostly excuses. You gonna stay on the *Titanic* when it starts sinking? Keeping pumping away for the Captain so he has time to get in the lifeboat?"

Scipio dropped the reins and smashed his fist down on the board they sat on. "Motherfucker, *that's* a story, okay?" He lowered his voice as if trying to reason with a madman. "I'm a goddamn country nigger, but as far as I know they wasn't no niggers on that boat, see? And if they was, the white folks woulda been using they dead bodies for rafts, so you can uplift my nigger ass all you want, but I'm just trying to live another day, brother." He was pleading now. "Get everybody in this town their forty acres."

The first buildings appeared around a bend. "Where do you think Fortune went?"

"Don't you get *nuthin'*? I don't care. I just don't want him acomin' back, that's all. Look here," said Scipio. "I don't have no grudge with Fortune. I watched him grow up, cuffed him when he needed to learn what it felt like to get cuffed. I stopped other folks from cufffin' *him*. I took care a him like a baby brother. An' I known *her* since we was babies. This still be a good place to live for *every* one if Ellanice break up that land. Hand it over to the rest of the niggers, give everybody else their forty. What'd be wrong with that? What'd be wrong with me and her being married and givin' that land away so that there'd be just enough for everyone to have?" Scipio looked at Walter, his voice sincere and very tired. "I mean it, White." All the roles, all the voices, were wearing him down. "What's *wrong* with that plan?"

Walter couldn't answer that, so he put it out of his mind. The station was finally in sight. "Drop me in front of the bank."

"I'm gonna find you wherever you is and put you on the six, dead or alive."

Walter smiled. In the last twenty-four hours he had prepared for death at least three times, and it was only getting easier, his mortality now an unpleasant acquaintance he kept running into at a party. "Oh, I think Tate and Miss Warren would have something to say about that now, don't you? No, that bag's at least another day away. I got some work to do. Know what I mean?" They'd reached the station. "Changed my mind. Let me off here."

Scipio did nothing to slow the mule, so Walter hopped out of the moving wagon. "You only walkin' the streets because of Ellanice. You be smart."

As Scipio's wagon went left and crossed the tracks, Walter walked faster and faster until he was trotting into town, but to where and to what ends he had no clue as he passed Sundy's Barber Shop and found himself standing just where he'd been a few hours earlier. He was looking for a boy he didn't know, in a place he'd never been to before. He was searching for truth and justice, but the definitions he carried now seemed imprecise, the victims and the guilty all squirming in the same bag. Scipio would kill him if he wasn't on the next train. He had three hours to save the life of *someone* in this town.

Standing at the intersection of the two main roads, Walter let the meager flow of Saturday in Sibley Springs curl around him as if he were a large rock in the Elk River. Horses and mules swerved past as he searched for clues in the wagons, on the boarded front of the butcher and the faded letters around the doors of Vine's. The pale brick of the bank offered nothing but permanence amid all the wooden buildings of Main Street. Walter scanned the second floor. Under a set of blinds slightly askew, painted in a script that identified more than it announced, the words. *Lee Palgrave, Esq.* stared down at him from a window. Cleon Quine's destination before he'd run into the boys.

He'd left a very large stone unturned. Stepping in front of a slowly moving Ford flatbed, Walter went through the single entrance along the bank's otherwise blank side wall and headed up the stairs to a frosted glass door painted with the same *Lee Palgrave, Esq.* in similarly discreet letters. Putting his ear to the glass, Walter heard nothing. He tested the knob and found it unlocked, so he gently pushed the office door open.

TWENTY

The office of Lee Palgrave, Esq., was a world unto itself. Blinds on the windows kept the room dim, the sounds of the street distant. Legal bookshelves fronted with glass and filled with identically bound volumes made up most of one wall beside two tall stacks of filing cabinets. A brown leather couch sat under the windows abutting on the left a most unusual thing to find in Sibley Springs, an ancient Chinese vase at least three feet high, cast in vivid blues and red and golds. An immense desk, angled in the corner, faced the door. Framed photographs, documents, and maps covered every free stretch of wall; an ancient baseball made of thick leather stitched with thong, a bronze trophy cup, a stuffed bear paw, what appeared to be a genuine Indian tomahawk, and more of the like covered the cabinets and the desk, mounded on legal files. The only space not covered with ephemera was the center of the desk where, under a pool of light from a lamp shaded with green glass, a man lay face down, arms at his sides, eyes closed, atop his blotter.

At first glance, Walter feared he'd come across a dead body, but in a second he detected air moving in and out of the man's nose with the leisure of a good nap, saw his chest rise and fall, and imagined Palgrave succumbing with a thump to the demands of Morpheus. He smiled. Indeed, the room would put anyone in the mood for

241

sleep; silent, warm, and cossetted with memories, it hardly encouraged an activist mind.

So this, thought Walter, is what a lawyer does. Palgrave wore a hunting jacket of heavy brown tweed with leather patches on the elbows. Nicely cut and apparently cozy enough to pull extra duty as a blanket, the jacket was the first object Walter had seen in Sibley Springs that he genuinely coveted. A little good taste earned the lawyer a longer nap; Walter let him sleep on as he stole a long look around. The largest thing in the room was something he hadn't noticed. On the wall to his right, not visible behind the opened door, hung an oil painting of a man done in a rustic style, though clearly attempting to emulate Gilbert Stuart or some other vision of epic American heroism. The subject depicted, an elderly gentleman in a hunting jacket not unlike Palgrave's, hounds swarming at his feet, stood with one hand on a ruined pillar amid a forest clearing. A shotgun, cracked opened to symbolize the man's peaceful nature, lay in the crook of the other arm. First glance presented a distinguished work, but it crumbled upon closer examination; one noticed that the eyes were not level, the fingers had been stretched to an abnormal length, and the impressionistic rendering of the trees surrounding the hunter appeared in truth a matter of inability not aesthetic intention. Walter moved on to the photographs, all of places that he now recognized: the spa, looking very much like the resort he had pictured, or at least its clientele, a crowd of women in long dresses with frilly hems dusting across the pines needles as they assembled for a portrait in front of the newly christened gazebo. Four houses, the grandly styled ones down by the river, standing alone with a dozen children in knickers and pinafores; an intact and clearly thriving Timmons Flour Mill; a group shot of a uniformed band surrounding the Vale of the Confederate Dead. The shiny bell of a tuba had caught the light of that day however many years ago and a lanky and familiar man, despite the seriousness of the occasion, beamed like a boy on his birthday.

"I'll be damned," whispered Walter as he reached out for the photo.

The sounds of great stirring—wool shifting, a chair creaking, deep breaths and finally one powerful snort finished with the smacking of lips—announced that Lee Palgrave, Esq., had awakened.

Before Palgrave could say anything or, for that matter, rise much above a crouch, Walter stood over him with an outstretched hand. "Walter White. The door was open, so I took the liberty . . ." Still bleary, Palgrave blinked a few times like an old man, though he was not yet old, not quite yet, and nodded as he shook Walter's hand. "I'm sorry if I disturbed you . . ."

Pushing himself up from his chair, he worked out some knots with a twist of his neck. Erect, Palgrave showed himself to be well built and flat stomached, accustomed to an active lifestyle, though the softness of his hands pointed to a genteel sort similar to the one portrayed in the painting. A full head of dark brown hair curled across his head in long, dense waves, one of the features that still held him on this side of life's later borders; a young woman could still possibly find him attractive, though not for much longer. Unlike the sickly white and jaundiced yellow of so many in Sibley Springs, Palgrave's skin had a ruddy, rich cast. "No suh. Ah'm the one to apologize," he said with a mossy gentry burr. "Ah have not been sleeping well of late, and by this tahm a day it seems to catch me. How ah you, suh? I heard your name spoken on the street this morning. Seems you performed some act of great charity or . . ."

Walter fended off the complement. "No. In fact, the other men saved Fentress. Not me."

The lawyer inclined his head to indicate Walter could have it his way if he preferred. Like the vase, Palgrave's patrician manner, both benign and edifying, passed a kind of judgment on the viewer, who could never be as old or as beautiful as the object, nowhere near as wealthy or wise as its owner. And yet the dust that Walter saw on the frames, the slanted blinds, the midday nap for whatever the reason, placed Palgrave not at the head of some hidden Sibley Springs nobility, but as a remnant of what it may once have been, and this office was the museum that housed it. Though a taste for Jack Daniels' whisky was as likely a reason for the lawyer's slow pace as Southern gentility, no crystal decanter sparkled on a silver tray, no jug peeked from under the desk, nor did Palgrave give off the stench of a drunkard.

Too kind to ask the cause of this pleasant visit, Palgrave assumed a pensive expression as he waited for Walter to explain himself. "Mr. Mitchell mentioned he had a parcel of land he was interested in selling, and I'd like to take a look at it." Walter made a show of checking both ways for eavesdroppers; with an oddball like Palgrave before him, he rediscovered the fun in stretching some truths. "I told him I wasn't interested, but I think you and I are smart men. I wanted to speak to an independent party. Someone who could steer me right."

Palgrave gestured for Walter to sit in a leather club chair in front of the desk. Yawning briefly, he took his own seat again, pressing his fingertips together while they sat in silence. There was no picture of a wife or children on his desktop. The younger man started tapping his toe and turned to the portrait. "Is this your father?"

"Oh no. No. That's Mistuh Gosmer Sibley."

"The founder of . . . ?"

"The very one."

Walter shifted into high Exelento salesman gear. "Well, *he* was a smart man." He drummed his fingers on Palgrave's desktop, hoped to keep him awake if not entirely aware. "This is a mighty pretty place, pretty favorable to man's living. I could see myself settling down here." One of the big houses down by the river, maybe; Louisa carving away at a mound of wet clay. As soon as he imagined it, though, he wondered why he hadn't pictured Ellanice.

"Cherokees have come to the spring for centuries, so they'ahs always been a settlement around he-ah of some sort, but Sibley caught wind the railroad would be passing through. He bought up just about every parcel he could. Made himself quite comfortable. And then, of course, the War. There were a number of interesting holding actions in this area . . ."

The history lecture rolled off Walter. Although Palgrave showed no signs of drink or any other sapping vice, his shoulders sagged, and as he spoke he leaned forward in a way that made Walter fear he would flop onto his desk again at any moment. His jacket, his shirt, the pattern of his tie all had a timeless quality to them, as easily worn by his grandfather as bought on a business trip to Memphis. He sighed. Remaining in the present was hard work for Lee Palgrave. "Your friend Mitchell has a small lot." Kept in his chair by ennui, he pointed to a map on the wall. "In town. Inherited it from his wife's family. Good for a shop, but . . ." He smiled in a greasy way, as if delivering bad news that secretly pleased him. ". . . you need a clientele. The butcher just boarded up. No trade."

"That's a bad sign."

"Yes, it is." They sat again for a moment. Though Palgrave clearly didn't like to say more than he had to, his reticence seemed unrelated to any client privilege. Walter fixed on a photo over Palgrave's shoulder, a shot of a lively downtown Sibley Springs lined with carriages and buggies, people three wide on the sidewalk. "Just how much land you lookin' fo-ah? I will say to you that farming's still a good living in these parts."

"You must be joking, Mr. Palgrave. I may not be from these parts, but I'm nobody's fool. I've seen some hard cases out there."

"Mr. White, my family no longer *farms*," He raised his voice on the last word with a Southern inflection that intimated that they now did some other terribly lucrative thing. ". . . but I do know that it demands as much thought and intelligence as any other occupation.

For those who treat it like a business and a calling, these have been very, and may I stress *very*, good years. Those who simply dig holes in the dirt . . ." He tilted his head toward the window. "They have suffered." He shrugged dismissively, then realized that he sounded a bit more Utilitarian than a good Christian should. "Which is a great shame." They both nodded, commiserated on the unfairness of life for as long as Palgrave could hold back his interest in making a deal. "There *are* two sizable parcels that are available. There's the Quine estate, which I assume they'll be liquidating without Cleon." He grimaced, then held up a restraining finger. "Unless that Scipio marries Ellanice." Palgrave picked up a horse's hoof that held down a stack of papers, examined its bottom. "You know he was near about the biggest landowner in the county?"

"Who? Quine?"

"Yes." The lawyer kept looking at the hoof, did not make eye contact.

"Colored landowner, you mean."

"No." Now Palgrave put the hoof down. "The biggest landowner of any race. He was on his way here to buy out Miz Fentress when . . ." He wriggled his fingers in the air, unwilling to speak the words. "That would be the *other* idea. Bank won't foreclose now, but Miz Fentress would still like to move that parcel." Palgrave noticed Walter's amazed expression. "Surprised?"

"Well . . ."

"If he had closed the deal with Miz Fentress he would have been flat out the biggest holder in Franklin County." Palgrave said this with a pride that puzzled Walter. "For a nigger, that Cleon was a hell of a man." He folded his arms and leaned back into his chair. "His mother's side was ours. If you weren't ours, you were the Timmons. Some of the farmers would rent out a nigger here and there, but the Timmons, the Sibleys, the Palgraves, and the Quines were the only real landowners before the War. Slaves would get sold back and forth.

246

Families only married with each other. By now there's more than a few drops of every family's blood in all us Timmons. And Palgraves. And Quines. Every family."

Surely that blood spread across race lines as well. Walter caught Palgrave's eyes to deliver a doubtful look but as he did so, he noticed that the lawyer was looking at him just as deliberately and just as silently. Palgrave had not limited what he'd said to simply the white families. He'd been careful to make that point. Walter squinted at Palgrave's outdoorsy complexion. The color spread well beyond his face. His hands, his ears, his neck, were all the same cast, and Walter had to fairly bite his tongue not to ask if he . . . *was* . . . Maybe he'd never been told. Or maybe he'd just been out grouse hunting last week and took too much sun. Maybe it was just warm in the room and he was flushed.

The lawyer tapped his blotter with his fingertip. "When that boy set his mind on something, he did it. He up and went to New York City, oncet."

Ludey Fentress was certainly not the mayor. He lived on his mama's land. Next to a small engraved trophy—Walter made out the words *Princeton University*—a rectangular brass clock with a handle on top suddenly rang three. Time was running out. "So you were here the morning of the lynching."

Palgrave winced at the word, lifted a quill pen, and twirled it in his fingers. "So aberrant for our town, Mr. White. We take care of our own. But Stiles and Mathers were bad business and Trick, well we all knew Trick would get himself killed sooner or later. Cleon got out of his buggy, and they start up their business which . . ." Palgrave's voice pitched stronger. He pulled his head back as he spoke now and gesticulated with his hands as if laying out the case. Walter realized that he'd be the lawyer for whoever they could pin the lynching on. Or Quine if he'd been allowed a trial. ". . . I must point out was something they did to nearly every person in Sibley Springs, namely to throw pebbles and hurl insults. They were thugs, I give you that. I do." He hit his palm with his fist on each word, making his closing argument. "But they—were—not—*men*! That's what Cleon got wrong. They weren't playing a man's game. They were not throwing rocks to *hurt* him. They were throwing pebbles to *annoy* him, and that's nothing they haven't done to me, nothing they hadn't done to any number of people in Sibley Springs, Negro and white, every day of the week."

Walter tried to imagine how long he could put up with having pebbles thrown at him every day. "Wasn't the daughter there as well?"

Palgrave averted his eyes and nodded guilty admission. "Yes. Yes, she was, and that was surely where the boys overstepped their bounds. Ellanice is a fine colored girl. She can be a fresh one, though. Got it from her mother." He smiled here, lolling back pastward again. "You know, Dulcie and I were raised together, nearly brother and sister. Her mama was my mammy."

"Really?" As hard as he tried, Walter could not *tell* and so hungry was he for that Livingstone out here in the wilds, he considered some kind of subtle testing of how deep Palgrave went. Yet a mistake would be more than embarrassing; it would kill him. All his life, he'd heard the old line that Southerners should be left to deal with the Negroes because they knew them, because they loved them in a way Northerners didn't, and every time he'd heard that the top of his head nearly flew off, but Palgrave proved it to him. Southerners really did know Negroes better because they were family. Just about every person, black and white, had some sister or brother or aunt or uncle or cousin or niece or nephew somewhere close or with some removes that was of the other race. Southerners didn't have family trees; they had thick vines of lineage that swallowed everything near them. In their lonely fields, they'd allowed unsolvable tangles of blood to grow that not only made race abstract, but strained every idea as well as to what made up a family. Their crimes were not the calculated hatred of chilly Northerners; they were crimes of passion against the families they denied.

"Indeed. Dulcie was a *fiery* girl. I imagine one of boys tried to have his way with Ellanice sometime. She's a pretty one, and she isn't one to have a white boy. No sir." Walter couldn't tell if Palgrave spoke with regret, pride, or admiration. "Anyway, Cleon shouted, and I heard this from right here at my desk, he shouted to the boys exactly these words—'Ahm jes' about set to own the county, so's you should drop by mah place if'n you want jobs.' Well, that just set the whole thing off."

Walter breathed hard through his nose to stifle a laugh. "I will be goddamned." He suddenly felt small in his clothes, small in the general scheme of things. Cleon had been a warrior, a guerrilla fighter as tough as General Forrest, holding off the white hordes until he was swamped. "Did he *really* say that?"

"He absolutely did." Palgrave shook his head in amazement, but he did not accompany it with any curses, had not curled his lips into a sneer. Were they sharing the same thought?

"Ever heard of a place up in the mountains called Diddy Wah Diddy?"

Palgrave looked at him a long time and didn't even pretend to think about the question, didn't scratch his chin or wrinkle his nose, before he said no in a brisk way that could mean many things, none of them a definitive no. If there was more he could tell, he wasn't telling.

"So Quine never actually bought the land?"

"No. Miz Fentress and Ludey was up ahere watchin' with me when it all started. Ludey was pretty upset at first, 'cause he thought they was 'bout to lose out on the money." The lawyer slumped, exhausted by his delivery of the facts, eager, it seemed to get back to his nap. Walter stopped himself before he asked about Cleon's money; that would show that he knew too much. "Now, you could easily take a look-see at both parcels, if you care too. Don't even need me along. The Fentress land is on the highway just out of town heading north, on your left. The Quine land starts right back of the Camp-bellite church on the right side of the road. Right about where the . . . lynching took place."

"They lynched him on his own land?"

Palgrave picked up the quill again, paused before he spoke. "Yes, they did. The Negroes were wise to stay inside their homes."

"What about his boy?"

The lawyer shook his head. "He has some big boots to fill. Always has. It's a hard thing when your father is such a fighter. Cleon rode him hard, but he taught him some things too, so you don't know which direction he's gonna go."

Walter stole a look at the clock, stood up. "Mr. Palgrave, you have been a tremendous help. With your permission, I'm going to take a look at the properties right now. I plan to be on the train tomorrow, or as soon as my sample cases come. You see, I'm a . . ." His work fin-ished, Palgrave's eyes had glazed over, and he nodded like a mute, devoid of any interest in Walter. "I'll stop by once I've had a look."

He closed the door behind himself, waited for a count of five, then opened it again. Palgrave's head had already hit the desktop.

"Fentress left, Quine right. Yes?"

The lawyer didn't lift his head or even open his eyes. "Correct."

"Thanks." Walter gently shut the door.

Back on the street, evening neared. Walter wondered where to head next. The person he most needed to see right now was Ellanice, but crossing the tracks was simply not possible. Whatever Scipio threat-ened to do to him, Walter would have to wait until nightfall. As he was trotting down the sidewalk with the Mitchell House in his sights, Baxter Vine burst through the doors of the store and planted himself in front of Walter.

"Just the man I was looking for."

Walter swallowed. The dubious trophy still sat in his pocket. "Well, hey, Bax. Awful sorry about that mess I made. If that's what you need . . ."

The grocer turned up his nose at the thought. "Naw. That was nothing. No." He opened the door with his right hand and waved Walter in with his left. "Come on in. Come on. I want to talk some business wichu." Not quite sure what Baxter meant, Walter returned his grin and entered the store. Vine had turned the lamps up high. "Wanna order me some a that hair straightener you peddlin'," said the storekeeper, but in a sly way that suddenly charged the air as if storm clouds had massed on the horizon. "Scipio was here lookin' to buy some."

"Bax, I don't know if you've noticed, but he's bald."

"For his mama, he said."

"Oh." No one else was in the store. "Hey, where's Feldon?"

"He gone home. Things pretty much thinned out for the day." Baxter came back around the counter and stood before a particularly ominous display of knives, hatchets, and other potentially deadly objects, shining in the lamplight. "Jes' you and me now, Mr. White." He placed an elbow on the counter and put his chin on his hand, made a small, smug grin. If he'd been a kitten playing with a string yesterday during the card trick, he was now a cat batting a mouse with his claws. "Jes' you and me."

Walter talked quickly; words were his only weapon. "Now you know I don't have my samples. That's why I haven't bothered going through the show with you. Lord knows I'm dying to sell you everythin' in my case but I can't in any kind of conscience expect you to place an order without having seen or touched or otherwise experienced for your own self the full line of Exelento products. I mean, I'd be happy to take an order from you. Sure. I mean I'd have to go back up to Mitchell's and pick up my order book 'cause I just don't have it on me . . ." He pulled his pockets inside out to prove that they were empty. ". . . I'd be happy to run on back there, get my book and log up an order from you but you know what? I believe that once you get your hands on what we offer, you're gonna order twice as much as you would right now. Hell. Forget twice. I think you'll order three times what you want to ring up right now once you see what we can offer you and your customers. That's my risk, see? That's the risk I'm gonna take because that's how much I believe in Exelento products."

About halfway through this speech, Baxter Vine had pulled himself up off the counter and leaned against the racks of trowels and spades. As Walter took a breath, Baxter grinned again, sucked his teeth, and said, "You ain't no drummer, White. You been lyin'."

Twenty-One

Five years before, a Howard linebacker had put a shoulder into Walter's gut and knocked the wind out of him, a suffocating sensation that came close to what he fought through now to speak. "Well now, Bax, that's a fine . . ."

The grocer stroked his jaw. "I mean, you're good. You got the lines down, brother. But you ain't no drummer."

He'd gone too far with the finger. Walter was sure of it. "Bax, you got me wrong . . ." Content to let his prey writhe some, Vine kept sucking his teeth and grinning. He wasn't buying the Exelento salesman bit, no matter what Walter said.

He dropped his shoulders in resignation, took a deep breath. "You got me, Bax. You got me good." They both nodded. "I'm not a traveler." Walter leaned in toward the counter and beckoned the grocer forward with a finger. "But since you caught me, I'll tell you." Like at Palgrave's, he checked the room to make sure it was secure.

"Jes' you an' me, White," said Vine warily. "Jes' like I said."

"Good." One more shift of his eyes, and Walter whispered, "I'm a newspaperman." He nodded slowly. "Reporter for the *Chicago Daily News,* and let me just tell you that more than a few people up there think the right thing happened down here." The suspicion on Vine's face crumbled. "Trainloads of niggers coming into our town every day, and I'll tell you, folks up North starting to understand what we been saying all along." Walter winked and pressed on. "I'm down here trying to get the truth. And I mean the *truth*. No more Yankee lies." He spat in the direction of the stove, though it landed only halfway there, right in the center of the aisle.

Vine lit up, unconcerned by the oyster on his floor. "You Southerner?"

Walter touched his heart as if taking an oath. "Born in Atlanta. Just doing a job up North, but I'm a Southern man through and through, and I'd like to get our side of the story out there."

"Oh hell, I thought for a while there you was some kind of gov-amint agent or something."

Walter winked again. The reporters he'd met had been inveterate winkers, desperately in the know. "The worst of a bad lot, my friend. Ink for blood. No lyin'. So hey, listen. I done interviewed everybody else. I been saving you for last because you know the *real* story."

The grocer arranged his tie, brushed the front of his apron. "Well, I . . ."

"You got a piece of paper I could borrow? I was just aheadin' back to Mitchell's for my notebook when you jumped out."

Vine couldn't be helpful enough, pulling his own order book out of his pocket and handing it to him with a pencil. "Will this do? I got a few other . . ."

Walter licked the tip of the pencil, wiggled his arm to loosen it up. "No, sir. You got me all set up here now. Alrighty, let me ask you a couple easy things first off. What's your full Christian name?"

"Baxter A. Vine."

"Age?"

"Forty-six."

"Married?"

"Eighteen years to Miss Goldie Parker of Cowan." Vine suddenly looked nervous and tried to get a look at the pad over Walter's shoulder. "Could we . . . ? Do you think you could say 'eighteen *glorious* years to Miss Goldie Parker of Cowan'?"

Walter clucked his tongue. "I knew you were a smart man the minute I saw you. Consider it done. Children?"

"Edgar. He's eleven."

"Alrighty. Eleven. So Baxter A. Vine, proprietor of Vine's General Store in Sibley Springs . . ."

Vine grinned, saw the words in print already. "Hardware our specialty."

". . . Hardware . . . their . . . specialty. Got it. Mr. Vine, did you know this Cleon Quine?"

"Well, hell, sure I did. Everybody knows everybody round here."

"You do business with him?"

"Sure. I do business with all the niggers. Cleon's the only one I gave credit, though. Son of a bitch had money, I'll tell you that. Came in with an envelope first day of every month, paid his bill in full."

"Hard to make a living that way."

"You telling me. And he was a talker, too. During harvest he come into town alaughing, saying he got a better yield than anybody in the county. I mean the boys with the scales made sure he was a liar, but damn if that didn't get folks ariled up."

Walter wrote down *talker* and *yield*. "Now what about those poor young men he killed? I haven't heard enough about them."

Still clogged from his cold, Baxter cleared his nose and added his own oyster to the floor. "Po' young mens? They was near ta dogs is what they was. I mean you ask most folks in this ahere town and they'd tell you justice was done all around. Cleon took care a three of the worst sons a bitches we ever seen in these parts, and then we got shed of the uppitiest nigger to boot. If it weren't for all them Yankees circling around, we'd be happy to wipe our hands clean and figure this whole story for over."

Shoving his hat back up to the crown of his head, Walter screwed up his face. Time for the hard questions. "So we have Ludey and Hillman and Nip to thank for this? They were the ones who chased him down? Ran the show?"

By this point, Baxter would pretty much tell him what he liked to do with Miss Goldie Parker of Cowan in their marriage bed, so thrilled was he to be in personal contact with the fourth estate, but the grocer shut down, pressing his lips together as he visibly struggled with what to say next. "Well, you know, those three is good fellers mostly, and there was a lot a people involved."

"How many you think? Pretty much the whole town?"

Again, Baxter hesitated, scratched behind his ears and otherwise behaved like someone with something to hide. "Well, we had a good three trainloads a people come into town. I'd say a few thousand was walking around by the time the train brings him back from McMinnville."

"Now, I know that, Bax, but Hillman told me that him and Nip and Ludey was the ones that really brought it on. Brother, I'm not lookin' to turn 'em in; Hell, I'd throw 'em a parade if I could."

As he did when nervous, Baxter began rearranging things in their cases; right now it was tin cutlery. He did not look at Walter as he spoke. "I imagine you seen by now that Ludey likes to tell a story."

Baxter went no further, but Walter couldn't follow the leads yet. "So?"

"Well, let's just say that everything those three saying about it ain't true."

Walter's grip on the pencil tightened; he flipped to a new page. "Like what?" The grocer bit his bottom lip as he considered whether to say more. "Listen friend. I seen them boys bitch like schoolgirls 'cause you sold a bottle of Black Draught, and all you's trying to do is make a living. Am I right? I mean you an' me both know they's buyin' here 'cause you let 'em. You cut off their credit and they're on their ass an' starvin'. Am I right?"

Vine nodded at the truth of that, smiled at his power. "Let's just say they ain't the heroes they stylin' themselves out ta be, all right?" In the land of Nathan Bedford Forrest, it was a safe bet that anyone Vine considered a hero would be somewhat farther down Walter's list. "Not like you with Ludey last night . . ."

"Forget about that. Let me tell you what Hillman told me, and you tell me if that's what really happened to Cleon Quine."

In great detail, Walter recounted the story Hillman had told him the night before, during all of which Baxter nodded in agreement, right up until the flames consumed Cleon's body, and he was gone.

More to himself than to Walter, Vine said, "Those boys don't buy nothing half the time they in here. Use up my logs to warm their asses. Well . . ." He looked Walter square in the eye. "None of it happened that way, for one." Walter did not move. "Say, you ain't writing any of this down."

"So you're telling me it's all a lie?"

"No. What Hillman told you is exactly what happened. But him and Nip didn't do nothing. They was there when Cleon got brung back. Yeah, okay. They was standing there in the crowd, watching like everyone else, but since then they been walking around town talking that they was the men who hunted him down and such, and they was the ones who lynched him and it ain't true. The only one to go up to McMinnville was Ludey, and he didn't lay a hand on no one."

"What did he do?"

"You got enough for a story there, I think. Lot a people'll wanna read the truth, for sure."

"And the truth is that the three of them didn't kill Cleon Quine."

"Now don't you go tellin' anybody I told you that. 'Specially not them. Somebody gotta make a living hereabouts, and it may as well be me, but they been boastin' that, yeah."

"So who did it? Who was behind it all?"

"I dunno. People I never seen before or again. Few folks just mad with it, pushing things along and three thousand more just goin' along like a herd a cows like the devil come down and everybody just follow him. Hillman and them is as innocent as anybody else in that mob."

And just how innocent was that, wondered Walter.

"Most people don't even feel like it was them that was there." Baxter pursed his lips and for a second had the look Walter imagined him having just prior to his death, as the great pearly gates came into view. "More like it was somebody take 'em over or somethin'."

The fact that his cover was blown fully registered with Walter, let him not think about the night before. "Now you won't tell anybody who I am, will ya? 'Cause if you do, everybody'll start tellin' me lies agin. People say anything to get their name in the paper. You keep my secret, and nobody knows who told me the truth, all right?" Baxter winked, but Walter wanted a little more security than that. "Lemme toss in something else to make it worth your while, Bax. Have you heard of the mail order business? Montgomery Ward's up in Chicago has constructed a special vault in the First National Bank of Illinois to house the excess funds it's gotten through that line of business. Now our friend Ludey got one thing right—that ole Piggly Wiggly gonna mean trouble for you. But one advertisement in a paper like the *Chicago Daily News* could lift a concern like Vine's Southern Department Store to heights its owner . . ." Walter pointed at the storekeeper. "has never even dreamt of. You see where I'm headin'?"

Vine's eyes bulged dangerously, trying to take in the full import of what Walter was offering. A Northerner in the making, greed came before color for Baxter Vine.

"You keep what I'm adoin' here hushee hushee—not a word to even Miss Goldie Parker of Cowan—and as soon as I'm back in

Chicago I drop by a certain feller in advertising who didn't back up his promises at the poker table, and he owes me one. *Comprende?* All you gotta do is keep your lips sealed until I get on that train." Vine couldn't nod fast enough. "And what about this preacher he left with? Lewis?"

"Sheriff kilt him up in McMinnville. Folks didn't bother hauling his body back. I mean, he didn't do nothing really. 'Cept talk." Baxter coughed hard.

While a few drops of arsenic turns a whole glass of water to poison, the human heart works on more complicated formulas. Evil of the blackest sort can exist hidden within a man for a lifetime while in the same world, good people lose control of their better instincts and perform acts that haunt others for lifetimes. We humans no longer share in the essential flow that lets a dog sniff and decide that one is worthy of its trust. We must calculate. Like Louisa, we must consider all the facts, weigh the reasons and the effects of our actions and those of others, and be grateful that we can apologize afterward.

Knowing that he'd been right, that maybe there was a bit of the dog still left in him, Walter had to keep himself from skipping as he left Baxter Vine's store. Hillman was not a lyncher. Nor, for that matter were Nip or Ludey. As much as they may have thought about it, talked about it, liked to pretend that they did, some saving grace had stopped them from doing the deed itself. Where they were on the moral spectrum Walter had not yet discovered, but at least they'd not gone all the way to the Devil. His report now had no names save the victim's, captured only the shadow of evil's passage through town rather than its regular growth here as a staple. Mr. Johnson would have to be satisfied.

Walking north on the sidewalk, he tried to imagine three thousand people thronging the streets, a false return to the vibrant Sibley Springs of the photos in Palgrave's office. Hatred had always been a part of its nature, an acid in the soil that didn't kill living things as much as retard their growth. A sort of balance had indeed held Sibley Springs, just as Scipio said; a balance of good and bad, of past and present, and black and white that remained predictable until the day when evil rushed through the streets, seeped into the ground, summoned up the worst in people and then flowed on. The stain of it still darkened this land and, having seen it, Walter had assumed at first that Sibley Springs was beyond hope, but if three of its basest sorts remained within view of humanity, he had to wonder if maybe the town itself was redeemable. He decided to stay the night.

TWENTY-TWO

The market day activity had died down by now, but knots of men stood and spat at the entrance to Pullet's and outside of Sundy's. A month ago, Fortune's wanderings would have brought comparisons to a barnyard cat, and that would have been the end of it, but now white heads nodded together as if resolving something. Walter recognized this spreading silence, a gathering threat too embarrassed of its intentions to speak them out loud. Little coals of danger burnt in twos and threes, men and women and teenaged boys all ignorant and vaguely angry, looking over shoulders, wondering if they were having the same thought as everyone else, waiting for one person to set them aflame with the right word.

Creeping on toward dinner, the sun not yet down, the klatches had yet to grow larger than any gathering of gossips you'd see on a Harlem stoop or street corner. Once the night came, and the groups of threes and fours met other groups of threes and fours, it would all change. Where in this muddy little Cumberland universe, bounded by mountains and flat, plowed fields, would he find Fortune? On the other side of the railroad station were Ellanice and Dulcet Quine. With all the eyes of Sibley Springs on him, he couldn't just steal away over those tracks. He'd guaranteed Scipio he'd find everyone and solve everything as if he were some Negro Sherlock Holmes, and so far all he'd found was who had *not* lynched Cleon Quine. He began to take longer steps toward the Mitchell House—six o'clock was coming soon.

When he arrived, he noticed with a catch that the Studebaker was not in front. Walter reminded himself that he had many more important things to worry about as he trotted up the walk and entered the house. In the dining room, a girl whispered as a young woman instructed her in some way. Edging around the door frame he snuck a view of Louisa bent over Goose, her hair hanging down like a shirred curtain of gold, as she showed her the proper way to set a place. Though the plates and silverware were completely mismatched, cracked, and tarnished, Louisa had laid the table with great care and arranged a few candlesticks in the center for a flourish. A pendant glittered as it swung from her neck. Back in the kitchen, grease from a frying chicken snapped in a pan. He had passed on the hard-boiled eggs at the gazebo and now realized that he was famished. An odd and pleasing sensation embraced Walter, the sense of how it would feel to open the door to his own home, a place full of light and new things, nothing at all like the velvet box he'd imagined with Cornelia. Not the home on Houston Street, but the home he would someday have. "And then the fork goes here. Fork has four letters, just as left does. That should help you remember." Goose used the heel of her hand to wipe her nose. "Why don't you do the next one."

With the same hand, Goose laid down the forks. Louisa looked up toward the door, her hair falling over the two sides of her face, and she smiled, her eyes slanting in genuine pleasure. "Hello," she said. "We'd given up on ever seeing you again."

Goose reached up and nearly ripped the pendant off Louisa's neck. "Ain't this the purtiest thing you ever seen? What happened to your bag?"

"Drake had the wrong one."

Louisa bit her lip. "I thought you were leaving on the two? Will you still be on the six? We've only set for eight."

"Well, the good news is that I got a telegram. Looks as though the meeting's postponed until Monday, so I'm staying the night."

Goose waddled around the table yowling, "You got a telegram? Lemme see it! I never seen what they look like!" Walter and Louisa exchanged shy smiles, turned away before it became anything more.

Shoving his hands in his pockets, a pantomime search for the telegram, Walter finally shrugged. "Oh, I'm sorry, Goose. You know, I tore it up at the station. If I get another one, though, I'll save it for you." His mountain of lies shuddered with the weight of another one. His fingers hit the pearls, rubbed against the finger.

The little girl's head sunk forward into its usual position, an imitation of her mother's bent neck. By the time she was old enough for high school, Goose would probably have her mother's same hump. Back in the kitchen, Pettey asked Gladys if she thought the chickens were finished yet, wondered if the others would lay enough tomorrow to sell, told herself it was the right thing to do, to cook two.

Louisa repositioned her hair into its more formal intention, a glowing thing that seemed to have its own source of light. "We're leaving tomorrow after church, so Mrs. Mitchell is frying some chickens. Why don't you freshen up, and we'll call you for dinner?"

Feeling fresh enough already, Walter picked up a knife and handed it toward Louisa. "Do you need help down here?"

Goose's eyes went wide and nearly dove across the table to grab the knife away. "Don't do that! Give it to me!" With great ceremony and calm, she presented the implement to Louisa. "If a boy hands a girl a knife, it cuts their love in two."

Louisa, Walter, and Pettey all shouted, "Goose!" at exactly the same moment, though it was her mother's voice that caught her attention. "Leave those two young folks alone, would you now? Come in here!"

A finger in her nose, Goose plodded out to explain herself. Louisa's cheeks had flushed rose, a most delicate and delicious shade that eased into a heavy cream at the edges of her embarrassment. Why did white people only call themselves "white," he wondered, for all their pinks and beiges and tans and creams. Even taking into account the fact that they only paid attention to themselves, it was as if white people never truly saw themselves, as if they lacked the ability to describe themselves as they really were, didn't realize who they were exactly, what they looked like, and what they were made of. Maybe white folks really were ghosts, he thought, walking the earth but never actually a part of it. They were ghosts to themselves.

Louisa had turned back to the table to avoid looking Walter in the eye. "Goose is such a silly girl . . ."

This would only get painful if he remained in the room any longer; things would be forced or trampled on. In the kitchen, Goose practiced her fa sol la singing. "I believe I'll go upstairs after all, Miss Warren."

Walter made his way up the stairs to Gladys's room, where he removed his coat and sat down on the bed, frustrated and safe. It was five-thirty. Scipio would be on the streets looking for him. If he crouched a little, craned his head so he could peer through the opening between the curtains, he could see the Quine house, the place he most needed to be. He pictured Ellanice sitting by the window, peering through her own curtains, waiting for Reverend Lewis to return; the news of his death would crush her. She'd probably have to marry Scipio. Unless they moved North. And yet though they'd been there, it was hard for Walter to imagine them strolling down 135th Street. Like Miss Dorcas in London, as large as they may have lived at home, they were still Country.

Unable to sit still, Walter dug out his notebook. He scribbled down the details he'd picked up from Sundy and Palgrave and Drake, then nibbled at the pencil, reviewing the contents of his bag. The toothbrushes he stuck in his jacket pocket; Shy and Pettey would profit from fresh breath. The fortune cookies, though, remained a mysterious impulse that he'd thrown into his bag as he'd walked out the door two days ago, though right now it felt at least a week. What had happened back in New York since he'd left? It seemed too macabre to eat dinner with Quine's finger on his person, so he moved it to his coat. After dinner, when it was dark, he would dash out for a long cigarette and get lost again, sprint over to Ellanice, and learn what he could to find the boy. The hard part would be avoiding Scipio. A door slammed nearby. Dorcas scolded Tate for his rascally behavior as their steps grew fainter away. The noise from the dining room increased; Dr. Moody growled about whether there would be grits; Dorcas asked with no sincerity if there was anything she could do to help; and the dead babies slept peacefully through it all.

Walter stowed away his notebook, sneezed a few times. The cold hovered around him, tried to sneak into his bones when he stayed still for more than a few seconds. Until night came again, he told himself, until he could sneak back to his people, all he could really do was eat dinner. He went into the bathroom to splash water on his face. Despite some concerns after this morning's strange encounter, the mirror showed him his same old self. He twitched the moustache a few times in a caddish way, raised an eyebrow to compliment such a dashing fellow, and got down stairs to the dining room in a surprisingly good mood, well before all the chicken legs were claimed.

This was their final meal together, the Warrens and the Mitchells. Like a low herding dog, Goose shoved Walter and Louisa together at Shy's end of the table, along with her and Dr. Moody, who, remembering his gracious days as a student at Vanderbilt or Tulane, pulled out a chair for Louisa. The candles had been lit, the flames flickering in the waning light off the tin implements. Apparently Goose considered hers the fun side of the banquet; she announced, "Ah have a good joke!" even before a fork had been raised.

265

Pettey pointed a finger at her from the other end of the table. "Miss Warren go to all this trouble, and you actin' like it's a church roast. You sit down *now*." As Goose deflated in her seat, her mother turned to Tate at her side and requested that he say Grace. Hair parted down the center and slicked down, wearing a broad plaid jacket belted at the waist, he looked ready for a day on the links with Lawyer Palgrave. Nodding once to accept the awesome responsibility, Tate closed his eyes and pressed his hands together in the prim steeple of a child or the conspicuously devout. "Oh *dear* Lord Jesus Christ," he said, coyly asking for attention, his "dear" dripping with sincerity, "Accept our grateful thanks for this *most* humble meal." Pettey's eyes opened with a start as she surveyed a plate piled with the parts of two perfectly healthy laying hens she'd offered up, a bowl of steaming grits and another bowl filled with biscuits. "In your wisdom you have given each of us what we deserve as a sign of your grace." Goose stared at Miss Dorcas's earrings, swaying now not from the wind of a fast drive in the car but from the vigorous bobbing of their owner's head. The candle flame made them glint; the large portrait of Christ looked on noncommitally. "May we be wise enough to accept your truth, and your word, as you have revealed it to all men in your Bible. Amen." Before anyone had raised their head or unfolded their hands, Tate said, "Ah must have a breast" and shoved his fork at the plate.

Once the boy's divinely ordered needs were attended to, the plates and bowls went about the table amid a silence generously passed off as hunger. It was nearly six. Walter listened for Scipio's boots on the back porch. At the far end, Pettey's lips moved as quickly as Walter had ever seen them move, and at the moment she appeared set to leap across the table and throttle Miss Dorcas. In the manner of a fine woman, Pettey asked, "Was your day pleasant, Miss Dorcas?"

Slicing small shreds of chicken off the bone, Miss Dorcas then forked one of them and placed it on her outstretched tongue as if she had received the Sacrament. As she chewed, she said, "*Delors*. Ah am be-*reft* at the loss! To think that we will no longuh be comin' he-uh positively rends me in two."

Goose pulled a spoon out of her mouth, emptied of its load of grits. "Maybe we come visit you in Nashville."

If possible, the table became more quiet, the polite smiles brittle as crystal. No one dared speak to Goose's suggestion, so the floor was left to Tate. He took one bite of the breast, pushed away his plate, then leveled a fork at Walter. "Pray, sir, tell me what that nigger man desired from you."

"Well, the trouble with the bag seemed to be that Drake still hadn't gotten it."

Goose held up her chicken leg. "And he had a telegram! Tell 'em you had a telegram!"

"Yes. Mrs. Mitchell, I'll be staying one more night, if that's all right with you. I don't need to leave until tomorrow." The screech of train wheels covered his last words. The six o'clock ground to a stop. Walter didn't move, tensing his body for Scipio's knock at the door.

Tate kicked a leg of the table, shaking everything atop it. "I was mightily displeased with his presumption. He ought to remember Cleon."

Moody nodded in a dignified manner. "Indeed." He worked something out of a tooth, then continued. "I believe the Nigroes had to be shocked by the passion and the violence of the white man's response to that boy's crime." In his mouth, the words *passion* and *violence* came drenched with their meanings, sibilant and trembling with what he no longer had the strength for.

No, thought Walter, smiling politely. *Actually we expect you to rob and rape and hang us. It's kindness that comes unexpected.* He poured some milk into the enamel mug of coffee, turning it from a burnt black into an umber. Another dash took it to tan, one more into a sandy color. It was still coffee with milk in it, but if he kept going, at a certain point it would become milk with coffee in it. What would he call it then—a cup of coffee or a cup of milk?

"With all due respect to you, *Tate,* as a Southerner, born and bred in Atlanta, Georgia, I look forward to the day when I can sit down to a meal and not discuss the Negro."

This option seemed never to have occurred to veterans such as Dorcas and Moody, who suddenly looked up and considered it. "Here, here," said the doctor.

The six o'clock seemed never to leave. Walter sat with his hands on the table, chewing the same bite of chicken as the steam hissed in the station. Louisa's foot bumped his, sending both of them nearly jumping into each other's laps. She placed the tips of her fingers on the back of his hand. "Are you all right, Mr. White?"

The train blew its whistle.

She had the lightest touch, and once he said yes, she did not lift her fingers but rather she pulled them across his hand for an inch before she place them back in her lap.

Goose pointed at the one unclaimed biscuit. "Anybody but Miss Louisa can have that biscuit," she said.

"Why's that," asked Pettey.

She rolled her eyes, delivering information she considered so obvious as to barely warrant being spoken. "Because then she'll end up an old maid."

Pettey was speechless with embarrassment, so Shy wrangled his daughter, "Goose! Why don't you tell us something nice for a change. What was that joke you started?"

She didn't hesitate. "Why do boys smoke?" she asked, looking at Tate. No one knew. "Because they're green."

It took a moment to sink in, and Shy pounded the table and Walter howled, rocking in his chair as the whistle faded down the tracks, heading west and he was left here, a willing captive of Sibley Springs. Pettey's chicken, against all his fears, suddenly tasted quite good, as did the grits, and he could hear Louisa's stockings occasionally rub together, a remarkable sound. Goose's joke led to a long string of schoolyard groaners and riddles whose humor value, though minimal to any society wit, pleased Walter immensely. Once the girl had exhausted her collection, he dipped into his. No bawdy Exelento salesman numbers; the sillier the joke the better was his rule. Walter White was a pie-in-the-face man. Though he knew the punchlines to all of Louisa's contributions, Walter kept silent in order to guarantee her the applause—chivalry demands many kinds of armor.

The room warmed up, the sun finally sank down, and soon the candles were necessary. Walter thought he saw a lantern bobbing outside on the street, the black form of a mule wagon, circling. Suddenly, he remembered something. "Goose, you clear the dishes," he said. "I'll be back in a second." Dashing upstairs, he grabbed the box of fortune cookies out of his bag and skipped back down, barely able to contain his excitement. Raising it before him with both hands as if it was a sacred object, he entered the dining room. In this bare chamber, it did seem to possess magical powers; all eyes fixed on the bright scarlet package and the black dragon wrapped around it, the equine face, fire blazing forth from the nostrils. Hypnotized, even gasping ocassionally, the eight followed it as Walter took the long, stiff strides of a priest entering the sanctuary. He placed the box at the head of the table in front of Shy and with a hushed and ominous voice, said, "I present—Mr. Chee's Genuine. Oriental. *Fortune Cookies.*"

There were oohs and ahhhs. Pettey clutched her heart. Though fascinated by the exotic, by the flash of Ming red and simply the word "Oriental," she couldn't help seeing the face of Satan on the dragon and anything having to do with telling fortunes was right out in the Mitchell home, so she began to wave her fingers and shake her head, stunned by this visitation. "There shall not be found among you any one that maketh his son or his daughter to pass through the

269

fire," she babbled, "or that useth divination, or an observer of times, or an enchanter . . ."

Goose drowned her out. "I know how to tell fortunes! If you see a red bird, you start saying your ABCs, and the letter you're saying when it flies away is the first letter of the name of the person you're supposed to marry and if the bird lights on a fence . . ."

Louisa winked at Walter and held a restraining hand out to Goose. "Calm down, honey." Undaunted by the mystical cookies from the East, she bade Walter continue. "Let Mr. White tell us what these cookies know." Then she looked back up him, ready for whatever he wanted to do. Shy appeared more puzzled than anything, while Miss Dorcas simply wanted dessert.

Opening the box and pouring the contents into a bowl, Walter went on in his spooky tone. "In the fourteenth century, the great and powerful Emperor Chee ruled China with a cruuuuuel hand. To the terror of his people, he burned their homes. He imprisoned the men, sent them off in his armies to conquer other peaceful lands." Walter swirled the cookies about in the bowl with a dramatic flourish. "The women and children? Well, they were put in factories to make vases and, um . . . robes. Yes. To make beautiful, ornate robes that he, the cruel emperor, would wear around his palace as he counted his gold. He was a glutton, too. An enormous man with *terrrrrrible,* terrible appetites."

Walter now held the bowl out to Dr. Moody. "Remove a cookie whose ends are facing you and place it on your plate." Then he turned to everyone with a grave expression. "Do not—I repeat—do not, open your cookie until every person at the table has one."

The doctor raised a finger. "Now there's a goodly chance I grown a bit hazy in mah dotage, but I recall that in fact the fourteenth century China was ruled by the Khanate. Kublai Khan, the grandson of . . ."

Louisa assumed a worried expression. "Doctor, please take your cookie. Ah truly must hear the rest of this story."

"Thank you. Doctor?" Moody selected his cookie with fingers shaking with age and Walter continued around. Overcoming his doubts, Shy took one and Goose had to be restrained from grabbing more than her share. "Now these people had no one strong enough to challenge the evil emperor. He had told them that he was a god, stronger than any of them, able to crush them with one mighty hand!" All of which Walter demonstrated with broad gestures that kept the party in his thrall. "Miss Dorcas?"

Miss Dorcas leaned her head toward the bowl. "They have a most delicious almond scent!" Tate had folded his arms in refusal. "Oh, Tate, they smell so good. Here, have one." She dropped one on the boy's plate and then took hers. "Thank you *very* much, Mistuh White."

Walter arranged her cookie so that the ends pointed at her. "Please, Miss Dorcas. We must allow the cookie to divine."

"Well, of course."

"But up where the Chinese gods live the Chinese dragon god whose name was Chee—you see the emperor had even stolen his name—got wind of what the emperor was doing. So one day he took the form of a humble baker. He presented himself to the emperor's guards, saying, 'The gods have sent me to reward the emperor with the most delectable, most mouthwatering, most amazing cookie the world has ever seen! I have been sent with a cookie that will tell him his *future!*'"

Swept up by the moment, by the faces glowing in the candlelight and the story, Pettey absently took hers. "So the guards told the emperor that the gods were the giving him the gift of food, and magical food at that, and the emperor said, 'Let him in, let him in!' So the baker entered the grand palace with his plate of five cookies, identical to the very ones you have before you, each with a fortune nestled inside. And when he reached the throne, he knelt down and offered the emperor the tray with the exact instructions *I have just*

given you. Now, one of the fortunes said, *Today is your last day to live.*"
There were more gasps around the table as many recoiled from their
dessert. "A most horrible fortune and surely one that no one here
will receive, I guarantee you. But four of them said *Eat just one and
you shall live.* See, the dragon god wanted to give him a chance. So
the emperor cracked open the first one." Walter let them wait a
moment. "It said, *Eat just one and you shall live.* And if he had been
satisfied with that one cookie, the emperor could have stayed alive,
but he couldn't resist. He threw the fortune away, gobbled up the
cookie, and then grabbed all the rest of them!" Walter played the
emperor, cracking, and gobbling imaginary cookies before his
entranced audience. "He cracked them all open with a blow of his
hand and even as he ate the cookies, he read his terrible future. And
then Chee the dragon god baker brought fire down upon the cruel
emperor, and the people of China lived happily ever after." He
paused. "You may now open your cookies."

Though Walter had hoped for a slightly more appetizing end to
his own story, on the whole he was satisfied. The cookies were
cracked. To Walter's disappointment, Chee the cookie god advised
Tate that he would have a long and happy life. Pettey was a loyal
friend, and Goose learned that the sun rises every morning. Miss
Dorcas concentrated on the cookie itself and rated it an absolute del-
icacy. It was while he and Louisa marveled that they'd both received
warnings that things are not always what they seem that Walter
noticed a tear running down Shy Mitchell's cheek. The man pushed
back his chair without a word and paced quickly out of the room.

Walter picked up his fortune. *Others have committed the same error,*
it said.

The table fell silent. "What's the mattuh?" asked Miss Dorcas.

Walter read the fortune again. "I think something disagreed
with him."

Pettey got up to follow her husband. Ignoring the news about

Shy, Miss Dorcas thanked Walter loudly for the cookie, and the party broke up with this slightly sour end. Goose walked along the table, eating whatever shards of cookie remained, and when questioned by Dr. Moody claimed that a fair day followed a clean table. As Goose searched for more crumbs, Louisa angled Walter into a corner near the living room window. The only light came from the moon outside. Feigning annoyance, she glared up at him. "What do you really do for a living, Mr. White? You're not *really* a drummer."

Walter twitched his moustache, scratched his ear nervously. Pulling back into the darkness, he wondered what to say. He could tell her that he was going to law school in the fall, surely that would impress her. In fact, he could tell her just about anything, but what he really wanted was to tell the truth, to explain the man he was, a man who would be exalted for the good works he performed for his people. He wanted her to meet his parents and embroider next to his sister Madeline on lazy Saturday afternoons. "All right, all right." He brought his voice down to a whisper. "You found me out. I am with a larger concern than Exelento. A *much* larger concern. I'm down here learning the lay of the land. Working my way up, so to speak."

"So you're not with Exelento?" This news made her eyes crinkle again in that way Walter liked.

"No. It is something much more important, and I truly wish I could tell you, but my outfit is expanding. You see, they have plans to take over this part of the country."

Louisa leaned her head in close to his. "Are you with Piggly Wiggly?"

Letting out a surprised burst of laughter, Walter had to hold himself back from touching her arm. No one would see them in this room. Most likely, they'd all found other things to do for this very reason. He looked out the window into the settling night. It was dark, and he had no idea where he'd ever hunt down Fortune out there.

Why are you still here? Walter asked himself. *Have you decided to stay tonight for Fortune, or for yourself?*

273

He could kiss her. He could kiss this white woman. This woman. All the possibilities spilled into his mind, beautiful ones and deadly ones, and Walter could no longer say whether he was still tricking all the white folks by living their white life, or whether he was just being himself.

The moment grew heavy. His hands left his side and reached closer to Louisa's bare arms.

The rumble of a truck outside destroyed whatever was about to happen. Hillman shouted, "Hey, Walter! Hey, Walter, come on out!"

The others in the house drifted down to the hall as Hillman made his way up the path and Walter met him at the door. "Hi do, Hillman."

"Hey, Walter. We getting' up a posse. See, Fortune done run off. We was awaitin' to see if'n he'd come back for supper, but he ain't, and we don't like it. We gotta find that boy."

Nip waved from the cab of the truck, with Ludey behind the wheel.

"I thought he was home. Dr. Moody's orders."

Hillman shook his head. "Too important, Ludey say. Gotta take care a this probbim oncet for all." He had an unusual fire in his eyes.

From the back, Shy pushed himself forward. "We gotta really do that, Hillman? Maybe the boy just run away to Memphis or Chattanooga."

"Aw, come on. Hey, Doc, you remember when they strung up that elephant in Kingsport? Damn thing went crazy and done stepped on the keeperman. They brought up a crane and some cables? Done hanged the elephant." The pitcher cackled in a way he'd never seen him do before. "We gonna show you what Sibley Springs can *really* do fer itself." Hillman clapped his hands. *But you didn't do it,* thought Walter. "That's what we gonna do. Gonna give you a show!" For all his crazy talk, Hillman looked unsure, like he needed to prove something. Whatever seeds the lynching had sown around this town suddenly looked to be sending down roots, trying to claim Sibley Springs forever like the vines crawling over the ruins of the Timmons mill and the Vale.

"Oh, you don't have to do that. That's . . ."

"Aw hell, White," said Hillman, bouncing on his toes. "You been asking about lynchin' the whole time you been here."

All the Mitchells, from Shy down to Goose, stared at Walter, who pointed at himself. "Me?" Louisa seemed to sneer at Hillman's presence, a scowl that made it wonderfully, painfully clear that Walter had to risk her disapproval in order to save Fortune. "I was just making talk, Hillman. That's all. I . . ."

"Come on, White!"

He had to stop all of this; he had to save Fortune's life and he had to stop these men before they became who they said they were. Mr. Johnson always said it: We *must save black lives and white souls.*

Walter looked at Louisa, whose face had fallen. The only consolation he could take was that if she wasn't upset, he wouldn't have cared about her. "What if I told you a secret?" he asked. "Would you be able to keep it?"

She had retreated into coyness. "Maybe. Why don't you try me?"

The eyes of everyone in the hall were on them. Ludey honked the horn.

"Try me," she asked again, more of a demand, now.

Walter turned away. "Hillman, I'm tryin' to get on the morning train tomorrow, so I got me a few things I gotta settle first. You an' the boys meet me back here 'round eight, all right? Tell Ludey I'll join you then." It was 6:45. Hillman nodded and walked out the door as the horn bleated again. Walter held his hand an inch away from Louisa's arm. "I'll be back soon."

TWENTY-THREE

As Walter came down the stairs in his coat, Shy reached over the banister to put a hand on his arm. "Don't do anything foolish out there. Them boys . . ."

"Mr. Mitchell, nothing would make me happier than to see Fortune Quine back home with his mama." Louisa had retreated to the darkened living room, holding herself close as she stood at the window where they'd just been together. Walter raised his voice so she could hear him. "I'm going to do what I can to make sure nobody does anything they'll regret. First, I have to check if my bag came in, so let me do that." Digging into his jacket pocket, he produced the toothbrush sets and handed them to Shy. "Put some of the cream in the tubes on the brush and then rub the brush all over your teeth like you're scrubbing 'em. Don't swallow the toothpaste, though. Spit it out when you're done and rinse your mouth with some water. Show Goose, too."

Shy and Pettey stared at the toothbrushes as Walter left the house with no further goodbyes. Goose and Dr. Moody watched from the porch. There was too much for him to do now to be scared. Though he'd originally planned to head straight over to the river and cross from there, with them keeping their eyes on him, now he'd have to actually go to the train station and somehow get past Drake.

The lights burned at the depot, under siege from the mounds of chairs and sinks and trunks circling the station now that the spa had officially closed. Walter slowed. Afraid he'd already worn this alibi down to threads, he knocked on the glass of the station door. Drake looked up, shook his head no.

That done, now Walter had to dissolve into the night with only an hour to find Fortune. Ten yards across the track stood the knotty boards of the Negro homes, and light from the Quine house glowed over the roofs to his left. He considered sprinting across the tracks; it would only be a matter of seconds before he melted into the gloom, but if Drake or Dr. Moody saw him, everything would go up for grabs. Over in the white part of town, a dog started barking; some family pet agitating for a bone. Walter reached a hand forward as if he could touch the wall separating this town, an invisible divide as forbidding as any canyon William S. Hart and Fritz ever faced and for a second it seemed he could actually feel a gelid sensation, pushing back.

Another dog poked its head out from a hole in the wall of one of the shacks and howled in his direction. Walter ducked behind a stack of large trunks piled at an angle that covered him from the Mitchell porch. Each had been freshly painted with the word *Records*, along with a year. Very much in the mood for a cigarette, he sorted out his actions. The simple dash across the tracks was out. He considered heading along the tracks to the bridge and then crossing there, either just over the tracks or under and along the riverbank, or else heading back into town, sneaking to the bank and crossing from there. Both were plausible—he'd get to the Quines sure enough— but either way would take too long. Through the cracks between the trunks, he spied Moody craning his neck, wondering where the mysterious salesman had gone.

Walter turned his back to the Mitchells and sighed. Shadows moved across the tracks. As he squinted into the dark to make them out, a lantern blazed and a large hand set it on the board of a wagon. Scipio's mule wandered over the tracks in no particular hurry toward the towering remains of the spa. He'd seen Walter; no question about it. The wagon halted in front of his hiding place.

Scipio whistled random notes as he slid down. Wiping his brow with the back of his hand, he gave the trunks a once-over, contemplating the big job ahead. "I thought I told you to get out of town," he growled. "*Nigger.*" A pair of shiny new boots stared Walter in the face. Scipio checked to see if they'd drawn anyone's attention. "You don't know when to quit, do you? Nigger. You still playing games." He opened the trunk marked *Records 1918* just enough for a man to crawl inside. "Get your ass in there." Walter didn't move. "I said get *your white ass* in the box." Scipio's voice dropped into an urgent whisper. "Drake's comin'!"

The message was clear—this was theirs to settle, black man to black man. If Walter stood up and greeted the stationmaster, he'd be safe from whatever Scipio may have had in mind, but everything else would be gone. He flipped into the trunk and let Scipio hoist the whole thing onto the bed of the wagon.

The trunk was dark. It wasn't hot inside yet, but it would be very quickly, and the smell of old, dark paper rotting under him already made it hard to breathe. Before the mule could move, Drake's sharp voice cut through the leather and cardboard. "Where the hell you goin' with that, Scipio?"

"Nurse Mansley done sent word this one brought down wrongly and she needs it now." The cart did not move; apparently Drake remained unconvinced. "Somethin' in it she needs, she say."

Walter took shallow breaths, kept his eyes open, though all he saw was black. Drake's voice came closer. "Lemme get a goddamned look at this thing."

Shifting among the reports of sulfur treatments and daily water intake, Walter reached up and grabbed hold of the two strips of leather across the underside of the lid so that if Drake tried to open it, the lid wouldn't budge. Scipio sunk into his deepest, most abject dialect. "See, Mistuh Drake. That's jes' some ole box. Somethin' she want. I dunno know what it is, but she sho wants it. One a the niggermens that be wukkin' up there come on down jes' as I was afinishin' mah . . ."

Someone tapped on the box, right where the latch was, fiddled with it a bit. Wound into a ball, Walter's own sweat now swirled with the crumbling paper. His moustache wiggled from the dust, from his lingering cold.

"Records," said Drake. The sound of his finger scratching across the letters went up and down Walter's spine. "1918." His nose began to itch, the dust rolled into a cough in his throat.

"Lahke I sayed, I dunno . . ."

Clearly Drake wasn't listening to a word Scipio was saying. "That's this year," said the stationmaster. Walter let go of a strap and clamped his nose shut.

"That's *this* year?"

"That's right, Scipio. This here's 1918. Another goddamned year of our Lord. Ain't you got a calendar?" Walter's eyes teared through a few more eternal seconds until Drake's said, "All right. Go on ahead and take it." A hand slapped the box. "Make sure that tie holds; don't want it all fallin' out. How's your mama?"

"She fahn. Thank you," said Scipio. "'Bout as fahn as can be."

"Your mama's a good woman. You tell her that. You tell her Eugene Drake ast after her."

"That I'll do, Mistuh Drake," he said as he lifted the trunk and slammed it down up near the seat like a passenger. "Don't you worry, ole box. Scipio gonna take goooood care a you!" Chattering away loudly, he whipped the mule onward and away from Drake.

Walter waited as long as he could, then at last sneezed convulsively into his hands. He pushed at the lid of the trunk, desperate for air, but it didn't move. Scipio had sealed him in.

"Scipio!" he shouted. "Scipio! Open this trunk! Open it now!" Old paper absorbed most of the sound; the rest packed into his ears so that all he could hear were his own words blasting back at him. Scipio didn't answer. "Scipio! He's gone! Open the goddamned box!" And then he knew that Scipio had no intention of opening the box. And they weren't heading to Ellanice, either.

Walter stilled himself so he could think. Outside, Scipio whistled another flock of high notes that danced about in search of a melody. Walter rubbed the walls, knocked them lightly with a knuckle; they were made of heavy cardboard, not wood, a hopeful detail, and so he pushed his back up against one wall and set his feet against the opposite side and pushed as hard as he could.

"How you doin' in there?" asked Scipio. Walter listened for cracking, prayed for something to give way at his feet or shoulders, but the trunk was too strong. "You fall asleep?" After a breath, he tried again, tried to burst out of this prison before panic set in; already the arm he was lying on had gone numb, and he gulped for air after each attempt. He heard Scipio laugh to himself, and then a few slaps of leather on the mule's hindquarters. Walter closed his eyes and tried to guess their path from the movements of the wagon. It seemed as if they'd turned right with the slap of leather. How long had he been in here? Though it already felt like fifteen or twenty minutes, it could have been five or maybe less; he'd lost all clues, the moon and the stars and the dimming lights of the town.

Sweating heavily now, sipping at the air, Walter decided to stop moving. Though it wasn't clear yet whether Scipio intended to kill him, why else would he have locked him in here? The wagon creaked, and Scipio whistled on. "Come on, White. You got nothin' to say?"

"You couldn't hear me if I did! Open up!" The darkness was making him nervous. His eyes were wide open, and still they saw nothing. They seemed to lunge forward, his need to see something almost as desperate as his need to breathe fresh air.

"What's that? Open up? Is that what you said?" Scipio laughed.

If Scipio was just moving him someplace, he'd have to open up the trunk eventually. Walter figured that he could burst out of the trunk, surprise Scipio for a second or two, and run for it. His hands were free; he could just spring out at his throat.

But what if Scipio had something more diabolical in mind. What if he was planning to throw him off a cliff or dump him in a lake?

Not yet, thought Walter. He hadn't been killed so far and he promised himself that it wouldn't happen now. Not at Scipio's hands. The foulest curses he could imagine rolled out of his mouth, and he stomped his feet at the walls of the trunk. At first, Scipio laughed at the panic inside, but then he tried to calm him.

"I'm just takin' you to McMinnville, is all! Just getting' you out a town, like I said!'

But Walter couldn't believe him. He needed to breathe, to escape, and as he kicked, he felt the trunk shift around on the bed of the wagon. And then he remembered: Scipio's wagon had no sides!

Rolling back and forth in violent waves, Walter took all of his fear and anger and set it to getting up enough momentum to shake the trunk off the wagon. Inch by inch, he could feel it move, and he knew he was making progress when he heard Scipio shout back for him to stop it. The wagon slowed. He'd have to make a final push. The fact briefly crossed Walter's mind that for all he knew, they were on the ridge of a hill, and he was about to kill himself, but the thought struck his as less awful than allowing himself to be killed. Whatever would happen next would hurt, but at least it would be his choice. With a few small rolls to start up, he finally flipped himself against the back wall of the trunk so hard that he could feel his whole body rolling over into space. He'd tipped the trunk, and now for an endless moment he was falling, falling down four feet or forty or four hundred—he couldn't guess, but as soon as he'd known it worked, he clutched his knees and squeezed his eyes closed and in a second the trunk slammed into the ground. A loud crack, and then the trunk began to roll and he could hear Scipio shout. Another crack! As Walter tumbled and papers surrounded him in a tiny storm and old keys that smelled of rust landed on his face along with some pencils and a doorknob, the corners of the trunk gave way and one side cracked open and with a great and final wallop he hit the base of a tree to emerge, newly hatched from this most horrible egg, papers strewn about and settling like massive flakes of snow.

He was dizzy and it was dark, but not as dark as the inside of the trunk. The fresh air rushed into his lungs, and he looked to the sky to see the wonderful rising moon. Unfortunately, it offered only enough light to avoid the most immediate obstacles. Above and behind, he heard crashing through the leaves and empty bushes—Scipio. They were at the top of a low hill, and below lay the lights of a small house at the end of town that he immediately recognized as the Quines'. Half a mile as the crow flew and he'd be at his destination. And then back to the safety of the white men.

The safety of the white men. Walter gagged as the words formed in his mind, but the sound of Scipio's pursuit pushed him down the hill.

He now existed between two small lights. Juking around the trees, he kept his eyes on the blur of the Quine house windows at the bottom of the hill. Behind him, Scipio's lantern came closer, his pursuer stomping over the forest muck. The ground varied from patches of dark mud and leaves to dry mats of dead pine needles and back to mud, studded throughout with rocks Walter never saw but simply stumbled over as he tried to maintain some kind of regular pace. Though the leather soles of his shoes were smooth and smart and perfect for the streets of New York, what he wanted was a pair of cleats for dodging the complications of this forest. Below, the Quine house continued to glow, a fixed light as constant as the moon.

As he ran, Walter searched for a boulder to hide behind or another thicket of sumac, but there was none. Digging into himself for a deeper, lung-clearing breath, he heard Scipio pant and then the clatter of his lantern being tossed aside. After about five city blocks the ground sloped dramatically. The house was now as close as the subway train from the office on Fifth Avenue, the Candler Building from his parents' home. A wheeze clung to Scipio's breath; he was losing ground. All Walter had to do was get across the road, through the field, Cleon Quine's field, and he'd be at the house. The trunks and branches up ahead thinned. He'd beat him again.

And then gravity took over for speed. Walter's feet all of a sudden shot out from under him, and he landed hard on his rear end with a grunt, grabbing at the passing trees for support, holding his body back as the hill pulled him down.

Scipio shot forward across the road and into the field about ten yards deep. He stopped there and crouched low, facing Walter like a linebacker.

"You ain't getting past me, White."

Walter dusted himself off, stretched his legs. Scipio wasn't rushing him. This was their final meeting, the confrontation they'd been meant to have from the first moment they saw each other yesterday. The trip up in the trunk and the hard roll down the hill had left Walter aching, and Scipio was one big son of a bitch standing there amid the ragged leavings of last year's corn. He rubbed the shoulder he landed on when the trunk first hit the ground.

"You know, Ellanice doesn't love you."

Scipio pawed the ground as Walter crossed the road.

"And even if she did, you think these white men gonna let all you have that land? You think they gonna let all the Negroes have jobs and responsibilities? You think they gonna let you be *men*?" Walter edged closer through the dead stalks, tried to sneak an angle on Scipio that the bigger man blocked with a quick move to his left.

"Listen, you need the white man's laws to tie up the white man—don't you see the beauty of it? Ellanice don't owe you—the white man does. Tie them up with their own ropes. Use their color *against* them. What you think law is don't matter to them. And God's laws don't matter to them either. Only laws white men care about is the ones they cook up on their own. That's what I'm trying to do, Scipio. Tie 'em with their own ropes. Why don't you just marry Tansy Portis and make yourself a daddy to Booney?"

"'Cause he *got* himself a father, White. That's why. Works up in Sewanee. *Christ,* you stupid." He circled to Walter's right, the side closest the house, to cut off any move that way. He'd had his hands open before, but now they were fists. "You really don't know what color you are, do you, White?"

"Fuck you. I don't need you to forgive me for having white blood." About ten yards away, Walter prepared himself for the open field move of his life. "I'm a ghost. I'm *their* ghost. And I'm gonna spend my life scaring the shit out of them, making them wonder if they're niggers too. It's a shield to take into battle, friend, and the way I see it, I'm risking my life a hell of a lot more than you these days. No white man in this town gonna lynch you 'cause you're one a the *goooood* boys. You a *goooood* nigger. They'll wait until the end, until you dug all the graves for all the other black folks in this town, filled 'em up and then dug your own. That's when they'll come a knockin' at your . . ."

He took one final deep breath and broke out of the blocks, aimed directly at Scipio whose outstretched arms seemed to circle the world. AU vs. Morris Brown. 1914. Walter had scored on a busted quarterback draw. *Bite! Bite!* Either the corn stubble would give him what he needed or send him sprawling on the stalks. Three yards away, he slowed down just enough to cut left, and as Scipio threw himself, Walter spun his body around in a three-sixty and jumped clear. Scipio landed on his knees. Walter stretched out into long strides, took the advantage all the way to the light gathered around the Quine house.

Scipio screamed back, "I was just takin' you to McMinnville!"

Safe now, Walter eased into a walk and finally stole a glance, his imagination giving him Scipio raging on the crest of the hill, tragic and Shakespearean, but he'd gone. Ellanice opened the door.

Twenty-Four

"Who you running from?" she asked, as he caught his breath. It was an accusation, not an expression of concern. "Was that Scipio?"

Walter pushed past her into the house without answering. Ellanice had changed from this morning's flashy outfit into a gray work dress. "They're hunting Fortune. They want me to join the posse." He nodded to Dulcet, who sat in an arm chair, gripping the doilies on the arms of her chintz throne. "You have to tell me where you think he is. Did he say anything to you, give you any idea of what he might be planning?"

Despite the dangers ripening around them in the trees, Ellanice remained composed. "He went out for a long time last night, but I saw him come in and his bed was slept in. When I got up, he was gone. I think he went to find Reverend Lewis, like he said."

Without thinking, Walter said, "He's dead." She shook her head, and at first Walter thought she simply didn't believe him, so he forced the facts on her with impatience. "No, he's definitely dead. Vine told me the sheriff shot him up in McMinnville and left the body up there." She formed a No, then covered her mouth with her green Veronica's rag, absently fumbled behind herself in search of some kind of support.

287

He regretted his heartless delivery of the news. Walter touched her arm, but she withered from it. He tried a softer tone. "Ellanice, I have to find Fortune. You have to help me."

Now she had vanished too, like Scipio, but she did so behind a vacant expression. As smart as she was, her hopes had ridden on the same miracle as Fortune's. The clock on the piano remained stopped at 4:38 P.M. Neither woman seemed able to move. Dulcet's head had dropped onto her chest, as if she'd slipped off into a nap. If she hadn't been born a slave, she'd grown up among people who had, and in her life she'd probably been mauled, robbed, Ku Kluxed, and burned out, and yet she'd kept moving up. Until now. Losing Fortune would leave her dead, even if it didn't kill her. They'd placed Cleon's photograph back on the wall, and though he stared down on his women from within the black frame, his powerful presence had sunk to portraiture. The Quine house was now a vulnerable place, the free movements of the two women made on borrowed time; even as they sat, the piano, once a musical instrument, decayed into a relic of happier times.

And an hour ago he'd been cracking open fortune cookies. The guilt ate at him, though for what crime he couldn't say. Lacking confidence in his ability to console, only his actions to offer, he leaned into Ellanice's carved face. "Tell me something!" he shouted. "Anything! Where's his room!"

She managed to tilt her head, indicating a thin hall that Walter went straight into. He pushed open a door to his left, already slightly ajar. Inside a room about half the size of his own small one in Harlem lay a low bed on a spindle frame next to a night table built of the same spindled dowels, both pieces heavy with a dark, last-century feel. Unlike the living room, no one had plastered these walls, content to leave them just a step past papered boards; a reminder that the Quines' wealth was a relative thing. On top of the ornate table sat a glass kerosene lamp along with a tin of shaving powder, a few cast-iron trucks, and a penny bank depicting a clown luring a skirted beagle through a hoop. A bottom shelf held some books—*Tarzan of the Apes,* Howard Pyle, Paul Dunbar. Over his bed, on the wall, Fortune had pasted photos cut from newspapers that had somehow found their way—maybe from Reverend Lewis himself—into the Quine home. But rather than just display full photos, with a careful hand he'd trimmed away everything not wanted and over the years had created a massive collage. Above his pillow, a yellowing Jack Johnson, legs spread, fists raised to gut level like a dangerous paper doll, faced off against a more recent clipping of a line of Negro doughboys, bayonets all thrust forward to protect Charlie Chaplin and Matthew Henson, identifiable only because of his fur parka—How many Negroes wore fur parkas?—from the threats of the heavyweight champ. The Woolworth Building, the Pyramids at Giza, and the Eiffel Tower provided backdrop, as a camel, apparently en route to the tomb of the Pharaohs, strayed through the spread legs of the Tower. The *Titanic* docked at the skyscraper's tip. A procession of motor cars, all makes and sizes, bordered the bottom while two dark suns, the heads of Dr. Du Bois and Booker T. Washington, hovered over it all. Down low, at eye level, Theda Bara in a costume made solely of rope coils offered her kohled and smoky eyes as inspiration for the young man who slept here, his mind already a bit too fertile. He'd left his stuffed blue felt dog, probably made by Dulcet, on his pillow.

Walter sensed Ellanice over his shoulder and said, "He's got quite an imagination." He looked at Du Bois again; once he might have done the same thing with the doctor's picture in his own bedroom, but some of the awesome magic had evaporated now that they were colleagues. When he saw his face now, he thought of his officious attitude, his dramatics around the office, the tension that froze any room he entered. Du Bois's theories weren't helping these people; they needed the Law. He noticed a tin locomotive identical to one he'd had as a boy.

"Imagination isn't always such a good thing."

"You sound like your friend Scipio." Walter felt bad the moment he said it. He had no right to feel jealous of either man, no right to begrudge her anything. "I'm sorry about the Reverend." Walter picked up the tin train as if it held some clue. "I'm sorry about what I just said."

"He's out there looking for him." Ellanice ran her hand over the quilt, large blocks of blue and green. Only the reddish cast to her eyes hinted at any problems afoot. "Mama made his bed this afternoon." As she patted her brother's cold pillow, her eyebrows slanted downward, and her lips pursed as if holding back a harsh laugh. "Usually he does it himself." They'd never let them keep the land. Soon, she'd probably wear this gray dress into another woman's home, thus completing the rise and fall of the Quines in two generations.

"Who's been looking for him?"

"Couple men went out after lunch for a couple hours, but they came back in oncet all the white folks started massin' on the corners."

"Did he have a suitcase or a bag? Maybe he ran off to join the army, or . . ."

She snorted. "I doubt *that*."

"Why?" Walter pointed at the wall. "He's got a picture right up there."

"He got a picture of Henson up there too and he ain't going to the North Pole," said Ellanice, amazed at his stupidity. "Papa would never let him go kill Germans for the white man. Only reason he'd do it was for the uniform." She reached over and picked up the felt dog, shook it in Walter's face. "Don't you get it? He ain't a man yet, White! Between mama boiling his milk and Papa dragging him out into the rows, he don't know if he's the boy prince or a field nigger."

"Did he have a place he liked to hide? A secret place?"

Rubbing the dog with her thumb, Ellanice shrugged. "He'd run away, say he was going to look for Diddy Wah Diddy, like Daddy told us. He'd pack up some eggs and go marching around for a few hours to work it off."

"But there's no such place."

"I never said *that*. There's a lot of mountains. Lot of coves where folks can do whatever they got a mind to, as long as they own a gun." It was 7:35. Fortune could be anywhere. "Maybe it's best if he goes," said Ellanice.

"Scipio's been talking to you."

"Yes." Embarrassed by even the mention of such things, she'd turned away, but then she turned back and met his eyes. "I need a man that's gonna fight for me. It don't have to be with guns, but he has got to fight." Ellanice set the dog gently back into place on Fortune's pillow. "Not too many fighters left around here."

"He wants Fortune gone. Then he wants to marry you and give all your land away, give every Negro in town their forty acres." Walter framed this with great disapproval, but the expression on her face did not change, defiantly so. She had already given this some thought. "Tell me why your family should give up theirs because the *white* folks are greedy."

"Because you have to start somewheres. Maybe not everybody's gonna rise . . ." She extended her arms as if presenting the whole Quine house to him. ". . . But it's pretty clear one man isn't enough. It's harder for a rich man to enter Heaven than for a camel . . ."

"You think God's gonna keep you out of Heaven because you're not hungry? Because you visited New York once? And what about Fortune?"

"I don't want to marry no theories! I want to marry a man that's gonna love me and take care a me! You got any other ideas? White man won't let two black women and a nigger boy own all the land in Franklin County. You gonna be on a train tomorrow morning, and you never have to see this town again. Scipio coulda turned you in a dozen times by now." Her eyes looked darker and larger than ever before and at her full height, she now stared down at Walter with them, setting his moustache twitching, as her voice rose. "Could've done it the minute he set *eyes* on you. He gave you the chance to talk at Papa's service, gave you the benefit of the doubt *awww* day, and you ain't done anything *close* to that for him. Scipio wants his people to live. You want 'em to *rise!*" She said this last in a mocking way, like a magician levitating.

Dulcet called from the living room, "You stop it, Neecie! I can't hear screaming tonight. I can't . . ."

"You could leave. Go to New York or Chicago or . . ."

"I'm not leaving!" she said. Then her face softened, "It'd be like dying."

"Then Fortune should," said Walter. "But I'm going to get him out of here alive, like a man, with a clean shirt in a bag, and some money. I can help get him into a good school up north or in Atlanta. Get him a job. That's what your father would have wanted. I can *do* that."

He put his hand over the finger in his pocket, imagined Ellanice recoiling in horror at the sight of it or, even worse, Dulcet cradling it to her face. Scipio was right; carrying a dead man's finger was a horrible thing.

Something small and white at the base of the lamp caught Walter's eye—a perfect white pearl the size of a pea.

He bolted to the door. "Stay here."

Muddy waters ran along the tracks; Walter ran from tie to tie as he dashed toward the iron bridge, aiming there for the narrow space between the tracks and the siderails. Crouching down low enough so that his eyes cleared the top, Walter took light, quiet steps on the gravel until he reached the center of the span and scanned the river below. A good sixty feet wide at this crossing, the Elk lapped at its banks with short waves, running southward with the sort of greater purpose Walter had failed to find in most people here. For such a large, strong thing it made little noise, a constant rushing flecked at times with the bright tinkle of higher notes, and it quickly faded as he strained to hear a word, a cough, a breaking twig, any evidence of Fortune.

The night was clear, and so the moon quivered atop the water, illuminating the banks closest to its light. Outside this charmed circle, all fell back into blacks and grays that Walter methodically scouted for signs of life. Low branches tugged by the river's tide masqueraded as kicking legs and fishing poles, rocks on the sandy shore became shoes, but patience and focus revealed nothing but forest mirage. If the boy truly didn't want to be caught, he wouldn't be within an easy sniff of the dogs, anyway. Instead, Walter turned to the sliver of island that poked up through the river south of the Timmons Mill ruins.

A dot of white light flashed on its eastern side. Walter held his breath. The moon glinted once more off the sharp blade of Fortune's knife. Walter crossed the bridge to the bank and wound through the trees without a path, certain now that the boy was exactly where he thought he'd find him.

TWENTY-FIVE

Twenty feet of fast water separated Walter and Fortune at a spot where a patch of rocks forced it to bubble. The rocks ended in a bank of increasingly smaller pebbles on the island's shore, and there sat Fortune on a log, slicing open mussels just as Walter had seen him doing the day before. Unlike yesterday, though, when he moved slowly and sadly through his pile of bivalves, tonight he twitched as much as Walter, prying them open with quick sloppy movements. He flung a pebble in the boy's direction, but Fortune didn't flinch. The pile of shells reached halfway up his left shin. He'd been waiting all day to be found, had planned this scene for whoever came to talk him out of running away, but no one had come, and he'd been left shaking by the shore, worried that now he'd actually have to do something. Walter guessed that even *he* had the sense to know that it would be something irredeemably stupid and dangerous.

Though Fortune hadn't tied off a raft or rowboat, Walter couldn't see any other way across. It looked shallow enough to walk, but his shoes had suffered enough the last two days. Slipping off his shoes and socks, he rolled up his cuffs until his white ankles showed, then with a final check to make sure no one watched from the bridge, he stepped into the cold water, groping tentatively with his toes as he held his shoes to his chest. The bed was indeed shallow here, made of rocks the size of a big dog's head and slick in a slimy way that made Walter cringe at the same time that he began to shiver. After five of Walter's mincing steps, Fortune finally said with teenaged exasperation, "Jesus Christ, it's only a foot deep."

Walter splashed to the other side, gesturing for him to be quiet. "Shut up!" he whispered harshly. "They're looking for you!" Walter tugged at the arm of his coat, already impatient with Fortune's attitude. "Come on. You gotta get back home."

The boy shook him off with a powerful flick of his arm that surprised Walter. Last night, his suit had disguised his strength, but tonight he didn't want to hide his neck and broad shoulders, the evidence that he was man enough to do what he contemplated, whatever that was. He wore traveling clothes—a cap, overalls, and a heavy denim jacket—but with no suitcase or bag visible, it appeared he preferred contemplating flight more than actually flying. Caught between a petulant day of hooky and an adult disappearance with implications for all of Sibley Springs, Fortune tapped at the shell in his left hand with the knife blade. "Fast, cold water, that's what the pearlymussels like." He wasn't ready to listen yet, hadn't had the say he'd spent the day preparing. Enough moonlight hit the island to make a branch on the sand reveal itself to Walter as a shotgun. "Nothing wrong with getting rich the easy way. That's what he used to say. Enough white folks ain't never worked a day in their life." Fortune flung a half shell so that it skittered across the water. "Daddy was always looking for that extra dollar."

Walter dropped his shoes, put his hands in his pockets, pressed his arms close to his sides. When he was eighteen he was a bellboy, working to pay his own college bills. If Fortune sold a few acres, even at the cut rate white bought from black, he'd have himself a comfy start. Gun or no gun, this was a boy. He'd be damned if he'd treat him any other way, and yet he wasn't much older himself, so Walter didn't feel the need or the ability to present his news wrapped in an avuncular tone. "Reverend Lewis is dead."

"He said you find one pearl every three thousand shells, and even that one mayn't be so good."

"Did you hear me? He's dead."

"I used to think you had better odds finding a good person, but even they all seem to be twisted somehow. Pretty much everyone except the Reverend."

Walter crouched down, put his face into Fortune's, the way he'd seen an army officer do at Fort McPherson on his three days in the service. "Goddammit, listen to me! Sheriff shot him in McMinnville! We have to get back to the house!" Fortune stared at the moon in the water, the muscles twitching in his face as he fought back the tears. Walter held his voice down, though it was becoming a challenge with this boy. "And what the fuck are you planning to do with that gun? Where'd you get it?

"Daddy," came out of Fortune's mouth, pinched and almost a call for Cleon's protection. He hung his head, scratched at the back of his neck.

"You know what they'll do to you if they find you out here with a gun?" Walter took a breath, reminded himself that a few days ago this boy's father had been burned alive less than a mile away. "Listen, if you're not in your own bed tonight, strokin' off to Theda Bara, you gonna be lynched."

Fortune looked up at him, angry and embarrassed. Walter decided to go in for the kill; there wasn't time to play. "Yeah, I went to see your mother and sister. Remember them? Your mother's near to crazy with grief, and your sister's about to marry a man she don't love just so there's someone can take care of her, 'cause you're still too much of a child."

"I'm going to *find* him," insisted Fortune, pounding a fist into the rocks. "I'm gonna find the Reverend, and we gonna come back here and set it all right!"

"Holy Jesus, what do I have to say for you to hear me? He's not out there! Get some sense in your head. He's not coming with the cavalry to save you, and he's not out there in the swamp building up some magic army! He's dead, goddammit." Fortune had buried his face in his hands. "He's dead." Walter took a step back, cleared his throat a little, and watched the water roll over the rocks. After what he judged to be a reasonable interval, impatience finally overtook his pity. "You gotta deal with the real world. Figure out how to change things the way they get changed, 'cause you can't wave some god-damned magic wand and expect people to start doing what you want 'em to do. And that's true, even if you're trying to get 'em to do the right thing." He kicked a pebble with his toe. "Far as I can see, the only true man in this entire town, black or white, was your father. All he cared about was being himself. Just a *man*."

Fortune stopped crying and wiped his nose on his sleeve, tried to pretend he hadn't been weeping seconds ago.

"If you want to fight, stay here and fight. Start an NAACP branch here. I wasn't much older than you when I started. But if you want to leave, you leave like a man. The way your father would have left here; with a ticket and a suit and a place to go. Don't go running off to find your dead preacher and then end up greasing tools in some garage in Huntsville, for chrissakes. You gotta be a man now. Your *own* man."

Fortune let his shoulders sink and his hands fall to his sides. "I'm tired all the time."

Ruling out an empathetic pat on the back, Walter sat down on the log next to Fortune. "Well, brother, then you're *already* a man."

He pulled a wry grin at his own joke, but the boy's face remained stone. "Daddy hated white men."

"Wasn't he always talking about Diddy Wah Diddy? All those

white folks and black folks living together back up in the mountains? Neecie thought maybe you were out hunting for that."

Fortune spat onto the shells. "Diddy Wah Diddy doesn't have no white folks. Forget *that*. If heaven got white folks, then count me out, nigger." The word sounded petulant in his mouth, as gratuitous and ugly as it was ever meant to be. Walter glared over at him, but held himself back as Fortune's nostrils flared, his face contorted. "I want to kill *all* these white motherfuckers."

Walter nodded. "I know. But the problem is, you can't. There's too many of them and not enough of you. The other reason . . ." He paused, amazed at what he was about to say. "The other reason is that they don't all deserve it. You can't give up on all the white people." He sounded like his mother, but it had to be said. "The world isn't made that way, black or white, good or bad. We have to fight the evil where we see it so the good can come through."

"Holy shit!" Fortune looked at him with disgust. "I thought you *was* something. I mean, you just some kind of bullshit preacher man?" Astonished at hearing something other than fighting words, he threw another shell into the water as he shook his head. "Scipio's right. You *are* white."

Walter grabbed the front of Fortune's shirt and pulled him toward his face. "I know you trying to insult me, but both my grandmothers are white women and I'm not happy about the way you're talking about them, son. You hear me?" He shoved him down. "You turn the world upside down so black means good and white means bad and you think you solved everything." Despite whatever physical advantage he might have had on Walter, the younger man was too surprised and too accustomed to being pushed around to do anything other than dust off his pants and set back on the log. "You know, white folks don't hate just *us*. They pissing on each other alllll day long. You *know* that. You *seen* it. They hate each other—shit, they hate themselves—just as much as they hate us. A white man is just about the loneliest thing on earth."

"That ain't my problem."

"Well, no, it's not. But as long as they keep kicking black asses because of it, then I think it is, young man. All them shoulds and oughters and supposed tos don't matter. These white men up here hunting *your* ass, they're like little babies who can't talk but for what they eat and shit and fuck. We can't let 'em keep being our masters. That's what Scipio wants. Keep the baby happy and do your own business, but the truth is that you gotta pass the laws. Get the better white folks to make the rules and whup the crackers till they learn for themselves, like your daddy surely did to you. Do it till they grow up and find some God or good sense. Maybe someday they'll do it because they want to, but until then, there's got to be some *laws*." Walter put his hand in his pocket. Cleon's finger didn't belong to him, and he didn't want it. He held it out to Fortune. "Here."

As soon as he realized what was being offered to him, Fortune looked to Walter very much like someone who'd still have a felt dog on his bed. The boy ran his finger down the side of the black object, closed his eyes and squeezed it as if he'd been given the chance to hold his father's hand for one last time. "Daddy," he whispered. The tears began again.

Walter watched the bridge until his toe started to tap. Hillman and the boys would be coming back to Mitchell's in ten minutes or so. "Here. Let's give him his rest." With a mussel shell he quickly dug a thin, deep trench in the sandy soil not far from the shotgun.

Fortune laid his father's finger into its grave, then packed the earth back around it, leveled it so that it couldn't be found among the rocks. He reached into the small front pocket of his overalls, pulled out a pearl and set it atop the miniature grave.

"You the one who gets 'em for Miss Timmons, right?"

The boy shrugged.

It was still possible to get him home alive. Walter worked up an encouraging smile. "Maybe the odds aren't as bad as your father said." With a hand on Fortune's shoulder, he guided him across the shallows, toward the bridge and home.

And then a dog barked.

At first it sounded like any other dog over in town, scaring off a raccoon nuzzling through the bones of tonight's dinner, but soon more joined, and they were coming closer. Seconds later, he saw the lanterns up near the trestle bridge, heard the truck, the first heavy steps of the boots clanging off the metal, the nails of the dogs scratching.

Fortune snatched up the gun.

Grabbing his shoes, Walter used his other hand to pull him by the gun's barrel into the thatch of trees. "Are you crazy?" he hissed. Wrenching the shotgun easily out of Fortune's hands, Walter was just about to toss it into the bushes when he decided that right now at worst Fortune was only missing. If they came across this gun, though, they'd kill him no matter where and when they found him. Walter unbuttoned his coat and stuffed the shotgun inside, cradling it with one arm as he fumbled at his socks and shoes.

The voices of Nip and Hillman called out Fortune's name from the bridge. Dogs bawled.

Without a raft or boat, the bridge taken and the moon up high, Walter could hardly breathe. No logs to float away on. He gestured for Fortune to sneak with him deeper into the slight cover of the island's bushes and trees where the two crouched down. They shuffled over to the boulder in its center and pressed against it. As the white men proceeded down off the bridge and along the near bank, Walter and Fortune very gently and gradually slid across the face of the rock on their stomachs so that now at least the boulder blocked them from their pursuers.

"I swear I seen something," yelled Nip.

"Oh, lahke hell," said Hillman. "Y'all didn't believe *me* before."

"On the island. I'm not lying." Paws started to splash into the water. "See, ain't deep here a'tall."

"I'd lahke to see Ludey now. Where'd he have to go so important?"

"Dunno. Said he'd pick up Walter when he done."

Walter nudged Fortune and pointed at the river in front of them, whispered as quietly as he could, "How deep?"

Fortune shrugged, then showed flashed ten fingers at him three times.

The other shore was ten yards away. He could see the columns of the Vale. Thirty feet of water, and they'd be into the woods south of the Timmons Mill. Thirty long feet. Ludey last night; tonight it was *his* turn to drown.

"Shee-*yit*. That's cold," said Hillman. "Let the dogs go."

Walter had no choice but to get his ass in the water and swim. Mouthing *Come on* to his companion, he slid his shoes into the Elk River with as little sound as he could, tiptoeing forward until his jaw hit and he pushed off, dropping the shotgun so that it sank to the bottom. Usually a passable swimmer, tonight Walter felt a clench in his stomach as he splayed out into a float and let the current pull him, moving his fingers as little as he needed to stay up and move forward. Clearly the better swimmer, Fortune dove under and made it at least halfway across under the surface before he broke through for a quick breath. Going back down for the rest of the way, at the far shallows he slid out, the water running off him in a high sound that made the dogs bark.

Midway to the other shore, Walter suddenly pulled his head up and swallowed some of the river. He thrashed, his coat, his heavy shoes all dragging him down to where the gun had already gone.

"Goddamn! You're right," shouted Hillman. "Come on!"

Gulping for air, positive he was about to die the death Ludey Fentress had avoided, he didn't hear the dogs behind him, or his fellow Joe Williams fan calling for reinforcements. A swirl in the current pushed him further south and closer to the shore until his wildly pedaling feet hit a stone and he found enough will and toe-hold to thrust himself forward into the shallows where Fortune could extend his arm and drag him into the bushes.

"I just seen him on the other side," shouted Nip.

"Let's go 'round and catch him on over there." The white men darted up the far bank, their lanterns bobbing across the bridge.

"Now," whispered Walter. Bent over, he dashed to the Vale of the Confederate Dead and slid into the two-foot opening under the platform. Fortune scrabbled in after him and protected by the town's forgotten dead, the two tried to catch their breath. They couldn't stay there long, just long enough for Walter to decide as the lights came closer, the dogs barked louder, where they'd go. They'd never make it through town and across the tracks to the Quine house. He'd have to hide Fortune somewhere here in the white part of town.

Tugging the boy's arm, he crept out from under the Vale, pulled Fortune along the darkened row of large homes, all black now, but as they approached the main street, he stopped and headed north, crouching behind a pile of firewood as the dogs passed by them toward the ruins.

He was freezing cold. There was only one place where he could possibly stow the boy long enough.

The lights of the Mitchell House burned just ahead. It was almost eight. Ludey would be waiting for him.

Could he trust Shy Mitchell?

In this dark, shriveling town, thrashing to stay alive, the Mitchell House represented his only home, and he prayed that it would now do more than just represent home for him, that the place where he laid his head would offer shelter from more than rain.

As Fortune shook his head, Walter pointed to the Mitchell House and pulled at the boy's jacket. His own coat streamed water down the backs of his legs so he grabbed up the hems to keep their wet slap from attracting notice.

TWENTY-SIX

Shy's head bobbed in the kitchen window. He was talking to someone else in the room. The dogs had taken a turn north. Walter knocked hard, but the innkeeper didn't move.

Walter knocked again and was about to try a window when the door cracked open and Shy's long face tilted to see who was out there. Shoving Fortune ahead into the crack and into the kitchen, Walter shut the door behind them.

"Shy, you've got to help."

The two black men shivered in front of the door, a vast puddle of river water spreading beneath them, Walter's prized shoes all but ruined. Next to Shy, Goose dropped her jaw. Faint white lines of toothpaste rimmed her lips. She had cut the dragon out of the cookie box and fashioned a necklace out of it, tied with twine.

"Oh Lord in Heaven! That's . . ."

Shy's hand shot across her mouth. He leaned over to her ear and calmly whispered, "Ah *know* who that is, Goose. You jes' be quiet." But he didn't remove his hand.

Walter tried to read the innkeeper's face. He had some toothpaste at the corners of his mouth, too. Walter held to the fact that Shy had not shoved them right back out the door or called for Pettey to bring down the shotgun.

"He hasn't done a thing, Shy. Just stayed out too late pearling."

Shy bit his lip, and Walter couldn't tell if the tensing jaw that had replaced his usual absentminded quiet signified anger or some kind of resolve taking shape. Pettey could be heard in the room above, talking to herself and now heading toward the stairs. Shy squinted one eye; he wasn't buying the story.

"Just hide him. Soon as I get rid of the posse, I'll come back for him. Ludey here?"

Pettey called down. "Shy, who's that?"

"Nothin'. I jes' threw something out for the birds." Goose couldn't help but let out a low, astonished moan. Shy whispered, "Not a word, Goosie. Not a word," in the firm way one calms an overexcited dog. "No, Ludey ain't come yet."

Pettey began stomping down the stairs.

Walter stared hard into Shy Mitchell's eyes. "This is your chance, Shy," he said. "Others have committed the same error." In the band photo, Shy had looked just as lean and long and leathery as he was today, but he'd all but burst out of the frame in Lawyer Palgrave's office. Walter searched for that same spark in Shy's eyes. "Please!"

The innkeeper pushed Goose, hand still over her mouth, toward the door and shouted up, "Pettey, going outside for a minute."

The dogs were closer, maybe a house or two away. Shy had clearly meant to put Fortune in the cellar, but there was no hope of that now, so he opened the pantry door and pushed the boy in without a word. He gestured toward the stairs. "Tell Pettey you fell down in a puddle. Git her to give you some a my thangs."

With no time for thanks, Walter made his way to the stairs and intercepted the innkeeper's wife, who put her hands to both sides of her mouth in a silent scream. "Oh my goodness! What happened to you?"

"I slipped and fell into the biggest pool a water over by the station and I'm just soaked. Shy said I could borry some a his things."

"Well yes, all right, but you gotta get out a those wet clothes." Two steps ahead, already halfway up the stairs, Pettey mumbled, "Fouling up my whole house. I'll be up all night!"

Back in the kitchen, Shy said, "Goose, that cough a yours is soundin' pretty bad."

"What cough, papa?"

"The one you been having, Goose. You know, the real bad cough. Why don't you see if Doc Moody can have a good long look at you. I think he got in a new thermometer."

After a sound of happy recognition, Goose fell into a sudden wave of hacking and began yelling for Dr. Moody.

At the top of the stairs, as Pettey paced into her room still muttering to herself, Walter met Louisa. She'd been hanging over the railing, listening to everything and smiling. "Everything's going to be all right," he whispered, undoing his tie as he opened the door of his room. "I just have to get out there before . . ."

The disembodied voice of Aunt Dorcas bellowed through her door. "Is that Mistuh White? Louisa? I said is that Mistuh White?"

He gave her a hopeful smile. She raised her eyebrows, then winked like a conspirator.

"Yes, Auntie. He's going back out with the men. Everything's fahn."

"Good," came the answer, as if from beyond.

Walter pulled off his coat and tossed it onto the floor. "Keep them busy up here."

Louisa nodded, locked eyes with Walter as she called back to her brother, "Captain, could you please remind me why exactly Mr. Durwood is going to France? I fear we may need to reread some of the early chapters . . ."

He turned into the room, dark but for whatever glow the moon could lend through the window. His hands cold, he fumbled with the matches until he could get the lamp lit and then tore off his clothes.

Naked, wet, and white, Walter closed his eyes, took a breath and tried to remember what the office at 70 Fifth looked like. He'd been there only two days ago, had eaten a tuna salad sandwich at the Automat. Next week, Barrymore at the Shubert Theatre. He would buy a book at Brentano's.

Someone knocked on the door.

"Yes?"

"It's me. Pettey. Miz Mitchell. I got them clothes a Shy's."

She thrust a pair of pants, a coat, and a flannel shirt through the cracked door. A pair of battered shoes hit the floor. As he thanked her, his heart fell. It was the muddy pair he'd seen Shy wearing around. Out front, Ludey's truck rumbled up to the gates, and Fentress shouted, "Come on, White!" It was ten after eight o'clock.

Buttoning his last button, he desperately tried to recall whether Shy had been wearing new shoes in the kitchen. Mitchell's scent descended over him as he put on his pants and shoes, all too long and large, but reasonable enough.

"You dressin' for a party up there?"

Walter came down the stairs in Shy's old shoes.

TWENTY-SEVEN

Compared to the Studebaker, the Ford was a basic machine, only a few dials in front of the driver and a steering wheel as big as one of the tires. As he stepped into the truck, Walter kicked a small box on the floor—a box of shells—then took Nip's usual place at shotgun. He funneled his urge to claw at Shy's clothing into efforts to stay warm, rubbing his arms and blowing into his hands as he tried to conjure a diversion. A burst of breath fogged his side of the windshield.

"Sorry I'm late," said Ludey. "Had some business to attend to." He looked jolly, his eyes lively in a new way.

Beating death had that effect, thought Walter. "How you feeling?"

Ludey hit the gas. "Got a cold." Chains meant for the legs and hands of Fortune rattled on the boards of the truck bed. "Why you wearing Shy's clothes?"

For centuries Negroes had danced white folks away from the truth of who they were, protected themselves with songs, and told tales that sent Charlie off hunting skunk when he thought he was trapping fur, but Walter had a reedy voice, and his sack of stories was feeling uncomfortably light after these two days. The words came out too fast.

"Mine were all wet. I was havin' a smoke and I slipped in one the goddamn puddles out back and then I ran into the house because

I was so goddamned cold." Barking away on the far side of Mitchell's, the dogs now moved north toward the train station. He expected Ludey to be throbbing and eager, but the big man seemed more relaxed than he had earlier, after dinner, as if he was just out for a little air. "I say we get the boys and the dogs and look up by the spa. I bet that's where he went. Nobody's up there. Lot a places to hide. You know, I was up there today. Saw the gazebo."

Walter drummed away some of his nerves on the dashboard, the smell of gasoline in his nose. He wondered if it came from the truck or if they'd packed a few extra gallons for Fortune. A few minutes ago he'd told the boy not to give up on anyone, never to surrender to despair. Right now, he was probably hunkered down behind sacks of flour and cornmeal.

The streets had emptied. Ludey smiled at Walter, who had not missed the fact that the other man hadn't yet thanked him for last night. "You know, I saved a man's life once. Me an' Billy Stoker was . . ."

Apparently this was his way. Walter's foot hit something else on the floor. A shotgun.

". . . so the man says he'll race us in his buggy, and it ain't fifty yards 'fore he loses the reins. Billy's laughing like a sonuva . . ."

He lifted the gun up off the floor, sighing, as Ludey regaled him with another epic tale of deliquency. In the last two days, Walter had held more guns than he ever had in all his twenty-four years, and he particularly disliked the immediate sense of comfort conferred by holding this one. Good way to end a lynching before it started. He interrupted the story. "It's a beaut."

Ludey snapped, "What the hell you doin' with my gun?"

"Sorry, Ludey. Just lookin' at it." Walter laid it back down.

And then, just as quickly, Ludey was all smiles again. Maybe Dora had taken pity on him, let him have an extra roll in the hay for almost dying; that always put a man in a better mood. "I say we hook up with Nip and Hillman and get ourselves a plan."

"I guess." Ludey shrugged.

A strange answer, to say the least, thought Walter.

Ludey hit the brakes hard. The headlamps shone ahead onto Andy and Lickbone pulling at Nip and Hillman, who'd both tucked their shotguns into their armpits. Standing on the fringe of the vacant field across from the station, the two men shook their heads and shrugged. The truck pulled up next to them.

Hillman waved at Walter. "Hey, White! Listen! We saw 'em comin' cross the river, then the sonofabitch just disappeared over by Mitchell's. You get your business done, Lude?" The driver nodded, for once not interested in talking about himself. "*You* hear anything, White?"

"Well, I think you mighta been seeing me. I was atellin' Ludey I was out having a smoke before, and I slipped and arun back in for some dry clothes."

Nip scowled. "Naw. We seen him on the island and then we heard him swimming over. Nigger nearly drowned."

Ludey spat. "Niggers can't swim."

The others kindly let that pass.

"Probably just a big fat coon," said Walter, sticking his arm out the window toward the dogs. "Anybody think of that?" For a moment, the exhaustion of the day and night hit Walter, and he leaned back against the seat. "I bet he just gone to Winchester to get himself some ass."

He offered his hand out for a pat, but before the dogs reached him they both reared back and bawled madly as if confronted by something they hated. Clearly Shy's clothing did not hide the scent of Fortune still clinging to his body. "What the hell's wrong with the dogs, Hillman?" Pulling back his hands, Walter stuck them under his arms.

Ludey smiled as if Walter was a boy mobbed by puppies. "Them dogs shoooore do lahke you, don't they?" But his eyes grew wider and his smile thinned as the dogs continued to scratch at the side of the truck, bark into the open window.

Walter pulled away from the door. "No, I just think they're a little off." Ludey shouted at Hillman and Nip to get the goddamned dogs off the truck, and the two men did what they could to calm them. Walter took a deep breath. "I think that's the problem, boys. Maybe the dogs just tired or crazy. You know, I bet they're upset about . . ." He ducked his head in deference to Ludey's loss. "You know. Poke. And now they just can't tell me from that boy or a raccoon up a tree." The dogs kept at it, though, and Walter shouted over the howls, more and more desperate as the dogs tried to convince someone that they'd found their quarry and it was right here, right here in front of them and yet no one was doing a thing. Walter had no plan yet; thankfully, they didn't seem to have one either.

Hillman yanked at Lickbone's chain hard enough to bring the hound's face down to the ground with a strangling sound, a brute display. "Nip, what the goddamn hell is wrong with these dogs?" Reduced to whining, Lickbone dropped his tail between his legs and circled with his head held low. Nip did the same with Andy. Throwing a guilty look at the dog, Hillman ran a finger around inside his collar and said, "That boy could be anywhere, getting aready to kill somebody or start a fire, maybe. How we gonna find him?"

As tough as Hillman meant to sound, he checked the other men, made sure he wasn't the only one still angry. Nip nodded. Walter considered calling their bluff, asking with a guileless look what they'd do once they caught the boy. Would the word be said? Or would it be case of a word *not* being said—the chains would go around Fortune's legs and then step after step toward death without anyone asking why, without one voice saying stop. If Simso had screamed, "Stop!" instead of "Let's kill the niggers!" maybe something different would have happened. They could go anywhere that wasn't the

Mitchell House. "Well then, why don't you all pile in and let's go search through them ruins."

Though he couldn't make out Nip well in the dark, Walter saw him flinch at the suggestion. "Naw, we been through there already."

"I don't know. A thousand places a nigger could hide over there, even if you got dogs. I say we go back and do a thorough job. The Vale too. I bet he's hiding under the platform or something. If I remember right, there's a good two feet beneath a man could tuck himself under. You boys look there?"

Nip sagged and rubbed his chest in a circular motion. "I don't see the need to go back there. We done been through there already."

"But did you go through the Vale?"

Hillman hoisted himself and Andy up and onto the bed. "Come on, Nip. Walter probly right. You and me jes' let the dogs sniff around; we didn't do a right search. Maybe the boy swimming put the dogs off a him or something." Hillman put a hand on Lickbone's forehead as if taking its temperature. "You got yourself a fever, dog? Huh? You not feeling right?" He nuzzled up the flap of the dog's ear with his nose, whispering an apology.

Nip reluctantly climbed aboard with the other dog, and Ludey turned the truck around so they were headed back through downtown Sibley Springs. The clutches of men and women had disappeared back into their homes. God was passing through tomorrow; Reverend Mincer at church and a Sacred Harp singing, so everyone had to get themselves Heaven-ready. The dimming lamps, the final tepid bath for the oldest as the other children shivered under cold sheets, the smell of lye soap drying into their hair. Some last-minute pies went into the oven while elsewhere, women who'd waited too long pulled jars of pickled rind off their shelves and hoped God would understand. Men drew dull razors drawn across their chins. Meanwhile, these three who had learned how to lynch from watching the visiting masters accepted their charge to find the missing boy and mete out whatever punishment they deemed proper for the crime of not being where the white folks expected him to be. The people of Sibley Springs would know when to come out, when to let their pies cool and stop shaving just long enough to watch. Walter recognized some of those faces now, though, knew they were also capable of kindness. Maybe they'd just gone to sleep.

Ludey leaned over to his passenger, the fingers of his right hand splayed out on the seat, clubbed ends like knobbed heads. "Say, White. You wouldn't have any more of that Choco-Lax, would you?"

Like Dr. Moody, Walter had no pity for any man who willfully denied the ability to control his own bowels. "Darn it, Lude, I wish I did."

The face of the laxative fiend twitched. He balled his clubbed fingers, ready for a fit that he would've thrown if only the man sitting next to him hadn't ostensibly saved his life the night before.

"You orta kept some for him," said Nip.

Somehow, thought Walter, this cracker who couldn't even shit without help had convinced the world he was its master. For the second night, he saw the child beneath Ludey's wrinkles. He was The Man of this town only because he was still a nasty, fat bully of a child who thought of nothing but himself. It was that simple. The child wasn't the father of the man; the child *was* the man.

"You know," said Walter. "I met your mama this morning." Back in the truck bed, the dogs tried to get up another round of howling, but a sharp chain snap from Nip stifled them. "She looked healthy as a hog. How old is she?"

"Seventy-eight," said Ludey, sounding somewhere between loving his mama to death and wanting her dead.

"You take good care of her," said Walter, winking wisely, "and she'll live a looong time. I heard a doctor say once you're over sixty you ort not eat meat with fruit. You might wanna try that."

They'd turned left at Vine's store, now headed toward the ruins.

Ludey's puffy lips pursed back and forth as he squirmed. Walter briefly imagined them nuzzling around for mama's teat, an unpleasant but very effective distraction from the fact that he had no plan here.

Hillman shouted, "Stop here, Lude!"

The hulk of the Timmons Mill lay before them now, long and black and dead. Moonlight hit the lines of skewed metal, lit the puddles and glass all the length of the ruin. Running with Fortune, he hadn't been able to notice how striking it looked in the dark, and the small bit of a poet in Walter tried to assemble words to describe the rhythms and angles that could only belong to this century, to the quick horns of James Europe's Hell Fighters Band, automobile races, and stainless steel. Rather than a ruin, the wreck now appeared very much of its time, a sharp, fast, and frightening place with a new definition of beauty based on destroying the past. Nip cocked his rifle, a sound that made Walter picture the doughboys on Fortune's wall jumping out of their trenches. Just behind, the columns of the Vale pushed up in romantic gesture, in the cold, silver light easily mistaken for the final pillars of a fallen Grecian temple.

Ludey didn't open his door. Neither did Walter, and for a few seconds the two sat together silently in the cab, staring out the windshield as the other two unloaded. "You know, I seen the face of God, White. Seen him in the water." Ludey turned to Walter. He displayed the bland, gently stunned expression of the newly saved. In a grave voice, Ludey said, "I just wanna see justice, White." He grinned now, a mad sort of grin that Walter found easy to attach to the overnight conversion of a bastard such as Ludey Fentress. "I need for you to go out there and show me what you think justice is." And then he laughed. Walter couldn't tell how serious Ludey was, but a blessed sort of smile took over for the laughter, tempering the challenge with a clear-browed look.

"Ah mean it. I seen the face of Jesus, and now all sorts a people tellin me you're a special kind of man, the kinda man who does *good*." He spat that out, still unable to say that word without sarcasm. "I wanna learn from you. I wanna be different."

"So you want me to . . . ?"

"I want you to help me do the Lord's bidding."

"Was that the business you were doing? Gettin' born again?"

"Don't go tellin' the boys. They'd git all over me." Ludey reached across and opened the truck door so Walter could stumble out.

Looking back to check if the driver was indeed the same constipated thug he'd let flail in the pond, Walter directed the troops. "Come on, Hillman. You and me check the Vale, and, Nip, you start at the Mill. I'll run on ahead." Ludey got out of the truck and stood between the other two. "Lude, you . . . you just . . ."

For the moment, Walter gave up making sense of the new Ludey Fentress and instead dashed on to the Vale. He touched every surface he could, got on his knees and pressed his palms into the mud, the underside of the platform, the columns, putting the dogs off him as he pretended to search for Fortune Quine.

Bawling and barking, Lickbone dragged Hillman toward the Vale. "Anything here, Walter?"

Walter wiped his hands on his pants legs. "That dog's just not right, is he?"

Hillman shrugged as if he wasn't all that concerned anymore. "Ain't much of a show so far. Sorry for that."

Like Ludey, he too seemed to have lost his edge. Hillman released the dog, who dove under the platform, its barking now muffled by the Vale as the men regarded the glimmering river through the columns, the moon through the branches of the trees. Walter took a deep breath of the night air, released it in a grand satisfying rush so as not to be breathless. "Pretty spot." He pointed to the pillars. "Your family up here?"

"Naw. After the War, our people moved down from East Tennessee."

"Lots of Union folks there . . ."

Hillman spat off toward the river instead of answering. "I know I seen him swimming across."

"What's your wife's name again?"

Hillman looked at him for moment before answering. "Janie Dale."

"How old your babies?" Walter wanted them with him and Hillman, on the ticket line at Griffith Stadium.

Lickbone continued his accusation of Walter. Hillman looked down. "Yeah, yeah. Go on, dog. Harry? He the oldest. He fourteen. Then Fran and Peter and Johnnie the baby. He just two."

"Any ballplayers?"

"Oh hell, I try to talk 'em out of it, but they play anyhows." He laughed to himself. "Yeah, Harry throwin' a curve now, but Peter's a hitter."

"Harry wants to be just like daddy, right?"

"Well, they don't say that, but you see 'em walking after ya, you know?" Hillman shot him a knowing look. "You remember that when you bringing up yourn."

Walter made a show of examining a few more pillars, sneaking quick looks around each as if Fortune had been hiding behind it all along. "You like it over at Pullet's?"

"When I started, Pullet didn't take no cars. I mean, I kin fix a car, but I don't got no feelin' for it. Not like horses."

"You got some?"

Hillman had quit even pretending that he was searching for the boy. "Me? Naw. We did? But we had to get shed of 'em 'count of how much they costed. Uncle Dick got 'em now."

"Up in Gassaway?"

"Yup."

"Wherebouts that?"

"Coffee County."

"You been there?"

"Oh sure. Big farm. Corn, mostly."

"What's the town?"

"You got Tullahoma."

"That's big."

"It ain't goin' nowhere."

"And you say they play some ball there."

"Got a proper field and everything."

"Where *you* boys play?"

"Usually that field across the station. No seats or nothing." He snorted and spat again. "Barely any grass once summer come."

"And your uncle said you can bring up the whole family?"

"Yeah. He my daddy's brother."

"You know, Hillman," Walter hopped off the platform and splashed into a puddle, shattering the moon. "I'd be home apackin' up if I was you, instead of foolin' around out here. I mean . . . Do you *really* want to do this?"

Leaning against the car, his arms folded as if supervising the whole scene, Ludey seemed to smile. Walter felt a new rush of sympathy for these complicated idiots, these religious fools, these nuggets of good men wrapped in dirt and dung and the American flag.

"I mean, are you *really* afraid of that boy? He's what—seventeen?"

Hillman said nothing, but Walter went on in a low, insistent voice.

"Don't do this 'cause you want to impress me. You an' me is . . . well . . ." Walter had the word on his tongue, and it teetered there as he stared at the drawling, slump-shouldered redneck before him. A dirty-faced, coon-hunting cracker that had become, in some definite ways, his . . . Walter still couldn't say it. He remembered the light in Hillman's eyes when he described the day Kingsport lynched the elephant." We got a . . . you an' me already . . . we . . ."

"Friends?" Hillman smiled as if he'd just won an award.

Walter clapped a hand on Hillman's shoulder for an answer, steered him back away to a more casual place. "You really want to be here?" Hillman shook his head. "Then let's go. Ludey drive us home. I gotta go ask Nip something, all right?"

He looked to Ludey, who gestured in the direction of Nip, over toward the ruins, with Andy, whimpering before a twined mass of iron and wood.

Before Walter could reach him, Nip had lifted the shotgun and aimed into the rubble of the mill. The roar of both barrels discharging hit Walter in the chest and stopped him for a beat that let Nip reload and shoot again. Andy howled. Walter had the panicked thought that Shy had thrown Fortune out, that the boy had run here to hide.

"Wait up!" Walter ran right into Nip, bumped him accidentally so that he couldn't get off any kind of accurate shot. "You see something?"

Nip brought his shoulder up to his ravaged cheek as if scratching an itch. "No." Andy had stopped howling to sniff at a rotting beam of wood. Nip reached down to haul the dog away. "Get your goddamned nose out of there!"

"What are you shootin' at?" Stumbling on hidden rocks and clots of metal, Nip mumbled Cloda's name, trying to escape his memories. Vengeance filled Walter. "Was there an explosion? Was that what happened?"

Nip stopped. He shuffled, moved his lips, and though some sounds came out, they were only that—sounds, indicating so much more raw emotion inside than could never be crafted into words and thoughts. Walter knew that Nip had never read a book or poem, but he hadn't fully imagined what that could mean until now, until he saw Nip's eyes grasp for meaning. A book could have told him that others had had experiences such as his, that other men and women had their own tragedies. Shakespeare, Milton,

Sophocles, Goethe—those rivers of words that connect mankind were off the map for Nip August, and so other humans were a mystery to him; he was a mystery to himself. Everything he felt, the intricacies and varieties of beauty or the blinding pain in his chest that struck whenever he pictured his wife and son, Nip could not describe. Instead, a dark prison held him, and he was too confused to even look for a way out, save for lighting the occasional match or seeing his dead son in Curtis.

Nip held out his hands and pleaded with the wreckage. "It was an *accident!*"

Walter finally understood. It was his fault.

He had caused the fire that had burned up his family, killed the town. If anyone should have been lynched, it was Nip.

Walter couldn't forgive him. But he could help him speak. "What was it like?" he asked.

The man stared into the ruins. When he spoke, it was without hesitation or even unease; glad, it seemed, that someone had finally asked him. "Feels hot at first. You think it's gonna stop but it, it . . . it just keeps getting hotter."

"And then what?"

"And you think for sure it's gonna stop now, 'cause you already swearing. I mean you're cursin' God and Jesus and your own mother but the fucker just keeps getting hotter till you start to *melt* inside, like your bones *meltin'* in you." Nip turned to Walter and actually smiled a little as he said that. He nodded. "That's right. Like your bones *meltin'* in you." His arms shifted into odd angles now, one leg twisting around the other as if the fire had caught hold of him again, and he crumpled into himself like a leaf ignited. "Right about then, it starts to hurt less 'cause the fire done et everything up, and they's just as well chop whatever it is burnt right off a you, but the probbim is that the fire keeps slidin' all over you, know?" He shook his head; the words rushed on now. "You think you gone as crazy as you gonna go, and you can't feel your feet. Fire's tearin' at your shins. Then when those die on you, your knees is burnin'. And it jes' keeps going up and up until somebody puts you out."

Nip shriveled as the talking stopped, as if he'd been doused himself.

The field stayed quiet. Walter wondered if Quine would have described it that way. That man had known there'd be no relief before Heaven.

Nip rattled Andy's chain. "Still hurts when it's cold. Makes ya tired." He rubbed his shoulder and began walking down the ruins again. "Oh my god, I do miss them. Miss my son." Walter stared at Nip, imagined the bizarre swirls and valleys of skin underneath Nip's clothes. Nip noticed, and after a few seconds averted his eyes, wiped at his tears.

"That's not Fortune's fault," said Walter. "He's just a boy, not much younger than Little Roy, right?" Nip bristled at that. "He's just running it off 'cause he can't think of anything else. Hopped a train north and now he's gonna end up shovelin' cow guts in Cleveland or drinkin' gasoline in an alley somewhere. That's the truth now, innit?"

Walter held his breath.

Nip lifted his shotgun.

"Killing Fortune's not gonna help, Nip." But Nip wasn't aiming into the ruins; the barrel pressed up into the soft space underneath his own jaw.

"I shoulda died. I just shoulda died."

Walter grabbed the shotgun away.

"Come on. Get back in the truck."

The dogs had strayed off, distracted by a raccoon in a nearby tree.

Ludey, now in the cab, stuck his head out the window as Nip silently clambered in. "White, let's get you back to Mitchell House. I need to ast Pettey somethin', too."

Walter grabbed at the cold air, as if something had just slipped out of his palm. Fortune being found hiding out there wouldn't be good—that was way too close to way too many white women. The hunt would start up again, and this time he'd never be able to stop it. Where had Shy hidden him?

"Oh, they been asleep for a long time by now. In fact, why don't you just drop me by the station. I could use a little exercise; haven't done much today but sit around."

The Ford turned over with a snap of Ludey's wrist. "Naw, we make sure you get there safe. Mama wants to know when the preacher comes in." He slapped the wheel. "Tomorrow gonna be a big, big day."

Hillman's laughter snapped in the back of the truck. "Since when you got business with Shy Mitchell? You meet Jesus, Brother Lude?"

The truck surged ahead. Ludey shouted over the engine, "Brother Hillman, they's some mysteries of men you 'parently just don't know."

Amen, thought Walter. But they couldn't go to the Mitchell House. They could go just about anywhere but the Mitchell House. "I'm guessing Shy's asleep by now. They're early risers, from what I can tell. Haven't seen them up past nine, nine-thirty the latest." He touched his temple with his finger. "You know, I heard Pettey say something at dinner about eight o'clock and you know, I'm sure that's what she was talking about because Goose was asking her when she had to wake up and Pettey said, 'Seven o'clock, because the sing started at eight.'"

Ludey appeared entertained by Walter's protests. "We all got a lot a work to do before tomorrow. Having a big gatherin'. Invitations going out; folks comin' from everywhere."

Hillman yelled forward, "Didn't know you was going, Lude."

"Well, I'm againin' in understandin' since I spent so much time close up with Walter here . . ." He whacked Walter on the shoulder and laughed, almost ferocious in its sudden intensity. "Look like everything I heared about you is right after all."

Lickbone shook his chains. "Janie wants to go. Maybe we oughta do that," said Hillman out loud. "Say, White, you going to the sing? 'Cause if you are, then maybe you meet my family there. Want them boys to shake your hand."

This amused Ludey, who whacked Walter again. "I got a feelin' you gonna miss that eight o'clock. You invited to the party, you know."

Walter scratched his neck. If he could steer them clear of Mitchell's, it would indeed be a miracle, and though he was borrowing every minute here, he absolutely wanted the chance to stand next to Louisa one more time. "Lemme see how I feel in the morning. We do need some good direction once in a while."

"Oh, the Lord'll see you get there. Somebody'll get you there, for sure. We're gonna miss you, White." He spat out the window and laughed. "Damn, we will miss *you*."

As the truck slowed down in front of Mitchell's, Walter saw a small silhouette in Dr. Moody's window; Goose, bouncing up and down, doing her best to annoy the old man to distraction. Other windows glowed as well; no one was asleep. Walter blushed.

"All right, let me get out here. You know, I can ship you down some more a that Choco-Lax soon as I get to Chattanooga. I've seen more at the home office, and it's no problem to . . ."

Ludey stared out past Walter at all the lit rooms of the Mitchell House. "Looks pretty busy in there." He put the truck into park and turned it off.

Walter opened the door and hopped out. "See, boys. Just Doc Moody tendin' to Goose. She got a bad cough. Everybody else gettin' ready for Reverend Mincer tomorrow. Lude, I'm sure Pettey said it starts at eight, so you don't have to bother stopping."

After a long look at Mitchell's out the cab of the truck, Ludey said, "Alright then, I guess you right. We just gonna take a last stop by Dulcet. Give it a good goin' over. See if they still keepin' any secrets we should know about. Say, didn't Cleon have himself a shotgun? . . . You ever see it again? I didn't!"

"Me neither," said Hillman, some pepper back in his voice. "I forgot all about that! You right, Ludey! Let's go up to the house!"

Walter waved his hands too eagerly. "No, I'm tellin' you, he's gone from this town. He's run away but good!"

Hillman gave him a funny look. "How you know that for sure?" The dogs sensed the quick change in mood and began a whimpering that Nip did nothing to quiet. "I wanna know where that gun is. If the boy took that gun, well excuse me, Walter, I gotta protect my family."

All three stared at him, Ludey smiling as he started up the truck. "You comin'?"

Walter jumped back into the truck. Where moments ago they'd been muttering to each other and yawning, suddenly the prospects of a confrontation, any sort of confrontation, even if it meant one with a recently minted widow, had them all chattering again, and the night's momentum crashed ahead.

Rumbling over the tracks, Walter could swear the Ford made a different sound than it did on the white side. Here, the engine announced itself, echoed off the thin walls of the homes, the chains rattling in the bed. This side of Sibley Springs was buttoned down tight, but not to prepare for the arrival of Reverend Mincer. Little eyes peeked through slats of wood just as Walter had eleven years before, and he cringed to know that they saw him, saw his face, and would always hold it in their memories of this night. He prayed none of them held a gun the way he had then.

Ludey hit the brakes, throwing them all forward. Like last night, lamplight spread a circle around the Quine house. At the ruins they'd all simply piled out of the truck, but now they checked their guns and reloaded, making metallic clicks and snaps. With Fentress in the lead, guns ready, the white men advanced. Piano music came from

inside, the notes that he'd heard Scipio whistling in the trunk—
Walter could tell now that it was Chopin. He tried to get in front but
the other three tromped up the steps around him, barrels pointed
forward. Ludey actually knocked once before he remembered his
manners and kicked open the door. "Dulcie!" he shouted. "Dulcie,
we come to . . ."

Ludey and Hillman removed their hats.

"Well *there* you are, Fortune," said Ludey. Walter pushed between
Nip and Hillman to see Dulcet in the same chair Walter had left her
in, eating a slice of cake off a china saucer. Fortune lay sprawled over
a corner of the couch with *Tarzan of the Apes* in his hand while
Ellanice sat on the other corner, needlework in her hand. Scipio was
at the piano.

"I was just out apearlin', Mr. Ludey," said Fortune, ". . . and I lost
something. Then I just lost track a the time. I'm agonna 'pologize to
Mr. Sundy soon as I see him."

"See, Walter. Scipio, he's a good boy," said Ludey. Scipio ducked
his head and grinned, met the eyes of Ludey Fentress. The two men
laughed as they both looked at Walter. "Scipio, why don't you play
some a them blues for Mistuh White?"

Twenty-Eight

From the shotgun seat of this muddy Ford truck, Walter asked the heavens if he had not done well the Lord's commandment these two days. In a violent land, he had driven men to righteousness without recourse to violence himself. Mr. Johnson would be proud. He had touched hearts, awakened minds, and, as he saw two lights on in the Mitchell House, reflected that most importantly, he had learned to have faith again in his fellow man. Somehow Shy Mitchell had done his part, and that was because of *him*. He'd breathed life back into that dying house with trust and new toothbrushes. He, Walter White, had lifted up white men as well as black because if the crackers didn't come too, none of it was going to work. Ludey himself had said it—he was the kind of man who did *good*. The other light in the house came from Louisa's room.

With the glory of the Lord pulsing in him so, and powerful thoughts of how he had broken one of the links in the chain, cracked it open in front of these white people without them even knowing, Walter burst into grateful laughter.

"Well, Ludey, the world is full of surprises. That's all I can say."

Ludey grinned in a sly, feline way. "You got *that* right."

Mr. Johnson would find Fortune some kind of job somewhere in New York. Ellanice probably would marry Scipio, it was the best thing, really. The man loved her. He'd take care of her, and he was sincerely trying to care for the people of Sibley Springs even if in only the most primitive fashion. With the information that Walter brought home, the uproar it would cause, the Negroes in this town would be protected from above, and Scipio could worry about whether they'd plant cotton or corn. He'd beaten him, thought Walter, even if he'd helped in the end. Brer Rabbit had switched skins on everybody, put Fox's skin in Bear's house, Bear's skin in Fox's house, and made the whole damn world better. A parade in Harlem was not entirely out of the question. Walter wanted to celebrate. "Hey Ludey, you got a jug here?"

Ludey sneezed. "Nope." The truck stopped in front of the Mitchells'.

"Well, boys. Maybe I see some of you tomorrow."

Hillman extended his hand. "I'm not sayin' good-bye." The two men shook with great solemnity. "You always welcome here, White." Nip touched the brim of his cap by way of salute.

"Life is long," said Ludey. The gears ground deep in the truck. "An' this town is small. Tomorrow gonna be a *big* day. Boys, let me fill you in . . ."

Walter waved at the men as they rolled on. Unlatching the gate, he made his way quietly up the path and onto the porch, wincing at the creak of the door as he pushed it open, eager to get out of Shy's clothes. He headed straight to the stairs, but a rustle in the parlor made him stop. There in the dark sat Shy on the couch, looking off toward the window he'd stood next to with Louisa.

As he walked into the parlor, words drifted up into Walter's mind, a near sermon of thanks and admiration for such courage and goodness. Hope burned forth from this house—yea, it shone forth as a beacon brighter than any devil's fire. The spark of love in this one man's heart would lead the way for the rest of the town, for smaller deeds had changed the world, so mighty was the power of the good man. Of all those bowing their heads before the Lord tomorrow morning, surely this one deserved His favor most. Walter sat down on the couch next to Shy, sighed like a workingman taking the bar stool next to another workingman.

"How'd you do it?"

"Scipio come by. Said he just seen Ludey, and he was alookin' for the boy." An owl hooted outside the window. "I just put a coat on him. Scipio walked him on home while you was gone." Shy shrugged. "Drake always gone by seven-thirty on Saturday."

So simple and pure, like drinking cold water or hugging your mama. Walter got up, noticed Shy's bare feet on the wooden floor. "Thank you, Shy," he said. The owl hooted again, and it felt like enough for both of them. As he headed upstairs, where the dim light from an opening door spread before him, Walter told himself the right thing had happened.

Louisa had not taken off her dress yet, though she looked quite ready for sleep as she met him at the top banister. She tucked some unruly hair behind her ears. "Hi," she whispered.

"Hi," said Walter, in a whisper just as urgent as hers. Louisa raised her eyebrows, expecting news. "Everybody's safe. The boy, the family. Everybody."

She smiled. "I'm glad." Then she leaned back with both hands on the banister, her head forward and looking up to Walter and the light still washing in from the small round window in the hall.

"I am too." She didn't move. Everyone else was asleep.

Such an uncertain future freedom would bring. Walls tumbling down, old roads paved over. New places discovered, and millions hopelessly lost without directions handed to them. How would we know when the future was happening, wondered Walter? It could be starting tonight. He could be starting it right here. When exactly would a man be allowed to be nothing more or less than a man? Should he . . . ?

The moment swelled, Walter as frozen as he'd been the night before watching Ludey drown.

Her head began to shift down a little. "Are you coming to church tomorrow," she asked, "before you leave?"

Walter put his hand into the pocket of Shy's coat, but he did not find the pearls, and his heart fell into an empty space.

A creak on the first floor warned them that the landlord was on his way up. Louisa suddenly stood up straight in the posture of a good Southern girl, and Walter shifted toward his own door. "Yes. If you're . . . ?"

She smiled and nodded through the fine veil of propriety sliding back down. "We're attending, yes," said Louisa. Shy had not started up to his bedroom quite yet, so she let them have one more long look at each other. "Good night, Walter," whispered Louisa with the sound of farewell, then she ducked back behind her door as if exiting the stage.

His pants and jacket laid out on the bed greeted Walter, grateful again for Pettey's quick hands. He checked his damp jacket pocket for the pearls and to his relief discovered them. Unfortunately, Louisa's door had shut.

The energy had to go somewhere. Walter opened up his bag and took out his last shirt and drawers, packed what was dry back in for tomorrow's departure after the Sing. As much as he couldn't wait to get home, a couple of hours more wouldn't make a difference. He put his notebook into his coat pocket so he wouldn't forget it and resting his head on his pillow desperately wished for something more interesting to read than the book he had packed, Wallace's windy biography of his great-grandfather, the slave-owner President William Henry Harrison. Even *Quentin Durwood* would be better.

Down to his underclothes, Walter resigned himself to sleep, lying under his white sheets in this white room, the last glow of the moon slipping through the curtains, across his hands. Looking out the window he saw the very top of it over the Cumberlands, sliding away behind mist rising from the valley. He turned his hands over and let the light shine in his palms. *We are all made of that stuff,* he thought, falling into the moon, falling asleep.

Twenty-Nine

"Wake up, Mr. White!"

He felt a small hand light on his shoulder, then shove him hard. "You gotta wake up now, Mr. White, or you gonna miss the service!"

Without opening his eyes, Walter identified his tormentor as Goose.

"All right, honey. I'm getting up. Just give me . . ."

She shoved him again with a vigor Walter found quite overly familiar. "You gotta see what Daddy gave me!"

On principle, he refused to open his eyes and with a gruffness that belied his general lack of patience with children he growled, "Leave me alone, Goose! I'll be down in a minute."

He listened to her sulk out, scuffing her feet across the floor until the door clicked shut, at which point he opened his eyes to a very sunny day. Sunday. Church back in Atlanta had long ago become more of a social obligation for Walter than a spiritual one, and he'd yet to find a congregation in New York—a search that would yield better results if it ever began—but today he felt pulled to the Cross and the Resurrection, and even this little slight to Goose appeared to him as a dot on his snowy white robe. Jumping out of bed now with a springtime energy, Walter looked out the window at the hardening mud, the drying lots, and imagined the buds just under the bark. Despite the flame, despite the rope, Sibley Springs was about to be born again. Resolving to apologize to Goose at his first chance, Walter put on his dry clothes, checked that he was packed and ready for the noon train, and opened his door with great hopes that Louisa would be standing there waiting to greet him.

She was not. In fact, the entire second floor seemed empty, so Walter scooted over to the bathroom and washed his face with a splash of cold water that kept his mind well in touch with the body that carried it, brushed his teeth, and then put on his jacket. The night had mostly dried it, though thicker places at the cuffs and seams still felt damp. In the right hand pocket, three pearls remained tucked in a corner. Smiling, Walter put on his coat, heavier than usual but dry enough to wear, and went downstairs toward the smell of coffee.

The rest of the house had gone on ahead on their own, doubtful probably that a traveling salesman had any actual intention of attending Sunday service. Pettey had left a pair of biscuits for him; he popped both into his mouth, and washed them down with a cup of the cooling coffee, left five dollars on the table and then shut the Mitchells' door behind him. Twelve dollars and forty-six cents remained in his pocket, just enough to get back to New York and hop the subway uptown.

He pulled open the door and stepped into a warmer day, no bite in the air, birds singing in the empty branches. The town's sulfurous stink put him more in mind of eggs than of brimstone.

"Hi do, Waaaalter."

Hillman stepped away from the wall next to the door, as Walter stilled his heart with a hand on his chest. Unshaven, with the collar of the shirt he'd been wearing the night before peeking out from under a buttoned flannel jacket, he looked haggard, had the sour edge of liquor on his breath.

"Well hey, Hillman. Jesus, didn't expect to see *you*." The pitcher's eyes didn't meet Walter's, instead they roved the boards of the porch, the eaves, the windows over Walter's shoulder. He pulled his chin in tight, so he could look at his shoes as if he were sad or angry and too scared to admit it. "What's wrong?"

"Ummm, Ludey sent me. Make sure you find the *Meth*odist Church."

Walter reached out and slapped Hillman's arm. "Hell, I didn't know you knew how to get to the Methodist Church." Hillman didn't laugh. "It's just you ain't a churchgoin' man, is all."

"Sometimes you git surprised." Hillman spat over the railing. "You gonna be late." He gestured down the stairs, moving with the logy bitterness of a man who had the bad luck to stay awake through a binge, forced to sober up as dawn broke on the other side. "Get a move on."

To the left, a crowd of people filled the low stairs and doorway of the Methodist Church. "Hillman, it's two blocks away. Janie Dale gonna meet . . . ?"

"I sayed, 'Come *on!*' " It was the same harsh tone he'd used on Lickbone the night before.

The boys had probably taken a few pulls from the brown jug after the evening's disappointment, and then Ludey had impressed Hillman into hospitality duty. He had no reason to fight, so Walter went down the steps at his side, joined the procession of people walking past the house, many just come from the train station. It was a fine spring day, most everyone was smiling. "You oughta take out your mitt today, Hillman. Look to me like the ground's firmin' up."

Hillman said nothing. He'd yanked the bill of his cap low, pushed up his shoulders under the coat, a heavy thing that looked awfully warm to Walter, given the balmy air. Recalling some of his own mornings after during his college days, the feeling that someone was squeezing your eyes, mucking about in your brain, he left poor Hillman alone so he could search the crowd for signs of Louisa Warren. As much as he liked Hillman, if he was spending a few more hours in this town, Walter wanted to spend them at *her* side, and he hoped she had saved a place for him at the church. He offered pleasant nods to the people around, a good many staring at him and Hillman.

While four steeples rose out of the rude streets of Sibley Springs, none signaled a building larger than the Methodist Church, at best the size of a modest barn. The windows on the side were thin and vertical, made of the same clear glass as any house or store, the colors of the rainbow too papist for these stern worshippers. An odd sound came from within the white walls, a louder version of the music he'd heard on the street yesterday, that jouncing rhythm now writ large with four parts in unfamiliar harmonies.

Walking up the short stairway, he wondered if Louisa had ever been to New York. He put a hand in his pocket and rolled the pearls through his fingertips, imagined leading her into the Shubert Theatre to see Barrymore. A late dinner at Delmonico's afterward. Fighting past his regrets that he did not simply take her in his arms last night and kiss her, he decided that at some tedious moment in Reverend Mincer's sermon, he would reach over and place a pearl in her hand. The delicious pressure of not being able to speak would make her eyes flash, turn every inch of her skin into satin, make the sound of her stockings rubbing together echo off the barren walls of the church interior.

Hillman stopped at the door, seeming to dread what came next. He had both hands over a bulge on his left hip. "You don't have to come in," said Walter, but Hillman pinched the arm of his jacket and pulled him in. A cross on the back wall and a lectern of dark wood to one side were the only signs that this place served as anything other than a meeting room. God had to be created from scratch here. Rather than pews, wooden chairs had been arranged into four blocks of twenty or so that all faced an empty square in the middle, taking the emphasis away from the cross. Woman and girls formed two blocks, while men and boys made up the other two. He wouldn't be sitting next to Louisa.

A bonneted woman with protruding front teeth lifted her head to Walter before he stepped into the square. "Are you a tenor or are you a bass?" she asked solicitously, as if inquiring after his health.

"Tenor, thank you." He gave her a pinched smile.

"You'll be right here, then." She pointed back over her shoulder, at the group closest to them, facing the cross and the sopranos. Hillman stayed at his side. A quick scan of the room revealed no one Walter knew. Certain that he did not want to be in the front row, but eager to find Louisa, Walter settled on a row in the middle of the tenors and took a seat on the end. Instead of hymnals, everyone held or shared with their neighbors the same wide book that Goose had been practicing with yesterday, and a copy rested across his seat as well, a thick book, bound, or rather upholstered, in a flowery fabric that made it soft. "Come on, Hillman," whispered Walter, patting the next seat. Leading this man to a better life was indeed hard work. Hillman shuffled in, never letting him out of his sight.

The door behind shut, and the assembly, until now rehearsing stray bits of music and chatting among themselves, greeting newly arrived friends from other towns, hushed, and a white-haired man Walter assumed to be Reverend Mincer, prosperous and proper in a gray suit, took the center of the square.

"Brothers and sisters . . ." he said, tucking his thumbs into the arms of his vest, lifting his chin in a senatorial fashion. From his ramrod back and air of command, the Reverend Mincer clearly found Justice to be the most winning of Christianity's teachings. As the congregation warmed under words of praise, Walter searched the parts for people he knew. Over to his right, among the basses, sat Shy, with Tate at this side. Pettey and Aunt Dorcas sat among the altos and under her long bonnet Goose, in a freshly ironed dress of blue gingham, had gotten to church in time to be in the front row of the sopranos. Next to her was Louisa in a sensible frock of pine green

337

cotton, with a rounded collar and placket of white lace. Mother Fentress and Dora both sang alto, but Ludey was nowhere to be seen.

Reverend Mincer yielded the center to a bald, bespectacled man, of considerable age, in a black suit who could barely manage both his cane and the Harp book—a full two feet wide when opened. In a dusty whisper, he announced that they'd begin with *David's Lamentation*. After a moment of furious page turning in the seats, he raised his cane for attention and pointed it at the basses. He flicked the end just a little higher, like a baton, then brought it down and the basses growled out a line of what Walter thought were nonsense words until he saw on the page that they were singing "fa sol la."

Hillman was no help. He sleepily swayed into Walter's shoulder, but then shot up into his usual fine posture and stared at Walter as if he'd somehow been offended by him. Sweat beaded along the line of his hair. Figuring Hillman profoundly in need of some hair of the dog, Walter concentrated on the book. As the basses kept on, the old man turned to the altos, who did the same with their line, then all the men around Walter suddenly took a sharp breath and began to sing.

He could read ordinary solfege, and he quickly saw that the simple notation made of squares and triangles and circles was even easier. And yet the bounding canter of the Sacred Harp bore no resemblance to any music Walter, now bouncing on his toes to keep time, had heard before. The singers created harmonies, but made no effort to submit themselves to an overall choral effect; each man, woman, or child blasted forth sound with as much power as they could. Though all kept surprisingly on key and true to their part, the qualities of their voices ranged the spectrum, especially in the case of one woman in a wide hat, possible unhinged, who belted with startling aggression and volume. With no vibrato, they sang fast, pure notes, formed polyphonies that compared to ragtime if it were played on a pipe organ or the pumping insistence of the accordian. Its acid quality, like the piquancy of the bagpipe that expresses the scoured, dense emotions unique to those who live in the heaths, felt old and unrefined. Under the title, Walter saw that *David's Lamentation* was written in 1778, a time when America was still brewing.

After one complete turn of the song in just sounds, they launched into the proper lyrics—David's words as he wept over the death of his son Absalom—and stopped after two verses. Then the old man shuffled back over to a seat in the front row of the tenors. It was simple enough to understand what the spirituals expressed, but Walter couldn't get a purchase on the Sacred Harp. Mother Fentress rose from the altos, and took her turn in the center.

She cleared her throat. "Now we'll do *Loving Jesus.*"

This announcement brought a happy titter from the crowd, and Walter saw why; as soon as the tenors launched into the melody, the other parts chased right in like a gallop, as they all sang of the ransom of Christ's blood, tossing the melody back and forth from part to part, all rambling ahead with an insistent, snappy beat. Walter's fellow singers held themselves rigid, raising a hand to witness or lead with all the verve of a timid schoolboy asking to be excused, white folks traveling their own thorny trails with their own music, releasing at most a passionate, pitiful anger. Emotions were named, but never expressed; for all their different voices, the women didn't roll back their eyes or stomp. Nothing flowed. It was pushed through, souls forced to march on a certain path, no matter how insistent all these people were on their God-given constitutional rights to be hearty individuals.

He looked across at Louisa. Like his, her participation was half-hearted. Through the entire song he stared at her, at the way her blonde hair curled across her brow and at the pink nub of her tongue when it slipped past her teeth in song. The pearl would have to wait, though he was not sure how long he could stay if every person in the room led a song. There had to be ninety people in the church.

Loving Jesus finished, and Feldon, Vine's helper at the store, now came up to lead the next selection, *The Morning Trumpet.* It too had been written in the eighteenth century, back when the slaves were using the same English hymns and common songs to create their music. Walter decided this Sacred Harp was a freak of musical evolution, a strange divide in the progress of music that had found its one and only perfect climate among the people of the South.

After enough staring, Walter finally caught Louisa's eye, and he smiled his most winning smile, something entirely appropriate to the holy setting but tinged with a daring twinkle of the eye. Across the void, Miss Warren clearly registered his existence, then looked away without signal or smile, a slight that landed like a blow to Walter's gut.

You are an ass, thought Walter. It was shamefully obvious in the light of day that last night *he'd* been the one to chatter on about Trollope when all that was called for was a kiss. She'd closed the door behind herself.

You are an ass, thought Walter again. But for what? For not kissing her, or for thinking that he actually should have?

The song was of glory and the final trumpet sound. Where *was* Diddy Wah Diddy, wondered Walter? Where was the nation where no one cared where his people came from, the land where all that would matter was a man's soul, his sweat, and the sound of his voice singing with everyone else? It wasn't Africa. Walter didn't want to go back to Africa. *This* was his home. America. The South. He wanted to realize the dream of America. Even the slaves had known the blueprint was right, but the white men who'd built it did a foul job of executing it. What now existed on this continent bore little resemblance to what the plans laid out, just the way religion had only a passing relationship with God.

Then he noticed Goose staring at her own hand, smiling a delicious smile, shy and thrilled all at once, as if something wonderful had happened. Whatever she had in or on her hand was blue. And gold. A gold ring with a large blue stone.

Dulcet's ring.

The next song began, but Walter did not see who started it, nor did he look at the book in front of him for the shape of the notes because he was moving his jaw up and down like a puppet, like someone being played.

Sometime, somewhere, during the lynching of Cleon Quine, Shy had stolen Dulcet's ring.

The weird harmonies, the thudding rhythms, droned in Walter's head. They wheezed and whined now like an organ poorly keyed, and his dizzy mind saw the eyes around him rolling back in ecstasies, but in a different place far from this church, up on the top of Quine's hill. The green ribbons tied into buttonholes and around women's hair were made of the same tweed as Ellanice's rag, the same tweed as Cleon's coat. The room was hot. Hillman finally unbuttoned his jacket, as close to succumbing as his friend. Inside, Nip August's holster laid a black band across Hillman's chest; the revolver gleamed on his hip. Hillman stared at Walter, but not with anger, not like Simso Clark. Instead, sad to the point of being tortured, Hillman just gaped helplessly, completely puzzled not by Walter, but by the unanswerable question asked by his friend's existence. He opened his mouth, moved his lips, and though no words came out, Walter understood. Ludey hadn't found Jesus. It had all been a put-on. He had to get out of town as soon as possible.

In the twinkle of a blue stone, Walter could no longer say whether he'd accomplished a single thing here in Sibley Springs, Tennessee.

Goose met his eyes, and after the squint necessary to identify her friend, she grinned a wide, happy smile, the kind of easy, confident smile every child in the world should make, but here it sent Walter clutching at his stomach as she waved her graciously laden hand, eager to show him.

He shoved the Sacred Harp book back into Hillman's hands.

Tumbling out of his seat, Walter shot past the bucktoothed woman guarding the doors, burst them open with both hands and stumbled away from the music, reeling in the sunlight. He closed his eyes and took deep breaths.

The doors above him opened, and little feet came down the stairs until they stopped next to him. Walter could smell her.

"Where'd you get it, Goose?" he whispered, hesitant to hear the answer.

She spoke without shame. "Daddy gave it to me last night. Said it come from Cleon." As if he should have known better by now, Goose lowered her chin and said, "Daddy said Mr. Ludey took all the money out Cleon's pocket, said 'No use all this burning,' and he done gave it out to everbody in town like a present." Goose waved her hand out like she was newly engaged. "Ain't that *somethin'*?" she exclaimed, confining her wonder to the magnitude of the gift and none of its horror.

"But Goose, honey. That ring belongs to Dulcet." Goose's smile froze. "It's *hers.*"

The little girl looked down at her hand with enough doubt to prove that indeed there was a human being under her bonnet. "But I *really* love it. I never had something so pretty before, and Daddy said I could have it because I was his special baby."

Walter had dropped to his knees by now. He lifted her plump chin with a finger. "You *are* special Goose. You're a fine . . ."

Her face began to redden, and her cheeks and brows pressed closer; she was about to cry. "I want something pretty! Something just for *me!*" Tears slipped from her eyes. "I never had a pretty thing in mah *life!*"

Starting on this day of February 1918, Goose Mitchell would look at a Negro face and see either a human being like herself, or a thing to be used. Music pushed out of the cracks in the door frame and the chinks in the wood, the words about entering Jerusalem hard to understand through the insistent, whiny tone of the sopranos, the cloddish bass line. Trembling now, Walter dug into his pocket and found the pearls. "Look at these, Goose! They're just as beautiful as that ring!" The urgency of his voice scared her and she stepped back. "They're pearls! Fortune gave them to me. The boy you helped save yesterday. He got 'em out of the river!" Walter grabbed her hand, turned it over and shoved the pearls into the pink flesh, forced her fingers closed around them. "See Goose, there's beautiful things all around us! People find them every day, and they don't have to take anything from other people to have happiness!" He could tell that he was crying, that his voice was cracking as he said all this, and Walter did not like to cry, but he could not stop himself. Goose looked to both sides, her own confused tears rolling down, and Walter grabbed her shoulders now, pulled her close to his face. "Don't you think that would be a better way to live, Goose? The *best* way to live?" He was shaking her hard now. "Let everyone have their own."

By now, he had embraced her in an embrace that he could not tear himself from. He felt the thin bones of her back, the grease of his hair on his cheek, and, as disgusted as he was by the contact, he remained pressed to her. She did not pull away; she only shook with her own tears of guilt and longing and mostly fear as to why this man was weeping this way.

Walter opened his eyes. A knot of people stood in front of Vine's store, and now he recognized many of the faces: Dr. Moody rubbing his hands together; Nip jawing with Mr. Toomer; the pig-eyed farmer and the leathery man managing a whole new brace of even more dogs that circled and tangled themselves amid the crowd, growing even as he watched. Though it was nowhere near noon, a train sat in the station, a special, and people streamed off it in a picnic mood, racing down the street as if they didn't want to miss a minute of what was about to happen. They were not stopping at the Methodist Church. Dressed for an outing or a sporting event, some families and old folks, they were mostly men buzzing with pregame excitement. Many had guns. Surrounded by unfamiliar faces, Baxter Vine pointed at his store as he recounted some recent event. In the center of it all, Scipio, hat in hand, spoke with great animation to Ludey Fentress, who nodded offhand approval of whatever Scipio said, his shotgun tucked under his arm. Booney stood next to Scipio, but he suddenly ran off, and Walter didn't know, would never know, whether Hillman had come to warn him or escort him to the executioner's block.

Bending down so that he couldn't be seen on the steps, he said, "Goose, I have to get back to the hotel." Walter let go of her shoulders. "I want you to think what the right thing is, you hear? I want you to think whether you ought to give that ring back to Dulcet."

The church door opened. Without seeing Hillman inside, holding his head in his hands and crying, before he could ever see Louisa Warren come out after him looking as if she'd just stared ahead many years into the future and seen him there, Walter had slunk down the stairs toward the Mitchell House.

Thirty

With no clue as to where this train was going, Walter paced along the road, certain that if he ran, he'd attract the attention of everyone passing him as they went toward town and the lynching party. He would hide out in the Mitchells' cellar with his bag until noon, when the train North arrived. Swimming against the current, he felt his heart beating and the notebook in his coat pocket thudding against his leg.

Suddenly, Booney stepped out from behind a shed and blocked Walter's way. He had no time to chat. "Booney, I don't . . ."

The boy had no interest in what Walter had to say. "Mistuh White, you gotta get on that train."

"I'm just stopping to get my bag . . ."

The boy shook his head, checked both ways once or twice as if pursued, then fixed him with a look as weary and sadly experienced as any adult Walter had ever met. "Mistuh White, get on that train *now*." It was an order. "Oh, an' Scipio tell me to say to this to you—'Hannibal got his ass *kicked*.'" Booney took two quick steps, but then stopped as if he'd just remembered one last thing. He showed his teeth, a hard and expressionless motion meant to be a smile. "That candy was *good* to me. Yes it was." Then he dove through the taller legs of the white folks, losing himself among

345

them as they laughed, pounded each others' backs, marched on downtown Sibley Springs.

Walter pictured his bag. Cornelia's photo. The book. He tried to remember what else he'd be leaving here, but decided as a plume of steam blasted up from the depot that it didn't matter. His trot became a sprint as the train whistle blew, and the special to Sibley Springs ground out of the station just slightly faster than a walk.

Dashing past Drake, he leapt onto the last car. From the doorway, Walter saw people begin to turn toward the station, the realization beginning to grow that their quarry was escaping. Walter urged the train forward, and the bell rang. Booney's black face darted through the crowd until the boy popped up next to Scipio. The older man nodded at a job well done, then the two of them faced him and both waved goodbye.

Walter slouched in his bench, torn between trying to appear white, chipper, and expansively salesmanish on this beautiful Sunday morning when hopeful blossoms of early flowers waited to burst open, or of keeping the kind of unobtrusive, low profile that would save his life.

He was a Negro. That much was true. As long as black men were hunted with guns and dogs, burned and tortured, treated as anything less than white men, then he was a Negro, even if he had only one drop of Negro blood in his veins. Even if he had none. Even if the thought of kissing Louisa Warren still lingered on him as a fading perfume. He breathed deeply to remember.

"Where you think you going?"

Walter straightened up in his seat. The conductor, this one younger, red-faced and full of high spirits, loomed over him. "Chattanooga," replied Walter.

"Six dollars."

Walter handed over the money. He'd do his expense report once they hit Washington.

The train was nearly empty. With nothing else to do, the conductor leaned over the back of the seat in front of Walter for a chat. "Shame you're leaving Sibley Springs. Seems they got themselves some yaller nigger in town, and they about to do a little business with him. Didn't expect to be takin' anybody *out* a town this morning."

The conductor's tongue slid forward over his bottom lip as he laughed his breathy pant of a laugh, as if his tongue was too large for his mouth. It remained held back by his teeth when he finally stopped.

"I'll be damned."

"Yep. One thing I hate is a yaller nigger. How 'bout you?"

Walter managed a rueful shake of the head.

Biting a nail, the conductor nodded, then looked around the car to make sure no one was listening in. "You know, they all around us. Um hm. That's true. They looks white an' all, but they's niggers through and through. I can tell 'em every time."

"Really?"

"Oh yeah. You just look at their fingernails." He held out a fat hand. "Lemme see yours."

Walter did not move.

The conductor said it again. "Lemme see yours." But this time it was a command.

Walter swallowed. He held out his hands.

Rubbing his chin, the conductor suddenly became very serious. With a cluck, he tapped a few of Walter's fingers like piano keys. "Works every time." He pointed at the nails. "See, if you had nigger blood in you, I could see it right there on the half-moons."

Walter took back his hand and looked at his own fingers. Under the buffed nails rose an arc of light skin—the moon in his hands. "Golly, that's pretty sharp, fella. I gotta remember that." He wanted to slump back in his seat and make sense of Sibley Springs, but no one could ever make sense of it. The conductor's lips smacked, and his fat fingers drummed on the seat. He would never have time to relax. A black man could never relax. In the end there was no certainty, just a human calculus, always changing, always begging to be solved.

He straightened his tie and cleared his throat. Walter White, Exelento salesman extraordinaire, twitched his moustache and winked. "So buddy, whaddya hear about that other lynching over in Sibley Springs? That Cleon Quine. Were you there?"

Afterword

The real story of Walter White is complex, controversial, and too
rarely heard.

Born and raised in Atlanta, White was blonde, blue-eyed, and
exceptionally light-skinned, even though he was "legally" black. He
attended Atlanta University and worked for Standard Insurance before
James Weldon Johnson recruited him to come to NAACP headquar-
ters in New York City in January 1918. As assistant field secretary,
White investigated lynchings, started and managed branch offices
around the country, and assisted in the association's lobbying efforts.
An attendee at the first Pan-African Conference in 1921, White was
also the author of what is considered by many the first novel of the .
Harlem Renaissance, *Fire in the Flint* (1924). In 1926, White published
his next novel, *Flight,* and received a Guggenheim Fellowship.
Throughout this period, White formed the center of a vibrant social
circle that reached across color lines and personally provided support
and arranged publishing contacts for such writers as Langston Hughes,
Claude McKay, and Countee Cullen. In 1929, he became acting secretary of the NAACP and succeeded James Weldon Johnson as secretary the next year. From 1930 to 1954, White led the charge against
lynching, inequality, and segregation in housing, education, and the
military, culminating in the landmark *Brown v. Board of Education* ruling

in 1954. He fought with Hollywood to promote realistic black characters, wrote regular newspaper columns, magazine articles, and four books of nonfiction. Though it seems at times that Joe Louis and Jackie Robinson were the only spokesmen for African-Americans before the civil rights generation, White, as well as many others such as Johnson, W. E. B. Du Bois, Ida B. Wells, Charles Houston, Roy Wilkins, Thurgood Marshall, and A. Philip Randolph, laid the foundation of legal challenge, vocal opposition, and sacrifice upon which the modern era of civil rights was built.

And yet despite the towering role Walter White played in racial issues in the twentieth century, politically, practically, and often at great risk to his own life, his story has been largely forgotten by Americans both black and white; at best, avoided. It's true that Walter White was not an easy man. His reputation today, among those who know of him, is checkered by his name-dropping, his ambitious and quarrelsome nature, his conflicts with W. E. B. Du Bois, and his divorce of his wife of twenty-seven years and subsequent remarriage to the white socialite and cookbook author Poppy Cannon. Clearly, White was a man of aspirations, but I'm not certain that he needs to be forgiven, since it was ambition that drove him to the kinds of risks I've tried to portray in this book. Researching his life, I found scholars who'd never heard of him, and of those who had, most whispered as they discussed a man who'd offered every moment of his adult life, publicly and privately, to the cause of civil rights, a man who'd willingly faced not just arrest but death literally dozens of times. Unfortunately, the issue of whether someone who was considered black in 1918 would be considered black today raises some difficult questions about race and identity; White challenges so many of our preconceptions and prejudices that I fear America simply decided it was easier to forget Walter White than learn from him. While he's no candidate for sainthood in anyone's religion, White deserves his place not just in the pantheon of African-American history but in the annals of this entire nation. We do not have to love the man to accord him his due and include him in the conversations of race and history.

Novels do not usually come with acknowledgments, but in this case they are necessary. No one will ever know just what exactly Walter White experienced and felt on those journeys South, but many people helped me step onto the uncertain ground of imagining the life of someone so different from me and yet one with whom I felt a deepening affinity every day I worked on this book. The following people and resources contributed each in their own way to my conception of Walter White, and I am greatly in their debt not only for their generous help and support, but for the work they do.

The Library of Congress, in particular the NAACP papers; the James Weldon Johnson Collection at the Beinecke Library, Yale University; Cathy Lynn Mundale of the Robert W. Woodruff Library at Atlanta University Center; Janice Sikes of the Auburn Avenue Research Library in Atlanta; Susan Haskell of the Peabody Museum, Harvard University; the Schomburg Center for Research in Black Culture, New York Public Library; Jessie Ball duPont Library, Sewanee, The University of the South; Floydaline Limbaugh of the Franklin County Historical Society, Winchester, Tennessee; Butler Library, Columbia University; Anita Martin of Herndon House, Atlanta, Georgia; Mary Rose Taylor and the staff of the Margaret Mitchell House, Atlanta, Georgia.

I am also grateful to my beautiful wife Suzanne for continuing to put up with me; Will Balliett and Lisa Bankoff for always being there when I need them; Lewis Hyde for inspiration; Adriana Trigiani for much-needed encouragement; and Thelma Carmon for her stories. Rose Palmer, Walter White's niece, generously shared much about her life and the history of the White family. Susan Fales-Hill deserves special mention not only for being a brilliant, elegant, and most honest woman, but also for her kind introduction to Jane White Viazzi, Walter White's daughter. Without question, my greatest debt is to Ms. Viazzi, who has never told me anything other than the truth, be it a detail of her father's life or her annoyance at my late arrival to a meeting. Her honesty and encouragement made this book possible, and I only hope that I've written a book deserving of her trust.